Angell, Pearl and Little God

Pearl had never been looked at like this before. A small black leopard waiting to climb on its mate.

She said: 'When we get to Victoria, Godfrey, if you follow me, I'll go to the first policeman and complain. That's the truth. I can't bear the *sight* of you.'

Godfrey said nothing until they were crossing the river. Then he said: 'O.K. little Oyster, but you haven't done with me. I've got you in my system. And I think maybe you've got me, even though you won't admit it. Deep down in your guts. Think about it. I'll be around.'

Available in Fontana by the same author

Cordelia
Night Journey
Fortune is a Woman
The Little Walls
The Sleeping Partner
Greek Fire
The Tumbled House
The Grove of Eagles
After the Act
The Walking Stick

Ross Poldark
Demelza
Jeremy Poldark
Warleggan

WINSTON GRAHAM

Angell, Pearl and Little God

Collins

FONTANA BOOKS

First published by Wm. Collins 1970
First issued in Fontana Books 1972

© 1970 by Winston Graham

Printed in Great Britain
Collins Clear-Type Press
London and Glasgow

FOR MIKE

BOOK ONE

Chapter One

'All right, you can get dressed now,' Matthewson said.

Angell put on his vest and pants, noticing almost without seeing a flaw in the silk of the pants as he flipped the elastic round his waist, leaned against the head of the couch to step into his trousers. A man is always at a disadvantage in such circumstances, feels himself ridiculous. One is always tensed up and at the same time on one's dignity, as it were – fearing the terrible words, the sentence that will cut away the future from under one's feet, and yet resenting being so much at someone's mercy.

'There's nothing wrong with you, Wilfred,' Matthewson said abruptly. 'Really nothing at all. I told you last year and there's no change. For a man of your age you're really in very good shape.'

'These pains at my heart?'

'Purely functional. Everyone gets pains somewhere, sometime. And if you're worrying about what I told you last time, forget it.'

'A murmur.'

'A systolic murmur. So slight as to be barely detectable. Of absolutely no significance. Sorry I ever told you.'

Angell put on his French silk shirt, buttoned it up the front, tucked it in. A slightly reluctant relief was seeping in – the reluctance of a fear to believe the best, an incredulity still in some part of his mind, the part that always refuses light. He stared down at Matthewson: a quiet-spoken sallow man, dried up, apparently tireless; great reputation as a diagnostician; did very well for himself with these handsome consulting rooms in Queen Anne Street, two hospital appointments, and a small discreet lucrative private practice among the great. A house overlooking the river near Cheyne Walk, a titled wife, two sons at Cambridge.

'Of course, there's the same old trouble, Wilfred: you're far overweight. But I don't suppose it's any use my talking.'

'I certainly don't consider myself fat,' Angell said. 'With my height. And it's healthy firm flesh, not flabby. Your diagnosis confirms it.'

'Stand on those scales a minute.'

'Nonsense.' He was fastening his blue knitted tie. Merely being dressed again made one feel more in command of the situation. 'My weight's beside the point.'

'Well, seventeen stone, I'll be bound. If you're worried about your heart give it less to do. There's absolutely nothing wrong with it but it's no better for being over-loaded. Nor is any part of your system.'

This was the old sore spot, but it was not the object of the consultation. The point was that Matthewson said there was absolutely nothing wrong. (Anyway he had *found* nothing wrong, muttered the Disturber, still not quite appeased.) Angell took a deep breath, and it was clear and unimpeded. He grew in stature as he did so. Somewhere, somewhere along the road now, and not so very far distant, the final anxiety was going to give way. Normality and peace of mind lurked, as yet just out of his reason's grasp. He knew from past experience, for this was not a unique occurrence in his life, that in a few minutes it would all be different. The minutiæ of living would become important again. Take away the menace, and the sun and the stars become visible.

'By the way, how's Lady Vosper?' he asked, chiefly to divert Matthewson, who he could see was about to return to the attack on his weight, with absurd suggestions of exercise and diet charts.

'Who? Lady Vosper?' Matthewson had peculiar eyes: they were of slightly different colour and never seemed quite to focus together. Sometimes one was reminded of putting sixpences in a fruit machine, when a lemon and an orange turn up.

'You still attend her, don't you? I haven't seen her since January and I heard she was unwell.'

'Yes – yes, that's so.'

Trained mind, surfacing from the weed-grown depths of

6

the last few days, was alert enough to detect some nuance in the physician's voice. The casual question producing the casual – unexpected – answer. But it could be important – important in that life that he was now preparing to resume.

'D'you mean she's seriously ill?'

Question not liked. 'Well, yes. She's not well.'

'How seriously?'

'She's not well.'

'Dear me. I'm sorry.'

He buttoned his check waistcoat. Then he bent to tie his shoes. This he would have been glad if Matthewson had not been watching; it was the only activity where his weight did cause an appearance of strain. The consulting room was over-warm, conditioned for human beings in undress, with their defences awry.

He said carefully: 'You know of course that we are professionally concerned in Flora Vosper's affairs – chiefly through Mumford, my partner.'

'Oh. No, I didn't.'

'And, of course, as you know I am her friend too. It's a matter of both professional and social concern to me if she is – if she is ill.'

Angell waited, but Matthewson did not speak. Instead he went to his desk, picked up his pen and began to write.

'She's quite young.' Angell straightened up, puffing out his lips. 'Much younger than her stepson, the present viscount. The old man was a great marrier.'

'I never knew him.' Matthewson pulled across a new sheet. My records no doubt, Angell thought. Over fifteen years. Not much to complain of there. Three or four false alarms of which, thank God, this was the latest. Little in doctor's bills. All told they'd broken about even so far. He'd done two wills for Matthewson, conveyed a house, made covenants for his two sons. It had *cost* Matthewson more.

'Talking of marrying,' the doctor said. 'You never thought of getting married yourself, I suppose?'

'Not for twenty-five years. Why should I? Women only complicate one's life.'

'They add something too.'

One thought of the Hon. Belinda Matthewson, thin-nosed and greying, and wondered what she added. And a poor bridge player, too.

'I'm not the marrying type, John.'

'Never met the right girl, I suppose. Sometimes one doesn't. Who are you going to leave all your money to?'

'No one, I trust for a long time, if you know your business! Anyway, I'm not a rich man.'

Matthewson smiled and put down his pen. 'Go on. Tell that to your more gullible friends.'

'I spend all I have in the sale rooms!'

'Well, possessions, then. I suppose you've got a nephew.'

'What for?'

'To leave your possessions to when the time comes. Still, it's not quite the same as a wife or son.'

Eric. A weak-kneed young man who'd been to Lancing and some red-brick university and was now struggling to make a living in electronics. Sooner a cat's home. The whole subject brought up again the disagreeable landscape of thoughts and emotions which he had just been preparing to ignore and forget. He said, turning away from that scene, pursuing the other, the more impersonal topic: 'Old Viscount Vosper had too *many* wives. It's already made enough trouble for his estate, and the present Lord Vosper is sitting in Geneva on what he can salvage. If anything should happen to Flora Vosper . . .'

Matthewson swivelled in his chair, fingertips together. 'Oh, you can have too much of a good thing. I agree. Marriage is habit-forming. But d'you remember old Leo Marzel at the Club, the ex-Indian judge. He'd been a great womanizer in his time, but he used to say to me: 'D'you know, John, I've *enjoyed* women. The one mistake I made was never to marry one. I realize it now, when it's too late.'

'Are you suggesting it will soon be too late for me?'

'Not at all. But you're forty-seven and –'

'Forty-six.'

'Well, whichever it is. My records say –'

'Your records are wrong. I was born –'

'Well, whichever it is, it was only an observation on my part that married life has its compensations. You're your own master, Wilfred, and must live your life as you think best. D'you want a diet chart?'

'Of course not. How much do I owe you? Five guineas, is it?'

8

'Six.'

'Even for cash?'

'You know that's less than my normal fee.' The physician smiled up at Angell, eyes never quite hitting the jack-pot. 'You *are* an old rascal, Wilfred. Who are your friends, apart from me? I've known you all these years, and yet . . .'

'I've friends. Enough. I'm self-contained. No use for endless prattle. That's why women don't attract me.'

'Don't they at all? I mean, at all?'

There was an inquisitive look on the doctor's face, slightly embarrassed, Angell thought, as if he knew he shouldn't have put the question. In fact perhaps he was the only man with a right to put it, but one resented it all the same – and also took interested note of the embarrassment. How *did* a man practise quite brilliantly for twenty-five years and yet still retain a sort of *pudeur*?

Angell said: 'I fell in love when I was twenty-odd. It was a ridiculous piece of nonsense, and of course it didn't work out. Since then with every year I become less and less interested. It astonishes me *perpetually,* the amount of time and energy and money and thought and sheer pre-occupation that many men lavish on their love affairs. It's such a waste, such a pouring away of vital humours on something that must be futile in the end.'

'What isn't?' Matthewson said, turning the cap of his pen round and round.

'Well, indeed. But even in the short term. My furniture and paintings . . .'

'Last longer than love? But what sort of companionship do they provide in later life? . . . However, perhaps you're lucky to be able to choose. Sex is such an integral part of the human *soma* – to say nothing of the *psyche* – that few are able to escape its claims entirely. Thanks.' The six shillings had been paid in shillings and sixpences and Matthewson carefully counted them. As a deliberate affront, Angell thought.

He said: 'Well, I have. But don't let it worry you, John. I lead a very full life, as you know. I have one of the most thriving practices in London. I live well, eat well, sleep well. I am universally respected – and in some quarters admired. My opinion is sought not only on legal matters but on questions of art. I am on the governing board of

9

three large charitable organizations. I am always starting something new, going into some new line. I am just as much abreast of modern life as you are. If –'

'Oh, I know, I know. Peace be on you. But d'you know, you came to me for a consultation, so anything relevant to your general life is relevant to your general health . . . You come to me with pains at your heart which I find have no organic cause. Now broadly speaking – well, how can I put this? – broadly speaking an "outward-caring" man is less likely to suffer from functional pain than an "inward-caring" one. An unmarried man with no family ties of any sort is probably more likely to be more concerned – to have more time and attention to *be* concerned – with his own symptoms than a man with a wife and family to look after.'

'So you pretend to think –'

'It's a very complex subject, Wilfred. Not one I can pontificate on, I assure you. But it seems that the human creature – at least the human creature of today – needs a certain degree of worry to keep itself balanced and healthy. There are states caused by over-anxiety and states caused by under-anxiety. Between lies a large, variable norm.'

Angell smoothed his hair in the mirror. It was still plentiful, grew strongly, almost luxuriantly, with only a little greying at the sides. It was a strong face, he felt, the nose straight and aristocratic, the chin slightly cleft: altogether a distinguished reflection. Although one was not conceited, there was no point in denying the plain facts.

'In somewhat cruder terms,' Matthewson said, 'I'm really telling you to think less about yourself. Whether you take my advice – and how you take it – is entirely for you to choose.'

Angell wasn't quite ready to leave yet. Through the mirror he could see the other putting away the pound notes he had received. *They* wouldn't go on his income tax, he suspected.

'How is your wife?'

'Belinda? Pretty well. You must come in sometime. I'll arrange an evening of bridge.'

'Thank you. That's a pleasant little John Piper collage you have there.'

'Oh? Yes. Belinda gave it me for Christmas.'

'Where did she get it – at a gallery? There was an

exhibition, I remember.'

'D'you know, I never asked. Being a present . . .'

'You haven't the right approach to collecting, John. But this you never did have. I suppose for me collecting is like a second profession.'

'Or even an alternative religion?'

Angell smiled. 'Quite so.' He continued to stare at the picture, his mind not on the picture. 'What *is* the matter with Lady Vosper? Is it the dread complaint?'

'No . . .'

'If it's serious my partner, Mumford, will have to know.'

Matthewson got up. 'She's been in the Clinic for a couple of weeks. It's a nephritic condition. Normally one can do a lot nowadays for that sort of thing . . .'

'But in her case?'

'No, not in the circumstances of her general health. A transplant is simply not on.'

'D'you mean she's not likely to live long?'

Matthewson stared at Angell broodingly. 'I tell you this in confidence, of course . . . Naturally she doesn't know. Her daughter has been told.'

'I'm sorry. I'm very sorry. A great character, Flora Vosper.' With new calculations at work, Angell stood a little apart from himself, contemplating the sympathy that he could give to one less happily circumstanced. He could observe but he did not wish to alter the dichotomy in his own nature, the shrinking away from sickness even in another, and the well-balanced calculations as to what that sickness could mean.

'Do you put a term on it?'

'On her life? Why should one attempt to? Six to twelve months perhaps. It depends less on what we can do than on how quickly her system succumbs. She's an unpredictable creature, but of course her way of life does not help.'

There was a taxi passing as he came out but Angell did not raise his hand. Feeling so much better already; pains at the heart gone as if touched by a miracle healer; energy returning. The final traces of anxiety, of disbelief, were only dregs in the mind, washing away. New interests and old caught at his arm, moving him away from the old dreads.

He caught a 59 bus down Wigmore Street to Piccadilly, and then a 19 up Shaftesbury Avenue. A roundabout route, but it cost no more than a taxi-driver would have expected as a tip and barely a thank-you for it. Besides it gave him time to think.

The offices of Carey, Angell & Kingston are on the north side of the Fields, and they are neither hygienic nor ornamental. But Angell owned the freehold, which was worth a lot of money, and he was waiting the right opportunity to sell and move west as a number of his more fashionable colleagues had done. Owen Angell had virtually taken over the firm when the last Kingston died in 1944, and Wilfred Angell had come to a more responsible position than he had ever expected in his early thirties by the sudden death of each of the three partners within a few years, his father of a coronary, Mr Gomme of tuberculosis, and Mr Hunter of a mental aberration which led him into his potting shed with a length of rope. Solicitors are known to choose this way out sometimes when fearing an investigation of the Law Society, but Mr Hunter's rectitude was a model for all. One could only assume that in his early fifties he had faced up to life and found himself going nowhere.

At least this was a question Wilfred had never yet had to ask himself. Under his energetic leadership the firm had moved steadily forward, both increasing its business and being more selective in the choice of business it took on, so that the work it did was angled towards the more profitable sides of law. There were now two new senior partners in addition to himself, Mumford and Esslin, and three junior partners, each one specializing in one subject or a group of allied subjects. Angell's speciality was property, and Company Law.

As soon as he got in he rang Sir Francis Hone at his office and said he wanted to see him on an urgent matter.

Hone said: 'I'm frightfully tied up. If you could give me some idea . . .'

'Well, I'd prefer not to say too much on the telephone but it's to do with Handley Merrick and the Vospers. Circumstances have changed and I think we could make a new approach.'

'And this is urgent?'

'It could well be. If you agree when you hear the facts

12

I'd like to act on them immediately.'

'I could make it ten o'clock, if that's not too late. I have a dinner but I can get away.'

They agreed this, and Angell called Miss Lock and asked her to get him a flight to Geneva. She said: 'First class or Tourist, sir?'

'Neither. There's a cheap night flight at this time of the year. See if you can get me on it. It's about £13 cheaper than ordinary tourist fare. I'm not sure of the time but last year it left about three in the morning.'

She went out and he riffled through the afternoon post. Old Mrs Montague was still haggling about the size of her bill. He dictated on to a tape a letter offering to reduce it by 15% provided she withdrew the word 'extortionate'. Parkinson & Parkinson were hinting at a settlement in the John Haig case. They still did not seem to realize – and it would have to be brought home to them – what little room they had for manoeuvre. Another number of the magazine *Health For All* had been delivered. He made a note to cancel it.

Miss Lock buzzed to say she had got the last seat, and take-off time was 3.20 a.m., so he asked her to bring him the Vosper file and he studied it for a few minutes and made some notes. It was a thin file but he hoped it would thicken now.

He saw both Mumford and Esslin before he left. Mumford was a heavy dark untidy man of fifty, clumsy in his movements, with long strands of hair streaked across his head like a pedestrian crossing. Esslin, a Czech, ten years younger, Angell had taken into partnership only three years ago, recognizing the acuteness of his mind and the value of an intellect not inhibited by his English legal training. Mumford was slow and solid, Esslin ambitious and volatile: a good pair in harness but they needed the coachman.

Angell did not mention Lady Vosper to Mumford because it was in fact none of his business. He had used Mumford's name to lend impersonality to his inquiries from Matthewson. If he had given Matthewson the impression that his firm acted for the Vospers as family solicitors it was in the circumstances, he thought, an excusable tactic.

When he left he took a tube from Holborn to Bond

Street, but it was too early for dinner at his club so he went into Claridge's Causerie, where one can get several helpings of smorgasbord at a single fixed price. He had three helpings this evening, and a pint of beer – since there was no point in paying fancy hotel prices for wine. By the time he had finished this, dinner was on at his club so he strolled up to Hanover Square and had a simple meal of smoked trout, saddle of lamb, and Stilton, with a bottle of 1959 Bel Air.

He was well known in his club, which he used a great deal, and if not exactly a popular man was prized by the other members as an eccentric. Angell would have been startled to know this. He thought himself a quiet senior member – senior at least as to membership – with the distinction only of eminence. This evening he had time after dinner for only one rubber of bridge; then he walked down to the Hones' flat in St James's Street and spent an hour with Sir Francis. After that he took a taxi home.

Eight years ago some property near Cadogan Square had come up for sale at a very reasonable price: numbers 24 and 26 Cadogan Mews, and Angell had bought them before they came on the open market. No. 26 is on the corner of Milner Street, and here he now lived, having let off No. 24 at a rental that more than paid for the outgoings on No. 26. They were both small Georgian houses, on two floors only, with spacious well-proportioned rooms. Occasionally when delusions of grandeur came over him he thought of having them both for himself and knocking them into one, not to provide more space for living but to house his collection of furniture and pictures.

Alex was not there when Angell got in: he had forgotten about the half day. He looked with displeasure at a thin film of dust on some of the furniture, at two pictures awry, unwashed plates in the kitchen and cigarette ash and a cork tip floating in a Coalport saucer. Alex was more and more trading on a belief that he was indispensable, his service increasingly half-hearted and careless. Angell bore his shortcomings from a dislike of change, after five years, and because when the boy felt like it he could cook like an angel. Less and less did he feel like it. Alex was 33 and a homosexual.

Angell rang the exchange and asked for a call at one a.m., and set the alarm for one-ten as an extra precaution. As he undressed and climbed into his crimson curtained French bed his heart was as steady as a rock, everything he had eaten and drunk, including two brandies at the Hones', having been perfectly assimilated. He mused on the strangeness of the human mind which could allow fear and apprehension to grow so large that all else was blocked out, yet twelve hours later the fear, having been adjudged groundless, was so far shrunken as to be hard to re-imagine. One couldn't quite believe it was being correctly remembered. *Was* I so upset? *Did* I believe those pains were an early coronary? Am I not now recalling it as worse than it truly was?

. . . The waking telephone call came in the middle of a dream. He took off the receiver, answering it from a dinner party at which the long-dead Anna was his wife, and Alex and his boy friend and Lady Vosper and Sir Francis Hone were guests. It is always bad being wakened in the middle of the night from a short sleep. One feels terribly alone. The sound of distant traffic had almost stopped, and he lay between the cool sheets with a curious sense of desolation as if he would never again have communication with the outside world. It was as if the loneliness were so intense that it became claustrophobic. One fought for movement and air. One was buried alive in loneliness, tied down by the silence, struggling to have someone to speak to, to confide in, to care.

Perhaps it was the dream: Anna, the charming hostess, yet a conviction that the dinner party would end in death and disaster. At times like this one *did* lack companionship, the confidant, the friend . . .

He fought his way out of bed, rang for a taxi for 1.45, dressed, made coffee, put a few things in a briefcase and was waiting at the door when the taxi came.

Drive through a half-silent London, check in at the soul-less, sleep-walking, de-hydrated, hygienic, impersonalized air-terminal; wait in the bar, buy sandwiches for the journey, follow the crowd to the bus, elbow someone aside to get the seat by the door, jog through the night, half yawning, half afraid, debouch at the other end, passports, flight cards, wait in the departure lounge, edging towards the most likely door; British European Airways announces the departure of Flight B.E. 562 for Geneva; another bus; then out on to the tarmac; again hurrying while not appearing to hurry, contriving to reach the steps first to get a back seat (supposed to be safer). A motley crowd, he thought; cheap clothes, shabby hand luggage, the ineffable air of lower middle class and upper working class, people without quality of any kind, except perhaps the quality of respectability. He despised them all. They herded, they scraped their feet, they self-consciously took off coats and hats, and the stewardess stowed them away. Many, he thought from their clothes, were going for a ski-ing holiday – one of the numerous sports he had never tried. This was what you got, travelling in March.

It was going to be full, but he hoped if he kept his briefcase on the next seat, and there *was* an empty seat, that this would be it. He had taken the right hand window, next from the end. He was always nervous in flying, but constant usage had dulled the edge of apprehension. He called to one of the stewardesses and ordered a double brandy; she did not like this, being still busy with passengers arriving, but he prevailed on her to keep the order in mind.

'Excuse me, is this seat taken?'

A woman's voice. Pretend not to hear; take notebook from pocket, jot down some figures for Viscount Vosper's attention.

'You'll pardon me, sir,' said the stewardess, 'this seat is free, isn't it. Can I move your briefcase?'

'Oh, I'm sorry.' He took the case onto his lap and glanced briefly up at the person who was forcing herself upon him.

It was quite a shock to him, quite sudden, quite a little shock. Because the young woman standing there bore a marked resemblance to the Anna he had been in love with twenty-five years ago.

Of course it was a casual resemblance, no more, and even if it had been a speaking likeness, it would have been of no great importance. But all the same there was this trifling sense of shock. For a moment it was just as if a quarter of a century had slipped out of sight, with all its experience, its wear and tear, its hazards, its achievements, its formula-

16

tion and change and consolidation of character, and he was a callow youth again (even after several years in the army), not yet through his finals, under his father's severe observation, groping at life, not knowing what it was all about, pretending to be adult, pretending to be sophisticated, fascinated by Anna but perhaps more interested in the sensation of being in love than really in love.

Then as this young woman sat down he lowered his eyes to the notebook and paid no further attention to her.

The plane took off, wobbling in that disconcerting manner planes have before they clear the clouds, then settled to its steady flight; they unfastened their belts and the stewardess brought him his brandy. In an hour and a half they would be there. He briefly rehearsed his approach to Claude Vosper. Then his thoughts went back to his interview with Matthewson yesterday.

Only one tiny irritant remained, pricking when one thought of it. Reading between Matthewson's comments and his questions, one got the impression he still seriously doubted that a man – a strong vigorous man in his forties at the very height of his powers – could really live without sex. So – reading from the denial that women were of interest – what was left?

Of course it was not the first time Angell had sensed such an implication in people's talk. Living alone with a man like Alex – and before him Paul – was clearly reason enough for tongues to wag. As if I care, thought Angell. It's only that one is irritated to be taken for one when one is not. Alex had his boy friends, whom one sometimes met when not supposed to; but his life was entirely his own to lead so long as it did not interfere with his work. That he meant anything more than a servant was perfectly absurd.

Angell finished his brandy and the stewardess bore it away. In the fashion of the time the girl sitting next to him was showing quite six inches of her legs above the knees, and he stared at them for some time, expecting to make her self-conscious. She was not self-conscious. Perhaps she did not even notice. They were excellent legs and would have been an asset to her in any beauty contest, but he noticed with satisfaction that he could stare at them with complete detachment; he could appreciate them in exactly the same

17

way as he could appreciate the carving of two Louis XIV acanthus leaves, but with noticeably less wish to possess them. She was quite a bit bigger than Anna, a shade statuesque, and less blonde. Her clothes were inexpensive but in fair taste. Her voice when she spoke to the stewardess was of a good timbre but with a trace of accent, south London probably.

Anna, of course, had lived in one of the fine houses of Regent's Park. A rich architect's child, she had really been too good for him socially, and the match from his point of view could hardly have been bettered. (Not that he thought of such things in those days: common sense had hardly activated him.)

But it was not to be . . .

The lights in the plane had been lowered and many of the people were dozing, but his earlier sleep had refreshed Angell, and he ate the sandwiches he had brought, disposing of them carefully one by one like houses in a property deal. The girl in the next seat continued to read magazines all through the flight. Only once she raised her eyes to his to apologize when a magazine slipped off her lap onto his feet.

Presently the note of the engines changed. They were coming down. Angell's ears crackled but there was no safety-belt sign so he went on with some last minute notes. It occurred to him to wonder whether Claude Vosper would resent this uninvited call. One thought not. Yet one wished one knew him better.

They had flattened out again and were climbing. Angell rang the bell.

'Yes, sir?'

'We're ten minutes late! What is the delay?'

'It's a slight hold-up at the airport. We'll be down in a few minutes.'

Other people in the cabin were stirring. The girl began to make up her face.

'Good morning, ladies and gentlemen, this is Captain Holford speaking. I must apologize for the delay, but I have to tell you that Geneva airport is at present closed because of fog, so we have been re-routed to Zurich. We are extremely sorry for any inconvenience this may cause you.'

One of the most maddening things about air travel, Angell always felt, was that people on the flight deck could talk at will to the passengers in the cabin but the passengers could never answer back. This breeds a degree of frustration that makes the blood pressure mount. A buzz of conversation now broke out, partly humorous, partly nervous, and he found himself caught up in the common impulse and communicating his feelings to the young woman beside him.

It was in repose that her face most reminded him of Anna. In talking she did not have Anna's vivacity or quickness of thought: she seemed a gentle creature, rather placid. She had the beauty of a good piece of sculpture of the old school.

She lived near Croydon, was off on a ski-ing holiday to Zermatt. She had been delayed two days because of a chill and was joining friends there. She knew she had several hours' train journey from Geneva and had no idea how much further it would be from Zurich.

By now they were circling again. There were minor air pockets and a good deal of unsteadiness, and Angell found himself becoming increasingly alarmed. There are few things more unsettling than to be several thousand feet up in the sky over mountainous country where the peaks can be just as high as you are, wobbling around in a 65 ton aircraft with 100 other people, precariously preserved from death by a thin shell of alloy and steel and four infinitely complicated engines, and the skill of two men – and nowhere to land.

The man in the seat in front said: 'We'll never get down in Zurich, I can tell you! They *built* the airport there in the one district where fog *always* settles.' He had a loud, coarse, knowing voice.

'Do you often travel this way?' the girl asked. 'Do you have a business in Switzerland?'

'Not *a* business. Business,' said Angell, with fear gripping his bowels. 'I am a solicitor and have business overseas.' Why had he decided to come at night, when there was so much less probability of fog during the day? This was *false* economy, Heaven knew, to jeopardize one's very life for the sake of £20.

They were climbing again. He wondered how much

petrol the plane carried: did they always fill up the tanks for these short runs?

She said: 'I work at D. H. Evans. On the beauty counter. It's quite nice really. Only the journey. It takes so much of the day.'

'Please fasten safety-belts and extinguish cigarettes.'

They were lurching about now in a completely drunken fashion. He had never known anything like it before. The landing wheels went *bump-bump*. The engines changed their note. It felt as if the plane would break up under the buffeting.

He asked her about her family. He was not in the least interested in her family and made no attempt to listen to her replies. Words were just a means of keeping in touch with the normal when confronted by the grotesque. There were no lights visible through the window.

She said: 'It'll be awful if I miss another whole day's ski-ing. That'll only leave me nine. You know what it's like after you've been off it for a year. It takes about three days to find your legs again.'

The stewardess came down the aisle unsteadily, clutching to each seat-back for support, doing her duty and making sure everyone was obeying orders. A man in the opposite seat was vomiting. Lurch, flop, lurch, flop. He could well have come by train, channel and train: the *old* way, the *safe* way, so simple and so safe. One tries to save perhaps twenty-four hours and so puts at hazard the last twenty-four years of one's life.

The girl took her light tulle scarf from round her neck and re-tied it. She put her magazines away. Clearly for her the flight was over. He felt annoyance at her calm. A total lack of imagination, docile, commonplace, ignorant, one of the crowd, cannon-fodder, just slightly but deceptively different because of her looks. A shop girl. Millions of such bred and lived and died unnoticed all over the world. As they deserved to. There was a bruise on her neck or a dirty mark. She looked otherwise very clean. For a brief and inappropriate moment the annoyance he felt for her changed to desire as he thought it would be nice to discover how clean she was all over. Something he had not felt for years; it was thrown up perhaps by his fear of sudden extinction, a purely primitive reaction just as an old tree will try to flower when its roots are endangered.

Then the feeling quite passed, leaving only normal terror again. In one sense she was quite right: the flight was over for all of them. In two minutes they would all be unbuckling their seat-belts and reaching for their coats, or else they would all be dead, twisted and broken and burnt-out corpses, deprived of life, sensation, future, by the gravitational pull of the earth, insects attempting presumptuously to move out of their proper element – and failing.

They dipped and Angell saw a light. Then the murmur of the engines changed to a roar, one had a sudden sensation of swishing past something that was very near either in the sky or on the ground, and then the nose of the plane lifted and they began to climb again.

'I told you we'd never get down,' said the man in front. 'See the way he brought her nose up! He damned near stalled her then! Here, miss, what's wrong?'

'Nothing,' said the stewardess unconvincingly as she brushed past.

Angell took out a handkerchief to wipe the sweat from his forehead. They were gently banking, the worst of the turbulence gone. Were there high mountains round Zurich? He said with sudden friendliness: 'I once had a superb meal here, at a hotel overlooking the lake. Some of the best food in Europe. Caviare, a poached sole with Normandie sauce, croustade of snipe with truffles, a soft French cheese whose name I – I forget . . .' Why was he chattering like this? It was not in his character to prattle to a friend, let alone to a stranger. He had never spoken to a stranger in a train in his life.

The girl was talking too, pleasantly animated, smiling. Angell's pencil fell to the floor and they both bent unsteadily to pick it up, heads almost bumping. He thanked her. They were coming in for their second run, wings swaying gently, the lurching ended. But could the pilot see anything at all? '. . . cooking,' the girl was saying, 'but at the end of the day I'm glad to get what's given me. You don't feel like making an extra effort, do you.'

Down. A perfectly sickening lurch. The wheels touched, lost touch, touched again, they were racing, running far too fast towards the end of the tarmac. The jet engines roared in reverse; seat-belts tightened; they began to slow. To slow. The intercom crackled. 'Ladies and gentlemen, we regret any inconvenience you may be caused by this landing. Refreshments will be served in the transit passengers' lounge. We hope to be able to continue our flight to Geneva in about an hour. Kindly remain seated until the aircraft has come to a standstill and the engines have been switched off.'

'*Epoisses*,' said Angell.

'Pardon?' said the girl.

'The name of the cheese,' he explained, but as they were safely down he said this only to himself. Nothing would have induced him to speak to her again.

Chapter Two

Angell had first met Claude Vosper in a dispute over a painting five years ago. He had been called in because of his expert knowledge of the art world, and he had acted for him then, and they had had brief correspondence once since. The impression he got was that the fourth viscount had withdrawn just as much as he possibly could from the English scene and had no financial interests there except what existed through his father's will and by virtue of their being in a trust that could not be realized.

Vosper was a tall bony man of fifty-nine, and his new wife, Charmian, whom Angell had not met, was a pretty dark girl of twenty-eight, Jewish and vivacious. He had done well for himself, Angell thought, and Vosper himself confirmed this view later in the day when he said: 'Best of the quiver so far. Excellent organizer. Since I married her I've had twice the service at half the cost. And never a hard word. Compared with Pamela, my God, or even Sue . . .' He brayed with laughter.

This of course long after the ice had been broken. The unannounced arrival had been attended by constraint. Angell might have been calling about the insurance. He had explained that he was having a few days holiday in Switzerland and had taken the opportunity to drop in with a proposition. Money, sums of money, had then come to be mentioned, and this had quietly cleared the air.

So lunch – delightful but frugal – Vosper was on some ludicrous *régime* – of turtle soup with sherry, a sole véronique and a soufflé; and afterwards his wife and youngest daughter left them and they sat in the glass-enclosed verandah overlooking the lake, smoking Lonsdales and sipping port, and Angell went into more details of the proposition he brought.

Vosper's expression did not change while he listened. His was an actor's face, the features larger than life but lopsided with wear. These and the mane of grey hair worn too long, the green velvet suit, the flowing tie, all suggested the artistic and the bohemian, where they should have implied the self-indulgent and the indeterminate.

He said: 'I did hear of the first offer through Flora. Not that we ever write – we're not on those terms – but the trustees felt they ought to let me know. Anyway I'd have refused even if she hadn't.'

'Why, may I ask?'

'Well, *cui bono*? Not I. If we sold the place for £60,000 the money would have to be re-invested by the trustees and she'd get the income for life. Money may lose in value, but property never. My son Harry's the one who'll get the best of it.'

'But this new proposition . . .'

'Ah, yes, it sounds attractive. But what's at the back of it?'

'What do you mean?'

'Well, let's start at square one. Why were you interested in the property in the first place?'

'My company takes a long-term view of its –'

'Your company. You mean this what-you-may-call-it –'

'Land Increments Limited, yes. Sir Francis Hone, M.P., is the chairman. I am a director as well as being their legal adviser.'

'Right, we've got that fixed. Go on.'

'My company takes a long-term view of its property dealings, and we've been buying land in both Hampshire and Suffolk as an investment for the future. Property companies do buy land from time to time, you know. Much of the stuff we buy will lie fallow for a generation, but it's necessary to have it in stock, as it were, for the future. Of course it's a gamble. But we reason these two counties are both too near London to escape.'

'Why Merrick House though? You're very much in rural England there.'

'It's a possibility for the future. And 200 acres of land go with it.'

'Farm land. Agricultural. A few cottages.'

'Yes. We think it a reasonable speculation.'

'Reasonable enough to come to me with an increased bid, eh? Why did you first go to Flora?'

'We thought she owned the property, Lord Vosper. But she told us it was left in trust for you at her death. Of course it could have been sold to us even then, with your consent, but since *her* consent was lacking there was no point in proceeding further.'

'She refused?'

'She refused.'

'On what grounds?'

'Sentimental grounds, I gather.'

Vosper grunted. 'I'd find it difficult to be sentimental about a monstrosity like Merrick House. I was always glad to get away from it.'

Angell nodded approval and waited.

Vosper blew smoke in a thin stream towards the alps on the far side of the lake. This morning Mont Blanc and all the other snowy peaks had been hidden in cloud; now they were as clear cut as cardboard scenery.

He said: 'You're now offering to pay me £10,000 – outright, in cash, is that it? – for an option to buy Merrick House for a fixed sum of £80,000 if or when the property becomes mine to dispose of. That's well enough. But you must know that the probabilities are I shall never inherit. I'm eleven years older than Flora, so by any actuarial reckoning she's likely to survive me. Then it would all go straight to Harry. I couldn't pledge for him.'

'No, of course, that's not possible.' Angell finished the last of his glass of indifferent port. How could a viscount permit himself to drink it? 'But do you see much of your step-mother?'

'No. We don't get on. Never have. Why?'

'I meet her now and then. She lives a fairly – how shall I put it? . . .'

'Randy life?'

'Well, of that nature. She rides very recklessly to hounds. She used to race cars, and I believe still drives very fast. Not to put too fine a point on it, she drinks a lot; and she –er – has had a variety of lovers . . .'

'Sex doesn't kill women,' said Vosper, 'it kills men.' He laughed his great braying laugh.

'But it all adds up. I think your actuary – if he were called in – would take these things into account.'

'Which your company has done.'

'Which my company has done.'

Vosper swung a bony leg over the arm of his chair and dangled it there, showing inches of scarlet sock. 'You know, *I* don't live in cotton wool. It still seems to me your crew are taking an unjustifiable risk.'

'We prosper by taking risks. I don't think you should consider us but only yourself.'

'Oh, quite, I agree. But when you get propositions like this, you can only see it plainly if you see what the other fellow has to gain.'

Angell began to wonder if this proposal was too generous. A meaner one might have been swallowed with less caution.

'I'm a cynic, Angell. Life peels off the layers of fluff we're born with and eventually leaves us starko. You tell me you're an honest man who has come to me with an honest proposition, and I'm inclined to believe you – maybe because I *want* to believe you: it'll pay me to. In the ordinary course of events I should never expect to see a penny benefit from what the old man left in trust for me. It'll all go to Harry – whom I never see from one year's end to the next unless he's in a scrape. But just because it looks a good proposition I've got to look at it all round.'

'Of course. By all means. Why not put it in the hands of your solicitor?'

Vosper glanced up in slight surprise, as if he hadn't expected this suggestion. 'Well, fine . . . I've a man in Geneva called Cornavin. He does for me out here –'

'Much better to employ someone in England, if I might advise. My firm clearly cannot act for you in this, but is there a family firm? . . .'

'Hollis did most of my legal work when I lived over there.'

This was what Angell had hoped. Hollis & Hollis. Alfred Hollis was old, could be obstinate and conventional; but he wasn't smart-alec and he had no finger in development pies. 'By all means. Would you like me to get in touch with him direct?'

The cypresses in the garden were beginning to throw long pencils of shadow. Lunch had been late.

'No, send the proposition to me first, Angell, and I'll forward it to him.'

It looked as if the fish was beginning to bite. But he was a wary old fish and had a reputation for being slow to make up his mind. 'You haven't asked,' Angell said, 'but perhaps I should explain that the option we propose should run for one year only. That is, we would be entitled to exercise it for one year after you had inherited the property. It would be unfair to you to make this of longer duration because you would have to be free to sell elsewhere if it didn't suit us to take up the option when the time comes.'

'Very fair. I still don't see the joy for your company in risking £10,000 on an outside chance.'

'As I've said, that's our problem. Frankly, at the moment, my company has a lot of ready cash that it wishes to re-invest. Your problem is whether you want £10,000 as soon as our agreement is signed.'

Vosper finished his cigar and got up. He had a strong, shambling walk. He emptied the ashtray into a wastepaper basket, closed the window against the afternoon air.

'I'm a bit out of touch with England at the moment. Maybe I should come over and see Hollis.'

'Of course. But I'll send you the propositions in detail here first. Talk it over with your wife. There's no great hurry.'

'You've increased your bid by 50% since January. It suggests there's a hurry somewhere.'

Vosper was nobody's fool.

'When you're buying something,' Angell said, 'it's common practice to put in a low bid first. But even £60,000 was more than realistic. By all means get the property valued. I doubt if it would be put at more than £40,000. The house is in a very poor state of repair.'

'And you're offering more than double.'

'Because we want it. Because it interests us. Because it's in the area where we are buying land. Those are the reasons, Lord Vosper. And although, as I said, there's no hurry, I think one has to bear in mind that Land Increments, although it is a big company, only has so much money to sink in future development. Sir Francis Hone – whom I'd like you to meet sometime – is a very busy man with a lot of interests in the States. He's interested in Merrick House, as we all are, at the moment. But this is the propitious moment, this spring. If it should hang on too long he might well give it up and turn his attentions elsewhere.'

Vosper laughed. 'That sounds like a sales talk.'

'Well, of course. That's what it is. We would like the property; that's why we're making such a generous offer. But of course it's entirely up to you. We shall certainly not bother you further if you decide against it. Do think it over and let us know.'

Knowing he could catch the cheap flight home at nine – the inconvenience of such flights often operates only one way – he refused a half-hearted invitation to stay to dinner and caught the bus back to Geneva. The tempting offer was already in Vosper's bloodstream; one had only to allow time for it to work.

He ate a hearty meal at the station restaurant, pleasantly conscious that he felt no fatigue after his broken night, and the better for knowing that he could charge Land Increments First Class return fare to Geneva. He did not feel he was cheating them, since the task had been as well performed as if the higher fare had been paid, and at greater speed.

On the flight home, which was quite uneventful, his companion was a brutish young man who slept with his mouth open all the way to London Airport. So his thoughts more than once strayed to the young woman who had shared the disagreeable journey out. When they had landed temporarily at Zurich he had avoided her. To do her justice she had behaved very properly, and when they resumed their seats for the journey to Geneva she made no attempt to make anything of their earlier familiarity. They flew on in silence, and as they separated in Geneva he had bowed to her and she had smiled and murmured 'good-bye'. That was all.

So memory now of any talk they had had must derive from the first part of the flight. It was as if conversation between them came back to him which at the time he had been too worried to hear. She was fond of music – when had she said this? He could not remember – some instrument, some unusual one, not a saxophone, not an oboe; she went to concerts – Pop concerts *and* Symphony concerts, she said. Now there was a centre in Croydon she went more often, otherwise it meant getting back late. The train service from Victoria to East Croydon was very good, but her home was a bus journey of ten minutes, and after eight there weren't many buses.

Her hair curled rather the way Anna's did in the one old photo he had: it was light hair, light in texture, that is to say, the sort that is always difficult to keep tidy. Anna used to complain at her own whenever there was a breeze; perhaps she complained more often so that he was given the opportunity to reassure her. This girl was quite three inches taller than Anna, and her eyes were darker and softer and more docile. Odd, that bruise on her neck.

Of course one did not know her name, nor would one ever have asked it. Her vanity case had P.F. on it.

Odd that one should think so much of Anna after all these years. If it had not been for that one photograph he believed he would have forgotten by now even what she looked like.

Lady Vosper had a flat in Wilton Crescent, where she spent rather more than half of each year. Angell's relationship with her was more than acquaintanceship, less than friendship. He had met her two or three times at the bridge table of common friends, and had rather gone out of his way to earn her liking. Titled clients are always good for a firm. He had first of all mentioned to her his acquaintanceship with Viscount Vosper, and when this clearly earned him no good marks at all, he had ventured to advise her on some investments she was thinking of selling. This had led to two small professional commissions, both motoring offences: defending her against a charge of careless driving, in which he had succeeded, and against a breathalyser test, in which he had failed. Then had come the proposal that he had conveyed to her to buy Merrick House, which she had rejected. Since then they had only met once, casually in the street. But on the Thursday after his return, in spite of his horror of illness, his genuine dread of even observing it at secondhand, he called on her.

She was a small woman, well built, dark and vigorous with a firm brisk walk and a tenor voice. Fifteen or twenty years ago she had been a beauty, but hers were the looks that harden quickly with the years. Her skin had become coarse, her fine black eyes seemed always to be narrowed with cigarette smoke, even when she wasn't smoking, and her hair was dyed a dark auburn that convinced no one. In spite of a mannishness in her talk and walk and dress she was feminine enough, as her marriages and love affairs showed.

Her little chauffeur-handyman showed him in, and he found her with her feet up reading *The Field* and just lighting one cigarette from the butt of the last.

'My dear chap,' she said, 'roses! Don't say you're courting me! No, maybe they're the wrong red. But it's very genteel of you all the same.'

'I heard you'd been ill, Lady Vosper; I heard only yesterday so I thought I'd call. Peter Werner told me. He said you had been in hospital.'

She screwed out the butt and drew deep at the new cigarette. 'Well, if the old Clinic's a hospital, he's right. I must say they feather-bed you in there. Delude you into thinking you're a film star while they do the usual ghastly things on the sly.'

Bulking large against the daylight, he put the roses on a table by the window. 'I hope it's nothing serious,' he said, taking a seat, unbuttoning his coat, resting and spreading his considerable body, eyeing her while trying not to. It's always difficult to tell with women: if they're sallow it is hidden under layers of make-up, if they're thinner they may have decided that week to go on a starvation diet.

'What the hell,' she said. 'I got my guts crushed eighteen years ago in that Aston Martin. Now and then it plays me up. This was one of the times, and a rather foul one.'

'Well, I hope you're quite recovered now and feeling better.'

'No, I feel as if I've been walked on. And I'm out of temper at missing two of the best weeks of hunting – and maybe two more yet, which'll nearly see the season out.'

'Is your daughter with you?'

Miriam McNaughton was a withdrawn mousy girl of 25 who was overshadowed by her ebullient mother and did things vaguely in the theatre.

'She's been around,' said Lady Vosper tersely. 'But her husband's in work at the moment: the first time for six months, so she has to hold his hand. And you, my dear chap? I hope you're not the bringer of bad news.'

'Bad news? I come simply to inquire after –'

'I'm joking, man. But my mother always used to say if a

solicitor calls on you it means somebody has died or is going to die.'

Angell shifted uneasily: she was too near the bone. 'Your mother was a cynic. Lawyers happen to be human beings like other men, and when a friend of theirs is unwell it's natural to be concerned. I was passing your door and thought I would call in and see how you were and if you could play bridge next week at my house. I have the Hones coming. That's Thursday of next week, a week today . . .'

'Well, that's obliging of you, but my fool of a doctor says I'm to rest for a week, and the minute I'm better I shall rush down to Handley Merrick to get the last of the hunting. But ask me when I get back. I shall be in town all of May.'

They talked of bridge and then of the sale-rooms, while the cloudy March day drew in its daylight like the lips of an uncharitable woman and Lady Vosper switched on a table lamp and the office workers hurried past the windows on their way home. Angell was never really sure what money Lady Vosper had. He knew well that upper class habit of always declaring oneself poor no matter what one's true circumstances were. Her last husband, the third viscount, had not left any large sum, but one never knew with what ingenuity money might have been salted away to avoid death duties. In January when Angell had called about Merrick House she had been properly downright. 'My dear chap,' she had said, 'Vospers have lived in the damned place for two hundred and fifty years, and that's where I lived with Julian for the best ten of mine. What Claude will do if he inherits, or Harry, is their business, but while I'm alive it stays in the family. I ain't got much sentiment about things as a rule, but I've some over Merrick.' This flat, too, he believed, had belonged to her husband: its contents were solid and worthy rather than distinguished; but there were a few nice pieces, some excellent silver.

He stayed for half an hour and then left. She clearly had no inkling of what Matthewson had told him. But the very lack of close friendship between them would make it extremely difficult for him to call again in this way, otherwise she would become suspicious of his attentions. All that could be done would be to try to meet her whenever possible, casually at the bridge table and elsewhere, to keep in touch and to observe from a distance. Certainly at the moment there was little to observe. She looked no different from when they had last met.

A reply from Vosper after a couple of weeks said he was interested in their formal proposal and was forwarding it to Messrs Hollis & Hollis for their consideration and advice. Angell rang Francis Hone with the news and Hone said: 'Come to dinner tonight and we can try to work out a time-table. There'll only be Angela and myself and she knows all about it.'

It was the day of a sale at Christie's, and there were three or four excellent things that Angell coveted, especially a John drawing which had captivated him from the moment he saw it. He didn't think it would be too expensive, but he never really liked to leave a bid with the auctioneer. So he got Mumford to take over his two appointments for the morning – which Mumford grudgingly did – and spent it in the auction room. He came away with the John drawing, which annoyingly had been forced up by a dealer, and a delightful small Chinese painting on silk, unsigned but entitled 'Crickets and Flowers'.

It was while he was bidding for this that the idea came to him that Lady Hone was responsive to the elegant gesture, and that to take her some small present tonight would be appropriate and polite. Crickets and *flowers*. But flowers were not enough, and chocolates ill-judged since she was waging the usual foolish war on weight. A piece of jewellery was far too expensive. But scent – perfume. What woman could resist perfume? It seemed likely that Messrs D. H. Evans would have a good selection.

It was just after five o'clock when he walked into the store and up to the board giving directions for finding the various departments. His was an important, solidly based walk, but with as yet scarcely any signs of the waddle that comes to so many stout men. Perfume was on the ground floor, and almost before he reached the department he saw her. She was not serving anyone so he went straight up to her.

'Can you advise me on some good French perfume?'

She looked at him with disinterested eyes, and then she recognized him and a wide, quite brilliant smile broke over her face.

'Why, Mr – er . . . Good afternoon. So you're back, then!'

'As I see you are.'

It was too warm in here after the cold day outside.

'Oh, yes. Only last Saturday! I had a fabulous time. Did you?'

'I came back to London the following evening. It was a brief business visit. One can see you have been in the sun. Very brown.'

'Thanks, yes.' She caught her lip under her teeth and glanced at a girl further along the counter. 'Only two cloudy days, and one with snow. I've never ski-ed in snow before. It's super. Do you ski?'

'No, I do not seem to have had time for it.'

There was a pause, and two or three women drifted past with shopping baskets and lizard bags. He noticed that the bruise or stain on her neck had gone.

'Did you say you wanted some perfume, sir?'

'Yes. For a present. D'you know. I thought of Dior, probably.'

'Oh, yes, certainly. As it happens we have a special Dior consultant here this week. Miss Porter, over there. She'll be glad to advise you.'

Stare over her head at the rows of boxes and bottles. 'What difference does it make whether she advises me or you do?'

He thought she flushed slightly. 'It doesn't really, but she's the expert. She just happens to be here this week and I thought . . .'

'Mme Rochas,' he said, still staring at the bottles. 'I've changed my mind. I'll have Mme Rochas instead. Can you advise me on that?'

She smiled widely, that very nice generous smile. 'Is it for your wife, sir?'

'I haven't a wife. It's for the wife of a business friend.'

There was really very little choice – one either bought Mme Rochas or one did not: it was simply a matter of size, but he contrived, sweating, to take some time over this. Would contrived be the word? Perhaps it implied something more deliberate than anything he had in mind at the time. While other assistants in the store began discreetly to get ready for closing, he eventually came to say:

'My name is Angell – Wilfred Angell. I have no account here, but I suppose I may pay by cheque?'

'Of course, sir. Yes, of course.' Even then she did not volunteer her name – which he thought showed good taste – so he asked it.

'Friedel,' she said. 'Pearl Friedel.'

'Is that an English name?'

'My father's Austrian. My mother was English. They say I take after her.'

'I knew someone many years ago whom you resemble. Her name was Anna Tyrell. She had some Danish blood, though she looked as English as you.'

Her head was bent as she put gift wrapping round the box, but he felt that she was pleased with his attentions – as she had every reason to be. Certainly he was pleased with her manner and her manners, and with her looks. There was a dignity about her. Or was he imagining this because of her height and her composure? The statuesque quality. But she was not a statue; her breast rose and fell.

Presently he took the packet and dabbed his forehead again and said good-bye and left the store, a little depressed. This was the end of the incident, of the meeting. Just as when the plane touched down in Geneva it had been the end of another meeting. One said good-bye and left; one simply went no further, because 'further' implied a step with incalculable ramifications, an incalculable future. He shrank away from that, all his legal experience stood in the way of committing himself so far. Like a man within a self-built wall, he could peer over it, but to break it down needed some impulse that his nature did not possess.

Angela Hone was delighted with the perfume. (He had spent more than he had intended, which was the only niggling regret.) But it did seem to him that such a gift might well be acceptable here and there in the future when the wives of influential business friends were concerned.

That week he discharged Alex. Suddenly the situation had become quite unacceptable – it was as if overnight the brink of toleration had been passed. In Alex's place he took a married couple but he did not think they would last long. When people were inefficient he was not good at hiding his contempt.

A successful solicitor has many contacts. One of a long and involved nature was Angell's acquaintanceship with Vincent Birman. They had been at Sherborne together where Birman, the elder by a term, had first tormented Angell, then dominated him, and finally had befriended him by protecting him from worse tyrannies. After the war they had taken their Intermediates and their Finals together and had qualified in the same year. Angell had gone at once into his father's firm. Birman had come into a legacy of £16,000 had spent it in a year, had then joined a distinguished firm of solicitors in Gray's Inn but after five years had got himself struck off the rolls by contriving somehow to become co-respondent in a divorce case in which he had been representing the injured husband. After that he had been a journalist, a travel-agent, and a P.R.O. before starting his own agency. The Vincent Birman agency was small but it was efficient, and its range was wide. Divorce inquiry work was its staple, but it would take on almost anything that Birman happened to fancy, from sending men to report for half a dozen newspapers at the Olympic Games in Mexico, to bringing over a giraffe from Africa to supply the needs of a film company. Because he spent his money freely, was well connected and a good mixer, he always knew somebody who knew somebody else; he was one of the world's great arrangers.

Angell employed him from time to time on occasions when confidential inquiries were needed or perhaps unusual contacts had to be made. In spite of his peculiar record Birman always kept his mouth shut; and it was far pleasanter to deal with a gentleman and a trained solicitor. Angell also had a long memory for favours as well as injuries, and although he had long since rationalized the terrors of thirty years ago, it pleased him to think of Birman as a school friend, and one to whom he could now be the giver of small employments.

In appearance Birman was a small, bald, cruel man with blandly innocent twinkling eyes and a candid smile. He had always been physically very strong and physically very brave, characteristics which in themselves fascinated Angell who lacked them but did so well, he considered, without them.

During these weeks Birman had occasion to call at the offices of Carey, Angell & Kingston several times. As a firm they avoided divorce when they could, but if you had a substantial client who got himself involved with an ambassador's wife, you couldn't suddenly tell him to take his business elsewhere. So Birman called and Birman saw Angell, and one day, just after he had discharged the married servants, and quite on the impulse of the moment, Angell gave Birman another little job to do. Almost as soon as he had spoken he was sorry, yet he allowed the conversation to proceed.

'Yes?' Birman said. 'But don't you know where she lives? That will take a bit longer won't it, old chap?'

'My client,' said Angell, uneasily resting his bulk against the desk, 'says that she lives a ten minute bus ride from East Croydon station. And of course her name's not a common one.'

'Have you looked her up in the telephone directory?'

'I gathered from what I was told that she was not on the telephone.'

Birman's hard smooth small shiny face showed only a cold innocence, like a child pulling a spider's legs off. 'What exactly do you want to know?'

'Our client was not specific. I think he means he would like a general sketch of her background: what her age is, where she went to school, her father's position in the accountancy world, what relatives she has, her hobbies and recreations, how she spends her spare time.'

'A sort of private Who's Who, in fact.'

'Possibly. One need not confine oneself to the facts she would fill in on the form herself.'

'I get the message, old chap.'

'Don't over-read it,' Angell said. 'As you'll see, the inquiry has nothing to do with divorce. So far as I can gather from our client's instructions, there is no question of litigation of any sort. Normally it would perhaps have been better if we'd referred him direct to you, but we've known him twenty years and sometimes one undertakes these things. I'm quite satisfied as to his bona fides.'

'That's your concern,' said Vincent Birman. 'I just do what I'm told.'

'The one thing that was emphasized to me was that every discretion must be used. It was put to me that it was better not to have information than to let her or her family suspect they were the object of an inquiry. I suppose it wouldn't be possible to do this yourself?'

Birman's bright eyes had been ranging round the office; now they settled on Angell for a moment in surprise. 'Of course. It'll cost you a bit more.'

'I'd be glad if you would.'

'Give me a week, old chap. I'll drop in a week today.'

After he had gone Angell abused himself for wasting money on an idle fancy. But for once in his life the expenditure of money was a secondary regret beside the apprehension that he had taken another step into the unknown. He comforted himself with the reassurance that he need never take another.

Chapter Three

Looking back over events as she did sometimes in a vague and unanalytical way, Pearl supposed that it had all really begun with the date she made with Ned McCrea. Perhaps the queerest part was that she'd never much cared for Ned; he was red-faced and he sweated; but he'd been on at her some time, and eventually it became easier to say yes than no.

It was the first week in March, and they made up a foursome with her friend Hazel and her fiancé Chris, and it was at Pearl's own suggestion that they went to the Trad Hall in Redgate because Geoff Houseman and his band were there, and she loved his clarinet playing.

The evening didn't start off too well because Hazel and Chris were in the middle of a row to begin with, and when they got there they found the hall only supplied coffee and soft drinks, which didn't please Ned, who loved his beer. He thought Pearl had done it on purpose because the only other time she'd gone out with him he'd got tight and this was another reason why she'd said no to him since. Hazel always told Pearl that she was too choosey about her men, but in fact it was a pure accident about there being no licence; it had just never occurred to her to think. You didn't go to a dance hall to *drink*.

The Trad Hall was fairly crowded when they got there, because Houseman was quite a draw. Pearl had a dance early on with Chris because Hazel had whispered to her would she because dancing with her always put Chris in a good humour and she said he certainly needed it. Chris Coke was heavy going both on the floor and off; Pearl always thought he took himself too seriously, and when he was dancing he twisted his elbows and scowled and moved his tongue against his teeth like a small boy learning to draw. Tonight she did her best with him, but obviously his row with Hazel was still simmering and he hadn't much thought for anything else.

After that one dance Pearl danced pretty solidly with Ned till about nine-thirty and then the band took a breather.

Chris said: 'I can't think why we came to a morgue like this. Come out for a quick one with me, Ned, while the girls powder their noses.' Ned grinned and said: 'O.K. by me, Chris.' It was just what he wanted.

As soon as they'd gone Hazel launched into a whole history of the row. 'Sometimes it's like walking a tight-rope. I can't put a foot right. I hope he comes back sober.'

'If it's like this now, what's it going to be like after you're married?'

'I don't know, honest I don't,' Hazel said, but with a flicker of dislike at the question. 'Oh, he'll be all right in a couple of days. He always is.'

'Maybe it would be better if you stood up to him,' Pearl said.

'It's all very well for you to talk, you can take your pick of half a dozen.'

'But *what* a half dozen!'

'They're all *right*, Pearl. Or all right as men *go*. You're romantic! You're a *snob*! You want a film star or something.'

'No, I don't. But I'd like something better than I've seen so far.'

They went off to the Ladies. Hazel was an age fiddling with her hair, and when they got back the band had already started again. There was no sign of the two young men.

Pearl began to feel annoyed. Chris was Hazel's headache, but she didn't appreciate being left flat by a man called McCrea who had gone off for a drink with an apologetic grin and not even invited her to go with him. And this after all his pestering for a date.

The place where you get coffee and snacks is off the side of the hall, through an arch, with a white painted fretwork fencing that you can sit beside with your sandwiches or lemonade and watch the dancing; or you can when there aren't too many people standing in the way. The girls had to go round the floor from the Ladies and past this part to get back to where they had been before, and Pearl had noticed two men eyeing them on the way out. Now they eyed them on the way back. Obviously Hazel hadn't noticed this because when the men came across and asked them to dance she looked quite startled and rather haughty and said, no thank you, I'm sure.

The one who had asked Pearl certainly wasn't her type, and her impulse was to say the same; but just then Chris and Ned came in at the door and Ned's face was even redder than usual and you could see he had been putting away just as much as he could in a short time. So she got up and said, thank you, and started to dance with this other man.

Pearl sometimes thought she would have hated to live in the days when people's idea of dancing was to clutch each other close together and stride about the floor. For one thing it must have been awful to fit your steps in if you were strangers; for another you more or less had to talk, and she was no talker with people she didn't know; for a third you were too *close* to look at each other properly. It was a sort of dancing that seemed terribly suggestive to her.

At least he was young, this man who had asked her, early twenties, but *small* for a man – at least four inches shorter than she was – with a mop of fine dark hair growing luxuriantly and falling like a cock's comb, and this seemed to help his height. Under it he was awfully good-looking in a rather fierce way. He had very dark eyes, deep set, a fine but sallow skin, a long straight nose, a wolfish, mischievous smile. One eyebrow was divided by a thin scar. Silk shirt, black bootlace tie, light-weight belted jacket, tight check trousers, suède boots. Everything of the finest quality. And he could dance. Not as good as a professional, but he put such *life* into it. You could hardly see his feet.

When it was over he just said: 'Thanks,' and looked at nothing in particular, and Pearl was going to turn away when he said: 'Like a drink?'

'No, thanks.'

'Oh, come on. It's thirsty work.'

The two young men had stood by the door till the end of the dance; now they were going across to where Hazel was sitting; they hadn't seen Pearl yet. She said on impulse: 'All right,' and went into the refreshment room with him. He ordered two milk shakes and they found a seat and he sucked his drink and eyed her. In the five years since she was fifteen she had got used to looks, so her skin didn't prickle any more.

'Pearl,' he said at last. 'Smashing name.'

'Who told you it?'

'Your friend called you that. Is it for real?'

'Yes.'

'Mine's Godfrey. God for short.'

She smiled politely at the joke and wondered how soon she could leave him. In spite of his fine clothes he wasn't much class.

'My surname's Vosper,' he said. 'What's yours?'

'Friedel.'

'Pearl Friedel. Quite a name. And where d'you live?'

'Does it matter?'

'Now we're introduced it's nice to know.'

'In Selsdon.'

'That's a few miles from here, isn't it?'

'Yes, a few. Just out of Croydon actually.'

'I live in a little village on the Thames,' he said. 'Called London. North bank nowadays. Moved up in the world, see.'

She said no more but finished her drink. She was not anybody's easy pick-up and she didn't want him to have ideas of that sort. As the band began again she could see Ned peering across the floor.

'Dance this?' said Godfrey.

'Thanks, but I have a partner.'

'That silly gett that kept you waiting? I tell you honest, if it was me in his place I'd never *dare*. I'd think I was on too good a pitch.'

Expressed more elegantly, this would have been rather along her line of thinking about Ned, so she danced with him again. Even his dancing was a bit common; one couldn't say how, it just was. Halfway through, Geoff Houseman took the music on his own, and she stopped dancing in the centre of the floor and listened. Godfrey said: 'What's up? What's wrong?'

When it was over she began to dance again, feeling good in the way only a clarinet could make her feel good.

'Is he a boy friend of yours?'

'Who?'

'The guy with the trumpet.'

'No, I've never spoken to him.'

'Is that other one your boy friend – that one sneering at us over there?'

'I came with him.'

'He thinks he owns you.'

By the time they finished they had moved round and were on the far side from Ned. Godfrey held her hand. He had awfully hard hands, hard and bony.

'You got a regular boy friend?'

She didn't answer.

'Not to worry. I expect you've got so many queueing up. It's the pie-faced ones like your girl friend over there who've got to snatch at any mug that's mug enough.'

'I don't think she's pie-faced.'

'Well, what does she paint her eyebrows up there for? Those bare bumps look as if she's got tumours.'

'Nobody's asking you to like her if you don't want to,' Pearl said, amused in spite of herself.

'Nobody's asking me to like you, but I can't help it. Once in a lifetime you get struck that way.'

She got her hand back as Ned came across. One thing about Ned, he was tall, a good six feet. That was one of Pearl's problems, not to look downwards at a man.

'How about coming back and joining us again,' he said sullenly, and without so much as looking at Godfrey. 'I reckon it's about time, isn't it?'

'Excuse me, I don't think you've met,' Pearl said. 'Mr Ned McCrea, Mr Godfrey Vosper.'

They just looked at each other, they never said a word.

'Well?' Ned said to her.

'Tell Hazel I'll be over in a few minutes.'

'And what about me?'

'What *about* you?' Pearl said, getting angry and breathless for once in her life.

'I don't know if you happen to have forgotten but you came with me.'

'I think you forgot first!'

'Look, Pearl –'

'Look, Jack,' said Godfrey, 'wrap it up. The lady says she'll come back when she feels like it. O.K., she'll come back when she feels like it and not before. Now fade.'

Ned turned on him, towering over him. 'I'll thank you to keep out of this! When I bring a girl to a dance I don't expect her to go off with some little twerp who hasn't even been able to find a girl of his own –'

'Don't press your luck,' said Godfrey looking at him. 'Run away and play with your toys before you get trod on.

You've heard what she says! Now – *beat it!*'

Pearl had only seen a fight once in a dance hall and that was in Streatham; there had been a sudden scuffle, a couple of angry blows, and almost while the men were squaring up again three attendants had appeared as if from nowhere and hustled them – almost thrown them out. It had been done with immense swiftness. She did not want that to happen here. Funny how the heart thumps, quite different from just beating fast when you're dancing. But thank God just then the band started up again and she began to move slowly in rhythm, and she happened to be opposite Godfrey, so he joined in and Ned was left glowering. After a few seconds when she was afraid he might take Godfrey by the scruff he turned on his heel and stalked off.

So that way the choice was made. She'd never taken up with anybody in this way before. Obviously Ned was in such a flaming temper that nothing but the completest apology would satisfy; and this he was certainly not going to get.

They danced most dances from then on, she and Godfrey. She was taken with his looks, a sort of dark dynamism that made up for his smallness. It was fun to kick over the traces a bit. About eleven Hazel came across and said she had a headache and they were all going. Unfortunately she said it as if she had been bitterly insulted as well as Ned, and this put Pearl out of step.

'Stay a bit longer,' said Godfrey to her. 'We're just getting in the slot. I've got my car outside. I can buzz you home in no time.'

'Please yourself entirely, I'm sure, Pearl,' said Hazel. 'But don't forget you're supposed to be *in* by twelve-thirty.'

That settled it. 'Thank you. I can find my own way home.'

'Definitely,' said Godfrey. 'I'll see her safe in, I promise you. Not to worry. She'll be there.'

You could tell by the way she put her heels down as she walked away that Hazel was annoyed. Pearl hoped it wouldn't start a feud that would last till their ski-ing holiday.

'Not to worry, Oyster,' said this odd dark small dynamic good-looking wicked-looking man. 'Little God'll look after you.'

They stayed through until the Queen, which was at mid-

43

night, and then with everybody streaming for the exit Pearl grabbed her coat and Godfrey was waiting for her and they went out to the car park.

This was the awkward part, this being taken home, because different men expected different things, and sometimes men who pick girls up expect a lot. Ned of course would have wanted to paw her about in the back of Chris's car on the way home, and they would almost certainly have stopped for ten minutes somewhere on the way; but ten minutes would have been all. Actually Pearl was not wild about that sort of thing, although sometimes it was better than others. But usually it simply meant that one's frock got crumpled and soiled and one often had a bit of a struggle not to let things go too far. It was different, Pearl felt, for those girls who right from the start wanted all they could get; she wasn't blaming them; only everyone wasn't made to a pattern and it was hard sometimes to get that point over. On the whole she found it better not to let men make too much progress, because the further they got before you stopped them the more offended they were. Anyway her view was that if she ever needed to start taking the Pill it wasn't going to be because of a fumbling struggle in the back of a car.

Ned would have known this, and so would Chris. Little Godfrey was the unknown.

Well, you never could tell what the next surprise was going to be, because they picked their way among the cars until Godfrey stopped at a great green monster all shiny and polished and chromium, and he unlocked the doors and said: 'Hop in the hansom cab. Right. In we get. Tuck in your frills,' and then he went round to his door. Unbelieving she sank back into a seat like a luxury armchair, and shaded discreet light showed up a glamorous interior with arm-rests and head-rests and a most peculiar central dashboard like the console of an organ; the whole thing could have been the cockpit of a luxury aeroplane.

So he put in his key and the engine whispered and they were suddenly in effortless motion, weaving among the others like a light craft in spite of their size, pushing and edging a way to the front of the queue; then they were out in the road and with sudden tremendous acceleration surged past a line of newly started crawling cars with their exhausts smoking, came to traffic lights and over-shot them as the cross traffic was just finishing. Horns blew, but they were left far behind, and there was just the rushing of air and a faint whispering murmur of power. Pearl felt a sense of pleasure, of exhilaration.

She said: 'Super car.'

'Yes. Cost over five and a half thousand. Not a bad bus. It'll do 140. Six and a quarter litre engine. Pass anything on the road.'

'Like now.'

'Like now. You got to have some kick out of motoring, else you might just as well own an old Morris 1000.'

'That's what Chris drives!'

'Who's Chris?'

'The other boy. Hazel's fiancé.'

He laughed. 'See it. And the face that came with you, the one as thinks he owns you?'

'Nobody owns me.'

'That's right. What does he do?'

'He's a radio mechanic.'

'And drives a little van during the day, eh? Knock, knock, excuse me, Mrs Smith, I've come to look at your telly.'

'It's honest work.'

'What isn't these days?'

She studied his face in the light of a passing car.

'You must be very rich to have a car like this.'

'Rich? No, I make do, see. But I'm going to be in the real money soon.'

'What do you do?'

'What would you say I did?'

She stared again, this time at his expensive clothes; then she glanced out. 'Are we on the right road?'

'No, but it's easier this way. Should join the Brighton road in a minute, no bull. Cigarette?'

'Thanks.'

He took one out of the cubby hole and lit it with the cigar lighter in the car. She said: 'Aren't you having one?'

'Don't smoke. You haven't guessed yet.'

'You run a garage.'

'Ha, ha, clever. No. Try again.'

She said: 'These are like ladies' cigarettes. Small and –'

'That's right. I keep 'em for ladies.'

They turned out onto a bigger road, swung left, snorted past four cars following two all-night lorries, began to climb a snakey hill.

'You work for the films.'

'Wish I did. Mine isn't easy mun. No, I box.'

'Box?'

'Box. That's why it's dead lucky for your flabby friend he didn't start anything.'

Of course as soon as he said it, it seemed the only thing he could have been, but she would never have guessed because of his size.

'Like to drive?' he suggested.

'Oh, heavens, no thanks!'

'It's easy on these big jobs. No gears. As much guts as a jet. Watch me put my foot down.'

They surged to the top of the hill, lights staring into the sky, swooped down the other side as if they were flying. There was just the rush of the dark countryside and the snort of the wind.

She said: 'What are you – middle-weight or what?'

'You joking?'

'No. I just don't know about things like that.'

'Feather-weight, me. That's nine stone and under. That's why they call me Little God. You've never seen nothing faster than me. I'm going to the top. You watch me.'

'You'll be going to hospital if you drive like this.'

'Don't you like it? It turns me on. What's life about if it's not taking risks?'

All the same he slowed down, and it was just as well, as they came to a roundabout and swivelled round it with a lurch of the great car. (She was relieved to recognize the road: they were heading in the right direction now.) It all fitted in: his wealth in one so young, the hardness of his hands and arms, the darting way he danced. It *was* lucky Ned hadn't hit him. She warmed to Godfrey.

'What do you do?' he asked.

'Oh, not very up-in-the-world. I'm a perfumery adviser at a big London shop.' She usually said this: it sounded better than 'selling scent'.

'You live at home, eh?'

'Yes. I travel up every day.'

'Where d'you live?'

'12, Sevenoaks Avenue. You turn off to the right in a minute.'

'Like to see me box sometime?'

'What? Oh, well, I never have –'

'Come on Wednesday. Next Wednesday, I'm meeting a fat little Mick from Liverpool called Ed Hertz.'

'I can't Wednesday. I'm going on holiday on Friday night.'

'That don't make sense. What's wrong with Wednesday?'

'Well, you know what it's like: I've things to do, pack, get clothes ready – You turn here!'

When he'd turned and she had given him the next direction she thought: there's really no reason why I *shouldn't*. He's not my type, he's common, he talks badly, he's too sure of himself. Champ's girl friend. Well, really. It doesn't suit me. The very opposite. People say I'm too quiet, too reserved, too choosey for twenty. Perhaps I am.

'Where now?'

'Straight on, and it's the first on the left. Number 12 is this end on the left-hand side.'

He did as he was told and they stopped outside the house among the other parked cars, and he switched off the engine and put on a low interior light that just showed things dimly, and they looked out at the small but respectable semi-detached.

'Well, thanks for the dance,' he said. 'How about Wednesday, Oyster? I'll come for you. Bring you back. All luxe. No effort. I'm on early so we needn't stay to the end if you find it a drag.'

'Where is it?' she said. 'The boxing, I mean.'

'Walworth. No distance. No problem. I'll pick you up here 7.30 in the old bus. Eh?'

'I really mustn't, Godfrey.'

'Call me God.'

'I really mustn't come. I have so much to do –'

'Which you can do Thursday just the same . . .'

There were no lights in the house. She would get a row from Dad if he heard of all this.

'That's fixed then,' said Godfrey, and leaned across and kissed her on a corner of the mouth. 'Little Oyster. Thanks again.'

'Thank you for bringing me home,' she said, surprised

and more than a trifle impressed that this apparently was all he expected.

'Think nothing of it. See you Wednesday. Be my guest. Seven-thirty here?'

'All right,' she said.

Then she stood on the pavement and listened to the low pitched well-bred bobble of the exhaust as the car accelerated away.

Frank (formerly Franz) Friedel worked as an accountant for Huntingdons, the great furniture firm, who have their headquarters in Croydon. He was not the chief accountant, and many people had felt – and said – that he could easily have bettered himself by taking work in London. But he had a sense of loyalty to the firm and a sense of belonging to the district in which for thirty years he had made his home. He prized this, this sense of having a root and a home, he who had been rootless under the shadow of Hitler during the formative years of his life. And anyway no one in his home ever lacked for the necessities.

Pearl's own mother had died when she was eight – she came from Nottingham – and her father had married Rachel a couple of years later and they had two boys and a girl. Rachel was Austrian like Frank, but unlike him her attitudes had been formed before she left. Frank had been careful to adapt, so that his speech was almost accentless and without foreign syntax. The boys, Leslie and Gustave, grew noisier every year and Julia, aged five, was going to be a little tyrant. If Pearl had been the bossy type she could have used her age superiority to keep on top, but somehow it never seemed worth the nagging and the disguised bullying.

A lot of things to Pearl didn't seem worth the effort. She was not lazy but she was placid. She lived a lot of the time in a quiet private world of her own, and this earned her a reputation for dignity and reserve. But she wasn't really shy; only a little slow-spoken and latent. She didn't much care what people thought – or if she did she never said so. She was ill at ease with children because they demanded too much of her. She liked cats but not dogs. She had herself a cat-like love of comfort and of being on her own.

She had joined the D. H. Evans' rota training scheme at

17, so that she could be earning her own keep and be out of the way, but went on living at home because her father would not let her leave. An intelligent man within narrow limits, his liberal English views did not extend to giving girls their freedom while they were still under age. Besides, a certain strictness towards Pearl was evidence of their special relationship: she was the surviving reminder of his first and English wife; more was expected of her than of the others. Pearl got on well enough with Rachel but often wondered why the marriage had happened – not because Rachel was not a good wife but because she did not measure up to his standards.

In spite of Pearl's being the odd one out, they were a fairly close-knit family, and on Sunday morning she was asked about the dance and had to tell a few lies and hope Hazel and Chris would back her up if need be. Pearl was never very happy at the sun going down on *anyone*'s wrath, so she made an effort to call and see Hazel that afternoon. It was a frosty meeting to begin, but after a bit they turned to talk of Chris, and Hazel unthawed. The last thing Pearl wanted was a blight over the start of their holiday. But she didn't mention her date with Godfrey on the Wednesday. Although she longed to talk to somebody about him, afterwards she was glad.

So it was Wednesday, and coming home she had the usual fight to get on a 25 bus, and she *just* caught the 6.14 from Victoria, and another bus from the station and was in by seven. It didn't give her much time, but Rachel was busy with her own brood and her father wasn't back yet, so she just called she would be out to supper and pretended not to hear Rachel's 'Where are you going?'

Working at a shop and living at home, she had made enough money to spend what Rachel called 'a fortune' on clothes, and her narrow oak wardrobe overflowed beneath a rail and curtain. She hadn't an idea what the done thing was at a boxing match, but Walworth sounded pretty sordid. After a lot of lip biting she put on a strawberry pink number of fine wool with a square neck line and a flared short skirt, and took her second best coat.

She had told him not to ring but to wait on the other side of the road, and sure enough by 7.25 the great green car was there, looking a monster among the shabby saloons and the family runabouts. She grabbed her bag and was going to leave, but suddenly remembered his size and kicked off her ordinary shoes and pulled on a pair of black patent leather with flat heels.

'Lo, Oyster,' he said. 'Wow, you look good. Smashing. Hop in. That's what I'm going to do tonight.'

'What?'

'Smash someone's face in.' He laughed. A harsh gasping sound, breath escaping. No mirth. 'O.K.? Let's go.' He started the car and they slid off.

He was in a polo-necked sweater and track trousers. There was a smell in the car of lotion or embrocation. He really *was* handsome in profile, and you could see a lot of girls would fall for him, and you could see he was used to it.

'Ought you to have come for me?' she asked. 'I mean, shouldn't you be getting ready or something before . . .'

'Oh, definitely. Robins is working up a head of steam because I'm not waiting around. But I've checked in, so what? I'll be back in time.'

'Who's Robins?'

'My manager. He's a wet fish, a fold, a drop out.'

'Why do you let him manage you if you think he isn't good –'

'Chance is a fine thing, lady. There's a lot to be learned in the boxing world; and three-fourths of it isn't to do with boxing at all. Someday I'll put you hip.'

They talked on the way in, but you could see that half his attention was lacking and that he was tense inside. Not surprising. Fighting and winning was his living, and he obviously made a lot of money out of it and couldn't afford to slip up.

'Is feather-weight the lightest weight?' she asked.

'Jees, no. There's bantam and there's fly. Light-weight's the next above me. I sometimes take on light-weights. That's the only time I got stopped.'

'Stopped?'

'I'll tell you all about it someday. Here we are. Just in time.'

They parked the car among a lot of others in the street and walked across to an odd town-hall-like building called *Manor Place Baths*.

50

'I got to leave you now, Oyster. Here's your ticket. I'll come and sit next to you soon as I'm through.'

'Why do you call me Oyster?'

'Can't you guess?' His hand on her elbow was as hard as iron. 'Here, Terry, look after my girl, will you. I got to buzz. See she's looked after.'

This big man with great ham hands and a bent nose showed her to her seat, which was three rows from the front. She felt conspicuous, out of her element. It would have been all right with Hazel there or someone to talk to. A biggish hall with seats like cinema seats, but otherwise very bare. In the entrance were tiled corridors and various notices about the baths.

It wasn't really as sordid as she had expected; the people were fairly ordinary, working class and some better, a sprinkling of ex-pugilists with their profession on their faces. There was one fabulously striking but fabulously common girl with platinum hair and imitation spectacles and a tiny skirt and great boots. Pearl decided to keep her coat on.

The thing started with two bantam-weights who lashed into each other for a couple of rounds and then one went down and was counted out. It was much like you saw on T.V. except that being live it was suddenly real and not on a tube in a box, and therefore different. Godfrey was third on the list. '6 (3 min.) rounds Feather-weight Contest at 9 st. between Godfrey Vosper, Kensington and Ed Hertz, Liverpool.' She was surprised this was in smaller print than two of the others. She wondered if it was anything to do with the weight of the fighters.

But it didn't seem so because the second contest, which was in even smaller print, was between two heavy-weights who scrambled and mauled for the full eight rounds before the black one won on points.

Then Godfrey came in in a red dressing gown with *Little God* printed across the middle of the back. He grinned at Pearl and climbed into the ring. The young man he was going to fight had a round pasty face and long fair hair. The M.C. announced the fight, the referee had them to-gether in the middle of the ring and then they both went back to their corners and took off their robes. Because she was below the level of the ring, they did not look particularly small, and Godfrey had a beautiful physique, a creamy olive skin, dark soft hair on his legs, muscles that only showed as he moved. By contrast Hertz looked white and bow legged, squatter, more bunched up.

At the bell they began to go round each other, sparring for an opening; and suddenly one thought he'd found it: there was an explosion of gloves: thump, thump, thump, hands going too fast to see; then it was over and they were circling round each other again. This went on all through the first two rounds: great flurries of violence mixed with sparring and weaving and circling. She couldn't for the life of her believe that she had anything to do with the small, beautiful, violent young man in the ring, that he had brought her here, or that she'd ever agreed to come. She was excited by it all but not thrilled. She noticed that Godfrey's left hand kept going out like a piston, and once in every two or three times it caught Hertz on the face, and Hertz's face was turning red and his nose had a smear of blood at the corner; but it was Hertz who was doing most of the rushing in, and several times he got Godfrey in a corner and there was a set-to before he got out of it.

She couldn't see his face between rounds except when he turned to spit water into a bucket; but when the third round started there was a change in the tempo. There was less sparring, more toe-to-toe fighting, gloves flailing, and the crowd began to roar. It went on like that for a full minute, and then the man next to Pearl said: ' 'E's 'ad it!' Pearl couldn't see what he meant because there was no change in either of the fighters. And then Godfrey stepped aside from one of Hertz's rushes and just stood there, his hands half lowered, dancing on his toes, as it were tempting Hertz to come on. Hertz rushed again and Godfrey did just the same again: it must have been maddening, Pearl thought, to hit thin air again and again and just have your opponent dodging and weaving, always near yet always just out of reach. People shouted. Then the gong went and the two men went back to their corners. But the referee followed Hertz to his corner, and after peering at him, walked back to Godfrey and raised Godfrey's hand. There was both cheering and booing at this. Then the M.C. came on and announced the winner, the referee having 'stopped the fight at the end of the third round to save Hertz further punishment.'

Catcalls and cheers, and Godfrey raised his hands, while his second put the robe over his shoulders. He hardly looked out of breath.

After that she watched another bout, but near the end of it the big man with the bent nose came behind her and breathed beer on her with the news that Godfrey was waiting outside in the hall.

She slid out and there he was – hair still wet from a shower – in a smart brown leather jacket and a white collar and a maroon tie over a striped silk shirt, and sand-coloured tight line trousers. He took her by the arm – that hard hand again – and again she felt a twinge of disappointment at his smallness, when he had seemed quite big in the ring. Walking to the car he explained how mad he was about the fight. 'Ref stopped it when it was all wrapped up. Next round I'd have thrown the whole book at Hertz. Just ready, he was, to be sewn up.'

'What does it matter?' she said. 'If you win, you win. It counts just the same, doesn't it?'

He handed her in and then went round and slid in beside her. 'You don't get it, Oyster. Boxing's not like needlework. It's like bull-fighting. You weigh up a man in the first round, see what he's made of, sum him up, if you're smart you plan for the next rounds, see. Then you get to work on him like you've planned, and when he's weakened, he's ready for the kill.' Godfrey put his hand palm upwards on the steering wheel and slowly clenched it. 'But just then a lily-livered ref steps in and says, oh dear me no, he's had quite enough and stops the fight just when you're getting ready to put him away. Refs, they ruin your life!'

'But couldn't you have hit him more in the third round instead of dancing around him?'

'Yes, yes, yes, yes, but it would have been the end of the *round*! I wanted another three whole minutes before I laid him out for keeps!'

Pearl shivered. He patted her hand. 'Now, come on now, didn't it give you a lift deep down? Didn't it turn you on?'

'Yes. Oh, yes. But it's a bit brutal, isn't it. I mean . . .'

'Life is brutal. I'm brutal. So what?' He dabbed at his lip. 'Is it swelling? Jees, I'm out of condition. I only did a week's training for this one. But mind, I run a lot. Every morning you see me padding it round the squares.'

They went to an expensive restaurant in Chelsea, a better one than Pearl had been in before. She drank a glass of wine but he would only have Coca-Cola. He ate badly and while he ate his mop of black hair slowly dried and seemed to rise into a comb over his forehead of its own vitality. His handsome dark eyes were always admiring, and something more. She got a tingling feeling in her spine. When they had finished he pulled a crumpled wad of notes out of his pocket and signalled the moustached waiter to bring the bill. It was nearly six pounds, and he gave the waiter a pound tip.

'Do you fight often?' she asked.

'Not like I want to. That's my crummy manager's fault: if he got around a bit more. Sometimes I do sparring as well; mind, punching up with a top notcher you learn things, but you only get two quid a round; it's not cushy.'

'But tonight.' She pointed at the roll of crumpled notes he was stuffing in his back pocket. 'Is that what you earned tonight?'

'What? This? Yes. Fifty quid. It's not bad for fifteen minutes, is it? Of course, there's the real money higher up.'

She frowned her perplexity. 'But you must fight quite often. Or else, how can you afford such a super car?'

He laughed that gasping, breath-escaping laugh. 'Shall we go?'

'Yes, yes, of course.'

They went out to the car.

'Home now?'

'Yes, please.'

It was a mild muggy night but she snuggled back pleasantly into the luxury interior.

'Do you have some other job as well?' she asked.

'You got the idea. Bright girl.'

He switched on the light and twisted the mirror to look at himself. 'It is swelling a bit. Nothing else though, is there, wouldn't know I'd been in a ring, would you. That's the way of it: the real smart lads never even get marked.'

'What else do you do, Godfrey?'

'What'll you give me if I tell you?'

'Oh, that's an old game.'

'No worse for being old, is it?'

'*Is* this your car?' she asked. 'You know, I mean . . .'

'What's the odds if it wasn't? I got it quite legit. It's mine to use when I want to. Little God's honour.'

'Of course,' she said quickly. 'Sorry I asked. It's not my business.'

'Could be, Oyster. Leather pushing's what I like doing and I promise you I'm on the up and up. Soon as I get a break I'll be in the big money. A man can make fifteen, twenty thousand in no time. Since I saw you last Saturday I thought about you a lot.'

'But you must be in the big money now in something. The way you dress, the way you spend . . .'

He said: 'I tell you I think a lot about you. That mean anything? How'd you like to be my regular girl?'

She opened the cubby hole, just for something to do, but the cigarettes weren't there. 'I'm not sure I want to be anyone's regular girl yet.'

'How old are you?'

'Nearly twenty.'

'I'm twenty-two. Why not? I mean, why don't you want to be anybody's regular girl?'

'It's just – well, it's just the way I feel.'

'Want a cigarette?'

'I have one in my bag, thanks.'

'You're a bit special for me, Oyster. I could do things for you.'

She managed to get the cigar lighter to work. It glowed a red end and she tasted the cigarette smoke.

'How about meeting next week?'

'I'm going ski-ing.'

He blew out a breath of disgust. 'Stone me. Going with that Ned McCrea, I suppose.'

'No, I'm going with Hazel and Chris. We're in a party.'

'When you come back?'

'Yes . . . Yes, thanks, I'd like to. But – you're a mystery man.'

He sighed in resignation, switched off the light, drove away. They wandered for fifteen or twenty minutes through the lighted car-choked suburbs of south London. He drove in fits and starts, would overtake a bunch of cars and bully his way to the front, provoking headlamp flashings of protest, then dawdle along a piece of road as if he were killing time or did not know the way. All evening he had been more tensed up than at their first meeting; this tenseness had not evaporated with the fight. He was still a coiled spring, impressive, dangerous.

'*Mystery* man,' he said, ten minutes after she had used the phrase, as if it had been rankling all the time. 'What's the mystery except you don't know where all the folding comes from? Typical woman. Don't be a typical woman.'

'Sorry.'

'You're not typical. You're the tops. See? What d'you want to know that'll make you happy?'

'Nothing. Honestly. It doesn't matter. I only thought you lived from boxing or something like that.'

'Who does? Maybe the first two in any ranking list. The rest . . . well, the rest work part time. Anything wrong with that?'

'No, nothing. Absolutely nothing.'

'I'm not a jewel thief, if that's what's worrying you. Wish I was.'

'Nothing's worrying me, Godfrey.' But that sort of thought had occurred to her.

They drove on a long way in silence.

'I could do things *with* you as well,' he said. 'As well as for you. *With* you, see.'

They were going across some open country, almost the first country they had found.

'What time is it?'

'Half ten.'

'Where are we?'

'Near Keston. You're nearly home. You don't trust me far, do you?'

'I was only wondering.' She felt depressed, let down. What had seemed like the beginning of an adventure was suddenly down to earth, tatty, rather sordid.

'That ref,' he muttered. 'I'd like to flatten that ref, knock him on his poop. Crummy old woman.'

They turned off the main road and bumped along a muddy lane. He drew in and stopped under some trees. For the last half hour she had been hoping this wouldn't happen but knowing it almost certainly would. He put his arm behind her along the seat and looked closely into her

56

face. He still smelt of the ring, a sort of carbolic and resin and Vaseline smell. It was quite dark here but she could see the glow of his eyes. He bent over and began to kiss her.

You could feel the slight lump on the side of his lip where it was swollen, but it didn't seem to trouble him. After a bit the kisses became more sexy. 'Look, can you get your coat off. Just as a start, like.'

'Let's make a date,' she said, 'for when I come home. I'm only away two weeks.'

'Right. Correct. Agreed. But tonight's tonight. Tomorrow, what say, we might both fall under a bus.' He started un-buttoning the top of her frock. She pushed his hands sharply away. It was more an impulse than anything – an instinctive reaction in which there was a twist of fear. If he had been one of half a dozen other men whom she would have expected to try this, she would have managed it much more tactfully.

He sat back and ran a hand through his flowering head of black hair. 'Little Oyster. You're fabulous. You send me, you really do. Where's the pearl? I've got to open the shell.'

He tried to slip her frock off her shoulders but the coat got in the way and it only slid back a bit. Then he changed direction and put his hand on her knees and ran them up inside her skirts.

She brought her knees quickly together and twisted away to get out of the car. She couldn't find the handle and scraped with her fingers all over the door. He sat back again gasping, and she realized he was laughing. His extra-ordinarily unattractive laugh seemed very out of place just then. She stopped fumbling along the door, feeling a fool but short of breath all the same, scared.

'Come off it,' he said. 'You must know what it's all about. There's no need to be shy.'

'Did you steal this car?' she said.

'Suspicious little oyster. No, I didn't, see. It belongs to an aunt. I work for her. She's got plenty. I borrow her car when I want to. Right? I'll take you round to meet her next time if you like, just to prove it.'

They were off the main road by a quarter of a mile: you could see the lights of cars passing. The night was hazy and the headlamps looked like searchlights. They were at the edge of a copse – low trees and the like.

He said: 'O.K., O.K. You'll not be happy till you know, will you. Not happy. Part time I work for an old girl as her chauffeur. She's not my aunt. That's all. That's all the diff. She likes me so she lends me her car. Any time I want it. That way and leather pushing I get by. Like I said. Money it's no problem. I make enough to get by. But any time now I'll be in the big money. See the way I wrapped up that Mick tonight. In a few months now I'll be a big wheel. Just that. Little God's honour. So now you know. Satisfied?'

'Thanks. Yes, I wondered.'

'So now you know.'

'Yes.'

'That makes a difference?'

'In what way?'

'Oh, now, it don't need spelling out. Look, – these seats lean back. You just wind 'em.'

'I'm sorry, Godfrey. It's just that –'

He patted her hand. 'Only take ten minutes. You won't come to no harm, even if you're not fixed up. Little God's honour.'

She sighed and wished her voice was easier, more assured. 'Sorry.'

'What's wrong? Not that corny old story. Or do I smell bad?'

'No, of course not. It's difficult to explain.'

'Try me. Don't be so scared.'

She didn't answer because she felt that whatever she said he would misunderstand. It's not always the moral thing that makes one moral. How can you claim to have a sense of dignity, a sense of privacy, of at least a little personal importance? How can you say that without inviting hoots of laughter? Pearl never could stand men who waded in, who seemed to think they owned you. But for heaven's sake, she'd dealt with this before. What was the difference between him and others?

He offered her another cigarette and she took it though she didn't really want it. He used his lighter this time on purpose and the lighter showed up her pure skin and clear features. It showed up too the intentness, the uncomprehending intentness of his own look.

They smoked in silence. She was anxious only for him to start the car, to move on, but she did not say so. She told herself that he *had* been nice to her, he had spent hard earned money on her, and he expected what he normally got. Although he was only 22, she felt she might be dealing with a man ten years older than that. Although she had in a sense been invited out under false pretences – and this irked – she could not show him this or he would think her a gold digger and a snob.

At last. 'Is that the time?' she asked, pointing to the clock.

'Yes. O.K., not to worry. Just one last good-night kiss, eh?'

So they kissed a few times more, and that was all right. It was less predatory than last time and she quite enjoyed it. But suddenly his hand slipped quietly under her skirt and began tugging at the elastic at the top of her tights. It was fantastic because it was so expert, she couldn't have done it quicker herself. She fought his hands away and they came back. For about two minutes they had a terrible sexy struggle: he seemed to have four hands and they were everywhere at once. She began to scream.

That stopped him, but one hand came up to her throat and clamped hard on it so that she choked. 'Hi! you'll have somebody coming!'

She clutched at his hand. 'Let go! You're choking me!'

He eased his grip but did not move it. 'That's a stupid piece of jazz. Lay off it, Oyster. If somebody heard you –'

'I swear if you lay hands on me again –'

'And if you scream again, what about that? What about that?' His fingers tightened again and then relaxed. 'Grip, grip, and you wouldn't scream no more. I won't stand for you trying to get me into trouble deliberate. Little God wouldn't stand for that.'

Panic kept coming in great waves. 'Let me *go*.'

'All right, *all right*. But there's got to be fair play, like in the ring. Screaming's not fair play. You could get me in the nick for that. They'd say I'd done things to you.'

Not so far away a car's headlights swung across the sky. The car came nearer, passed the end of the lane, lights like radar beams that didn't quite reach.

He was stroking her neck now, smoothing her down. 'You came out with me willing enough. It beats me what you expected . . . Jees, you're all right. Super neck, like a – like an urn. And as cold as ice, eh?'

'Will you drive me home, or shall I get out and walk?'

'Look, I got a proposition. There's three rugs in the boot. What say we get out and sit down among those trees for a bit? Nothing serious if you don't want it. I *promise* . . .'

She knew then with the most awful certainty that she was in real danger. Her heart was bumping like a car wheel with a puncture.

'I *promise*. Don't you *believe* me? Look, I'm in a way about you. I want to be friends *next time*. I won't *bite*. I don't *make* girls do things!'

'Yes, but you –'

'Think this is ordinary with me? Well, it's not. I'm dead gone on you. I'll only hug you a bit if that's what you say. I want you to be my *girl*. I'll buy you things, give you things. I want to show you off to people. I'll be *good*.'

'You promise?'

'Promise? I don't promise, I *swear*. You can trust Little God. He won't let you down.'

'It'll be cold outside.'

'Not on your life! Not wrapped in a rug.'

'All right,' she said. 'But –'

'*Good* girl. Good little Oyster. Little God's a man of his word. You'll see.'

He leaned over and found the door catch she had been unable to locate. While doing this he pressed his cheek against hers. Then he turned to get out. Before he could open his door she had slipped out and was running down the lane.

She heard him shout, then she heard him laugh, and he suddenly switched his powerful headlights on, and *there* she was, her flying shadow leaping about like a scarecrow strangled on a wire. She had never run so fast in her life, didn't know she could. Then she heard the car door slam and he was running after her.

In the struggle one leg of her tights had been ripped away from the top, and this rolled down and nearly tripped her. Then she turned her ankle on a stone and caught at a branch of a tree; anything to be out of this light; soon his shadow would be stretching out to reach her. A gate and she scrambled over it somehow, skirt tearing, into a field. The field was bare, no corn, ploughed or something; heavy going; he would catch her, no escape. More trees on the left. She angled for them and lunged over the second gate.

Dark in the undergrowth, lungs fit to burst, a ditch; she fell into it anywhere; it was dry; brambles scratched then closed over her.

He came panting up. He was half laughing, half cursing. She couldn't understand him: they might have been playing lovers' hide and seek if it had not been for her certainty that they were not. Perhaps he'd be laughing when he raped you. He was close by somewhere now listening. She put her hand over her mouth trying to filter air in silently, breath she had to have to live.

'Oyster,' he said cautiously, and his voice shattered her it was so close – could he *see* her? 'I know you're here, so be a nice chickie and call it a day. I'll not lay a glove on you if you do. Take you straight home. Little God's honour. It was all a lark, wasn't it, so let's go.'

No answer from her.

'It was all a lark, see; but if you keep me hanging around I may get cross. *So come out now.* It won't make no diff. I'll hang on here till midnight.'

Pearl was not really the praying sort, but when you're in a real panic the words come. 'Dear God . . .' And then she stopped because it seemed as if he had stolen the name and she was praying to him. 'Christ . . . Christ help me. Jesus Christ help me.' Because, whatever calmer thought might come later, she was certain then with an inner conviction that if he caught her he would rape her. And if she struggled he would strangle her as well.

He moved a bit away. He obviously had no torch, otherwise he would have seen her at once. But the car lights weren't far away. *They* wouldn't last for ever; if he didn't go back soon he would have a flat battery.

He stumbled over something and cursed, and he must have disturbed a bird because there was a frightened fluttering.

'Oyster,' he called, and began to come back. 'I know you're near by. I can wait. I'm not in all that hurry. I'll fix you yet.'

As his eyes grew used to the dark he would see her; her coat was dark but her face was white and one of her legs was white and she didn't dare move to draw it up under her.

He went away again. That is, his footsteps moved away,

but on the soft earth you soon lost the sound of them and you couldn't tell how far. Complete silence. She was lying just as she had fallen, and there was a branch digging in her shoulder. Something began to crawl over her bare knee. It was a snail. She groped round the shell, got it and pulled it off; the thing had a horrible suction on her skin. She dropped it away, and the shell made a rattle among the branches.

'That you, Oyster?' he said, still close.

Another bird fluttered and flew away.

He went right past. 'Now come on, chickie, enough's enough. I'm getting razzed. If you don't come out now you can walk home – and it's five miles or more – I'm going to wrap for the night. Jees, d'you think I want you now? I've gone right off, I can tell you that! Not me. I'd sooner have an honest tart any day!'

He was still fuming as he went out of earshot, back the way he had come. A car started and then it seemed to die away. But she wasn't absolutely certain, and long after it had gone she lay where she was, only shifting her shoulder to get away from that branch.

She began to count. She thought, when I get to 1000 I'll move on. I'll go then. I'll be safe. I'll wave a car down on the main road and . . . When I get to 1000. But it took too long and she was too cold. At 241 she lost count and jumped to 750. It seemed as if she couldn't lie there a minute longer.

And then suddenly his voice shouted at her close by: 'Well, chickie, I hope you rot in your ditch and get pneumonia! But remember, there'll be a next time. Don't you worry, I know where you live. There'll be a next time!'

A rough crackling in the undergrowth and she heard him move off. Almost at once she scrambled out of the ditch and knelt on the dry soil listening. And this time she heard him start the engine and the lights moved as he backed and turned. When the lights were pointing the other way she stood up and watched them flicker off down the lane and turn into the main road and flash eastwards. She ran across the field in the other direction looking for another road.

Chapter Four

Home without anyone knowing. Back on the main road at a crossroads, she took a chance at thumbing a lift. A middle-aged couple stopped and were sympathetic to her made-up story, drove her home right to the door.

But quite ill next day. A touch of flu maybe; there was plenty about, or lying in the ditch. She told Rachel she had a sore throat and did not mention the skinned elbow, the bruises on her arms, three nail scratches high up on the inside of her leg. Little God. The memory was hard to keep on her stomach, she would have liked to sick it up. The whole *pretence* of the thing affronted her, too. She was disgusted with herself for falling for such a tall story – smart (borrowed or stolen) car and the rest – and she was disgusted that she had let herself get into the position that she had. A cheap boxer's girl friend could probably only expect to be treated the way he had treated her – like a piece of *flesh* to be given over to his enjoyment. She shuddered and shivered in bed and loathed him and loathed herself. She was such a *baby* to have been taken in: it was the humiliation.

In the light of morning she was somewhat less completely convinced that he had meant to force her against her will. A girl, an ordinary decent girl brought up in England, comes to look on herself as inviolate, protected by society, self-possessed by personal right. Whether she is moral or immoral is not the point; she is still 'preserved', as one might say, for whom she chooses. Pearl had read plenty of news items about 'Nurse attacked in Railway Carriage' etc., and rather enjoyed reading them – it made the news interesting – but she hadn't ever thought it would happen to her. Now in the light of day she wondered if she'd read *too* many news items, if she'd panicked unnecessarily, if she'd made even more of a fool of herself than she needed to.

But there were doubts. Her confidence was shaken. Life for a brief half hour had become dirty and dangerous. And it was not just confidence in her safety she had lost for that short time but confidence in herself.

God, or Little God, or Old God, or whatever he called himself, lay on her memory, and she could not sick him up. His handsome head, deep-set dark handsome eyes, eager and lustful and wild eyes, beautiful miniature body, every muscle rippling and tuned, fine dark hair on legs, fine olive skin. And hands, *fingers,* powerful predatory obscene fingers pressing over the soft parts of her body, undoing her clothes with *lightning* speed, taking hold of her breasts, clutching her throat.

Iron strong fingers, but so much more dangerous than iron because they not only attacked your body, they attacked something in yourself.

Rachel was always too busy, too hard-worked, too disorganized, too interested in her own children, to spare much attention for Pearl, but in the evening her father came up and looked at her and sent for Dr Spoor, who arrived two hours later and said she had a high temperature and a relaxed throat and it meant a couple of days in bed. This was catastrophe because if he insisted it meant missing her flight to Geneva in the small hours of Saturday morning.

After he had left, her father came back and sat talking. Mr Friedel was not tall – Pearl got her height from her mother – but to his family he was an impressive looking man, with a fine fresh complexion and a short pointed beard going grey and an appearance of dignity about him. He might, Pearl felt, have been a financier or a surgeon or even a diplomat. He was always neat, always quiet, always dignified, and always carefully dressed, though he spent little money on his clothes. Pearl would see him coming down the avenue on a summer evening, stocky, respectable, in command of himself, and be glad to think such a distinguished man was her father, and at the same time perplexed that he was only an assistant accountant.

After he had smoked a small cheroot – he never smoked cigarettes – he said to her: 'Did you bang your neck somewhere, Pearl?'

'My neck? Oh, this mark. It's like a bruise, isn't it. I don't know where I did it.'

'Who did you go out with last night?'

'It was two friends from the shop. They were coming

this way and picked me up in their car.'

'Dr Spoor asked me if you had had a shock.'

'What? . . .' She laughed, but that hurt so she stopped. 'I shall have a shock if I miss the plane on Saturday!'

'Rachel said your shoes were very muddy.'

'We had supper at a restaurant in Chelsea and then drove round by Keston. We got out and walked a bit. It was a lovely night.'

He put his finger tips together and looked at her. 'I don't want to seem inquisitive. You'll excuse me, I'm sure. But you're barely twenty, and with your mother not being . . Sometimes one gets anxious.'

'It's all right, Dad. Thanks.'

He blinked, and his cautious elderly eyes went round the room. 'Often I wish you had a brother of your own age, someone to go about with. It would be better. If your mother had lived . . .'

They sat silent. He said: 'Sometimes I think this neighbourhood isn't quite right.'

'The neighbourhood? What's wrong with it?'

'Oh, nothing. Very good, in its way. Respectable. But you don't seem to meet the people you should. This trip you are going to Zermatt. Your party. Young clerks, electricians and the like. One hopes for something better.'

She wondered what he would have said if he had seen her last night.

'What's the matter?' he asked.

'What d'you mean?'

'You flushed suddenly.'

'I expect it's this temperature. But seriously, Dad, you *must* persuade Dr Spoor to let me go! I shall be O.K. After all, what's a sore throat and a temperature? By the time I get to Zermatt I'll be absolutely fine. It'll be an absolute disaster if I don't catch this flight!'

'It will be a disaster if you catch an extra chill.' He got up and rubbed his beard and looked at her. 'We'll see. Skiing, with all the exertion and getting hot and cold. But we'll see. You may be much better tomorrow.'

To her fury she wasn't better on Friday. Her temperature was 103° and Dr Spoor wouldn't consider the idea of her getting out of bed. There were panic discussions with Hazel

65

and last minute rearrangements. Saturday when it was too late the temperature came down with a bang and she crawled about the house waiting impatiently for Mr Friedel's return. When he came he told her he had been able to get her an ordinary B.E.A. tourist night flight for the Monday. This cost more than the charter flight of the Friday, but he whispered that he would pay the difference if she promised not to tell Rachel.

Even then her troubles weren't over, for the plane ran into fog and they were diverted to Zurich and reached Geneva four hours late, and she was afraid she might miss Tuesday's ski-ing too. In the plane she sat next to a fat elderly gentleman who got in a panic because apparently he was afraid the plane was going to crash. In his agitation he talked away at her, and in her agitation she talked back at him. Not that their anxieties were the same, but when you have only *one* real annual holiday and three days of it have already been lost, utterly lost; and when, except for a week in the summer which is too short a time to make much use of, you don't get another holiday for *twelve months,* then the fear of another day lost becomes almost as important as fear of a crash.

In the end she reached Zermatt in time for some ski-ing on the Tuesday, and Hazel and Chris greeted her as if there had never been a cross word between any of them, and anyway it had been snowing all Sunday and part of Monday, and the weather set fair from the Wednesday morning and she had a superb ten days and went on some of the upper slopes and learned to do an up-hill christie properly for the first time. The ski-prof took a fancy to her and gave her extra time on the slopes free of charge, and they ate and drank and she danced in the evenings, and it was all so good that she forgot England and only wrote three postcards the whole time she was there. It wasn't really until the last full day that she began to think of the dreary routine of her ordinary life and her ordinary work again.

Then for a fraction of time a nasty little fear stirred, like a worm wriggling out of a maggot. It was a fear that Little God might be waiting for her when she got home.

And of course he was not, and of course she settled back

into her ordinary life as well as anyone can after a wonderful holiday.

But the holiday was too unsettling. Everything about her job, which was no better and no worse than many others, seemed dull and boring. The long hours of standing, the forced politeness to difficult elderly women buying expensive perfumes, mixing again with all the other girls who all seemed just the same as herself, young, vaguely happy, vaguely unhappy, alternately bored and excited, wanting a man but not any man, talking of clothes, make-up, money, clothes, boy friends, clothes; being one in a staff of fifteen hundred; the struggle every morning by bus and train and bus; the crowds, the hour's journey; a cheap lunch in the canteen every day on the seventh floor; the struggle every night by bus and train and bus; home with its relative comfort and ease, its relative discomfort and shabbiness, narrowing, stifling in effect, like living in a cage. Money. Lack of money. Weekly pay packet with deductions. Money, clothes, daily travel. Money.

As soon as I'm twenty-one, she thought, I'll have a showdown with Dad; this endless waste of time travelling. Even change my job: this one gives me backache with standing, I'm too *tall*. But what else? Right height for modelling but they want scarecrows. Can't type so not secretarial work. Three 'O' levels, but in things like Art and Geography. As soon as I'm twenty-one I'll move. But that's thirteen months away.

One day soon after she got back the fat elderly man she had met on the plane came in to Evans's and bought some perfume. He was wearing a check suit that emphasized his fatness, and she remembered the one he had on on the aeroplane was also a check but not quite so awful as this. He made a point of her serving him and was friendly.

A young man called Gerald Vaughan started calling her up, and she went out with him a few times. She had met him at a social in Hammersmith, which D. H. Evans sometimes gave in conjunction with Harrods. He worked at Harrods, but in spite of an impeccable appearance and the whitest cuffs in Knightsbridge he nourished a left-wing hatred of all things English and American, and after a while she found this tiring and unfruitful as the only topic of conversation. So she began to choke him off.

Two weeks passed, and a letter came for her addressed care of the store. Although the address was typewritten the letter inside was in ink. Under an address of 26 Cadogan Mews the letter said:

'Dear Miss Friedel,

I am taking a few friends to a performance of Mozart's Clarinet Quintet next Thursday at the Wigmore Hall. Knowing your interest in this instrument, I wonder whether you would care to join my party? The time is 7.45 for 8 o'clock at the Hall, and there would be supper afterwards.

Yours sincerely,
Wilfred Angell.'

So there you were: you never knew. She was amused, pleased in a way, a little flattered. However stuffy it might seem to some people, it was quite a compliment to be asked to join a party of Mr Angell's obvious quality. Hazel, among others, had always called her a snob, but was it being a snob to like the best, to want the best, to enjoy mixing with well-educated people, people who had a thought beyond the next pay day or the next boy friend? Pearl had always liked taste and style and manners and breeding. Her father had encouraged her in her liking and had always coveted them for her.

Anyway, she had never heard the Mozart Quintet, and the thought of five clarinets playing together was dreamy. She wrote back accepting.

The week passed and the days were lengthening and she saw nothing of Gerald Vaughan; but one night she dreamed of Little God when he was some sort of golden idol sitting cross-legged in a temple and she had to burn incense to him.

She told her father of the invitation and rang her friend Pat Chailey, who had a flat, and Pat said yes delighted if you don't mind sleeping on a Li-lo.

Thursday was late night in the store anyway, and she was able to change in the cloakroom in the basement, and since the shop almost backs on to Wigmore Street she walked there and got to the hall exactly on time.

He was there already and she had guessed right, no black tie. But thank heaven he wasn't wearing the terrible check suit, and in blue he didn't look so fat. He greeted her politely but distantly like someone welcoming you on behalf of someone else; his hand was hot; he said would she like to leave her coat and she said no thank you, and then he led the way in. Rather impressive the way he walked, as if he were used to being in charge of things. It was only as they were going down the aisle that he said: 'Oh, by the way, Mr and Mrs Simon Portugal were prevented from coming at the last moment, so I'm afraid we are on our own.'

The concert was a fabulous success. After she had got over the disappointment of finding only one clarinet after all, she really got dug in to the music and completely forgot her host. But in the second part of the concert, which was chiefly a piece by a man called Howells, the enchantment thinned and her brain came to and did a little homework.

She thought, supper after? Oh come, Pearl, don't be *too* silly. It's Little God you've got on the brain. This stout, elderly, well-to-do solicitor. Of course it would explain the sort of impression she'd made on him in the plane, but then . . . How old *is* he? Perhaps it's being so fat that makes him look older. Not *ancient* actually, but old. Early fifties? Pearl hadn't much idea about men, once they were out of their twenties. Good skin, healthy looking, plenty of brownish hair worn rather like Jo Grimond with only tips of grey at the ears. Quite personable in an elderly way. Rather impressive in the way her father was. But so fat. He nearly overflowed onto her chair. Like Godfrey in the Chelsea restaurant. But so *un*like Godfrey. Thank heavens. This was a gentleman.

After it was over they walked to a restaurant farther down Wigmore Street. 'Not the most fashionable,' he said, 'but excellent food.' She was disappointed. It was not as good a restaurant as the one Godfrey Vosper had taken her to. Mr Angell ate twice as much as she did in the same time, and although his table manners were good they were not genteel in the way she had been taught.

He was very nice to her, called her Miss Friedel all the time, treated her with respect; it was the sort of treatment she liked but seldom received. Yet she felt he was not personally as forthcoming as on the plane. She felt he was sounding her out, that he was wary all the time of being *too* friendly. Near the end of the meal he asked her if she played the clarinet much.

'Oh, I don't,' she said. 'I love it, but I haven't got one. I've tried one a few times, that's all. I love it. By the way, how did you know I was interested?'

'You mentioned it on the aeroplane.'

'Did I?' She didn't remember. 'I did buy a recorder once but there wasn't really time to practise and we live in a small house. I've a step-sister of five who goes to bed early.'

He puffed out his fat cheeks and spaced his legs. 'A pity. I watched you at the concert. So absorbed.'

'Oh, I'd *love* to play the clarinet. More almost than anything. But it's too late now anyhow . . . Are you a musician, Mr Angell?'

'Far from it.' He helped himself hurriedly to the last two gris sticks before the waiter took them away. 'I *listen* to music, as you see. The other arts are really my hobby. I collect furniture – antique furniture – and paintings.' He crunched his gris stick with noisy concentration. 'You must see them sometime. On those I can speak with authority.'

They talked on. The bill came and he paid it and gave a five shilling tip. But he seemed well known in the place and she supposed it was all right. Somehow he got her talking about herself. It was not often a man, a cultured and quite charming man, asked her the sort of questions he asked her and listened with such flattering interest. He was clever in putting a question that needed a denial and then, as it were, an explanation of the denial. Perhaps it was his practice at the bar. Also the Algerian wine she had drunk had gone a little to her head.

She still did not quite believe that this distinguished old gentleman . . . 'You must come and see my pictures sometime.' She knew some men hadn't got past it in their forties and fifties, but somehow he didn't look the type. It crossed her mind that he might be thinking of her as a secretary.

At last he looked at his watch and said, dear me, I must be going, it's been very pleasant, can I drop you somewhere? And she said, well, if it's not out of your way, and he said, not at all, I've a car coming at eleven-thirty.

So she was driven to her friend's Li-lo in style, though the car was stuffy and formal compared to the one Little

God had borrowed or stolen. When they stopped he said: 'This has been an agreeable evening for me. Would you care to have dinner with me at my house next Friday at eight?'

She thought, so it *is* that, oh crikey, you never can tell, what do I say now? But before she could utter he added, 'There'll be four others, so I don't think they can *all* fail to turn up.'

She looked at him and there was a gleam in his eye for the first time. She laughed and said: 'Thank you, Mr Angell. I'd love to. And thank you for a fabulous evening.'

The next night she went to the pictures with Pat Chailey so was late back, and as there was no bus outside the station she walked. It was only twenty minutes and a beautiful moonlight night. When she got in her father had gone to bed but Rachel said: 'There was a young man called for you about seven. I told him you wasn't in.'

Pearl was cutting herself a sandwich and she wondered why Rachel could never be bothered to talk properly and how her father could let her go on without correcting her. 'What was his name?'

'He didn't give one and he wouldn't say what he wanted.'

Pearl could make a pretty good guess. Gerald Vaughan was trying to persuade her to join him in some sit-down demonstration in front of the American Embassy. She sighed. She never seemed to get suitable young men who behaved *normally*. Either they were political agitators or they were sex maniacs or they went off and got tight in the middle of a dance –

'What did he look like?' she asked sharply.

'Small. Thin. Flashily dressed but they all are now, in my day young men never flaunted themselves, not like peacocks. A scar over one eyebrow. A pity you was back so late, why don't you go to the pictures in Croydon, it's cheaper.'

The bread saw slipped on the loaf and just missed Pearl's thumb. She sucked the end of her thumb just as if it had been cut.

'What did he want?'

'I told you, he came to the door and just asked and I said you was out. Big car. Big green car with a big back

71

window. Too showy for me.'

'Did he say anything else?'

'Yes, he says he will come back later tonight. But I shouldn't suppose he will come you are so late now.'

Pearl looked at her watch. It was ridiculous. Her fingers were fumbling as if they did not belong to her. She concentrated. It was eleven-fifteen.

She thought of her walk from the station in the moonlit darkness. Of course it was street lit all the way, but being oldish property it was not lit too well. There had been no one in Sevenoaks Avenue when she came into it except the usual parked cars, no green monster with its God at the wheel.

She took a bite at the sandwich but the relish had gone. 'I'm tired, I think I'll take these to bed. If the – if this man comes again, could you just tell him I'm in bed and asleep?'

Rachel said: 'The washing machine is good but it does not iron, the hours I stand over this board. So you know him?'

'Oh, yes, I went out with him a couple of times. But he's not my type.'

'Now I think perhaps not, he is not your type. So I send him away, eh?'

'Yes, please.'

Rachel said: 'Just because you're not my daughter don't mean I don't feel a responsibility. Your father'd think I was to blame if you got into any trouble.'

'Well, you can stop worrying. I'm not in any trouble.'

'Your father is a great one for respectability. You know that. Maybe because he was not born in England is what makes him that way. He has lived in this house twenty-two years and everyone in the avenue respects him. It's Good morning, Mr Friedel. Good night, Mr Friedel. And both the boys going to the grammar school. So have a care for his sake as well as for your own.'

Pearl said: 'When have I given him the least worry? When?'

'No. No.' Rachel nodded, and a tinted curl fell over her forehead. 'You've always been a right thinking girl. But lately you've been more secret, not saying where you're going or where you've been. Your father has remarked this.

And you're pretty looking, even though you're big – that puts easy trouble in a girl's way. Pass me those socks.'

Pearl's bedroom was over the front, and before she put on the light she drew the curtains across and looked through a slit. The avenue was silent and empty. Then she saw a figure running. Her heart began to thump. But the figure went past, and she stared up and down again, trying to see if anyone were skulking beside one of the parked cars.

But there was nothing, and he did not come. And he didn't show up at all during the week-end.

She had to be at the shop by a quarter to nine, which meant leaving home at seven-thirty every morning to catch the bus for the 7.55 train. Everything looked different by Monday.

Yet she was half prepared when he took the seat next to her in the train.

The trouble is that being prepared doesn't really take away the shock, because you're not really prepared for the event, you're only waiting for it to happen.

It was one of those open-plan carriages where you sit two aside facing two other people, with a middle corridor. He must have been very close behind her because there was the usual rush when the train came in, and in no time people were standing. So she couldn't very well get up and move away, and they sat there not speaking until the train lumbered out. Two men opposite, business types, unfolded their papers in a cramped space. She opened her bag and took out a paper-back novel and began to read.

'You wasn't in last night,' he said.

Black sweater and black gaberdine trousers, plum-coloured shirt, yellow tie. It was a month since she had seen him, and he was at once different from what she remembered and exactly the same. Less terrifying, more ordinary, more utterly, utterly commonplace; a little chauffeur, a professional boxer on the lower rungs, bad voice, uneducated, *cheap*. How she could ever even have *looked* at him. Or been afraid of him. But the same handsome profile, the same dark darting eyes, clear olive skin, rich mane of hair, vivid vitality, bursting egoistic vitality, overflowing vitality, rippling muscles, hard and searching hands, rapier like, quick, living, obscene. She pressed the paper-back to open it wider at the page.

He said: 'Have a snorting holiday? Good ski-ing? I been busy. That's why I've not been round before.'

She said in a low voice: 'I don't want to talk to you. Please leave me alone.'

'Oh, come on. Maybe I was a bit pressing that night. But you got in a panic. I'd never have *hurt* you. Honest. That's not my way.'

'It's not my way either.'

'Well, I'm sorry about that night. I told you. I'm sorry. It just was a misunderstanding, see?'

The man opposite folded his *Daily Telegraph* and glanced over at them.

Godfrey said: 'You fair had me on toast that night. How did you get home?'

She did not answer.

'Is it because I'm just a chauffeur?' he said. 'Does that make the diff? Friendly with a big wheel, not with a little one? Well, it's only temporary, just to keep me going. All boxers take jobs till they hit the big time. And that's mine for sure soon. I got a match with Bob Sanders next month.'

'Will you please go away,' she said. 'I don't know how you've the cheek – the impertinence to come and –'

'Why? We got our lines crossed that night, that's all. I said I'm sorry. It's a gas when you've been fighting like I was that night, you don't relax all of a sudden. You don't relax. But going out with a girl helps you relax. It gets in your blood, like. So things weren't right between us that night. But another night it'll be different. You can stand on me!'

The train rattled along. His arm was touching hers. It felt like iron, but iron with some sort of magnetism in it. She felt suffocated, pursued. Suppose she said, this man is bothering me! Will you ask him to leave me alone? The *Telegraph* and the *Mirror* opposite would be embarrassed, disapproving. What else do you accuse him of, bruises and scratches long since gone?

'I got all today off,' he said. 'First for weeks. We could hit the town. Slap up supper. And I'll not lay a glove on you. Honest. Little God's honour.'

Clapham Junction. What when they got to Victoria?

'You're different from other chicks – other girls. It's something. You really got me on toast. Never happened

74

before, I promise you. I keep thinking about you. Don't you ever think about me?'

She looked at him then, met his gaze. 'No.'

'No? Honest?'

She had been looked at most ways in her fairly short life, from gentlemanly admiration to plain lechery, but she had never been looked at like this before. A small black leopard waiting to climb on its mate.

She said: 'When we get to Victoria, Godfrey, if you follow me, I'll go to the first policeman and complain. That's the truth. I mean it. I just can't bear the *sight* of you, so please go away and leave me alone!'

It took an effort to say, and she leaned back out of breath and feeling sick. He said nothing more until they were crossing the river. Then he said: 'O.K., little Oyster, you're paddling this time. But you haven't done with me. And that's honest too. I've got you in my system. And I think maybe you've got me even though you won't admit it. Deep down in your guts. Think about it. I'll be around.'

That morning she sold the wrong lipstick and broke an expensive bottle of toilet water and missed a sale because she couldn't take an interest in the woman wanting advice. But he didn't show again all that week, and she began to hope that in spite of his threats she had choked him off for good.

Thursday and the dinner in Cadogan Mews. Because she was nervous and afraid of being late she arrived early, but the four other guests were already there as if they had been invited for an earlier time. It was a super house, but the furniture was weird, much of it that bright brown highly polished walnut with masses of curves and gold ornamentations and marble tops. A bit too much like being in one of those furniture shops in Knightsbridge. And it was *over*-furnished so that you could hardly move freely for risk of bumping into something. And the walls were fuller of pictures than the National Gallery. He even had five in the toilet.

The other guests were a Mr and Mrs Brian Attwell; he was something in television and the theatre, and a Mr and Mrs Simon Portugal, in their late twenties, very smart and sophisticated; he was an estate agent, which didn't quite match with the estate agents Pearl had met before. She had some nervous moments during dinner, fear of using the wrong fork, etc., but it passed off fairly well. Fortunately everybody talked non-stop so she didn't have to say much. They were waited on by a butler, but Pearl did not think much of him and she noticed Mr Angell looked annoyed once or twice at the way things went.

It wasn't really until near the end of the evening that she realized he was nervous himself. This was a surprise because, except in the aeroplane, he had always seemed so confident, more than confident; when he walked he fairly breasted the air like a sultan, and he always spoke as if he knew he'd be obeyed. And obviously he was much, much richer than she had had any idea of. He spoke of having loaned eight of his chairs to an exhibition at the Brighton Pavilion last year. He was involved in some big development company with Mr Portugal. He had acted recently for Mr Attwell in a case involving Equity, and famous names were mentioned.

There was not much of this talk Pearl could join in, although Mr Angell with courteous good manners did not allow her to feel neglected. She sat on his right, and as her own nervousness went off she noticed his little habits. He was always rubbing his left thumb and forefinger together as if crumbling a piece of bread, and he would take up his wine glass to drink and then think of something to say and say it, quite long, so that you might think he was proposing a toast. And he blinked too much. He had good lashes for an old man, and they kept covering his pale eyes.

It was a long meal, and good food, all sorts of good food, things she hadn't tasted before, and wine, and liqueurs afterwards. But the evening was over at last, and this time she found Mr Angell had engaged the hire car to take her back to Pat Chailey's flat, so again she returned in style, a trifle drunk, satisfied with the sort of luxury evening that absolutely suited her, impressed by the money, the culture, the conversation, but still puzzled by it all. Of course Mr Wilfred Angell had taken a fancy to her, and had made these gestures of 'taking her up'. She was accordingly flattered and rather grateful, but she couldn't really see where it would lead.

She thanked him nicely when she left, and the following

day, having looked it up in a book on etiquette, wrote him to say thank you over again. The next three weeks passed, and almost daily she expected a letter back from him suggesting another meeting. Daily too for a time in spite of telling herself it was ridiculous she expected to find Little God waiting round some dark and lonely corner.

But at last she began to think she would not hear from either of them again, that they had each dropped her as quickly as in their peculiar ways they had taken her up.

Chapter Five

Godfrey was annoyed. He did not like ever to admit fault in himself, but now he realized that he had made a real mess out of this one. The only time a girl had ever got under his skin and this had to happen. There are hundreds of women with good looks and he had to pick on her.

That was the way it was right from the bell, and the second round did all the damage. He was not a raper from choice: he didn't have to be. Girls told him he was no worse looking than a film star, and if that was a bit of flannel it was not all flannel. Normally he had more traffic than he could handle.

But he *had* to pick on the one who played hard to get. Right from the beginning he had known she was different, and he had handled it very cool at the start. This often paid because they didn't know whether you were attracted or not, but it hadn't paid this time, at least not with his follow-up.

That time in the train he had tried hard to explain to her, but he wasn't very good at explaining. It was after a fight: it gets in your system: it's something to do with the bip-bip-bip of blood and muscle. Perhaps in a way like in the old days you killed a man and had his girl. So he'd not paid enough attention to the fact that she was different, and a bit superior and a bit haughty, and he'd hurt her feelings and maybe frightened her – though privately he thought that part put on; what girl is really scared of what all girls want?

But he'd gone *on* too long, shouting after her in the wood, using a few hard words. Because he always *had* had what he wanted – which comes surprising from an orphanage product, but true enough of the important things. What Little God wants Little God gets. So he'd been pretty mad. First he'd been done out of finishing off Hertz and then he was done out of her. He surely would have leaned on her if he could have found her. But he was sorry afterwards, sorry he'd got so snotty, and he'd tried to make it up. Still wanted to. Badly. Had to. He kept thinking about her. What Little God wants Little God gets. Even if what he wants doesn't want him. But he couldn't really believe that.

'Aggressive' was the word they used about him at the orphanage. 'Aggressive.' He always fancied that. It summed him up. But he didn't like to feel he hadn't a smooth line where women were concerned, no subtlety, that irked.

The visit to the Trad Hall had been a coincidence in the first place, all stemming from his 'aggressiveness' of twelve months ago. Because it was in the middle of his suspension that he was in Newmarket with a mate for the Cesarewitch – there's always extra work and pickings of some sort at a time like that – and he got a job driving a van for Sir George Wayland – or his stable anyhow, his steward – ferrying things from his place which was about twenty miles away. And Sir George himself seemed to take a fancy to Godfrey – not unusual, people often did – and Sir George had done some boxing when he was a lad, he said; so when the meeting was over Godfrey stayed on at his place where there was a house party, helping around the house with odd jobs of this and that.

And the day the party was breaking up, Godfrey was getting ready to go when Sir George sent for him and said: 'Lady Vosper's chauffeur has had a stroke and has gone off to hospital. Have you ever driven a Jensen?' He said no, he hadn't, but he could drive anything on four wheels; and this woman got up from her chair and came across and looked at him as if he was a piece of pre-wrapped sirloin in a Supermarket. She was a middle-aged woman who walked like a man and had skirts too short for her age and he hated her on sight. He thought, I'll tell her where she can stuff her lousy car, but just then she said: 'You're a boxer, are you, Brown? Warned off the course, eh? Suspended. Drunk in the ring or something?'

'Don't drink,' he said and gave her a look that should have dried up anyone.

But all she said was: 'I'm a *driver*, Brown. But I've been warned off the course. Suspended. Drunk in charge. So we're both more or less in the same mess.' And she snorted with laughter.

He stood there wooden, not knowing what to make of

this, whether to walk away or answer something rude, when Sir George said: 'Lady Vosper is not permitted to drive her own car, Brown, and would like you to drive her to her home in Suffolk. It's about fifty miles. I imagine you can do this. It's more or less on your way to London, if you're going to London.'

'It's worth a fiver,' said this Vosper woman. 'If you get me there safe. I'm otter hunting in the morning. Can you drive, boy? Speak up.'

So he spoke up. Try anything once. But when he got in the car she came and sat beside him and watched closely how he handled it, especially the automatic change which took getting used to, having nothing to do with your left foot. But after a few ghastly jerks when he tried to de-clutch with the brake, he mastered it.

She talked nearly all the way to this place, Handley Merrick, this village where she lived. After a bit you had to hand it to her, she was a game old bird. She knew more about cars than Godfrey thought there was to know. She had raced, actually raced, she claimed, at Silverstone, and after his first sneering disbelief he began to wonder if it might be true. She knew the inside of an Aston Martin like most women know the inside of their dressing table. She knew nothing about boxing, but hunting, racing, shoot-ing, climbing, all that, she'd done the lot.

So he got more at ease as they went on, and was soon telling her about his life, how he had moved from fighting in a fairground to the A.B.A. for a couple of years while he did odd jobs at a garage touching up hot cars, working on a building site shovelling hard core, bookie's runner, looking after the dogs. She asked him, so he told her how a man called Regan paid him £100 to turn pro and had put him in a few fly-weight contests. It was small time, but he had begun as Godfrey Brown of Birmingham and later he had moved up to the feathers.

Then there was a spot of trouble that had really been Regan's fault, but Godfrey carried the can for it, and he had been warned by the British Boxing Board of Control. After that things didn't go so well between him and Regan, and one night, the only night he'd been stopped, when he'd been matched against a light-weight called Carmel, Regan came in the dressing room before he'd had time to

80

cool off and started ranting at him for boxing so badly. And somehow in a flash things got out of hand and Regan had a black eye and a bleeding nose. So the next day he was out on his ear, and the B.B.B.C. had him up before them again and this time it was a fine of £20 and a twelve months' suspension.

All this the Vosper woman seemed to find very funny, and the fact that she found it funny helped Godfrey to see his grievance in a better light. She told him how she had been driving home fast one night, back to London, and near Chelmsford had skidded on an icy road and run into a van. Not too much damage but the police came and tested her and found she'd had too much so she was fined £100 and disqualified for a year – nine months still to go.

'Drunk?' she said. 'Of course I wasn't drunk. Damned fools! But I'd had a lot to drink. When haven't I? It doesn't make any difference to the way I drive, except to make me more careful. When I was a gel, used to have to drive my father home, big four-and-a-half litre Bentley, big as a steam engine. I used to drink much more then, so that I couldn't walk straight. But *drive* straight – that was second nature. I used to get in, shove the lever in first gear, and stay there all the way home. It was heavy on the petrol but safe as could be. Fools and their drink tests! It's intelligence tests people should take!'

Godfrey thought once of telling her that he had never bothered to get a driving licence, but he thought better not. And this was lucky because when they got to the house where she lived she said would he like to stay on as temporary driver until her own chauffeur came back. He said yes he would and thought it's not going to be so temporary if I know anything, seeing that chauffeur carried out of the house by a couple of body snatchers to an ambulance and him unconscious and snoring. He'd only seen one before like that, in the ring, and he died on the way to hospital.

So he stayed on and he was right, her chauffeur never came back, so the temporary became sort of permanent and the permanent sort of indispensable.

Lady Vosper had a handsome flat in London as well as Merrick House and she spent more time in London than in the country, but he seemed to slide into both pretty well. She had hardly any staff at either place, just a man and wife in the great place in Suffolk and a daily woman in Wilton Crescent – and Godfrey. Godfrey always because he drove her wherever she went.

Merrick House in Suffolk was in Godfrey's opinion as big as the orphanage where he'd been reared and about as beautiful. All the Vospers, Lady V said, had been army men, except the one that built it, who was a merchant and made a fortune in Victorian times and pulled down the original house and put this up in its place. But if he had built it, it was the army men who had left their ticket. The place was cluttered with souvenirs of this battle and that war, somebody's standard at Malplaquet, muskets from Waterloo, cannons from Sebastopol. Half the time you fell over the things. But there had been another war since then and the house had been used as a paratroop training school, and no one had spent much money on it since, so it was a fair shambles in parts. The small wing where Lady Vosper lived was cosy enough, but the main part was as draughty as a building site, and at night it reminded Godfrey of something out of Son of Dracula.

Being chauffeur was a good enough job while he was still serving his suspension, and he tried to keep in with Lady Vosper; because it occurred to him that she knew practically everybody, and when the time came a word from her might give him a leg up the ladder. So it was more than two months before he realized the way things were really drifting. It had not occurred to Rudolph Valentino Brown that Flora Vosper was fancying him for more than the way he drove a car. Modest Little God.

But she was not above dropping a hint, and after a little hesitation and a pause for inspection he was not above taking it. He reckoned from what she said that she was around forty-six, but he was not all that particular where there was good for Godfrey to be got out of it. And of course it was something to lay a real Viscountess. The first and only time in his life that he was nervous. Because this wasn't just merely having it off with a woman old enough to be your mother. It was something else again.

And of course she was not that bad to look at if the light wasn't too bright, and he had to confess she learned him a thing or two. And he pleased *her*. He'd plenty of go, and there was no training to think about. And there was one thing he specially liked about her, she never got sloppy. A lot of women get sloppy after and chat you up about love. They get clinging and cloying. Even just after it's over and you want a fag and a change of thought, they'll wrap their moist arms round you and want to talk about how wonderful it all is. She did not. She never did. When she wanted it she wanted it, and when it was over it was over.

So it was surprising and yet not surprising that their relationship changed so little. In the bedroom she called him Godfrey, but out of it it was Brown. And for a long time he never called her Flora to her face. It's hard for a woman to be bossy when she's looking at the ceiling, but she was always the one in charge at other times.

The only fly in the ointment, the only real nasty difficulty in all this was Miriam, Lady Vosper's sour-faced pimply daughter of 26 or so. She was married to someone on the stage, and it seemed to Godfrey that Lady V kept them both. So in a manner of speaking there was enmity between rival claimants on Lady V's generosity. It did not take long for Miriam to spot what was going on between mother and chauffeur, and she did her best to cramp Godfrey every way she could. Once Godfrey listened at the door and heard Miriam rowing with her Mum over all the expensive shirts and ties and jackets he had. Lady Vosper just laughed and said she didn't buy them, he did what he liked with his money, and Miriam said, then you must wildly over-pay him, and Lady V said, on the contrary, and she'd never had such a good chauffeur before.

When his suspension was up he had been in her employment four months, but he was not for throwing up such a comfy berth for a while. He was as flabby as Tottenham pudding, and he had to get in training again, and he put it to Lady V that he could do this in his off time and meanwhile look out for a new stable which wasn't going to be any piece of cake while Regan was telling his story of a black eye, etc. The name of Godfrey Brown was going to be a smear word for quite a time to come. So then she said: 'Why don't you change your name? People soon forget.' 'They'll take care to remember this,' he said. 'Boxing's a small world.' So she said: 'Yes, but it'll be easier under another name and Brown is such a dull name. Did you ever know your father?' 'I never knew my mother,' he said, 'the bitch. Brown was give me at the orphanage.' 'Given,' said Lady Vosper. 'Eh?' 'Given. Was given me at the orphanage.'

They were talking on their way down to Handley Merrick and suddenly he said: 'How about me taking the name of Vosper? Not for keeps but for boxing. Boxing as Godfrey Vosper.' He hadn't an idea how she'd react but she seemed pleased by it, amused, it tickled her fancy like having a racehorse named after her, so that was how it was fixed.

Soon after that he met Robins who was an old pug and managing two other lads and was willing to take him on. Robins was even less lively than Regan and not the man for a pressing youngster, but at least he was in London, so Godfrey signed up, but only for two years instead of the usual three because Robins would pay him nothing to join. Godfrey still hoped that Lady Vosper would be able to pull a few strings or put in a word for him with one of her friends, but no such luck.

He had two fights under his new manager – crummy preliminaries they were, while the audience were still scratching their way into their seats – and Lady V watching him win the first well inside the distance, when she had to go into Hospital for a couple of weeks and he was left on his tod.

So being free he took the big car and did a little joy-riding in it and after a row with his current girl he ended up one night at the Trad Hall Redgate, casing the talent, and who should he pick up with but this girl.

She was too big for him really, and not his usual style at all, he liked more glitter. And anyway she didn't want him. So he tried to forget her.

And he tried to forget her.

There was a woman at that first fairground in Yarmouth that used to sell love potions. Godfrey thought that maybe somebody had shaken some of this potion on his chips in place of pepper. Not that he admitted anything to do with the word love. It wasn't in his book. But he wanted Pearl the way he had not wanted anyone before, and he felt he wanted her for keeps. It was that bad. And what Little God wants Little God gets.

After chatting her up on the train and the second Big

Brush-Off he did nothing for a while. Flora Vosper had come out of her hospital and was temperamental and hard to get on with. He guessed she still had a hang-over from all the tests and things, and when you caught her without her make-up she looked a bad colour like she had had one in the solar-plexus and was trying to hide it. Usually he could make her laugh – she laughed easy – but it was not so easy now.

It was at this time that he first caught Miriam up to something. In the flat in London, the woman, Mrs Hodder, came in daily and cooked the midday meal and went home at four. Almost every night Lady V would go out to dinner, but once in a while she would stay in and cook something or have a salad and a glass or so of champagne. They always ate separately even when there was just the two of them, she in the dining room and he in the kitchen, but after, if she asked him in for a brandy, he would know what this meant. He would go in and sit down and talk and make her laugh, and she would swallow two brandies to his one, and after a while they would drift into her bedroom. It was dead smooth: he came in one door Brown her chauffeur, an hour later he would follow her through the other door, Godfrey her bed mate. Then after they had fraternized he would slip out and pad off to his own little room, Brown the chauffeur, back on his beat.

In the kitchen there was the usual cutlery but also a lot of odd junk that had been brought from Merrick House, clumsy spoons and forks with three prongs instead of four; and one evening when Miriam had been visiting he came in the kitchen unexpectedly and she was stuffing some of these in her handbag. He pretended not to notice but the next day he asked Lady Vosper what they were and she said they were Jacobean and had belonged to a Sir Henry Vosper, way back before the first Viscount. Godfrey guessed then they were worth a lot of folding so he told her he had seen Miriam putting some of them in her bag.

It was always a touchy point. Whenever he mentioned Miriam Lady V would get an attack of stuffed-shirtism, so there was the usual haughty answer, and it took him all the following day to get on friendly terms again. But the next week she suddenly said: 'I spoke to Mrs McNaughton about what you said. She was taking the silver to be cleaned and polished. Afterwards it will be lodged in the bank, as it's too valuable to leave about.' He didn't believe a word of it, not one word, because of Miriam's attitude.

Just after this Lady Vosper decided to go to Cannes and she wanted Godfrey to drive her down. This was awkward because he was now in training for a fight – it was out in Reading but was about the best he had had so far with Robins and likely to be the last of what you might call the season – and Robins would play up if he didn't train properly for it.

So he told Flora Vosper that he could not go. She had been feeling seedy again, but she still seemed badly to want him around and in attendance. Instead of giving him the sack, as he expected, she sent for Robins unknown to him and gave Robins a couple of snorting drinks and offered to let her chauffeur train in Cannes, and Robins was so impressed at talking with a real Countess – as he called her afterwards – that he said it was all right for Godfrey to go.

They were all set to leave on the Friday morning, so on the Thursday he asked if he could borrow the car for an hour or two. He wanted to see Pearl again before he left. It was crazy maybe, it was crazy. But he wanted to see her again. Somehow he'd got to make her. It was more of a challenge than being in the ring.

So he drove down to Selsdon thinking to call at 12, Sevenoaks Avenue, and wondering whether he'd get the evil eye from that foreign woman who opened the door before, or whether he should just hang about outside in the hope Pearl would not stay in the whole of such a smashing evening. And he was still very undecided and just turning into Badger's Drive a second time, which is the next avenue, when who should he see but Pearl herself stepping out briskly towards her home.

He came up slowly behind her. She had a light summery frock on, short enough to see all but the best part of her legs, and a thin mack over her arm and a green lizard handbag, and she was wearing her browny-blonde hair loose, but she'd had it cut a bit and it was shoulder length and swung and fell heavy as she walked. Not many women in short skirts look good from behind. She looked good from behind. He said to himself, play it gentle, God, take it easy, don't scare her,

But how do you play it gentle, when you're catching her up like this? If he didn't say something . . .

So he said something. He said: 'Hi, there, Pearl! Can I give you a lift?'

Well, whatever way it ought to have been done, that wasn't the way, because she threw a start like someone had given her the needle and stared open-eyed at him, looking as if she was going to drop her mack and run.

'Take it easy,' he said. 'I was just passing and saw you. Thought I'd stop and see how you was going on.'

Her eyes had glazed over after the first surprise, and she turned away and started walking on without saying a word. He followed her, kerb crawling, keeping pace.

'Look,' he said. 'I've not got leprosy or V.D. I *told* you I'm *sor-ry*. Can't you just stop and chat?'

They went on. It was a long avenue, and no parked cars here, thanks be.

He said: 'I'm going away tomorrow. I'll be away some while. Going to France.'

'Please *stay* away,' she said. 'Stay away from me.' And she seemed out of breath.

Just then a car came towards them and blew its horn loud because Godfrey was driving on the wrong side of the road. Somebody shouted, 'bloody fool!' as it swerved past. Godfrey tapped the accelerator and shot ahead, killed the engine, then got out and came back to meet her.

She came on and then stopped. It was still daylight although the sun had set, but there was no one about. There was this sound of a lawn mower somewhere, and a dog yapping, that was all. She came on and they were about twenty feet apart. She looked white round the gills. Then she looked at the house she was near, and quick as you please she had turned to open the gate. 'Oyster!' he shouted. 'For Chrissake!' and he jumped at her and grabbed her arm. It felt good but she wrenched it away and her sleeve tore and she went running up the path and banged on the knocker of this house.

His friends sometimes told Godfrey that in the ring he didn't know when to put up the shutters. But he knew now. The torn sleeve did it. For you can talk your way out of most things if you're smart enough, but not out of a torn sleeve. All they had to do was pick up the blower and dial the dicks. From then on he'd be in trouble.

So before the door was even opened he beat it back to the car, started up, roared off round the corner, and hoped no one had noted his number or he might be in trouble with Lady Vosper too.

They stayed in Cannes three weeks altogether, and as for training to meet Bob Saunders he did nothing, but nothing. Flora was in bed half the time, so he found a girl called Françoise and that way he got about as untrained as he well could be for six three-minute rounds against a smart little up-and-coming southpaw from Reading. But he thought he was getting Pearl thoroughly out of his system, and his mates in the Rob Robins stable had said that Saunders could box but carried nothing really dangerous in either hand.

When it came to the night he had only had one week of hard training but he was pretty confident of himself – he didn't ever really get soft, he found, not *soft* – so he took on Saunders with a will. But if his spar mates said Saunders carried no punch they had never been in the ring with him. By the fourth round instead of him having Saunders in a corner it was the other way round and he was bleeding from the old cut on his eyebrow and wearing lips like a Negro. In the end he got the verdict, which was a good thing for Lady V who was in the front row and had put £100 on him, but the decision was so narrow that most of the hall screamed and jeered for the other man.

The next day he was bushed: it was the first time ever since the fight with Carmel that he'd been marked, and he cursed his own carelessness and nervously felt his face to see if a bit of pressing would help it go back in shape. It was the only thing that got him ragged, damage to his looks, and in a way he blamed Lady V for putting the temptation in his way to get out of condition. They had a couple of rows – not about his face of course; rows always develop about something different – but to his surprise he found her taking sauce that a couple of months ago would have seen him out without a week's notice. It marked a change: she needed him and she couldn't hide it any longer that she needed him. They went down to Merrick House for three weeks – not that he minded this because he couldn't even *try* to see Pearl before his face was back in shape – but when they got down there Flora was ill again and he got pretty well landed as a nursemaid.

All the same, more or less against his will, he was developing a sneaking admiration for old Flora. Sick or well she was a good sport and she depended on him for light relief. He could make her laugh when she didn't feel like laughing, and it pleased him to have an audience for his jokes. Often he could get her to eat when she didn't feel like eating. The local doctor shook his head over her a few times, but she still drank enough to sink a row boat and smoked like Battersea Power Station; and the minute she felt better she was off on some jaunt or other.

He knew she would miss him when he went.

In Merrick House he caught Miriam at the same games as before on one of her visits. This time she had taken two little pictures off the walls in the gun-room. It was the purest chance he caught her, and he pretended not to see, and, after some think work, he decided not to mention it to Lady V.

Flora recovered and they returned to London. Summer is a close season for fights, at least for the small fry, so Godfrey kept his comfy slot and worked on her to help him in the autumn. Sometimes he suspected she was playing foxy, pretending that one day she'd help him but privately taking care not to lose her chauffeur.

During this time he thought a lot of Pearl. There was still the challenge, the picturing of what she'd be like.

So one dusty evening when he had taken Flora to bridge and had three free hours, he slipped back to the flat and changed into his new lemon yellow tweed jacket with a navy shirt and a pale silk tie. He thought he looked O.K., and more than one woman thought he looked O.K. when he stopped at traffic lights on the way down to Selsdon. He hadn't a mark left after the Saunders fight; they'd all cleared up great; only that eyebrow from the bout with Carmel and he had learned a new trick with that: you borrowed one of Lady V's eyebrow pencils and darkened in the break so that nobody would hardly notice.

He bought a big box of chocolates on the way down. They're a good excuse for a frontal attack, and surely after all this time . . .

A boy opened the door of the house, age fourteen or so, sticking his snout round the door as if he expected somebody else. Godfrey the disappointment.

'Is Pearl in?' Very polite he tried it.

The boy stared at him, hair like a ball of tarred string. 'She doesn't live here any more.'

'What?'

'Pearl doesn't live here any more, she's married.'

Godfrey stared, mouth open, like when you've walked into a right hook. Not out, quite easy to stay on your feet, but waiting for the bell to get a breather.

'Married? Get off.'

'Two weeks last Tuesday.'

'Get off. Who to?'

'A man.' The boy giggled.

'I know that, clever. What's his name?'

'Angell.'

'Angell?'

'Like they fly in the sky.'

'Leslie!' called a voice. It was that woman, Pearl's stepmother. 'Who is it?'

'A man. Wants Pearl.'

'She's not here.'

'I've told him.' The door was closing, Leslie disappearing.

'Hold on,' Godfrey said and felt in his pocket, fished out half a crown. 'Got her address?'

The boy looked at the half crown, then looked past Godfrey at the parked car. 'Tell you for five bob.'

Godfrey would have liked to beat the little gett's head against the door, but the foreign woman would be out in a second. 'O.K.'

The boy held out his hand. 'Pay first.'

Red spots dancing, Godfrey felt in his pocket, found a two shilling piece and sixpence, handed them over.

'In London,' said the boy.

'What? That's no good. Where in London?'

'Cadogan Mews. I've forgot the number. On a corner. Right in the West End. Smashing house.'

'What's the number?'

'Leslie!'

'Coming . . .'

Quick as if he was riding a punch he pulled his head

90

back and slammed the door in Godfrey's face.

Little God stood there, thinking of kicking the door in. But it would have spoilt his shoes, which were best calf that Flora had bought him in Bond Street. He looked around but there was nothing. Then he spotted a plant pot in the next door garden, with an old moth-eaten fern growing out of it. He leaned over the wall and picked it up, judged the distance to the edge of the street. He nipped in the car and started the engine, then got out and heaved the plant pot through the front-room window. It made a hell of a row on a quiet summer evening, and before the last bit of glass had stopped splintering he was in the car and revving up and away.

He felt mean. He felt mean like he only did usually in the ring. He could have crashed the car into the first car he met. He would have liked to get out in Purley and pick a fight with a policeman. Or go around with that guy he went round with in Birmingham, breaking up kiosks and smashing bus windows. Or taking a woman some place.

He drove home and got more curses from other drivers than he had ever had in his life before and he kept his window down so he could curse back. By luck there wasn't an accident, not even a scrape or a bent bumper. He stopped in Wilton Crescent and all the places outside the flat were taken for Chrissake, so he had to park two hundred yards away and walk back. And he let himself in and slammed the door hard enough to nearly bring the chimney pots down. And he went into the drawing room and switched on all the lights and slumped on to the settee and put his expensive calf leather boots up and wiped the dust off them all over a silk cushion, and looked up at the goddam ceiling and wished it would fall.

It wasn't all that easy for Little God to let off steam. There was a full bottle of Teacher's and a glass and two siphons, right to his hand, but Little God didn't drink. And there were cigarettes and cigars and what not, but Little God didn't smoke, not except after sex. When Little God was mad he wanted to break something.

After a while he got up and started thumbing through the first of the telephone books. There were thirty-four Angells, enough for a flaming heavenly host, but only one of them lived in Cadogan Mews. 26 Cadogan Mews, S.W.1. W. J. Angell, 331-9031. He stared at the book hot enough to make it burn, then fished out Flora's A-Z. The place was quite close by to where he was, not ten minutes' walk away. Ten minutes and he could go and beat up the house. Wreck it. Go in, force his way in and see her and then start breaking up the happy home. Mr and Mrs Angell. Send them up to heaven right away. Leave two corpses bleeding on the carpet and then go and pick Flora up from her bridge.

But by now it really was time to go and pick her up and he hadn't even time to fill in all the dramatic picture. On impulse just before he left the room he picked up the phone book again and dialled 331-9031. It rang four times and then a man answered. He hung up and went out for the car.

He had to take Flora to Brighton next day so it was a week before he had time off again. The next Saturday it was, he strolled along and looked at Cadogan Mews. It was a classy enough neighbourhood, same sort as Wilton Crescent, and 26 was on the corner as the boy had said. Maybe the mews had been stables once, but that was in the days when horses got better treatment than people. And No. 26 was bigger than the others. She hadn't married anyone like that red-faced nit at the dance. She'd married money, some weak-kneed fag with a voice like bed-springs creaking.

He propped himself up against the wall opposite and put a wad of chewing gum in his mouth. He chewed steadily for half an hour while there was no action. All the classy folk had gone off to their week-end cottages. Just now and then a solitary stroller would pass him or someone would come out and drive away in a shiny car. No action where he was interested.

He spat the chewing gum out and put in another wad. Just as he was about to give up in disgust a fat old man with a waistcoat like an oven door came out of 26 and walked off towards Cadogan Square. That was the end of activity but it encouraged him to wait a while longer. So half an hour later the fat man came back and this time Godfrey saw more of his face and realized he knew his face somewhere. Whether his picture had been in the papers or on telly or he'd been at some boxing tourney.

As Godfrey walked back to Wilton Crescent the name Angell seemed to mean something to him too.

Late on Monday afternoon he tried again. There was no shop around where you could ask, so he went straight up to No. 24 and rang the bell and asked for Mr Angell.

A smart boy looking like a King's Road boutique answered the door. 'Mr Angell?' he said, and looked at Godfrey as if he was something out of the drains. 'Next door.'

'It's the young Mr Angell I want, see. Not the old man.'

'Next door,' he said. 'No. 26.' And shut the door in Godfrey's face.

Godfrey spat on his doorstep and tried No. 22. No. 22 did not even know where Mr Angell lived, for Chrissake. So he thought it over and then tried across on the other corner from No. 26, No. 37.

A woman. Tarted and tinted and trying to look young which she never would be again except to a blind man with no arms.

'Mr Angell? It's opposite. The white house.'

'It's the young Mr Angell I want. Not the old man.'

'There isn't a young one – nor an old. Mr *Wilfred* Angell lives there.'

'A – a stout gent?'

'Yes.'

'But I thought there was a young one.'

'No, there's only himself and his wife. He's just newly married.'

Godfrey stared with his mouth half open and muttered something into his gum shield. Then just as he was turning away she had an idea. 'It isn't his servant you want, is it?'

'Pardon?'

'He used to have a servant called Alex Jones. He left about three months ago. Tall boy with a lot of dark hair and a sexy walk.'

It was lucky she couldn't hear what Godfrey said then, but perhaps he did not look too loving because she shut the door quick. Little God was left alone in the hot street with the sun streaming down and just his thoughts for company.

Because it altered a lot. It altered the way he thought about her. Her marrying this fat rich old man. He could hardly believe it. It would have been bad enough marrying a rich young one.

It altered the way he thought about her. He'd thought she was different from the rest, more superior, something out of the top of the bag. But she was the same as all the rest. She'd turned him down because he hadn't enough glue in his sock and sold herself to this fat merchant who was lousy with money. When he thought of that fat man pawing her he got goosepimples, and red spots floated.

But in one way it was better than a young man.

A few months ago she had almost been Little God's girl. He had picked her out at a dance and driven her home. Then she'd come with him to Walworth Baths as his girl, sitting there watching him box.

But she didn't want Little God with all his manhood and fire in his belly; instead she went for this old heavy-weight who could buy her diamonds and mink. The broad. The crummy stuck-up little broad.

Quite by accident a couple of days later Godfrey was looking at a picture of Venice in the hall at Wilton Crescent and he remembered where he had seen the fat man before. The fat man had called on Lady V a couple of months ago and had stopped to stare at this picture. Godfrey had opened the door for him and there he was, standing there in a suit that was first cousin to a draughtsboard and carrying a bunch of red roses. It was just after Flora had come out of her clinic.

So that night when he was playing rummy with Flora – she was having one of her off days – he brought up the subject in a roundabout way, and she told him who Mr Angell was.

'This bloke I was with,' Godfrey said, while the thumb-screws worked in his guts, 'this bloke says to me that this Mr Angell has just married a young girl, young enough to be his daughter. That right?'

'That's right. Some suburban miss he unexpectedly picked up with. No fool like an old fool. I went round last month to the reception he gave to introduce his blushing bride.'

'When was this? I never drove you!'

'No, it was that week you were in strict training after we came back from Cannes. I went by taxi while you were at your gym. There's a run for you! I throw my knave and I'm out.'

Godfrey totted up how much he was down on the hand. 'How old d'you reckon he is?'

'Who?'

'This Angell.'

'Oh, just the right side of fifty, I should say. Of course she's pretty enough in a rather sweet unanimated way. She was nervous at the party. One wonders what she is getting out of it. All his friends were absolutely astounded, I can assure you.'

'Been married before?'

'Wilfred? Heavens, no. Most of us thought he was a pansy.'

Little God watched her deal the next hand. Seven each. She made a click with each card. Her hands were strong but tapering and the nails had an orange coloured varnish on them.

'Mind you, it has happened before,' she said.

'What has?'

'An old queer gets rather past it, so he puts aside his boys and takes a wife so as to become one of the majority in later life.'

'Think that's the case with Angell?'

'I wouldn't know. He may have been a Don Juan all his life on the quiet . . . I'd hardly think so with all that weight. And anyway he'd be far too careful of his money!'

Godfrey thought afterwards it was strange how things turned out. He had been spar mate to Alf Manton two years ago before Alf hit the big time, and in September Alf was going to Boston to fight Joe O'Connor, and he thought he could persuade Bingham his manager to take one spar mate from this side for his three weeks' training at Boston. It looked a great chance, and if Godfrey had got it he would have left Flora flat and maybe thought no more of Oyster and how he would have liked to look inside and find the Pearl.

But Bingham played around with the idea and then wouldn't wear it, so it all came to nothing after all. This made Godfrey more frustrated than ever. Robins was useless and he was getting nowhere. And he would soon be getting to his peak now, age wise, and he hadn't for ever to wait. He needed a manager who was in with the ring, the real promoters, not a small time push-over who just hung around their offices waiting for a word, and when he got it didn't speak the same language.

So he was back with Flora V, and he had nothing to train for until maybe October when Robins was trying – and so far failing – to fix something up. So he thought more and more about Oyster and the closed shell and the Pearl inside. And he thought of W. J. Angell Esq. who had taken his girl. And of the firm of lawyers called Carey, Angell & Kingston where he worked. And of 26 Cadogan Mews only just round the corner from here. And he tried to think how he could put his spurs in. He tried to think how he could get in on their lives, how to keep the pot boiling, or maybe just simmering so that sooner or later Little God could get a taste of the soup.

Chapter Six

Lawyers are by training, by habit, and often by temperament, cautious people. It is of the essence of their profession that they look at all possible flaws in a deal or in a line of action before the deal is completed or the action undertaken, so that adequate provision be made to deal with the flaws before they arise. No good solicitor will approve a will which does not appear to be legally tight-bound against the worst that mischance can do to upset its intended provisions. No solicitor can convey a house or a parcel of land without 'searching' the previous deeds for the disadvantages his client may incur by completing the purchase. It is never the solicitor's function to be the optimist. It is never his lot to think: 'But of course this in all probability will never occur.' It is always his lot to think: 'What *else* might occur?'

So, not unnaturally, a professional habit becomes an ingredient of personal behaviour. More solicitors carry umbrellas on fine days than any other profession.

But that being said, it is surprising that these habits of exemplary caution, assimilated, ingrained and inherent, do not invade their private lives more than they actually do. At times there appears to occur a subconscious rebellion within the psyche which will launch a hitherto circumspect solicitor upon a course that naturally less cautious people would hesitate to take. The history of the Disciplinary Committee of the Law Society is full of such cases. And some of the most noted rebels of the past began in law.

Wilfred Angell of course would not have admitted even to himself that marrying Pearl Friedel, a relatively unknown girl less than half his age, was an incautious or precipitate act. There was naturally a degree of risk, but so there is in any human action. Logically there were many advantages. He needed a wife. This year, reluctantly, he had come to that conclusion, though not altogether for the reasons Dr Matthewson had suggested. The social and domestic advantages were clear. A young woman was both more attractive than one of his own age and less set in her ways; he did not think he could ever have tackled a woman of forty-five. Also Pearl reminded him of Anna: this was a sentimental thing but not unimportant. She was half Jewish and therefore more likely to appreciate a bargain whether in the market or the registry office; and Vincent Birman's unobtrusive researches into her private life had shown her to be healthy, of a respectable family though not well-to-do; modestly educated but with some accent on manners; she was fond of music, especially the clarinet, and she was reserved for a girl of these days. She went out with young men but had a reputation for being fastidious. She liked the good things of life, the things that money could buy, and she was not particularly comfortable at home. It seemed to Angell that he could offer her all but one of the things a sensible girl could desire.

Of course there had been moments in the courtship when he had been nervous, when he had had doubts. That first dinner party at home had been embarrassing because she arrived early and before he had had an opportunity of telling the story he had made up to explain her presence. However he swallowed his annoyance and noticed that she bore what to her must have been quite an ordeal with the utmost composure. Also she looked very pretty, and although this meant nothing to him in the ordinary way, she had for him something of the intellectually sensuous appeal of a Rodin.

After the party he did not make any further move for three weeks. He had directed an inquiry as to Frank Friedel's financial situation. Also it seemed good policy to leave Pearl alone for a while so that she might begin to be afraid he was letting her drop. Then he invited her to lunch at the Ritz. It seemed unavoidable to spend *some* money at this stage, and after careful consideration he came to the view that such a meal offered the most impressive surroundings for a not too extortionate outlay.

They talked there, and for the first time he allowed her to see that he was genuinely interested in her, not merely as a casual friend. He told her of his busy and interesting and prosperous life which to some extent lacked a centre, a focal point to which one might always hope to return for companionship, for friendship. He put this well, he thought, as a distinguished and important man might.

She did not seem surprised, and did not make any comment – it might not have been directed at her at all – and it was at this stage perhaps that he came nearest to giving up the pursuit altogether. At the end of the meal he found himself sweating and beset by doubts, and they separated without any future meeting being arranged. As he had said to Matthewson after the medical examination, his life at present was beautifully ordered and singularly uncomplicated. Was he not now in process of doing precisely what he had then derided others for? However little he might feel for the girl sexually, there had to be an element of sex in the association because of the very nature of her being. However equable now, she might in later years become temperamental, difficult, or – worst of all – extravagant, and one could not discharge her as one could Alex. One might be in for 'scenes'. Although she might by her good sense save some money in the house, inevitably she could cost him far more than he saved, in clothes, in perfume, in hairdressing, even in holidays. She might even want a car.

He thought of the paintings he could buy, the furniture, the tapestries, the sculpture. Meals, if they ate out, would cost twice as much. (Or anyway one and a half times as much.) Only a few months ago he had thought contemptuously of John Matthewson and his faded wife and his two public school children. What was he about now?

But the fact remained that he was steadily becoming richer. If this Vosper deal finally went through he was likely to become richer yet. Pearl Friedel was another acquisition. Over her whole life with him she could hardly be as expensive as a Ruoualt. If moderately extravagant she might cost him as much as a Guardi. With luck she might not amount to more than a couple of Louis XV armchairs. In return he would get gratitude from her for raising her out of the common ruck, some companionship when he needed it, and possibly even a little affection. He would have a table companion at dinner who was a quick learner and who already looked the part; his sexual position in society would no longer be open to misunderstanding. And, of course, she still reminded him of Anna.

The Vosper deal rather irritatingly hung fire. Old Hollis

had advised Lord Vosper against the agreement, on principle, Angell was certain, rather than as an informed decision, but Claude Vosper was sheltering behind this advice to avoid making up his own mind. A vacillator by nature, he clearly wanted the money but no doubt thought that a little reluctance might bring him even better terms. Francis Hone, Angell, Simon Portugal and the rest had decided against any increased offer: it could only raise suspicions that there was something behind the deal.

But there was not all the time in the world. News might leak. It balanced rather on a knife edge. Between attending to the business of his firm, playing bridge at his club or in select private houses, courting Pearl, haunting the sale rooms of Sotheby's, eating monumental meals and under-tipping waiters, Angell fretted over the chances and the sums involved. During the last two months he had only seen Flora Vosper once, and then she had looked unchanged. An uneasy fear stirred in his mind sometimes that in some way he might have misunderstood Dr Matthewson's prognosis, or that Matthewson himself might be mistaken. But an attempt to check with Matthewson had met with a rebuff.

Nor could he very well call on Lady Vosper again unless invited. Apart from his morbid distaste for illness of all kinds, such a visit would tactically just not do. He considered engineering a meeting with Lady Vosper's daughter Miriam; but he had never even met her, only seen her once; and to do this would be more noticeable even than calling on her mother.

Angell sat uncomfortably at luncheon in his club one day eating a double helping of baron of beef and listened to two young men, one an architect, the other a surveyor, speculating on the possibility that the government might pick on a site in Suffolk for its next satellite town. It was disconcerting.

So back to Pearl, his symbol of adventure in a rather grey and frustrating world.

A car-hire firm called International, in return for certain legal coverage and advice, offered Angell cars at a 50% reduction, so one splendid Sunday in June he hired a chauffeur-driven Princess and took Pearl out for the day. They went to Oxford and he showed her round his father's college and explained how the war had prevented him going there. He made an effort to talk well, and when he tried he could. She was impressed by his sharp caustic judgments, his wide cultural range, his sophisticated knowledge of life. Often she instantly saw that he was right in his opinions, though she would not have had the wisdom to think so first. She wished she were like him.

On the way home they stopped at a famous restaurant on the river and took a quiet dinner. Soon after the sun set he asked her to marry him.

She did not speak for quite a while, and Angell wondered a little how she would frame her acceptance.

At length she said: 'Wilfred – I've never called you that before, have I?' And she laughed apologetically. 'Wilfred, it's super of you to ask me. Really it is.'

He knew it was but he could hardly say so.

'It's fabulous of you to ask me, but, Wilfred, I don't love you . . .'

'What is love? Affection, friendship, companionship. Do you feel any of these?'

'Oh, yes, in a way. I have super times with you –'

'And could have many more. You see the way I live.'

'But isn't there – there should be something more to marriage than that.'

'Do you mean desire?' He picked up the wine basket but the bottle was empty. 'That's quite a different thing. I could hardly expect you to feel that – so soon. In any event I would never press you to feel that. It would be a matter entirely of your own choice.'

She wrinkled her brow and stared out over the river. A creeping mist was lurking among the shadows, like breath from the hot day. She had seen the proposal coming during the last few meetings but had still refused to believe it would really happen. It was like being offered a floor managership at D. H. Evans: flattering, but if you accepted would you ever be able to be yourself again?

'How do you mean, my own choice?' she asked.

'Well, you will know how marriages came to be arranged in the old days. Parents picked one's husband, one's wife on grounds of general suitability. One came to marriage often with one's feelings unawakened. Thereafter often it came about that one fell in love. You'd be surprised how many happy marriages developed from this sort of arrangement.'

'Do you mean –'

'Of course this is not so in our case. We have met frequently and we like each other. I believe we are well suited. You can offer me a great deal. I can offer you a great deal. We are complementary to each other. The rest can follow as and when it may.'

'Do you mean,' she said, 'that you love me or that you don't love me? I mean, I still don't quite understand.'

Angell was nettled by her youthful directness. She left no room for implications or nuances. It all had to be in words of one syllable.

'Of course there is – love in this. But I am suggesting to you first and foremost a companionate marriage. A marriage of true interests. Desire may or may not become a part.'

By now the lights were coming on in the restaurant. He thought she looked flushed. Her neck was flushed above the fine white sweater which so clearly showed the outline of her breasts. Angell sipped the last drop of wine from the bottom of his glass. He had known all along that he should have ordered the '59 instead of the '63. The '63 was 15/- cheaper, but the difference in quality was much wider than the difference in price.

She said: 'I – really don't know what to say.' She glanced up hopefully at the waiter who had stopped at their table.

'A liqueur for madame? Cointreau –'

'No, no.' Angell waved him irritably away.

'– as a matter of fact,' Pearl said, 'I'd simply love a liqueur, Wilfred.'

'Oh . . . then, waiter!'

'Sir?'

'Miss Friedel will – what would you like?'

'A crème de menthe, please.'

Angell suppressed a wince of distaste. 'A crème de menthe and – oh, well, yes, I'll take a brandy.'

In the silence that followed, Pearl rubbed her wrists which seemed to be suffering from prickly heat. 'I never thought, I certainly never thought when we met on that aeroplane. I never dreamed . . . Have you – never been married?'

'No, I was engaged once – or almost engaged, but –'
'What happened?'
'It broke up. It was to the girl who was rather like you.'
'Yes, I remember you saying.'

Wilfred said: 'Perhaps this is one subject I should touch on. I have made my life – as I tell you – as a bachelor ever since Anna died. This gives rise naturally to rumours. To-day the whole of life is so sex-ridden, such pressure is put on people by the whole ad-mass consortium, such reverence is paid to the words of a morbid Viennese Jew called Freud, that no one is allowed by public opinion to live without sex even if he wants to. Because I have chosen to do so, because I have had menservants to look after my house, people have whispered that perhaps I am a homosexual.'

The waiter came back with the drinks.

Wilfred said: 'Personally of course I have cared nothing for such tittle-tattle. It is unimportant; idle gossip. Anyway there is little prejudice against the homosexual today – indeed why should there be? in a world of over-population he can claim to be the best citizen. But I thought it necessary at this stage to mention it to you, and to tell you categorically that I am not.'

'I see what you mean,' Pearl murmured, rather lost what to say. 'Thank you.'

Neither spoke then for a while. Pearl sipped her sweet green drink and felt it go down burning gently. The restaurant was elegant and expensive, the food and the wine had suited her. She thought: I can do this all my life if I want to now – if I *want* to. No more travelling up to London on the 7.55, rain or shine, winter and summer, fighting for a seat, tramp, tramp, tramp among the thousands out of Victoria and queueing for the bus, standing in the shop all morning, 3/6 canteen lunch, standing all afternoon, getting backache, then coat on, queueing for the bus, tramp, tramp, tramp among the thousands into Victoria, fighting for a seat, bus at Croydon or twenty minutes walk, home to the small bedroom or downstairs Rachel and television and Leslie and Gustave arguing or fighting or whistling or doing prep, and Julia cross and being put to bed, and Dad coming home grey-bearded with quiet dignity; and afterwards maybe Hazel and Chris and some young man for me, an electrician or a mechanic or a clerk, with no

103

manners and common tastes. (And pawing hands. Temporarily at least she was very much off pawing hands.) No more two weeks' holiday a year, scraping for the package deal to Zermatt; no more thinking if I buy that crimson barathea it will have to do for winter as well; no more advising old women who can't possibly *look* nice how they can *smell* nice. If I say yes now, for the rest of my life I am *on the other side of the counter*. It's like being elevated to the peerage.

But. She looked at Mr Angell, as she still called him in her thoughts. *Enormous.* The breadth of his chest, the breadth of his waistcoat. What *size* would his pyjamas be? What would he look like in a bath? Or in bed? A good head – quite a noble head, if you looked at it right – and not *old* looking – a *strong* man, never seemed to feel his weight. Would he be generous? He might be persuaded. Would he lose weight? He might be persuaded. Of course there was no *romance*; not a vestige, there never *could* be. Nor could she ever love him, if love meant what it was supposed to mean. But this might even be an advantage, to be free from the unpleasanter obligations of love. And how unpleasant, thanks to Godfrey, these obligations at present seemed.

She knew what her friends would say. Pearl? Well, I always thought she was a bit of a snob, but it never crossed my mind. Just a gold digger. And an *old* man. Well, middle-aged. And have you *seen* him? There are some men in their forties who quite send me, but *him*. Maybe she's marrying money, but I'll say she's earning it! Pearl. Good-looking as well. For crying out loud, she could have done better than that!

So they'd say, but could she? Where was the romance with young engineers and clerks and shopkeepers and schoolteachers. Sex, yes. They all offered her that. In fact they thrust it at her like a hot potato before she was ready. All Little Gods in their own way. Little Gods but inhibited by the laws of the land. She shivered.

'Are you cold?'

'No, no, thanks.' She had quickly lowered her eyes so that he should not see their expression.

'You're not 21,' he said. 'You're not 21 until next May.

That may raise the question of your parents' consent.'

'Oh, that. It will only be Dad. I mean he is the one that cares. Perhaps you ought to meet him. That's if . . .'

'Naturally I shall wish to meet him. Could he come to see me on Saturday morning? Or shall I come down to your home?'

'No . . . I'll have to ask him, won't I? I'll have to ask him. But first –'

'Waiter, my bill!'

'Coming, sir.'

'But first,' she went on, 'I've – got to make up my own mind.'

For the first time Angell began to feel a niggling sensation of uncertainty such as he sometimes felt at Christie's when the last bid was his but the auctioneer had not yet brought down the hammer.

'You might prefer to think it over for a day or two. If there is –'

'Yes, I would. I would,' she said like a child let off an examination. 'It's – a big step.'

The waiter brought the bill and Angell took library spectacles out of his breast pocket and scrutinized it. After a moment he beckoned the man back.

'We had only one coffee. Miss Friedel did not take it.'

'Oh, sorry, sir.'

The adjustment was made, and Angell reluctantly took out his pocket book.

'Your father, I imagine, is a sensible man.'

'*I* think so.'

'So he will wish for his daughter's advancement and happiness.'

'Well, yes.'

'Does the question of my age deter you?' he asked suddenly, taking off his spectacles. His eyes were quite stern.

'Oh, well, I wouldn't say –'

'Because there are hundreds of cases every year of men in their forties marrying younger women. Statistics show that on the whole such marriages prove more lasting than where the parties are the same age.'

'Oh, I know it does happen. A girl I knew –'

'I believe we should get on very well. D'you know.' He

suddenly smiled, and that lit up his face. 'I have watched you very carefully – not merely for my sake but your own – and I have seen you enjoying the things I enjoy. I believe it would be a *companionate marriage*. I'm a very busy man, and you would have a good deal of freedom. But when we were together I think we should be very much in accord.'

'Yes . . . Yes . . .'

'But talk it over with your father, please. And let us arrange a meeting. I would like a private word with him. Can you see him tonight?'

'He'll be in bed before I'm home.'

'Ring me tomorrow at my office. You have my number, of course. I'd very much like to talk to him.'

He put some notes and some silver on the table, counted out the silver a second time and took two shillings back. Then he waited restively for her to collect her things and rise.

Not much more was said. They drove home in a not quite comfortable silence. He was slightly irritated with himself now that he could find no warmer or more affectionate things to say. But he had exhausted his vocabulary and his tongue would not frame words that might commit him too far or make him sound ridiculous. But in the back of the car he did take her hand and hold it all the way home. He felt this was expected of him and might make do in place of the whispered affections. She did not withdraw her hand or move it away.

Angell's meeting with Mr Friedel was a very distressing one.

His first impression on seeing Mr Friedel and shaking him by the hand was that Pearl's father was good-looking, dignified and better bred than the report had suggested. After five minutes' talk, with the sharp assessing eye of a lawyer, he still allowed Friedel his good looks but he had already seen through the dignity of a rather timid man who had sheltered all his life behind this wall of reserved impressive elegance, away from the harsh stress and judgment of the world. When he tried to be impressive he was pompous, and his rather careful accent broke down in stress words in which there were echoes either of south London or

106

Leopoldstadt. When you met him you felt he was born to command; after a while you discovered that he was born to be commanded.

This woke the bully in Angell, who in certain spheres knew all there was to know about timidity but was better skilled in hiding it. Mr Friedel, he felt, had come to inspect and possibly even disapprove of this wealthy but otherwise unsuitable husband for his little girl. In fifteen minutes Angell, spreading his hands and his waist, had disposed of all the objections Mr Friedel could possibly raise.

He was playing on his own ground, which too was an advantage, but to his surprise, having gained the major point, he came up against an utter and very distressing obstinacy in Mr Friedel's character, which might well be the obstinacy of a weak man but was no more removable for that. Like a swimmer on the point of drowning and clinging with despairing fingers to a tidal rock, Mr Friedel was not swept away. The condition to which he clung was that if Pearl married she must have a marriage settlement before the wedding. He wanted nothing for himself, he kept repeating *ad nauseam*, as if anyone in their right mind supposed he could possibly expect anything; but there must be some 'provision for Pearl'.

There was a considerable and devious discussion in which a number of irrelevant subjects were mentioned before Angell said in a cold and despondent voice that, sooner than allow any dissatisfaction to arise in Mr Friedel's mind, he would be prepared to make his wife a gift of a thousands pounds, though he was sure that Pearl would reject the idea outright and indeed be very offended at the thought. Mr Friedel said it was not really for Pearl to decide this, and that he considered a figure of ten thousand would be more appropriate. Bargaining, Angell said in a court-room voice, was sordid and distasteful in such a matter, indeed offensive, Mr Friedel agreed.

'Mr Angell, I have to tell you that I am still puzzled by all this. Pearl – I never thought Pearl was all that unhappy at home.'

'And her being willing to marry me proves she is?'

'Oh, please, I hardly meant to say that. There are –'

'But it does imply that, doesn't it. You underrate the

advantages she will have.'

'Oh, advantages, yes.' Friedel's eyes travelled over Angell's bulk. 'But we are much of an age, Mr Angell –'

'I doubt it –'

'Well, within a few years. And we both know that girls, that young girls are romantic. They feed on the idea of meeting some handsome young man –'

'Romance does not last long in a two-roomed flat in Notting Hill or a shared semi in Streatham.'

Mr Friedel stroked his beard to give him confidence and support.

'The money you are trying to persuade me to put in her name, that is unimportant,' said Angell. 'What is important is the automatic advantages she will have as my wife. She will become a lady –'

'I have always done my best to make her one.'

'She has far more chance with me of becoming what you have tried to make her than with some scruffy young man earning £25 a week.'

Mr Friedel picked up his greasy mackintosh which he had hung over the gilded beech back of a Cressent chair. He folded it twice and put it on the seat of the chair, since he had no intention of leaving yet.

'She will have to give a lot up, Mr Angell. I have been awake half the night thinking of this. It means leaving all her friends, all her *young* friends. She might not be happy with you. You might not be happy with her.'

'It's a risk in every marriage.'

'Her mother was killed when Pearl was still a child. It was a great shock. On the Clapham Line – quite a minor accident – she was the only one killed. I remember coming home after – after identifying her and thinking now I shall have to be everything to my little girl. Father and mother too. I have tried to be that. That is why I feel I have a special responsibility.'

'Very commendable of you,' Angell said, 'I understand exactly how you must have felt. But because I am older than she is, I too feel a special responsibility.'

'As for the settlement . . .' said Mr Friedel.

In the end they agreed on five thousand pounds. Somehow in the atmosphere of bargaining, which they both admitted they so much disliked, Pearl's assent to the marriage, which she had not yet actually given, was taken for granted.

Caxton Register Office, with only the necessary witnesses, a small reception the following day at 26 Cadogan Mews, to which Angell made a point of inviting Lady Vosper. (She still looked *exactly* the same, which perhaps was as well so long as Vosper refused his signature.) A honeymoon in Paris. Well, not quite a honeymoon. Angell had put forward his views to Pearl both before and after the wedding, and she had agreed to them with a willingness that he found slightly unpleasing. They stayed at a quiet hotel off the Rond Point and had separate rooms with connecting doors. They joined forces for breakfast on the balcony, he in a monumental black silk dressing gown, but apart from this they stayed in their separate territory.

She had never been to Paris before and seemed content to sightsee, usually without Wilfred, go to a few concerts, usually with him, and window-shop. She spent some money, but Wilfred took care not to let her near the Faubourg St Honoré district, so most of the purchases were fairly inexpensive. When he was on his own he browsed in the art galleries and showrooms and spent far more than the cost of the holiday on a painter called Bonel who was at present quite cheap and looked a good investment.

They got on surprisingly well. In numerous ways they did think much alike. Their honeymoon was companionate in the way he had thought of it being. There wasn't a solitary major disagreement; and although most often she fell in with his plans, he sometimes found an unexpected pleasure in pandering to her wishes.

There were also times, he reluctantly admitted to himself, when, catching sight of her through the connecting door accidentally left open, her long beautiful legs meant more to him than the Louis XIV acanthus leaves with which he had equated them on the aeroplane in March. There were times when the white swell of her skin around the shoulders and breasts, made his mouth a little drier than it normally was. But the whole purpose of this marriage was that it should be a civilized and intelligent contract. An eventual sexual relationship had not been altogether ruled out in the sub-clauses, but privately he had always determined that nothing of this nature should ever occur. Once such a relationship intruded, it could alter and distort the whole pattern. Their future together would then become unpredictable. At present it was almost wholly predictable. His life was pleasanter than it had been before and yet its ordinary rhythm had hardly been disturbed. Once let the act of sex occur and he would be down in the arena with the other poor fools.

'Mr Godfrey Brown' meant nothing in his appointment book, and when he asked his secretary she said the man telephoning had insisted that he consult Mr Wilfred Angell. None of the other partners would do. The caller, she said, had not a well educated voice, but he had said it was a personal matter and would explain it to Mr Angell when they met. The appointment was for 3 p.m. on the next Tuesday, which would be five weeks to the day since their return from Paris. He made a note on his pad for Selbury, his clerk, to vet his visitor first. One got such cranks.

However, at 3.10, Selbury put his head round the door. 'Mr Angell, Mr Godfrey Brown says it's a personal matter and he won't talk to me. He's – not much class, to say the least, but he seems quite normal. I'd say he was genuine.'

So Mr Godfrey Brown was shown in – a vital, sharp-eyed, handsome, small man in a sober blue suit and holding a peaked cap. Angell, with his memory for faces, recognized him immediatey.

'Aren't you Lady Vosper's chauffeur?'

'Yessir.'

'Has Lady Vosper sent you? Did she –'

'No, sir. She don't know I'm here.'

'Is she ill? Is she ill again?'

'No. Well, she's not what you'd call in the pink, but she's not ill. She's out for tea and bridge. I just took her to the Werners, see. I knew she was going, that's why I rung up and came to see you.'

Angell pointed to the worn old black horse-hair reserved for clients. 'Well, sit down.'

The young man sat down. There was silence. Angell put on his library spectacles and picked up his pen. 'Your name is Godfrey Brown?'

'Yes, sir. But you don't want to put that down. I just came to see you about something worrying me, as you might say. Seeing as you're Lady Vosper's lawyer.'

Angell's eyes strayed over the top of his spectacles. It was a sunny day. The sun showed up the dust on the piled law books. The moment passed.

'It's like this, Mr Angell, Lady Vosper, she got a daughter, see. D'you know her, eh?'

'I have met her.'

'Well, she comes in and out of the flat all the time, comes to see her mother, like –'

'Wouldn't it be as well to start at the beginning?'

'That's the beginning all right. You see –'

'How long have you been with Lady Vosper, Mr Brown?'

'Oh, near on a year. She's been O.K. to me. She'll be able to drive herself again next week but I don't reckon she reckons to get rid of me . . . Mind if I have a fag?'

'No . . .' As Godfrey looked around, Angell pushed forward a box on the desk. Confronted with a man of Godfrey's class he would not normally have been accommodating, but this man's employer gave him some importance.

'Don't often smoke, you know. Not me to smoke. But now and then, just now and then.' Godfrey blew twin streams down his nose like the exhausts of a sports car starting from cold.

'You keep in training, I suppose.'

'Yes. I keep in training. I'm a boxer. Didn't know you'd know.'

'Lady Vosper mentioned it.' She had more than mentioned it, had bragged to him about her little tough fighter at the wedding party. Something at the time in her voice. One could never tell with middle-aged women where their fancy would stray. Or how far. With a sick woman one knew even less.

'It's Lady V's – Lady Vosper's daughter that's the trouble. She's in and out of the flat couple of times a week; and she comes down to Merrick House now and then. Her husband don't often come – only seen him a few times – Lady Vosper and him don't get on. But Mrs McNaughton comes a lot. And things are going . . .'

'What d'you mean, going? What things?'

'Things in the house. It's like she's nicking them. When she comes down to Merrick House, and once every couple of weeks or so at Wilton Crescent, something goes. Little things, not big. It gets on your wick. Before you know, Lady V'll be thinking I've nicked 'em.'

Angell tapped his spectacles on the blotter. He eased off the top button of his trousers and swayed gently in his swivel chair. Underneath the young man's deference he detected an arrogance. Yet it was an engaging arrogance. One wondered at the muscular little body hidden in the conventional blue suit. A boxer. The exchanging of harsh blows upon eyes and nose and flesh. For money. For sport. As a way of living. It was something from another planet. Angell would have found more in common with a Chinaman.

'And Lady Vosper? Are you saying that she does not notice?'

'Lady Vosper, she's one on her own. She's not the sort to count over what's hers. But first time I did mention it, like, you know, just casual; I said, look, your daughter, etc. But she shuts me up like a match box. It's a dicey point between us, her daughter, so I lay off. But couple of days later she says to me, Mrs McNaughton took the silver for cleaning. After that it will be put in the bank. Too valuable, she says, to leave around.'

'Well, that's very reasonable.'

'And what about the other things? Pot figures off the mantelpiece, round little pictures in black frames off of the walls?'

'Always small things?'

'What'll go in a shopping bag.'

Angell regarded the young man thoughtfully. 'And why have you come to me, Brown?'

'Well, it don't seem right. I'll get the stick. I know it'll be that way.'

'I think I have to ask you at this stage whether you are consulting me as a client or asking my advice as a friend of the family?'

Godfrey narrowed his long eyelashes to the smoke. 'Well, I thought you being her lawyer . . .'

'I'm not the family solicitor.' He had to say it this time. 'I have acted for Lady Vosper on occasion.'

'Well . . . that's it, then. So I came to ask you what to do.'

'It seems to me it's my advice as a friend of the family

113

absolutely nothing to prevent a mother giving presents to her daughter.'

'But half the things she don't know, that's for certain. One day I hear her asking this woman that does for her in the country, this Mrs Forms, she says where is this miniature and Mrs Forms don't know because she hasn't noticed that it's gone, see. But before you know it she'll get the fault, or Joe Forms. Or Mrs Hodder that comes in in London. Or me. Most likely me.'

'Why?'

'Why me? Because I came without a reference. The others, they been with her years and years. And that'd just suit Mir – Mrs McNaughton.'

'Do they know you have come to see me?'

'Who?'

'The other servants.'

'Nah. No. They'd never say nothing. It's not their way.'

Angell made a note on his pad. *Brown. What sort of a liar is he? The old trick: complain someone else is stealing things when you're stealing them yourself?*

'And you think by coming to me that it is a safeguard in case you *are* accused?'

'Yes, Yes, that's right.'

'What gave you the idea of coming to me?'

'Well, I think Mr Angell's a lawyer, maybe he can speak to her, tell her it's not fair. If she wants to give her daughter things, she should do it straight, not let her pinch off with them under her arm!'

Angell was examining the situation that was offered to him and wondering if he might turn it to advantage. He added another note. *May be speaking the truth. When one considers all the circumstances, it's quite possible that Mrs McNaughton might seek to secure . . . But still question his motives in coming to me.*

'How is Lady Vosper? Her health, I mean.'

'Oh, so-so. Like I said.'

'Has it deteriorated of recent months? I mean has it got worse?'

'Pardon? Well, she never been right since her visit to that Clinic. It done her harm, that Clinic.'

'In what way is she ill?'

'Well, there's headaches. And she tries to fetch up and

can't. Like being sea-sick on an empty stomach, she says. Then she got no energy – just lying on this couch all day.'

'You wait on her personally?'

'Me? More than I look after her car. Like a bl – like a nursemaid.'

'Is she always like this?'

'Always?' Godfrey screwed out his cigarette, looked at the box and then overcame the temptation. 'Not always. Sometimes she's O.K. I just said I just took her out to bridge.'

'Does the doctor say what is wrong with her?'

'Not to me he don't. All she tells me is it's her kidneys.'

They stared at each other through the smoke signal that Godfrey's butt end was sending up. Angell picked up his pen, wrote: *If he is telling the truth about daughter, it is clear that* she *has few doubts about her mother's illness. But Brown* . . . He drew a pin man on the pad with little round balloons for hands. He was not convinced about this visit. It smelt of some subterfuge, yet what subterfuge could there be?

'If I speak to Lady Vosper about this, Brown, she will know you have been to see me, and it will make her angry. My advice to you is to go back and think no more of the matter. If at some future date there is trouble between yourself and Lady Vosper, you may mention this visit to her and I will confirm that you came. But I'm afraid it is no safeguard.'

'Why not?'

'You see I have only your word for what is happening and that would not stand up in a court of law.'

'Well, it is happening I can tell you –'

'No doubt, no doubt. I believe what you say. I was about to add that if it was of any encouragement to you, you could keep in touch with me on this matter.'

Godfrey stared and then blinked to hide the look in his eyes. 'You mean – me come here again?'

'Well, if you wish. It is entirely as you wish.'

'You mean, tell you when it happens again?'

'That or anything else that arises. Lady Vosper's continuing health is of concern to all her friends, but she doesn't welcome inquiries. I should be glad to know.'

'Yes. Yes, sure. I'll do that,' Godfrey said,

Another silence fell. It was the third of the interview, and during it much was left unsaid. They were like two chess-players making moves which seemed to fit the pattern of the other's play but which did not actually belong to the same board.

Angell at length spoke. 'If you feel you want to see me, ring my secretary before you come. I am very busy and can seldom see people at short notice.'

'You mean if –'

'I mean if there were any sudden change in Lady Vosper's condition or in the circumstances of her household.'

'Sure. Yes, sure,' Godfrey said for the second time and got up.

He looked as if he might offer his hand, but Angell nodded and pressed the bell. Miss Lock came to show Godfrey out.

Godfrey went, his mind active but puzzled. He had been prepared to call on Angell with a succession of excuses – or complaints – or at the worst even threats. Somehow, some way, he wanted to continue an association with him. He was prepared to ad-lib, to play it as the chips fell, but to press on somehow. But it seemed that the way forward – if only a little way – was open. He had been invited to call again.

That evening on arriving home Angell surprised his wife practising the clarinet. A month ago he had seen one advertised in an auction at Puttick's in Blenheim Street, and had sent his clerk round to put in a bid. He had got it very inexpensively, and though it was not a good instrument it would do.

He shook his head as he listened. It would do more than handsomely for Pearl who so far was no player and he suspected never would be.

When he went in she was just putting the clarinet away, and she looked up in surprise, through the curtain of her hair. He got a twinge, which he supposed was because she instantly and poignantly reminded him of Anna. It was rare these days for the resemblance to strike him, because Pearl's face had come to replace Anna's, and usually he had to make an effort to recall his long-lost first love.

116

She had settled down quickly after one or two early mistakes, and he was glad to recognize and appreciate her sense of money. Morning and evening meals were always on time and the house was well kept. He dined out less than he used to and often came home to dinner before going back to his club to play bridge, thus saving some of the extra cost of her being here; though her meals did not always suit him. More than once there had been a lack of substance, a lack of good meat and too much emphasis on fruit and vegetables, but so far he had not criticized her openly. This could come when they were more at home with each other.

For they were not yet at ease in each other's presence. She had irritating moods, and he wished he could understand them. She was always very straightforward while all the time his own mind sought for *arrières pensées* that did not in her case exist. Now and again he would decide that she was stupid, yet she was capable of coming to sharp decisions which showed that her mind could work as quickly as his. Many things, of course, would have to change before he was entirely satisfied with her. He had gone into the marriage with calculation and with pride. Already he found some of his calculations wrong and some of his pride recoiling on himself. For the first time in his life he was dealing with a young woman, and the act of marriage had put her on nearly equal terms.

He knew that by ordinary standards the marriage he had entered into was ludicrous. Most people, he considered, married solely to copulate, and they only discovered later whether any sort of civilized living together was feasible. He, with Pearl's somewhat withdrawn co-operation, had reversed the order.

But he wished sometimes that she was not so physically decorative. Tonight was one of the bad nights. She was wearing a sleeveless frock, and the part of her inner arm from elbow to armpit constantly drew his glances. It was pure and soft and faintly shadowed and not quite so round as the rest of her arm. It fascinated him. He thought it would have some slightly odorous, scented, womanly smell. In the end she looked down and said: 'Is there something wrong?'

'No, no, not at all. But I think that is a nice frock.'

'You've seen it before. I wore it to that first concert at the Wigmore Hall.'

'Did you? I'd forgotten.'

'Wilfred, I've been wondering . . .'

'What is it?'

'While I was dusting all the frames of the pictures today, I wondered if we could have a few less about the house. It's not the dusting I mind, but they seem – on top of each other. You can't see one for looking at the next one.'

Angell cut another slice off the breast of the chicken and put it on his plate.

'The trained eye is not affected. They give me great pleasure to look at.' He withdrew his glance from her inner arm. 'They should you.'

'Oh, I like them – or most of them. But I should like them even better if they were hung up in turn, say. Perhaps half of them, for a month at a time.'

'I already have plenty to make a succession. You've seen the boxroom.'

She sighed. 'It's difficult having so many. But couldn't you – no, I suppose not.'

'What were you going to say?'

'I thought perhaps you might sell some. Wouldn't it make you like the others better?'

'Not at all,' Angell said. 'There's the pride of personal possession. There's the special pleasure of looking at them constantly and getting to know them *detail* by *detail*. In time you will come to understand this – this pride of possession.' His voice was rather peculiar and he recognized it himself. He cleared his throat. 'More chicken, my dear?'

Pearl glanced at him in slight surprise. Since her marriage, terms of even mild affection had been lacking. She had also come to expect that her husband was always too interested in food to realize what was on *her* plate.'

'No, thanks. Have you finished? I'll get the pudding.' Before she rose she put both hands up to fix her hair, and this lifted her breasts and exposed both under-arms to his gaze. When she had gone out into the kitchen he shifted in his chair and took a piece of bread to chew between courses. He realized that this faint sickness – a sickness of desire – had attacked him before. But each time it was slightly worse. He realized that it would pass by tomorrow and rationally there was no reason why it should ever return. But in some way his aesthetic sense was awakening a physical sense. And there was another impulse at work that worried him, though perhaps it went too deep for rational examination. He had used some phrase just now to her. 'Personal possession' – that was it. Personal possession had always been one of the dominating motives in his life. He went to art galleries and museums, but only – or almost only – to compare what was in them with what he owned or might come to own himself. A tiny Picasso scarcely bigger than a postcard gave him more pleasure because it was on his wall than did 'Les Demoiselles D'Avignon' in the Museum of Modern Art in New York. A single William Kent chair, gilt on mahogany and decorated with dolphins, although in such frail condition that one could no longer sit on it, was more exciting in No. 26 Cadogan Mews than an entire Chippendale suite in Harewood House.

And now he possessed something new – something quite different from anything he had ever owned before. Was pride of possession beginning to work here too? And in so working, was it stimulating – or disguising itself as – the sexual impulse?

After dinner he would not so much as pick up the evening paper – whenever Pearl read a newspaper it was left as if she had been reading it on a windy promenade – so he sat for a while with a new book on French furniture, trying to concentrate. Pearl was busy in the kitchen and stupidly stayed there so long he felt affronted. But this was partly his own fault: he had never suggested they get any permanent maid – they had a woman six mornings a week – if he wanted more of her company in the evenings he supposed he would have to be prepared for it.

Eventually, feeling not at all sleepy, he got up, fastened his waistcoat across his broad silk-shirted body, and padded into the kitchen. She was busy rearranging some pans and looked up inquiringly.

'I feel tired, Pearl, so I'll go to bed early. Good night.'

'Good night.' She hesitated; there was no accepted routine. Then she put up her cheek to be kissed. He kissed it, resting his lips briefly on the satiny skin. He did not touch her arms. She smelt refreshingly of perfume.

He went up to bed and undressed and lay, a solid, middle-aged mountain under the sheets, staring at the Dufy flower painting over the Adam mantelpiece. He heard her come upstairs, and he listened quietly to her preparations for bed. Presently he put out the light and instantly went to sleep. Since marrying he had not had a recurrence of the claustrophobic loneliness which affected him on the night of the flight to Switzerland. All this summer he had kept extremely well, and he had no intention of disturbing either his mental or his physical equilibrium with ill-considered adventures into a way of life that other married men followed.

The next morning when he reached Lincoln's Inn there was a letter from Lord Vosper saying he had decided to accept the terms offered by Land Increments Ltd for the purchase of an option to buy Merrick House and 200 acres of land in the parish of Handley Merrick, Suffolk.

Vosper had taken four months to make up his mind.

Chapter Eight

On Angell's reckoning it would now take six or eight weeks to get the deal finalized. They needed Chancery Counsel's advice, and he went to see Saul Montagu, who was about the best man on property now in chambers. It would be quite a tricky agreement to draw up, since Lord Vosper had as yet no legal title to Merrick House or lands, and it was essential to bind him as securely as if he did. There were technical problems in finding the best way of binding a man to sell what he had not yet got.

Vosper's solicitor would have to draw up the draft contract of sale, and then when everything was ready for signing, the contract would be annexed to the option agreement. But when Angell called personally to see Hollis, the old man seemed unwilling to begin his part of the business until the draft option agreement was forthcoming. Hollis's view was that there was no need for undue haste and that the proper steps should be taken in the proper order. Also there would be the problem of obtaining sight of the deeds, and other information, from the solicitors acting for the trustees. This could no doubt be arranged, as the two firms had frequent dealings. But it would take tact, said Hollis, and it would take time. Angell came away irritated, and unconvinced that much would happen in that office until Saul Montagu had done his part.

In the middle of all this a telephone call from Godfrey Brown to Mr Angell.

He couldn't get round, he said, couldn't get away; but Lady Vosper had had a real nasty turn on Sunday; so he thought he'd ring. The doctor had been each day, so had Mrs McNaughton. Lady V was suffering from something else now, the doctor said. Tension, or something.

'Hypertension?'

'That's it. That's right. Doctor says she got to go slow. Some hopes. She'd sooner blow-up, she says to him. Says if she's better she's driving to Merrick this week-end, celebrate the end of her lay-off. Handle a car again, she says.

121

Do her good. You can't win. She gets her own way.'

Curiously this telephone call, this speaking privately, ear to ear, added a dimension to Godfrey's association with Angell that Angell didn't like. Instead of a visit to the office, where the difference of age and respectability and station was immediately clear, confidences on the telephone brought them to a level. It was as if Godfrey already understood too much, as if, without knowing why, he perceived that Angell was not doing him a favour by allowing him to ring.

'Bye bye for now, sir. How if I come round next week, when we get back?'

'That will hardly be necessary. Unless there is something really important to tell me.'

'If we're still in London. Minute she's better, we're off. Mr Angell . . .'

'Yes?'

'If I got something to tell you, maybe I could call at your house next time?'

'My house? Why?'

'So near. Five minutes' trot, see. I can nip round in no time. Your office is way out. I got to take two buses. When I'm out Lady V always wants to know where I been.'

'Yes. Well, possibly. But only if you . . . Well, yes you could. In the evenings. Monday and Friday evenings after six are best. Tuesdays and Thursdays I am always out.'

'Right. O.K. Thanks. If there's anything fresh I'll nip round.'

That night in bed Lady Vosper said to Godfrey: 'I think I'm going to die.'

'What? What d'you say? Oh, lay off it, Duchess, you give me nightmares.'

'Something Matthewson said today.'

'What'd he say? That old frost.'

'I said something about hunting next year, and he just said: "Well . . . we'll tackle that problem when it arises." It wasn't really so much what he said as the expression on his face. One felt pretty certain he believed the problem would never arise.'

'Oh, wrap it up. You're as tough as your riding boots. Made to measure. Can't wear out. Drink a drop less, that's all you need to do.'

'I'm not so damn sure, my little Godfrey. I'm firing on one cylinder only, you know. Have been for the last eighteen years.'

'Doesn't seem to me like one cylinder. You're a six-cylinder de luxe open sports with independent suspension and automatic transmission –'

'No, don't touch me any more. That's another thing.'

'What is?'

'I can only stand so much of it these days. You knock me over, you little devil. Listen to me –'

'I'm listening.'

'Oh, what the hell. I'm tired.'

'Tell me about Silverstone. You know. The crash.'

'I've told you.'

'Not properly. You just said it happened when you was lying second.'

'Well, it was a long time ago. At that time you were a squalling brat in an orphanage.'

'O.K., O.K., I was a squalling brat.'

'And I was lying second with only three laps to go. That mean anything to you?'

'Yeah. You'd got a chance of winning.'

'I'd got a chance of winning. A major event. *I* had, Flora Tower, independently entered, a *woman* driver. Two of the Italian champions in it too, and both retiring with transmission failures. I only had Lee-Turner to pass, and I tried to do it on Stowe and again at the Chapel Curve. Then on Beckett's Corner I skidded past him but I was going too fast and I spun off the course and overturned. The car finished on top and I was underneath. Proper place for a woman, you might say.'

'Want a fag?'

'You know I always do. Don't burn a hole in the sheet, man! This is the last of my wedding linen!'

'Which wedding?'

'The Bonny Mayhew, of course. It was the only one we got presents for.'

'So?'

Flora blinked to try to remove the black spots that were floating in her vision. She was no sentimentalist, and contrary tides of feeling contested within her. In reminiscence ran the danger of nostalgia, and she was not sure if she began where she would stop.

'So?'

'Why the hell should you be interested?'

'Why not? So I am. Why not?'

She stared at him through the smoke. He didn't look as if he was having her on.

'Oh, that wedding – that was a month before the outbreak of war. That was when we were married. I was just nineteen, and my dear mother thought we were rushing it. But we knew better. Bonny was the same age – he came to me one hot August day in a thunderstorm and said, "Russia and Germany have signed a Non-Aggression pact. Come on; we're getting spliced next week!" And we did. Mother was shocked; she thought the neighbours would think I was pregnant.'

'And you wasn't?'

She refused to be provoked. 'Miriam was born in 1941. Bonny knew there'd got to be war after that pact.'

'What's a Non-Aggression pact?'

'I'll tell you some day.'

'Whose side was Russia on in the war? I thought we were fighting Germany.'

'I'll buy you a book. Can you read?'

Godfrey rubbed his nose on the sheet. 'Bonny Mayhew. Kook name for a man. Like a girl. Did you like him?'

'His real name was Bonamy. Nobody used that. Yes, I – liked him, you insolent little man. We liked each other. He was hell-bent; one knew he couldn't last. He was shot down over Crete in 1941. I always felt he was one of those men who was half in love with easeful death.'

'I don't get you.'

'You wouldn't. Anyhow, I'm not. I don't welcome death any way it comes, any time, and it depresses me when my doctor looks as if he's at a wake.'

'Tell me about the next one.'

'What one? Paul Tower? But I've told you.'

'Not properly, you haven't.'

Flora Vosper drew at her cigarette. Her fingers these days would never stay steady.

'Paul was another play-boy. Maybe I attract 'em. But Paul was 46 when we were married. He'd made a packet during the war and had just sold his engineering works in Coventry and had money to burn. I helped him burn it. We sizzled all over the Continent for five years. It amused him to have a wife who was known on the Grand Prix circuits . . . Odd about that crash: I knew if I over-took Lee-Turner I had to take a risk that no sane professional racing driver would ever take, but I knew damned well that I'd never get as near winning a major race again. Both Ascari and Farina out with transmission trouble and almost all the other names had had mishaps. It was a vile day, greasy and windy . . .'

'What happened after the crash?'

'They fished out one kidney, mended my shoulders and rib. I was about again in a couple of months as bright as a bee. But Paul wouldn't let me race again, damn him. I suppose that began the break-up. Anyway he met his Judy the next year and I met Julian Vosper, so we had a double break and a re-splicing.' She yawned. 'You'd think you could go on for ever with one kidney. People do with one eye. And anyway you only have one liver to begin.'

'Bloke I knew used to box, only had one lung; never did him any harm; welter-weight; Sam Fox; wonder what happened to him; he had a greengrocer's shop; he's around somewhere, you bet.'

'Well, if you've only got one, it depends how that one works. Mine's packing up, it seems.'

The bedroom in the flat had a big bay window overlooking the garden at the back, and a sudden light from a flat opposite flooded across the thin curtains and cast stripes and shadows on the wall.

'Lord V was a lot older than you, was he? How many times had *he* been hitched before?'

'He was fifty when we married. Seemed a bit old to me then but it doesn't now. I was what? – thirty-two. Yes, I was his third, as he was mine. Everything considered we got on marvellously well.'

'Maud FitzGerald and Gerald fits Maud, eh?'

'Right. And it would be the same today if he hadn't had a coronary when we were in Bermuda five years ago. A bumper coronary, the doctor called it, the bloody fool. He might have been talking about a school picnic. Julian was sitting at the table having lunch and he said to me: "It's going dark, Flora," and I looked up and before I could get up and walk round the table he was dead.'

'You're in a right mood tonight,' Godfrey said. 'Know any more good funerals?'

'Yes, my own.'

'Oh, give over, Flora! Time I was hopping it and I can't leave you here moaning about yourself like a fog horn. Like a nice cup of char?'

'I don't mind telling you I'm scared, Godfrey. I don't want to die.'

'And you're not going to! Little God'll see to it. Little God's honour!'

She half laughed. 'I wish you were Big God as well.'

'Look,' he said. 'Like me to stay on? I always set my alarm for seven, to get in my run before Mrs Hodder turns up. What d'you say?'

'All right,' she said. 'Little Man, I think it would help. I seem to need the company.'

Pearl's premonition that most of her contemporaries would think her stark raving mad had been confirmed. Hazel and Chris, and Pat Chailey, and most of the girls in D. H. Evans, and those of her schoolfriends who knew, and various young men up and down Selsdon and Purley and Sanderstead.

She was also aware that there was a good deal of sniggering behind hands and bawdy speculation. She bore it with what even to herself was a surprising lack of embarrassment. So far as the girls were concerned she was certain that their derision was a way of hiding an element of envy. She had talked to too many of them and heard too many of them talking to each other to doubt for a moment that the second preoccupation of them all, after wanting to get married to some good-looking boy, was that the good-looking boy should have a super job with lots of lovely money. And if there was lots of money it wasn't *too* important that the boy should be so very good-looking or so very much of a boy. She had only carried this reasoning to an extreme conclusion. She had married someone without looks or youth but with what amounted to real wealth. So one balanced against the other. The swings and the roundabouts. There was no love but there was leisure.

There was no sex but there was satisfaction in prestige. Maybe there was no heady exaltation of young lips and young limbs; but oh, the heady exaltation of a large bank balance and a personal cheque book! Perhaps in time the joy of money and position would wear off. But so, everyone said, did the joys of love.

As for the young men, if they at once mourned her and sneered at her, what had they offered her but gauche compliments and furtive fumblings in the dark? She had married, they thought, a fat old buffer old enough to be her father; she had married, she thought, culture and good taste and the refinements of life . . .

Of course disillusion had set in early after her marriage. She realized quickly enough that the tips of the iceberg in Wilfred Angell's nature which had shown during their courtship were in fact only too truly representative of the massive elements under the surface. He was fat because he was greedy, no other reason at all. He was not generous – to say the least – though so far she had not used the word meanness even in her private thoughts. He was something of a bully, and would quickly raise his voice in restaurants if not given the best attention, in spite of the subsequent frugality of his tip.

He had a number of curious old-maidish habits. He usually bathed only in the evenings before dinner when he was going out, so that 'there should be no risk of taking a chill'. And every morning he counted exactly the same amount of money to carry with him: one £5 note, five ones, five ten shillings, three half crowns, three florins, four shillings, four sixpences, six pennies; so that he would never be short of change and would know at the end of the day just what he'd spent. And Sundays he didn't wind his watch, so that it ran right down . . .

All these were depressing failings and peculiarities, but Pearl was a patient girl and she did not despair. She was bent on a quiet re-education of his gastric juices, and so far he had not complained. She had £5,000 – five thousand actual pounds – of his money in a deposit account in her name, and this was hers to do with as she liked – thanks to her truly beloved and wise and distinguished and beautiful father. She found she liked the thrill of buying pictures almost as much as Wilfred, and she fully realized his

127

acumen. She loved going with him to a sale and sitting beside him enduring all the tensions and surprises of the auction rooms . . . And she sometimes suspected that his bullying had arisen out of his loneliness. When the world passes by unheeding, a small boy will shout to draw attention to himself.

Being a self-contained girl by instinct, she seldom needed company, and she was astonished when Veronica Portugal, whom she'd met at that first dinner, rang her up one day and asked her out to lunch. She was scared by the idea, and would much have preferred eating on her own, but when it came to the point they had it at the Caprice, which was fabulous if noisy, and she really enjoyed the whole thing. It occurred to her, by way of comfort, that Veronica, though married to a man of her own age, was more in need of company than she was.

Recently, during recent weeks, she had noticed Wilfred looking at her with a more brooding eye, and she suspected this might be an awakening interest. She didn't quite know within herself whether she welcomed this or not. She was enjoying her new life and there was plenty of novelty in it without the novelty of discovering sex in the company of a middle-aged man she liked but did not love. But, intuitively rather than by reason, she suspected that her influence on Wilfred might be enhanced if he began to desire her. And she wanted influence over him. Unless she had some guns on her side the contest would be unequal.

On the 12th August, which was a Monday, she spent all day shopping on her own. She loved spending money, but heredity, upbringing and her own nature were equally against extravagance. She bought frugally, wisely and with a sense of values. About 5.30 she staggered home in a state of subdued bliss, feet aching, parcels on her wrists and many more to come. She took a bath and while in it heard Wilfred come home. She speculated as to whether she should tell him of her shopping and whether she could possibly claim his interest in such things. She had to tell somebody and he seemed the appropriate person. He did not so much mind if she spent her own money, which was something already lost to him; but he had only rarely shown interest in her clothes. Indeed, if one faced the hard facts, he took little interest in anything unless it affected himself. Pearl felt he had to be gently prised out of this position. She did not underrate her task: he was an old bachelor deeply set in his ways and ruthlessly self-centred. But neither did she underrate her own good-tempered perseverance.

She had just dried herself when the bell rang, and she poised with the Chanel talc in her hand listening. Wilfred had early made it clear that he did not answer his own door; but as he was downstairs and she was up she waited to see what happened. Nothing happened and the bell went again. She took off her cap, shook out her hair, dug her feet into mules, put on the ice-blue silk dressing gown she had bought in Paris at the Aux Trois Quartiers and went down.

Little God was at the door. Her whole body seemed to lurch, to want to shiver.

'What do you want?'

Blue uniform, sober and tidy. All that black luscious hair subdued, face quite formal, without expression. Clear skin shining. He touched his cap. 'Beg pardon, ma'am, is Mr Angell in?'

'Go away!' She was beginning to shut the door.

'I got a message for Mr Angell! He told me to call, see.'

'Go *away*!'

'As soon as I give the message. I brought a message he asked me for, see. I've got a message.'

'What are you here for? Why are you pestering me again?'

'I'm not! Honest! Didn't know you were here.'

'That's a lie! You've come –'

'I've come to see Mr Angell. It's important! Let me in.'

She opened the door an inch or two further, drew behind it because his eyes, not as impassive as his face, had been looking her over.

'What sort of a message?'

'About Lady Vosper. I'm her chauffeur. Been her chauffeur for years. That's her car we went out in. Mr Angell's her lawyer. He asked for me to bring a message.'

Somehow he was inside, not very far from her. The hall was dark when you shut the door. It was the only dark room in the house, and even white paint didn't lift the shadows.

'You're Mrs Angell now, I suppose. I heard you was married. I went round to your old home, asked for you –'

'Yes and threw a flower-pot through the window!'

'What a dirty lie! There was some snotty-nosed kids round behind one of the cars when I left. Maybe it was them –'

'Yes, maybe it was them.'

'You don't need to sound so sarcastic. I never done you any harm, except that once I scared you. Anyhow don't give me away or I'll lose my job! I've come to see your husband, Mr Angell. I've not come to see you. I can't help it if you're here, can I?'

'No, you can't help anything –'

'You'd think I done you an insult being crazy about you. I *was* crazy about you, you know that. I'd – I'd have done murder for you if you'd asked, I would straight. That's the sort of sucker I was. But it's all over now. You're married, so that's that.'

'Yes, I'm married.'

'Happy, I hope?'

'Very happy, thank you.'

'Well, that's smashing, isn't it. Got a big car of your own now, I suppose.'

'No, as a matter of fact, we haven't.'

'Well, smashing place you've got here. I hope you'll be very happy.'

'Thank you. I'll call my husband.'

'You're still the tops, Pearl, for me. Groovy. Honest. Just to look at you –'

'If you begin again –'

'No, no. O.K., O.K., I give up. I've come to see Mr Angell. Right? I got a message for him, that's all. On the level.'

She left him there with his olive skin and his small rippling muscles and his gleaming eyes.

That night at dinner Pearl said: 'What did he want – Lady Vosper's chauffeur?'

'What? The chauffeur. Oh, he had a message for me. Lady Vosper has been very ill again, but she is feeling better.'

'Couldn't she telephone you?'

'Um? No. This is a private matter.'

130

'With Godfrey Vosper?'

'With whom?'

'Godfrey Vosper, the chauffeur.'

'His name's Godfrey Brown. No, of course not with him. How could it be with him?'

Pearl moved her Georgian silver fork so that the light reflected on it.

'Did you know I knew him before?'

'Godfrey Brown? When?'

'I met him two or three times before I was married.'

'No, I didn't know.' Angell looked across the table at his wife, but his surprise and disapproval were not sustained before her candid gaze. 'Very unfortunate. You met him. When was this?'

'Oh, at a dance. And twice afterwards. We weren't friendly. I didn't like him.'

'I'm glad you weren't friendly.'

'I didn't like him,' she said.

Wilfred, relieved of the need to criticize her taste, became judicial. 'Well I can't say I see anything to dislike in him particularly. As a particular type, one could even call him interesting.'

'I'd rather he didn't come here again, Wilfred.'

'What? D'you mean he was insolent to you in some way?'

'Not tonight. Oh, no, butter wouldn't melt. But I –'

'Of course it is embarrassing now you are my wife to have to meet people you knew before. Lady Vosper's chauffeur . . . unfortunate. Did you know he was that?'

'Of course not. I thought he was a boxer.'

'So he is – or so Lady Vosper says. But it's a part-time occupation.'

Silence fell. She had not combed her hair as much as usual, and it clung on her shoulders in heavy luxuriant folds. Her eyes were very bright, her cheeks flushed. She was wearing a frock she had bought that day, although he did not know this, and it diverted his attention from the six lamb chops he was eating. It was a sort of soft grey chiffon, very very light material, with a halter neck like a knotted rope and hundreds of tiny pleats falling straight down from the neck to the hem. The material looked too light and flimsy to be quite fair on him over dinner.

She said: 'He told me his name was Vosper.'

'Who, Brown? I suppose that was one of his jokes.'

'He boxes under the name of Vosper.'

'Does he, by Heaven. That is certainly impudence. Flora Vosper must know, for she told me she went to see him box.'

'And he borrows her car more or less when he wants to.'

'Their association may not be exactly a normal mistress-servant one. He's certainly very sure of himself.'

'Do *you* find him attractive?'

Angell looked up, and she smiled at him brilliantly. He put in another mouthful of food, chewed three or four times and then swallowed it. 'I don't know quite what you mean, my dear. A man who finds another man "attractive" can only have one name – at least in the charitable world of S.W.3.'

'I didn't mean that.'

'I trust you did not. But the little man is very personable in his way. I see that. His vitality has an immediate animal appeal. I can understand his being attractive to women – some women.'

'But not to me?'

'You have said not. I should be very disappointed in your taste if he appealed to you. Pass me the potatoes, will you?'

'They're finished. I didn't do any more.'

He blew through his lips. 'Not enough, Pearl.'

'They're fattening, Wilfred. Bad for me. I don't want to put on weight. You wouldn't want me to put on weight, would you?'

'Er – no. I have always been fond of them, though.'

'There are a few more beans. Do you find me attractive, Wilfred?'

He put the beans carefully on his plate. He took out his library spectacles, polished them, then did not put them on. 'Of course. You must know that. I asked you to marry me.'

'Attractive in the way that Anna Tyrrell was attractive?'

'Yes. In the same way. But I am older than I was when I knew Anna.'

'Did you make love to Anna?'

'I – made love to her. I never slept with her, if that's what you mean.'

'Have you ever with anyone?'

132

He froze up in a way that a month ago she would have found intimidating. 'I think you forget yourself, Pearl.'

'I'm sorry.'

'You've no *right* to ask me a thing like that! Good God! no right at all!' He took a sip of wine and then a longer gulp.

'Shouldn't I have the right? I'm your wife.'

'Well, I've no intention of answering you!' His face had flushed.

She said: 'I've never slept with a man.'

'So I should think not indeed!'

'Not so very many could say that at my age.'

'That's one of those silly statements that can never be either proved or disproved. Anyway, whether you're right or not, I'm not interested in generalizations.'

'But you are interested in me?'

'I'm interested in you, of course. In every way. Were you drinking before dinner?'

'Yes.'

'What did you drink?'

'Vodka. There was some vodka. It just happened to be there and I had a little vodka.'

'I've never seen you like this before.'

'Like what?'

'Wayward. Almost wanton. If –'

'I'm young.'

'Yes. Sometimes to me you seem very young –'

'You're not old, Wilfred. Are you? *Are* you?'

He slowly finished his last mouthful and put knife and fork together. 'What sort of pudding have you made?'

'None.'

'None? Then is there –'

'I forgot. I intended making something light. Light and cool. But I forgot. I'm sorry. I forgot.'

'Oh . . . it doesn't matter. For once. Don't make a practice of it. Is there cheese?'

'I'll bring it.'

She went out with a light and swinging step. When she came back he was standing by the mantelpiece with a glass of wine in his hand. She came over to him and buttered one biscuit and put a piece of cheese on it and offered it to him. He stared at it as if it were the apple in the

133

Garden of Eden, and his gaze travelled past it to the long hand holding it, and the wrist and the rounded forearm and the elbow and the upper arm with the slightly flattened plane towards the armpit. He took the biscuit from her and munched it, and she buttered one for herself and came and stood beside him and ate it with him.

'You're not *old*, Wilfred,' she said. 'I'm sure of that. You don't *look* old. You look quite a *young* man.'

'I am – a comparatively young man. But I am mature, not given to –'

She said: 'Why don't you kiss me?'

'What d'you mean?' he asked suspiciously, as if he were being offered an unexpected clause in a leasehold.

'It's easy. There's nobody to see us. Do you mind?'

Instinctively his fingers went up and brushed a crumb of biscuit off his lips. 'It's not a question of minding, Pearl. It's –'

'What is it then?'

'It's –'

'What is it then?'

They stared at each other for a very long moment. She was wanton and he despised her for it.

'Pour yourself another glass of wine,' he said.

She did so and buttered him another biscuit.

Chapter Nine

Among other things, Godfrey had come to say that Flora Vosper and he were leaving for Merrick House on Tuesday afternoon. On the Tuesday morning Godfrey went down to the Thomas à Becket gym for his last work-out with Alf Manter before Manter left for Boston for his title fight.

Godfrey drove the Jensen down the Old Kent Road at five to eleven, parked just off the main road and opened the side door of the big gaunt pub and went straight upstairs. He never cared for the smell of beer and the tinny music and the barmaids wiping down the tables and the early customers propping up the counter. Before a fight, even a sparring match, there was a sort of snarling austerity about him that he never let Flora Vosper see.

When he got up to the big bare L-shaped room above with its tall dirty windows, its ring and its punch-balls, Manter was already stripped and doing some shadow boxing while about eight people watched.

'You're late,' said Cohen. Godfrey glanced at the clock. 'Dead on time.' 'Ten forty-five, I said.' 'Eleven I agreed with Alf.'

'Kuh, kuh, kuh,' said Alf, delivering fierce short jabs at his unseen opponent. 'Kuh, kuh, kuh.' It was his way of pretending, Godfrey thought. Like a kid, making his punches land every time, hitting the other fellow. Well, he'd soon have someone to hit. There were two men in the room he didn't know, also a photographer from the *Daily Mirror,* a reporter from *Boxing News*; three or four other blokes he knew vaguely. He went in to change.

Fred Bingham was in there, Alf's other spar-mate. They nodded. Then Cohen, who had followed him in, said: 'I'm giving you the first two rounds, God. Then two for Fred, then two more for you. I want him to get a good work-out this morning but not too much rough stuff.'

'As if I could hurt him with these pillows and his motoring helmet,' Godfrey said sarcastically. 'Who's that dark joe out there? The one with the camel hair coat and the glasses.'

'Never you mind who's out there,' said Cohen. 'Just keep your thoughts on Alf. He's not going to pull any punches this morning.'

He went out and Fred Bingham began to tape Godfrey's hands. 'The man with the glasses, he's Jude Davis.'

'I thought I seen him somewhere. Doesn't he manage Tabard?'

'Yeah. And Bushey. An' he was the one that built Llew Thomas up from butcher boy all the way to the Lonsdale.'

Godfrey went out again and into the ring. It was prepared as though for an actual fight, except that there was no referee. Cohen from outside the ring would act as referee. Jude Davis was a thin dark Welshman of about forty-five, and he was talking to the press photographer and leaning on his umbrella.

The gong went. Alf Manter was one of the most generous men out of the ring, but in it he could be really mean. With his protective headgear he looked like a ton-up boy in a bathing suit. They knew each other's style well and most of each other's tricks, but this was their last meeting before Alf left, and a bit of extra competition came in. Alf had perfect style and perfect balance. His reputation was to win on points; rarely was he ever knocked down, his weakness was that he seldom knocked down anybody else.

This day happened to be one of the few in his career. In the second round he swayed his head back from Godfrey's sharp left, turning a fierce punch into an innocuous tap; but for once Godfrey had been able to disguise the right cross he had been following up with, and Alf grunted and slipped down and was on the canvas for about five seconds before he recovered himself. Cohen had half ducked into the ring, but seeing Alf getting to his feet again he restrained himself and they boxed through the rest of the round.

At the end of it no one said much; Cohen took off Alf's helmet and sponged his face and had a word with him; Alf shook his head vigorously and indicated he would continue. Godfrey got out of the ring, wiped the sweat from his forehead with his forearm and went to the window. Fred Bingham climbed into the ring and when the bell went he took on Alf Manter for the third round. Godfrey kept himself warm jogging around the empty part of the room, shaking his shoulders, kicking his feet out loosely from the ankles, relaxing. Then he went to the punch-ball.

'What's your name?' said a voice behind him. 'Vosper, is it? I haven't heard of you.'

It was Jude Davis, eyes narrowed as if with smoke, assessing.

'I been around a bit. Nothing much worth taking on – yet.'

'Whose stable are you in?'

'Rob Robins.'

'What fights has he given you?'

'Bert Bromley; I got a point decision. Ed Hertz; I won, r.s.f. in the third. Tiger Wedgwood; I won, k.o. in the fifth.'

'Bromley is not a bad win. The others are very small fry. How old are you?'

'Twenty-three.'

'How long have you been a pro?'

'Five years.'

'Well, what did Robins do for you before that?'

'That's all. I was with Pat Regan before that.'

'Never heard of him . . . Oh, yes, in the Midlands, isn't he?'

'That's right.'

Jude Davis leaned on his umbrella. 'You look as if you've got a punch, Vosper. That one really hurt Manter.'

'It would have hurt more if we'd had proper gloves.'

'Would you be interested in a move?'

'I sure would.'

'When did you sign with Robins?'

'Last year. But I only signed for two. I'm nearly through the first.'

'Um. Something might be arranged. I'll have to see what Robins thinks. When you're through come downstairs into the bar and we'll go into a little more detail.'

While Bingham was in the ring, the press photographer had been taking one or two shots. Now at the end of his second round – and Manter's fourth – Bingham climbed out of the ring, his face blotched where Alf had marked him. Godfrey got back in and boxed two more rounds with Manter. But this time Alf was making no more mistakes.

In the interval between these two rounds Cohen had

gone away, and, glancing over Alf's shoulder, Godfrey saw him in conversation with Jude Davis. It didn't improve his temper through that last round, but he contained it somehow, and when it was over Alf said: 'Thanks, God, you really worked on that.'

Godfrey went into the changing room, showered himself, put on his outdoor suit. When he came out Jude Davis had gone, and a couple of other boxers were doing some limbering up out of the ring. Godfrey slapped Alf on the back and wished him luck in Boston. Cohen was waiting with his money but he didn't look at Godfrey as he paid him.

Downstairs in the bar Jude Davis was talking to an attractive dark girl of about twenty with an impudent face, and a short stout man of fifty-odd with a bald head and no back to it. Godfrey went over and Jude Davis said, 'What'll you have?' and Godfrey said: 'Thanks, Mr Davis, I don't drink.' 'Then take a seat. D'you know Fred Armitage, the matchmaker?'

'No. How d'ye do. Thanks.'

Davis did not introduce the girl, who sat knees crossed, turning her lip-stick container over and over in small deft fingers and glancing up now and then into each of their faces in turn. Armitage and Davis went on talking for a while and Godfrey took no part in it, staring at the notices on the walls of all the old fights. Henry Cooper, Randolph Turpin, Len Harvey, Tommy Farr.

Armitage got up, and the girl drifted to the bar with him, and Jude Davis tucked his camel hair coat around his knees and looked at Godfrey.

'Your real name is Brown, then?'

'Well, if I have a real one. It's only one as was given me because people didn't know no other.'

'But you began boxing under the name of Godfrey Brown.'

'That's right.' Little God thought up new curses for Cohen.

'And you changed after you'd served your suspension.'

'I work for a woman. Chauffeur-handyman, see. She suggested to me, she said, you should change your name, so I did. She said, change your name.'

'People don't lose their identities as easy as that in the boxing world.'

138

'Didn't try, Mr Davis. I told the B.B.B.C.'

'You'd have been in trouble if you hadn't. But what was the idea?'

'The idea? I don't know. Making a fresh start, like. Thought it would help.'

'I hear you were suspended for being too handy with your fists out of the ring.'

Godfrey's eyes glinted. 'That's right.'

'No excuses?'

'I was needled. I was cheated.'

'It happens to us all, every week of the year.'

'Think so?'

'Yes, I think so.'

Armitage and the girl returned, Armitage carrying more beer, and that broke the conversation. Godfrey stayed on. He was going to be late back for Flora but Flora would have to whistle. Eventually they all got up and moved towards the door.

Davis said: 'I like the look of you in the ring, Brown. Or Vosper, if you prefer the name. You've got a classic left – which I think comes natural to you, and that's saying something; you're very quick on your feet and you're full of fight – anyone can see that! You need experience with good men, that's your chief lack and you ought to get it.'

'I could take on Alf Manter any day.'

'Maybe. But you've got to learn to keep your temper out of the ring, and that's yet to be proved. D'you say you've another year with Robins?'

'Bit more.'

'Well, I'll keep an eye on you. When your contract expires come and see me if you're still interested.'

'Jees, but I'll be twenty-four then! It's another year wasted! Can't you do something for me before then, Mr Davis?'

'Not wasted. You can find your way a few rungs up the ladder. See this next winter out with Robins and look me up, if you want, about next July. I'm in the telephone book. Or you can get me at Viking Enterprises.'

They were driving down to Handley Merrick at two, and Little God did not appear at Wilton Crescent until two-thirty. Lady Vosper was furious and Godfrey snapped back at her, and they had their first full scale row. And this time there was no titled lady and chauffeur about it. It was a young man and an older woman violently quarrelling on a level. Even their language did not differ, for Flora could match any Godfrey produced. It ended as quickly as it had begun – not with any apologies from Godfrey, not with any easier words to finish: it just dried up. Then Flora said: 'Get in the car, we're late enough. I can't help your troubles,' and Godfrey carried the two bags out of the house, flung them in the boot and Flora slammed the door of the flat and got in the passenger's seat.

Godfrey drove out of London with all the frustration of his angry body in the soles of his feet. They stormed up to traffic lights, shot away from other cars like a jet; as the traffic lights spaced out they were up to 80 m.p.h. from a standstill while they took three quiet breaths, then heavy braking at the next red brought them almost pushing through the windscreen. All this Lady Vosper took without comment. No word was spoken all the way down.

They stopped outside Merrick House with a long slither of tyres on the loose gravel, and the car ended diagonally across the drive.

Flora said: 'Right. You can get out tomorrow! A month's wages in lieu of notice. I want no insolent little rats in my employment!'

Godfrey said: 'I'm not leaving tomorrow and you needn't think I am! Now I'll tell you why I'm mad.'

'I don't care a bloody damn why you're mad! I'll not have servants of mine throwing nasty little fits of temper.'

'I got a chance this morning of being taken on by a *real* manager, a *real* manager. I missed it. I got cheated of it. Listen. I want to tell you. I got a chance.'

'Go to hell.'

'I been doing my first rounds with Alf. Alf Manter, that is . . .'

Lady Vosper took a cigarette packet from the ledge under the facia and lit up. She said absolutely nothing while Godfrey told what had happened. Then just as he was finishing, Joe Forms came out for the luggage. Flora went into the house without saying anything more to Godfrey, and he drove round to the rear and put the car away.

She dined alone that night and had no word with him at all. But no more was said of his getting the sack.

The next day she said to him. 'Get the car out. I want to go to Norwich.'

'D'you want me to drive?'

'Yes, if you know how.'

'Oh, I got over that. I was in a rage. You might say Little God couldn't take it.'

'You might say Flora Vosper doesn't have to.'

'No, well . . .'

'So I'd like an apology.

Godfrey chewed his bottom lip. 'Yes, well, I'm sorry. It was just one of those things. I got in a rage. You can see why, though. I got in a real rage.'

They stopped some distance outside Norwich at a factory. Flora went in, leaving Godfrey in the car; but in ten minutes she came out with a man in a track suit who had what to Godfrey sounded like an Etonian voice. They drove on through some gates and came to a smooth macadamed road almost like a race track. Two mechanics pushed a low-built sports car out on the road, and Flora and the man in the track suit bent over it and walked round it and inspected the engine and the chassis. Then Flora buckled on a crash helmet and walked back to the Jensen.

'Perhaps you'd like to come with me. This is a development car I've been invited to try out for next year's Le Mans.'

Godfrey slouched out and followed her. It was an open two-seater, blue, very low-built, small, streamlined to the point of having disappearing head-lamps. Lady Vosper and the man were discussing some technicality about compression that Godfrey did not follow. 'Get in,' she said to him, with a flick of her thumb. He got.

One of the mechanics offered him a crash helmet. He sneered his refusal. Flora climbed in beside him and slammed the door, started the engine. 'I'll try a couple of laps,' she said to the man. 'See what I make of it.'

'O.K. There's no hurry. I'll be around.'

They set off. For half a mile Flora drove normally, familiarizing herself with the gears and a few half stops on the brakes. Then on a straight piece she suddenly slid into first, screamed away, flicked up a gear, up another, and at 100 miles an hour charged for a clump of trees rapidly flying to meet them on a corner. When within shouting distance she changed down and down again, braked, flung the steering wheel round and they skidded on all four wheels towards inevitable death. Just before the crash the tyres bit into the road and they had somehow skidded a complete circle and were roaring away up the next straight. Here she got into top gear and climbed to 120 m.p.h., roared to the next corner, changed once only and swirled round its banked end. They came within inches of the edge and Godfrey had a wild sight of fields and countryside and quiet lanes into which he knew he would immediately be hurled.

This curve led to a straight downward slope and here the car seemed to take off as if it were being flung across country by a breakdown in the earth's gravitational pull. There was a slight rise coming, and they zipped at it as if there were no road beyond at all. Flora changed down and up a couple of times and they passed three men staring. It was only as Godfrey suddenly saw himself being projected at gun speed towards a familiar clump of trees that he realized the three men were those who had launched them on this suicide pact and that they were going round the course for the second time.

Another lurching screaming skid, and this time they came out of it badly and got into a speed wag that Flora kept over-correcting. Then Godfrey perceived that, far from trying to correct the tail wag, it was she who was creating it. At ninety miles an hour she was flicking the car from side to side of the road. They were approaching the banked curve and she took it much more sharply and lower down and braking hard. With a smell of tyres and with his stomach left somewhere by the roadside, they screamed full throttle down the other straight. This time only one man was there. Flora raised a hand.

Altogether she did four laps, the third time even more suicidally than the first two. On the fourth she did front wheel skids. They pulled up by the single man, who was the man who had brought them, and the two mechanics reappeared.

'She's all right,' said Flora. 'There's some rear-end breakaway under extreme pressure. Pity you haven't a chicane here.'

'You might come over to the Park sometime,' said the man. 'If you've the time, that is.'

'And there's a bit of surging from the rubber drive-shaft,' said Lady Vosper. 'Look, let me take you one lap. I'll show you what I mean. I don't know if it's too late to correct it.' To Godfrey she said: 'Get out.'

Godfrey got out. He found that he had some hair left and that he could just stand. There was a white mark across his hand where he had been clutching the side. The man got in and they roared off. One of the mechanics grinned at him. 'All right, mate?'

'Right enough for you, mate,' snarled Godfrey and went back to his own car. He sat there glowering and biting his lips until Flora joined him. 'We'll lunch in Norwich,' she said. 'The manager is staying on here, so we can go right away.'

'Thanks,' said Godfrey and put in the ignition key but did not switch on.

'You all right to drive?'

'Course I'm all right. But I never said Jesus so many times in my life.'

Flora Vosper said: 'Next time you have a fit of temper I'll take you to Brands Hatch.'

Chapter Ten

Pearl said: 'Aren't you going to your club tonight?'

'Yes, I think so. But I have no bridge arranged, and these catalogues to look through.'

'I was looking at some of your art books today. Fabulous illustrations. Nearly good enough to frame, themselves.'

'I'm glad you're interested. You have a sense of values.'

'Oh, not over pictures. Some of the pictures here, a few, don't look worth anything to me. The abstracts, as you call them.'

'They're more difficult. But rewarding with study. They have what is called significant form.'

'Well, Wilfred, to me form is significant if it – if you can recognize it as something. I don't so much mind a table with five legs or a woman with three eyes, so long as you know they're supposed to be a table and a woman. It's these lines and squares and dots that don't mean anything to me at all.'

'I hope last Monday night meant something to you.'

Pearl smoothed an invisible crease out of her skirt. 'Why, yes . . . If you mean what I think you mean.'

'You must know that it's natural these things don't come right the first time. As between, well, how shall I put it –'

'Between beginners?'

'I was going to say between a man like myself who has devoted his life to intellectual and artistic appreciation, and a young girl as yet unawakened. There is bound to be some – experimental period, as it were. I hope you did not find . . .'

'Find what?'

'I was going to say I hope you did not find Monday evening embarrassing.'

'No-o. Well, I invited it, didn't I.'

'It took me by surprise. D'you know. It went beyond the terms of our agreement when we married.'

'Did you mind?'

144

He looked at her with slightly uneasy dislike. 'Not if you did not.'

'Well, I'm sorry if I broke the agreement. You see I had had . . .'

'Had what?'

'Oh, it doesn't matter.'

'Had what? You must tell me.'

'Two vodkas before dinner.' It was not what she had intended to say.

'I dislike women who drink too much.'

'Well, it's fun occasionally.'

'I'm glad you found it – fun. With your not mentioning it for a week I thought . . .'

'Oh, I meant it was fun – just having the *drink*.'

'Oh, yes, I see.'

Silence fell. Wilfred cut the tip off a cigar and rolled the end of the cigar round in his lips to make it smooth.

'Lady Vosper's chauffeur hasn't been again,' said Pearl.

'You will be glad.'

'Have you told him I don't want him calling?'

'Not yet. He's in Suffolk with Lady Vosper.'

'He's very small.'

'Some people say he is going to be a champion boxer.'

'Oh, he's all right in his class. Feather-weight or something. Have you ever watched a boxing match, Wilfred?'

'No. I have no taste for any form of sport.'

'I think it might be interesting. Would you take me sometime to see what it's like?'

Angell had not yet lit his cigar. 'Possibly. Sometime. Brian Attwell, whom you met at dinner here, is concerned in all these things. Pearl.'

'Yes?'

He struck a match and carefully lit the end of the cigar, shook out the match, put it in a silver ashtray. 'I have thought a good deal about last Monday. Even though it was not altogether a success.'

'I'm sorry if it broke the terms of our agreement.'

'Oh, that. Well, it certainly did, didn't it?'

'Well, we can –'

'But what happened has happened. It has altered our relationship. Although this was not the intention of the marriage, it is clearly what all ordinary people would expect to be the outcome.'

'I'm sorry if it's made everything more ordinary. Perhaps it brought it all down to a lower level in your eyes.'

'A *different* level. We have – moved on. And I don't think there is any going back.'

Pearl uncrossed her legs and crossed them the opposite way. 'Could I have a cigarette?'

'Oh . . . of course.' Angell shook himself out of a temporary hypnosis, and reached up to the mantelshelf, found a packet, hesitated, then got up and offered her the packet, waited, lit one for her. It was the first time he had ever done this.

'Thanks. Thank you. I've often thought it was strange, our first meeting. If I hadn't been delayed at home with a sore throat . . . It's like fate, isn't it?'

'Very like fate,' said Wilfred, accepting the cliché without even a shudder. 'I may say, although everything was not as it should be last Monday evening, my memories of it are not distasteful.'

'I'm glad of that.'

'I put it badly, of course. Failure is a relative term. I am a man with a more than ordinary appreciation of the aesthetic appeal of beauty. You see the evidences all around you. But until Monday I confess that I had not fully appreciated the aesthetic and – and physical appeal of a young woman.'

'Not even Anna?'

'Too long ago, Pearl. It might have happened to another man. In my memory of Monday the – well, let us put it crudely – the embarrassment, the frustration, are not the predominant memory.'

Pearl rubbed a speck of ash off her wrist. 'What is the predominant memory?'

Wilfred had let his cigar smoulder in the tray. 'Frankly – if we must be frank – it is my memory of you unclothed.'

After a minute Pearl said: 'D'you mind if I open the window? It's such a warm night.'

'Someday I'll tell you about Anna,' he said, moistening his lips.

'I wish you would.'

'But not now. Sometime. Where did you get that dress?'

'I bought it at Harrods – last Monday.'

'I think last Monday was a very significant day for us both. Was it expensive?'

'What – the day or the frock?'

Only when he smiled did she realize how rare this occurrence was. He had all his own teeth, that was something. He was really a good-looking and certainly a distinguished man, if one ignored his bulk. Unfortunately on Monday it had been impossible to ignore his bulk. It was *her* predominant memory, that and a wonder that what was so great could produce so little. Yet she did not dislike him and she was not repelled by him. He was her husband, and after his own light was kind and had given her much.

She opened the window and drew in a breath, but only warm London air was available, air well used and flavoured with the smell of petrol and concrete and tired leaves and warm brick. The sky was a faded cinnamon. In a corner of the mews two people were kissing. No Little God came to menace or disturb her today, or to provoke her into calculated indiscretions. He was down in Suffolk with his Lady.

She turned back and Wilfred had got up, was standing by the fireplace, just as he had stood last Monday. Perhaps this was going to become a characteristic stance with its own significance. He was puffing at his cigar but did not seem to be savouring it. His fingers as he tapped off the ash were uncertain.

'I've had very little to drink tonight,' she said.

'That could be rectified. That could be changed. Let's change it. I think – myself – I could do with a *stiff* whisky and soda.'

'What happened to Anna?' Pearl asked. 'Did she die?'

'What makes you say that?'

'Something in your manner. Something. Is that right?'

'Well, yes. I don't want to talk about it. I don't want to talk about anything!'

'Now's the time, if ever.'

'It's a great pity that it has gone wrong again. I thought tonight . . .'

'It was better than last Monday anyway.'

'Don't let's discuss it. Things will come right in due course. That's if one wants to go on with them . . . Clearly it's a matter for some doubt.'

147

He stirred petulantly, angry with everything, hands trembling, wanting to get up and stalk away, his mind seeking an excuse to blame her, his self-esteem deeply hurt.

There was a long silence.

'Tell me about Anna.'

'This bed is too *soft*, Pearl. It is a modern mattress in spite of the Hepplewhite frame but –'

'It doesn't seem too soft to me –'

'Well, when you are alone! Naturally. With us both it gives too much, makes things more difficult. It stands to reason! I thought you would see that. Anybody could see that!'

'Tell me about Anna.'

'I have always been a big man,' he said. 'It's strong, healthy flesh. I am tall and have a big frame, that's where a lot of the weight comes in. Nothing flabby. Only a few months ago, Dr Matthewson, who's one of London's leading physicians, said I was exceptionally fit and well.'

'It isn't really any advantage to be heavy, Wilfred. And I think one looks younger.'

'I don't look old. I don't *feel* old. God knows in one's middle forties!'

'Of course not.'

'Naturally my body hasn't got your youth. But I don't feel old, even now, after tonight.'

'Why should you? Was she killed in an aeroplane accident?'

'Who, Anna? No. Whatever makes you think that?'

'I thought perhaps you seemed over-anxious in the plane when we met.'

'I wasn't at all over-anxious! One is often diverted to a different airport when flying. It's a natural hazard that the experienced traveller learns to expect!'

After this Pearl relapsed into silence. He lay there, quietly hating her for being the object of his humiliation. What an unintelligent common creature she was, with no sensitivity or finesse. She just *lay* there making small talk as if unaware of his anger. His marriage to her had been a desperate mistake – what he should have expected! And this *act* in which they had partly participated, how exhausting and common and unhealthy. Alley cats. Women set such store by it, pretended it was romantic and beautiful. Utter nonsense. It degraded the human spirit, and women knew it did. The aesthetic and the beautiful were not to be found in carnal things. Man's mind only could appreciate them, man's mind only was big enough, so women clung and clutched at him, trying to bring him down to their level. And he, Wilfred Angell, after so many years of triumphant isolation, had allowed himself to be caught. The tender trap! It was a rat trap!

This was the moment, he knew, the exact moment to end it all. Not of course the marriage but this horrible and degrading exercise which left him so spent and useless; with some care one could return to the relatively happy status quo, to the unambiguous days before last Monday.

Yet he made no move. He lay there as silently as she. Because, undermining his judgment, filtering through his determination like enemy troops moving into new positions, were feelings that he did not have to entertain before: concern that he should not offend her too deeply, and foreknowledge that his disgust would not last, a premonition as it were of future lust.

A car hooted outside and a door slammed. To Pearl it made a noise uncomfortably like the clump of the Jensen door, which she remembered so well.

She said: 'You've never told me about your parents. Have they been dead a long time?'

He shifted his bulk. 'My mother was forty-two when I was born – ten years older than my father. Yes, they have both been dead a long time . . . She was – she had been the headmistress of a girl's school before she married. You must realize that she was 23 when Queen Victoria died. All her childhood and adolescence were Victorian. It is no doubt hard for you to realize how close all this is in terms of the generations . . . She naturally had a strong influence in my early life. Her somewhat primitive beliefs . . . Even today it is difficult at times for me to escape from the consequences of her philosophy – the absolute relationship between sin and retribution, for instance, similar to that between crime and punishment. The Lord thy God is a jealous God. Very hard. D'you know. Very hard.'

The people were shouting and laughing outside, then the car accelerated away and the voices left behind subsided to a murmur. Pearl lay still. Fortunately she could not read his thoughts. Without conscious decision, she felt that it was a good thing to encourage him to talk at this time. The second fiasco had left him in the grip of some strong emotion, and he was a man to whom emotion came rarely.

'Do you like jewellery?' he said suddenly.

She could hardly believe her ears. 'Who? Me? . . . Yes, I love it.'

'There's some coming up at Sotheby's when they re-open,' he said, still tartly, almost in annoyance. 'Not too expensive, I should think. I've never collected jewellery.'

'D'you mean for me, Wilfred?'

'Well . . . not exactly. In a sense. You could wear it. It would be insured.'

'That'd be super. What sort of jewellery is it?' She sat up. 'Brooches? Ear-rings?'

'Oh, various kinds. Mind you, I'm not a rich man. I owe a lot of money.'

'Do you? I didn't know.'

'To dealers, to auctioneers. I buy things on hire-purchase, so to speak. I'm still paying for the Bonnard I bought three years ago. And the Sisley in my bedroom.'

'I'm very fond of emeralds,' Pearl said after a minute.

He said: 'The setting of a jewel is often more important than the jewel itself. To the connoisseurs, that is . . .'

'But that would be lovely, Wilfred.'

He sat up and leaned back against the head of the bed, rubbed a thick thumb over his forehead, pushing back his hair. 'Jewels. I think of Anna who had some good ones . . . She lived in one of those handsome houses overlooking Regent's Park. She had inherited the things from her mother. Her father was a widower, and a housekeeper looked after them. More frequently Anna looked after the housekeeper who drank too much but was an old retainer – they would not discharge her. One night when her father was away and we knew the housekeeper would be in her room and entirely unconscious until morning we made plans to meet – I made plans to come to the house. With, of course, the obvious purpose in mind. We were not so innocent then, you see. Some people talk and write as if the sexual act were discovered about 1960. But . . . after a few minutes, when – how can I put it delicately? – when this would soon have happened, she was taken with acute pain. *Acute* pain. I tiptoed down to the dining room and got her brandy. The attack did not go away. I stayed on, and wanted to ring for the doctor. She said she could not have him while I was there. But I could hardly leave her like that. In the end the pain went, but by then she was too exhausted for love. She was anxious for me to go. She said she would ring the doctor as soon as I was gone. So I went . . . Incredible though it may seem, I saw her again only four times after that.'

'What was wrong?'

'It was the dread disease – inoperable at that age! One can hardly believe. She was only twenty.'

'Oh dear, I *am* sorry. How awful for you. I never thought.'

'No matter.' Wilfred tasted the luxury of being comforted. It took some of the bitterness of tonight away.

After a while Pearl said: 'Why do you say it's of no importance to you now?'

'Because it's all buried – *long* buried with her, and best forgotten . . . It was of importance to me at the time, naturally. But it has long since ceased to be important.'

Presently he sighed and moved to get up. 'About the jewellery sale,' Pearl said.

'Oh . . . perhaps. I will glance at the catalogue again. Probably it is all too expensive. I am in no position to be extravagant.'

'Those two paintings in the bathroom, those you said you'd got tired of, by that Russian who lived in Paris. Why not sell them?'

'I couldn't do that. I wouldn't get my money back.'

'But you'd get something?'

'Oh, yes. Four or five hundred pounds for the two perhaps.'

'Well, then.'

Wilfred considered the matter in the dark. 'No, no. I'm only *temporarily* tired of them.'

Pearl said: 'Why did you see Anna only four times more?'

'Oh, it's all past and done with! I don't want to talk about it any longer!'

Godfrey next called on a Tuesday when Wilfred was at bridge.

She half shut the door on him, but somehow he managed to slip in and stand in the hall, hat in hand, apologetic and impudent at the same time.

He said: 'I've only come to see Mr Angell. Honest. I got a message. I'll not touch you. When've I touched you except that once?'

She found herself less afraid of him than hitherto. His uniform brought him down, hiding his physical arrogance. Wilfred's legal bonds surrounded her too. And within these defences she was growing up, maturing, becoming more confident.

She said: 'If you've a message you'd better take it to Mr Angell at his club.'

'If he's expected home soon maybe I could wait.'

'He's not expected home soon. It's one of his bridge nights.'

'So he's playing bridge . . . He'd thank me for bursting in in the middle of his bridge. Lady V would, I know. Maybe I could just write him a note.'

She hesitated. 'I asked my husband to tell you not to call here again. He'll be very annoyed if he knows you've been bothering me.'

'Bothering you? Oh, there, Oyster, that's an untruth if ever there was one. How am I bothering you, just nipping round with this message?'

'And stop looking at me like that.'

'Now I can't even look. O.K., I'll put my hand over my eyes. O.K.? That please you?'

'D'you want to leave a message, or d'you want to go?'

'I'll go. I'll be back in an hour maybe.'

'No, don't come back.'

'Well, it's important.'

'Then leave a message.'

Godfrey thought, and removed his eyeshade. 'Have you got a piece of paper, Pearl?'

She rummaged in a drawer in the hall and found a pad, switched on the table lamp there.

He looked round. 'And a pencil?'

She found a ball-point and put it on the table beside him. His hand gently touched hers before she pulled it sharply away.

He said: 'Don't be afraid of the dark.'

She said nothing while he pulled up a chair and began to write. Writing did not come easy, or he purposely delayed. She watched his strong short fingers, clumsy in their present work.

She said: 'Haven't you done?'

'Not quite. I ought to come back. That'd be best.'

She said: 'Finish your message, please, and go!'

He put the pen between his teeth and tapped it up and down, did not look at her. 'How d'you spell love? Is it with an o or a u?'

'Love! You don't know what love means!'

'Let me show you. I'd be different this time.'

'This is really what you came for, isn't it; this calling with messages is only an excuse you've worked up!'

He shrugged. 'Still can't see you settling down as an old man's plaything. It works on me. Gets on my nerves to think of it.'

'Do I have to tell you again that I don't want anything to do with you?'

He looked at her then with all the fullness of his eyes. 'Someday I'll believe you – maybe.'

'Believe me now. It's the *truth*. For Heaven's sake. What can I say to convince you?'

'It isn't always what people say that matters.'

She sighed, heavily, angrily. 'Listen. Listen, Godfrey. Just try to understand. All the early part of this year you made my life a misery. Then when I got married I thought I was rid of you. But now you're back again. I never know when the bell rings . . . Of course I could complain and we could get the police but I don't wish you any *harm*. I've tried to forget all that – that misunderstanding at Keston. It's not important any more. But I'm in a new life now, and I don't want you around.'

He did not answer, being apparently busy folding the message he had written. She wondered if she was getting through to him at all.

She said suddenly: 'Look, I've got money. Would you

153

promise to stay away from me if I gave you some money?'

He tapped his teeth, picked at his bottom lip. 'How much?'

'A hundred pounds?'

'My! More'n I get for a fight. Am I worth that to you?'

'It's worth that to have you out of my way.'

He shook his head. 'Can't take money from a woman. Never have. Can't start now.'

'What about Lady Vosper?'

His eyes showed he didn't like the suggestion. 'She's different. She gets value for money.'

'All right then! I've done all I can.' She moved to the telephone. 'You're set on your own way. So get out! And I'll see Wilfred never lets you come here again!'

'Don't get so angry! I don't see why you get so angry. Honest! I mean you no hurt. Look, I got an idea. I'll not take your money, because it won't help. But your – Mr Angell, he knows everybody, don't he. A lawyer and a public man. Gets around everywhere. Get him to get me a new manager. I got a bad one now. He's strictly a layabout. I got to have a new manager to get the fights!'

Pearl stared at him. 'What d'you mean?'

'What I just said.'

'You – want a new manager to arrange your fights?'

'Look, kid, every boxer has to have a manager. Right? But not anyone'll do. He's got to have a manager who's in with the matchmakers, the big-time promoters. That's what *I* need. If you're in Jude Davis's stable, or even Cohen's, you can get a fight maybe once a month just because your manager's in with the people that run the halls. This Robins has been managing me for a year, and it's been a complete fold. I want someone with know-how, someone like Jude Davis or Mel Anderson. Not the third raters. I'm too good for the third raters. You seen me fight, you ought to know that!'

Pearl fiddled with a piece of ribbon on the sleeve of her frock. For the first time he was talking out of his heart and not because he wanted to climb onto her.

'D'you mean you think my husband could arrange . . . But he's a lawyer – not in the boxing world.'

'People like him can do a lot if they try.'

'Why doesn't Lady Vosper – can't she help you?'

'Maybe she could, but if she could she won't. Frightened of losing me, see.' He grinned, and the predatory twinkle that had been submerged returned to his eyes.

'Frightened of losing me,' said Godfrey. 'Not like you, *wanting* to lose me.'

'And should I?'

'Lose me? Yes. I'm nuts about you, maybe always will be; but give me a chance in the big time and I'll soon grow out of it. I want to go places, get on. Maybe you haven't noticed.'

'I know your promises.'

'Listen, Oyster. I got one ambition in life and that's to be feather-weight champion. If I could be that I'd step on anyone's face to give myself a step up. So I'm not going to bother about a bit of tail if doing without it helps. You arrange with your old man; then I drop out of your life *complete*. Get him to get me in with Jude Davis so I can go places –'

'I wouldn't think he could help at all –'

'Look. Make a note. Jude Davis. He's the man I want to manage me. Write it down. He's interested already. He's more or less promised to take me on in a year. But I can't wait that long. I'm twenty-three. I only got five more years at the outside to get where I want to get. You grow old early in my business. So it's now or never like. Jude Davis is the man who's interested. Write it down.'

'I tell you, I've no idea –'

'Well, try. Real reason Davis won't take me now is he'd have to buy me off Robins. It wouldn't be much – maybe the hundred you said you'd give. But he thinks he'll wait and save the money and see how I get on. He only needs a push from someone up top and I'm in. Your Mr Angell could fix it.'

'I'll think about it.'

'I'll call next Tuesday, while he's out again. About this time. I'll nip round, see what he says, eh?'

'All right.'

Godfrey put his note for Angell in an envelope and sealed it. 'You could say you found this pushed under the door, if you like.'

'Why should I?'

Godfrey shrugged. 'Please yourself then. Only he told me not to call Tuesdays.'

'So you *did* come – deliberately.'

'Yeh. Can't keep away. But do me this favour and I'll do you one. Fix me this and you'll never need to get hot at me again.'

Chapter Eleven

Francis Hone said: 'Well, it's very frustrating, this further delay. Did he give you no idea of the time he'd be when you approached him?'

'He thought a couple of weeks,' Angell said, rubbing the crumbs together between finger and thumb. 'But he's appearing for Surrey County Council against West & Cassell, and the case keeps dragging on. I rang his clerk again yesterday but there's no immediate prospect of its ending.'

'Penalty of popularity,' said Simon Portugal.

'Yes, well, exactly. In law this is particularly true. I wanted Montagu because he is the best man. But because he's the best man everyone wants him.'

'There must be others,' said Hone.

'Oh, there are others – half a dozen nearly as good. But they are not without briefs themselves, and I hesitate to swop horses in midstream.'

'What has your man to report?' Hone said to Portugal.

'I gave Wilfred the details yesterday.'

Angell shook his head at the waiter who was about to help him to potatoes. 'It's all perfectly straightforward so far as it goes. The tenancies are varied as to type and tenure, but there's nothing we haven't tackled before. There are two rights of way that are indisputable, but these can very simply be developed as roads through the estate. And there were two public footpaths which have fallen completely into disuse; we should be able to ignore these, but if there is sufficient of a protest we can adjust accordingly. The only real problem lies in the land abutting on the B.1018 nearest to the centre of the village. It's not at all clear what rights the villagers have over it. As it's also the most valuable piece – about ten acres – we shall need to go into it carefully.'

'My man tells me there'll be a storm of protest once the Ministry's plan is known,' said Portugal.

'When has there not to any development? One can

hardly put down a row of houses in this country without a wail of complaint from everyone in the neighbourhood.'

'Oh, I know. Don't we all know. But Handley Merrick being a well known beauty spot, and Handley Oaks a few miles away. Constable painted two of his most characteristic pieces there.'

'One day a latter-day Lowry will be able to paint two more,' said Sir John, tight-lipped.

'That's all right,' said Portugal. 'I'm not casting doubts on the deal, only ensuring we know all the hazards. Ministries and governments have been known to yield to protests.'

Sir John lit a cigarette, a habit Angell much disliked with a meal half finished. 'This is too important, Simon. It's too much a part of a great complex. To yield to pressure here would be to put a whole wide project out of joint. Besides you ought to know democracy doesn't really work over a thing like this.' He moved his cigarette, and blue smoke drifted across Angell's sensitive nostrils. 'You know what happens, of course. A handful of highly-placed, responsible and dedicated civil servants have come to the decision that with the population explosion what it is and the drift to the south-east an irreversible tendency, a new complex of development must be sited somewhere in the area, say, north-east of Chelmsford. As to its exact position, they have studied the area in some detail, have carefully weighed the various conflicting interests, and after long and no doubt sober debate among themselves they have decided that the area taking in Handley Merrick is the best to develop. That's as far as it has gone yet, but for all practical purposes, the decision is made. From now on each one of those civil servants will support and defend that decision with all the very considerable power he can muster. And the minister responsible for the actual decision will be briefed in all the facts that make Handley Merrick the only possible choice. He will eventually announce it in Parliament, and later he will defend it in Parliament, largely in language written and drafted for him by those civil servants, and presently it will become a matter of personal face to him to see the scheme through. Even if there is a change of minister before the development takes place the chances are the new man will be equally pressurized, and anyway by then so much will already be sunk in the development in the form of plans and linkages with other plans that it will be irreversible anyhow.'

Portugal watched the wine being added to his glass by the waiter. 'So let's hope we wrap it up before there's a leakage.' To Angell he said: 'How is the old lady?'

'She's not exactly old,' Angell said stiffly. 'Forty-eight or nine, at most. I don't call on her myself because the last thing we want to appear to be doing is "gathering round", so to speak. I met her at the Peter Warners' last month; she seemed well then but I gather she's in very poor health at the moment; she's not been out of her bedroom for a week.'

'I was talking to a friend recently,' said Simon Portugal; 'he knows the Vosper household pretty well and he says it's in a very peculiar state. Apparently Flora Vosper has a chauffeur who has gained a sort of ascendancy over her. She depends on him absolutely. I suppose there is no special risk to us in this set-up?'

'Little as far as I can see,' said Hone. 'Even if she went queer in the head towards the end, the house and land are not hers to will away.'

'As a matter of fact,' said Angell. 'I am keeping an eye on it. I have had some contact with the chauffeur, and this I think is a useful precaution.'

'Contact with the chauffeur?' said Simon Portugal. 'Whatever d'you mean?'

'Chance has put me in a position where I may be able to befriend him,' said Angell. 'No more than that. I have done nothing unethical. But with the opportunity coming my way it seemed improvident to refuse it.'

They both stared at him.

'How?' said Portugal.

'How? How am I to befriend him? No matter. If it succeeds it will I think have a dual purpose. One, it will help to weaken his ties with Lady Vosper – which must be to the good of everyone. D'you know. Two, it will make him favourably disposed towards me – which, if there were any crisis in the Vosper household, again can do no harm.' Angell looked at the handsome menu the waiter had put in his hand. 'No, nothing more. I'll have coffee.'

'Well I'm damned,' said Portugal after a minute. 'You certainly get around.'

Francis Hone ordered cheese. 'You feeling all right, Wilfred?'

'Feeling all right? Certainly. What d'you mean?'

'Only that you've eaten less than usual. Half as much as usual, I'd say.'

'Oh, I'm very well. Never felt better. But I have an afternoon's work ahead of me.'

'I've never known you have concern for that before. You've always said food invigorates you.'

'So it does. But I've had sufficient.'

'Are you dieting or something?' Simon asked, smiling.

'Good gracious, no! What an absurd idea.'

'Well, my dear chap,' Vincent Birman said, 'I would have thought it could be arranged. I've met Jude Davis at the N.S.C. a couple of times. He's tied up with Eli Margam and that means he's in with the big promoters. Can you give me any more background?'

Angell swivelled in his chair. 'My client says that Davis has seen Brown box once and took a fancy to him. But when he knew that Brown's contract had a year still to go with his present manager he told Brown to come and see him again when it had expired.'

'So presumably he wasn't so keen on him that he was afraid of some other manager beating him to the draw. It looks to me a question of plain economics.'

'Economics?'

Birman's innocent bright eyes wandered round the shabby office. The child might have been busy dismembering the spider again. 'Jude Davis will do pretty nearly anything for money. And he's not too flush at the moment. He's got some promising youngsters coming on, but he's had no big money earner since Llew Thomas retired. I should guess he's interested in this boy but not interested enough to buy him. Just that.'

'Well then?'

'If your client wanted to befriend the boy he should offer to pay the purchase money, whatever it may be, so that Davis can buy the contract from – who is his present manager?'

'Robins.'

'Never heard of him. So that Davis can take over Brown without cost to himself. It should be arrangeable.'

'What will it cost? What would it cost my client?'

'I should have thought a couple of hundred. Might be more, might be less. It's a world in which a lot of money changes hands. And most of it is in cash.'

Angell's stomach rumbled. He thought of the rich loin chops swimming in gravy he had turned down today – and at someone else's expense. 'I don't think my client would go beyond a hundred.'

'A hundred isn't much. A manager takes 25% of a boxer's earnings, you know. Of course it depends how much Robins values Brown and how much he needs the money.'

'Well, put the matter in hand, will you. I'd like to give my client an answer next week.'

When Birman had gone Angell got up from his desk, pushing the chair well back to give himself room to rise. He padded to the window and looked out over the Fields. The tall plane trees hung motionless in the afternoon sun. Children were playing in the far corner: their thin shouts came distantly to him. It was nearly five o'clock and he was ravenously hungry.

Two cases needed work on them before tomorrow, but he felt disinclined to give them his attention. And one of his junior partners, Whittaker, was demanding a larger share of the profits on the grounds that his side of the firm's work was increasing out of proportion with the rest. (At present it was divided 40% to Angell, 20% each to Mumford & Esslin and 10% to the younger men.) One did not want to lose Whittaker to some rival. (He was very hungry indeed, but it would be the height of illogicality to eat now where one would have to pay for what one ate, having only two hours ago deliberately turned down succulencies which were paid for by Francis Hone.)

Never, thought Angell, had Birman even so much as hinted his awareness – though he must surely have known – that the young woman whose life he had investigated in the spring was now Mrs Wilfred Angell. It gave one a sense of confidence in his absolute discretion. One ought to try to put more work in his way. (Not that he lacked work, but one heard that some of it was a trifle shady.)

The Association of Fine Cotton Spinners were asking him for the latest interpretation of the Factory & Workshop Act and whether they had a case against Bromley & Preston Mills Ltd. The death of Sir James Grebe, his father's oldest client, raised intricate questions of Probate. And he was very hungry, too hungry to concentrate.

What was this insanity he was acceding to – whereby he deprived his fine vigorous body of strength and sustenance merely to come nearer to the conventional norm? He had always prided himself on being different from the herd. Even his appetites were larger, more expensive, of a finer more discriminating taste. Why should it not be so? What was there to be ashamed of in mere size? He had married a suburban small-minded middle-class woman who drew such ideas as she had from the society in which she had passed her formative years. And now he was suffering for it. What a fool to get so involved! He should have been content in his former happy state. Marriage had not merely brought him down to the common level, it imposed on him judgments which he knew to be the judgments of the herd.

He pressed the intercom for Miss Lock.

'Not the *office* tea!' he said testily. 'Tell young Richmond to go up to King's Restaurant in Holborn. It will only take him five minutes if he hurries. And some *fruit* cake, I want. Several pieces of good *fruit* cake.'

This done, he was able to spend a few minutes on the affairs of the Association of Fine Cotton Spinners. But not for long. He was aghast at his own foolishness, not merely in the matter of cutting down – voluntarily, and without any apparent pressure from her – his intake of nourishing food, but in his other insanity, that of offering to buy the girl jewellery. There were times, such as this, when he was surrounded by all the furniture and fittings of his profession and in full possession of his critical faculties, when he stared at his own actions and could not recognize them for his own.

Of course he could – and would – get out of his rash and lunatic suggestion. Nothing would ever get him to Sotheby's on the day. But he still could not understand the disrupting influences which had prompted him to have

162

the idea in the first place. It was not even as if he had held out the lure of jewellery as an inducement to her to sleep with him. This might have been conceivable. But she needed no such inducement; indeed they had already completed their unsatisfactory juncture, and a moment before he had been considering leaving her bed with cold dignity and making an end of their intimacies for ever. Then, like a weathercock in an errant breeze, he had swung round and promised her *jewels*. It hardly bore thinking of. That such a man as he should become so unpredictable . . .

He worked on at peripheral jobs for ten minutes. One wondered if Whittaker would be worth an extra 5% of the profits. He was a good man, young and restless and striving. But once you gave in, how long before his next demand? And whom could the 5% come from except from Wilfred Angell? It would leave him only 35%, plus his fee from various companies and of course his profits from Land Increments.

His tea came and he snapped at Richmond for being so long. Still working in a desultory but more satisfactory way, he ate all the currant cake that had been brought and drank four cups of tea. Then he leaned back in his chair belching slightly and put aside his pen and his papers and thought of Pearl.

Pearl had two further meetings with Godfrey, one when he called on the following Tuesday and she had no news for him and would not let him in, one when he came on the 17th September and told her that he had been seen by Jude Davis and arrangements had been made for him to change stables.

Through all this Pearl kept her strict distance, but the second meeting, when Godfrey was so obviously delighted, was hard to keep on quite the same level of hostility. What had begun as a hard bargain with enmity as its only motive became somehow a remarkable favour for which he was overwhelmingly grateful.

He said: 'Jees, I didn't think you had a prayer, didn't think your old man could fix anything. I put it to you like a challenge, just to see; didn't think it'd work but thought I could come back on you then. But it's worked – what a gas – it's worked! I'm on top. Swinging. Thanks.'

163

It is almost impossible to feel hostile towards someone you have just helped. You can work at it and get back to the old fear and dislike in due time. But it takes time. And Pearl was not by nature a grudge-bearer. Anyway the favour had cost her £200 – Wilfred had refused to bear any part of it – so she thought herself entitled to feel the benefactor.

Before he left he talked away to her about his boxing future, on and on, confiding in her like a friend, and his final words, that he now intended keeping his side of the bargain and she would see him no more, carried conviction that even the hot regretful look in his eyes did not quite belie.

Flora Vosper was not so pleased at the news. 'Does that mean you're going to leave me, little man?'

'Come off it. Wouldn't be such a rat.'

'Even rats have been known to desert a sinking ship.'

'You're not sinking, take it straight from me. You'll be bobbing about like a cork for years yet. I'll book you a ringside for my world championship fight!'

'You'll get your nice looks spoiled.'

'Not on your life! Look at blokes like Sugar Ray; they come through a hundred bouts and never a mark. I'd be scarred already if I was going to be. Anyway, you watch!'

'Doesn't seem that I have much choice.'

He sat on the arm of her chair and put his arm round her shoulders. 'Now what's wrong? You're a real old worry-cat. I just change my manager – get someone more go ahead – what I been wanting all along – what I wanted you to do for me and you said you couldn't.' He squeezed her arm. 'So that's what I got, a new manager. I'll have to be in stricter training, that's all. But his gym's handy – off Cranbourne Street – no trouble at all – I just nip over there at ten every morning, and I'm back in time to drive you anywhere for lunch.'

'It won't last,' said Flora. 'You horrible little man. Of course I didn't expect it to go on like this for ever; but I hoped you'd stay around long enough to see me out.'

'Why, you're better this week than you were last, aren't you? Isn't that –'

'Better only because last week I felt like death.'

'Well, it's on the up grade. Old Matthewson was pleased yesterday.'

'Pleased the way an anatomist is pleased when a frog's leg goes on kicking after the frog is dead. Don't try to comfort me.'

'When you're in one of these moods,' he said, 'you're murder, straight you are. Look, let's go down to Merrick again. I'm free these next few days. I can pack for you and we'll be there tonight – we could stay till Saturday. Maybe you'd like to drive. I'll sit in the back and you be my chauffeur, eh?'

She patted his hand. 'Damn you, I never thought I should be so dependent on a man! All my husbands and lovers. I was never the clinging sort. When you're sick the way I have been. Terribly difficult, you know, not to get sorry for oneself. Get me a drink, will you?'

'O.K. Shall I pack?'

'Can't go. Mrs McNaughton's coming to dine tomorrow, and the Dennisses. No, on the whole London's best.'

'Can I borrow the car this evening then?'

'Yes, I suppose so. How long will you be out?'

'Ah-ha, that shows you're better! Oh, I'll be back about ten if it's like that.'

'It's like that.' Her hand briefly grasped his sleeve and then let go. She got up, for a moment her old stocky authoritative self. 'Get me that drink, you lazy little tyke. And when are those suits coming I ordered for you? They've been long enough.'

Godfrey laughed at her. 'They said next week.'

'Well, see you keep 'em to it. If you're going to be world champion you've got to dress the part.'

Wilfred's determination not to have anything to do with the jewellery he had rashly mentioned was absolute when he was in his office. At home it was susceptible to the corroding influences of Pearl.

He told her that he had had a word with a man at his club who was an expert and who had warned him that the stuff coming up for sale was generally of poor quality and would mainly attract continental dealers. So there was simply no point in going any further. Pearl said, well, let's at least read the catalogue, it'll be fun to go through it. When they read the catalogue Pearl said how could Wilfred's friend be sure it was poor stuff when the sources of the sale were so different? 'The property of the late Countess of Didsbury', 'Sir Amal Siridabar Khan', 'Mrs Chester Caine', 'Mrs William Dunbar.' Would it not be a good idea to go on one of the viewing days and decide for oneself? Angell found himself agreeing to go on one of the viewing days.

They went. Pearl was enraptured, Wilfred disparaging. Everything she praised he found fault with. Presently she began to look downcast and hurt and he found himself hedging his disapproval and adding here and there a word of faint praise. At Pearl's suggestion Wilfred spoke to one of his friends in the firm, and presently about eight items were ticked in Pearl's catalogue, which they agreed to come and bid for. For the intervening two days Pearl allowed him to see how much she was looking forward to the auction.

On the day of the sale Angell was taken with acute stomach pains. He thought, he said, it was something he had eaten – or perhaps it was lack of food, lack of the correct nourishment to which his body had become accustomed. He stayed in bed and telephoned his office and had only lemon tea for breakfast. Pearl was for calling in the doctor, but Wilfred would not hear of it. A day's rest, he thought, would set him right; he could do a little work in bed and could be in constant touch with his office. When Mrs Jamieson came at ten Pearl said:

'Will you be all right now, dear?'

'Oh, I'm better, please don't worry about me . . . What d'you mean? Why are you asking?'

'I was thinking about the sale. You'll miss it.'

'Yes . . . yes, that's too bad. I'm sorry. But, well, there'll be another one.'

'I was wondering, Wilfred. If you're feeling better, could I go along and bid on your behalf?'

'Certainly not. It would be most hazardous. You have no experience. You might lose your head and pay far too much, or buy something we didn't want. It's very easy to make a mistake in those surroundings.'

'Yes . . . I suppose so. Well, we know what Mr Moreton

thinks of the pieces we're interested in. Couldn't you phone him your bids? Then I can go along and watch and see if we get anything.'

Angell stirred uneasily in his bed. He looked like a small boy feigning illness to avoid going to school.

'I don't like to do that. One can so easily be let in, even by one's friends. I think – as I'm feeling so much better – the pain has almost gone – if you'd do me some scrambled eggs and bacon – I'll have them and then get up and we can take a taxi there. I don't want to disappoint you, and I know how interested you have been in these pieces.'

So he had his breakfast and got up. But it took him a long time – naturally he was weak.

The sale began at eleven. By the time he was ready it was eleven-thirty. Most of the lots they were interested in were low numbers. The auctioneer in question was a man known for his efficiency and speed.

Still a little unwell, he reached the sale-rooms on Pearl's arm at five minutes past twelve, to find that because of some dispute over the earlier lots, the later ones had been taken first. They were in nice time.

Even so, he was not defeated. His keen sense of the sale-room, developed over many years, enabled him almost always to stop while he could still be outbid, and even Pearl's excited pressure on his arm only forced him into error twice. In the end they bought a peridot brooch – the nearest they could afford to emeralds – and two diamond clips, at a total cost of £150. Wilfred was careful to point out to Pearl that the antique setting of the pieces would appreciate faster than the actual value of the stones.

They went out to dinner that evening, Pearl insisting on treating him, and afterwards by unspoken agreement went to bed together. This time her gratitude overcame her embarrassment at his bulk and his ineptness, and this helped him to achieve more than he had done before. He was delighted, confident at last, even chuckled at her next morning; talked about it over breakfast, began sentences with, 'I flatter myself . . .' kissed her when he left.

After he had gone she went upstairs to tidy her room but instead went to the window and pulled the curtains aside to watch him walking off towards Cadogan Square. It was a sunny day and his coat was open and blew in the breeze. He walked like a big male swan breasting the air with his size, his satisfaction and his importance. She stood at the window for a long time after he had disappeared, her face expressionless. Then she let the curtain fall and went to examine her jewellery. But he had locked it away in the safe.

When Angell reached Lincoln's Inn Fields, Saul Montagu, Q.C. had at last delivered his option agreement. Immediately Angell rang up Hollis, but Hollis was on holiday in Bournemouth and would not be back till the 23rd. Spitting his annoyance, Angell spoke to Hollis's partner, Mr Quarry, who was guarded as to the amount of work that had been done on drawing up the draft contract. Angell guessed that nothing had been done at all. He said that he would send the option agreement round by hand that morning and asked Quarry to give it his immediate attention. Quarry promised to do what he could, although, as he pointed out, this was really Mr Hollis's concern as Mr Hollis had always dealt personally with the Vosper family. Angell retorted that Mr Hollis would be back from Bournemouth in ample time to deal with the final details personally; what he, Angell, wanted was to feel that an energetic start was being made. At this Quarry became rather stuffy.

Among the other matters to be considered and resented this morning was Vincent Birman's account of thirty guineas for arranging the transfer of Godfrey Brown. Much as he would have liked to, he did not feel he could come on Pearl for Birman's charges too. Pearl in the first place had told Wilfred that she wanted Godfrey helped because the young man otherwise might become a nuisance. Godfrey was convinced, she said, that Mr Angell was such an important man that he could do anything if only he would try. Godfrey had, in fact, said Pearl, got a sort of fixation on Mr Angell; *she* was only important now because she was married to him.

Wilfred, only half convinced, and not above a twist of jealousy, had nevertheless complied for his own good reasons. But thirty guineas was still a lot to pay, and he toyed with the idea of sending the bill back to Birman with a letter of complaint. This he knew would produce no result, and as a firm they could hardly afford to default.

One could only keep the man waiting as long as possible so that the thirty guineas would earn something in one's own account first.

He had been spending money far too lavishly since he was married, and he drew up on a sheet of the firm's paper a list of economies they might make. One of the great difficulties of married life of course was just this question of economy. It was very difficult to cut one's wife's indulgencies without cutting one's own. The list began: (a) Mrs Jamieson three days a week instead of six. Why not? (b) Impress on Pearl the foolish wastefulness of taxis. (c) Spanish burgundy instead of claret, except on special occasions. (d) Give up dining out with Pearl. (e) Cut evening paper; one can always see the headlines at one's club. (f) Less milk; it is often wasted. (g) Does Pearl know that Polish butter is just as good and quite a bit cheaper? (h) Salads are expensive; Pearls spends too much on these. (i) Stop buying cigars at the club; one can get them wholesale from Evans's. (j) Watch the lights. As the evenings draw in, careless use of them runs away with money. (k) Ask Pearl if she can manage on less per week. If she is short she can always draw a cheque on her own account. (l) Cancel those shoes.

At this stage he stopped and read through his list, then screwed the paper up and threw it in the waste-paper basket. At such a time, on such a day, with a knowledge of the night's triumph behind him, it was inappropriate to consider these things. Now of all times he knew himself to be a success, in business, in the home, in society, in life. To hedge now, to quibble, would be unworthy of one's destiny.

He took a deep, satisfied breath and pressed the bell for Miss Lock, to dictate the morning's letters.

Before he went out for lunch he rummaged in the waste-paper basket and found the crumpled paper. He folded it several times and put it in his pocket book for future reference.

Chapter Twelve

In early October Jude Davis said to Godfrey: 'Spencer's out on the 10th, the X-rays show a splintered bone. Think you'd like to tackle Vic Miller?'

'I'll tackle anyone,' said Godfrey. 'Give me half a chance.'

'I'm putting you in, then.'

Godfrey knew all about it. A welter-weight title fight at the Albert Hall. Nobody cared much who featured on the undercard: you drew the crowd in for the big fight, and the rest was any old thing you could scrape together. But it was the Albert Hall, and even if half the spectators had not yet come, because the big fight wasn't due until nine, or had already left, because the big fight was over, you still boxed before several thousand people, with a few of the Press at their tables, and if you put up a good show it was worth a lot publicity-wise. Miller he'd never seen; he was from Dundee and had only turned pro about a year, but they all said he was a rising man and he was managed by Karl English, who had one of the best stables in the business.

That night he wrote a short letter to Pearl: 'I'm fighting at the Albert Hall Thursday the tenth. Thanks to you. A title bill. I'm in the groove. Regards. Little God.' He walked over and pushed it under her door.

Pearl showed the letter to Wilfred. 'It was addressed to you but I opened it by mistake. Awfully sorry, dear.'

Wilfred stared at the note. 'Little God. I wonder if he thinks he is, with those striking looks and that small physique. Strange young man.'

'I think he's got a crush on you,' she said. 'Shall we go?'

'Where?'

'To watch the boxing. The Albert Hall is nice and easy to get to.'

'It's a Thursday, I can't. My bridge night. And anyway seats at boxing matches are very expensive.'

'I thought you'd never been.'

'Nor have I. But one gets to know prices.'

'Sometime I'd like to go. Just for the novelty.'

'Sometime you shall, my dear. There'll be other opportunities.'

The next morning, mindful of Wilfred's exhortation not to take taxis, Pearl walked to the top of Sloane Street and took a bus to the Albert Hall. When she had bought her ticket she put it deep in her handbag where it would not be pulled out by mistake.

Since his marriage Wilfred had given the occasional dinner at home – the Portugals had been twice, the Hones once and the Warners twice – but had refrained from asking people to bridge. But this evening he had told Pearl he was bringing three of his club friends back with him. Pearl had not met any of the three men before; one was a County Court judge, one was an antique dealer of great repute, one was the editor of a literary weekly. They were all scrupulously polite to her; their manners had been long groomed in unobtrusive courtesy. She liked them all. The youngest was sixty.

She watched the bridge for a time and noticed how the game affected Wilfred. It brought out the aggressiveness of his nature: this was the sort of combat he enjoyed, an intellectual battle which released his adrenalin and while there was no physical risk to carry it beyond the limits of enjoyment, there was a small financial risk which added to the agonies of failure and the zest of victory. Perhaps these qualities made him a good lawyer.

When she went out to get coffee and sandwiches she heard his voice above the others; it was the voice he would use to gain attention in restaurants, to put a case in the lower courts to silence a group if he wanted to recount an anecdote. During supper the three men were again beautifully deferential towards her, but she wondered if they would be so kind when discussing her among themselves.

After supper she cleared away and washed up, then slipped upstairs to bed. But she did not sleep and heard them leave about one-thirty.

The next morning at breakfast she said: 'You never told me you'd been in the army.'

'What?' He looked up from his *Times,* his lip damp and

discoloured with coffee. 'Oh, yes. Didn't I? I think I did. What makes you ask?'

'Judge Snow last night said something about you being in the Western Desert.'

'Oh, yes. It is not a period of my life I look back upon with pleasure.'

'I didn't know you were old enough.'

He blinked uneasily. 'I was just. It interrupted my university career. I told you.'

'Tell me about it again sometime. It's a bit hard . .'

'What?'

She was going to say she found it hard to imagine him with a trim figure and a youthful step undergoing the hardships of a campaign. 'It's a bit hard to think what the war was really like. I – wasn't born, you know.'

'I do know. Well, even for me, my dear, it seems to belong to another age, as if *I* were not born and it all happened to somebody else.'

'But you weren't in the fighting, were you?'

'I was in a non-combatant unit – the Pay Corps. But the war in the desert was so fluid that distinctions of that kind did not always work out. I was in considerable danger at times. And of course the hardships were endless. Have you more toast?'

'I'll get some. But there's Ryvita.'

He grunted and looked at his watch. 'Don't bother, then. I'll make do.'

Godfrey neglected his Flora for the week before the fight, as she predicted he would have to. Although he had kept in training of a sort all summer, he needed to be tightened up for a fight that, whatever the bored audience thought, might be a turning point in his career. Jude Davis's trainer was Pat Prince – an ex middle-weight of fifty-odd, with scar tissue sewn into the bags under his eyes, and a throaty voice. Godfrey despised him at first, but when it came to ring craft you had to hand it to him that he knew his job, and he put Little God fairly through his paces during the last week. He confided to Godfrey that if he had had his way Godfrey wouldn't have been in a single fight for the first six months while he unlearned his bad habits, but Davis had overruled him and said the boy needed extending and could learn while he fought. Godfrey was all with Davis in this.

He met his opponent for the first time at the weigh-in at the Dominion Theatre at midday on the day of the fight. Miller, a dour tough Scot, was making his first appearance in London and therefore was more dour than ever. In the evening they were told they would have to appear just before or just after the main bout, depending how the preliminaries ran. But in fact the preliminaries went their full time so it was after. Godfrey cursed his luck. More people are there just before: just after they all go out to the lavatories or the bars. He sat in the long shabby changing room with its dreary unshaded bulb and its endless shelves to contain the belongings of the orchestras and massed choirs of other evenings, and he listened to the sustained roar: one of the title fighters was Welsh and the hall was full of half drunken Welshmen singing and shouting at the top of their voices. And the top of a Welsh voice is very loud indeed. The coloured heavy-weight, Tom Bushey, who was one of Davis's coming boys, had just won on points, but he said to Godfrey that he had hardly been able to think how to box, the row had been so great. The audience wanted the main bout, and screamed incessantly and deafeningly for it.

Godfrey would have liked to see the title fight, but they weren't allowed out of the dressing rooms. If there was a sudden and unsatisfactory end they would be thrust on immediately to help divert the crowd from their frustration.

So he waited around talking to Pat Prince, hands ready bandaged and taped, gloves hanging from a convenient nail to be slipped on at the last moment, gum shield, Vaseline and towel on a ledge, green and white towelling coat over his shoulders with *Little God* stamped on the back. The din outside grew worse and worse. Jude Davis had been in the dressing room beforehand, but like nearly everyone else he had crowded out to watch the big fight.

'Nervous, kid?' asked Pat Prince, stopping his endless almost silent whistling to let out the two words.

'No more than usual. I know I'm good. That's all I care.'

'Well, take care you keep your temper. I saw you sparring last week when Nevil fetched you a nasty little uppercut.' He started whistling a tune out of *Oklahoma*.

'Nevil's a big head. One of these days he'll get it cracked open.'

'Well, I'm only telling you. Better now than after.'

Just then the screaming suddenly broke in a new wave and carried on. Bushey said: 'Sounds as if someone's got it! And it isn't Evan Morgan!'

After a few more moments of pandemonium a trainer came pushing in. 'Referee stopped fight! Lopez got a cut eye. Morgan's got the title!'

'Shouldn't never have been stopped! Lopez was only cut on the eyebrow!'

'Lucky it was that way round! Welshmen'd've wrecked the hall if it'd been their man.'

In the chaos that followed, Pat Prince jerked to his feet. 'We're on, boy.'

They fought their way through crowds of shouting Welshmen and got near the ring. Someone was singing 'Land of my Fathers' and everyone in the hall stood up. Then gradually the new champion was escorted out of the hall by half a dozen policemen, and Godfrey saw his opponent climbing into the ring. He followed, while people thrust their way out towards the bars and the few that were left settled into their places. The master of ceremonies appealed for quiet and announced the next contest.

The applause was as perfunctory as the interest. The arguing point of the evening was clearly going to be whether the referee stopped the fight too soon or whether Evan Morgan was a true champion. The arguing point would have nothing whatever to do with the two unknown, untried and undersized men in the ring.

The referee had spoken to them, they had touched gloves and gone back to their corners, backs to each other waiting for the bell. Godfrey hated a crowd that had no interest in him and he hated men with freckled skin and red hair. Anyway, unlike many boxers, he always hated the man in the opposite corner. When the bell went he came out into the middle like a demon king, only the green lights and the fiery breath lacking. He dropped his defence and went for Miller with both hands as if this was a fight in a back alley. Miller had only time to raise his guard, and this was swept away and he was back against the ropes. Being no

174

fool, he fought and blocked and dodged his way out of a hail of blows, but was pursued ceaselessly round the ring, as he tried to collect his skill. But there was no stop for the three minutes, and although at the end he had made up some ground he went to his corner puffing and sweating, his light skin reddening on shoulder and arm and rib and cheek where the blows had landed or where he had gone back against the ropes.

Somewhere in the middle of the round the audience had become aware of the fact that something interesting was still going on in the ring and had paid attention. At the end there was a ripple of applause that was more pleasant in Godfrey's ears than the string of curses that Pat Prince muttered in his ear with warnings that he would be pumped out by the end of the third round. Godfrey didn't mind now; he'd drawn attention to himself and was feeling fine. The second round went more steadily, with each man taking the look at his opponent that Godfrey's wild beginning had prevented. Miller was a good stylish boxer but didn't seem to have a really dangerous punch. Like a pawky farmer gathering windfalls, he picked up points just when they came along. He was taller than Godfrey and his extra reach was useful. In the third round Godfrey played him at his own game and encouraged him to make the running. He found that Miller didn't use his right a lot, but when he did he threw himself off balance for a second before he covered up. In the fourth round Godfrey invited a right cross, got it, shifting his head an inch to take it high up, and then hit the Scot with all his force, first to the body and then to the jaw.

Miller crumpled and was down for a count of six. Godfrey waited, his black hair springing, then went in to finish it off. There was a lot of noise in the hall now, and quite a few people had come back from the bars to see what was on. Miller survived the round and recovered quickly in his corner, and the next round made a determined comeback. At the end of it there was a roar of applause.

The sixth round began in the same fashion, but Miller had shot his bolt. He was on one knee for a count of five and got up visibly unsteady. The referee was moving to stop the fight but Little God was ahead of him and a right to the jaw put Miller down for the count.

Pearl, lonely in the early bouts among a crowd of bellowing Welshmen, had sat through the controversial title fight, and after it had suddenly found vacant seats all round her and a chance to breathe and stretch. So to the six rounds of the fight between Vosper and Miller, triumphantly won by a flamboyant Vosper, who left the ring shaking hands with himself in mid-air. Then, feeling conspicuous in her isolation and not wanting to make it obvious which bout she had come to watch, she sat through eight rounds of a dull middle-weight fight before getting up and climbing towards the exits at the back.

Round to the front door, where a lot of people were milling. Taxis would be hard to get but a walk would do her good: she was hot and sticky and empty of emotion, glad of a chance to peer at herself before she got home, ask, why come? Why risk exposure to a virus? Why want someone to win? Why foster unspecified discontent? Why get into this position at all?

As she was leaving: 'It's Mrs Angell, isn't it?'

A stocky dark-eyed woman with a silk Picasso scarf round her head: she looked dreadfully ill but her voice was strong.

'Yes . . . I . . .'

'Flora Vosper. We met at your wedding party.'

'Of course! I was just going to say Lady Vosper.'

'Didn't know you were interested in prize-fighting.'

'Well, no. But Wilfred was out – I thought a title fight might be interesting.'

'Bit of a fiasco, eh? I came to see my chauffeur – that virile little devil with the hair – he was on after the championship bout and won in six rounds.'

'Oh, yes. I remember. Is he your chauffeur? Yes, he knocked the other man out, didn't he.'

'Good win, I thought. Bit of a showman, of course, but the crowd like that. I'm just waiting for him. He's gone to get the car. Can I give you a lift home?'

Panic. Don't show panic. 'Oh, thanks very much, it's awfully kind of you, but I'm – I'm visiting a friend before I go home. I was just going to get a taxi.'

'Not our way? Can drop you off.'

'Thanks, no. As a matter of fact, it will be quicker to walk. Are you keeping better, Lady Vosper? I heard you'd been ill.'

'Death's door, my dear. But I kick like hell on the mat. And you? Enjoying life?'

Two more cars drawing up. But neither the car she knew so well. 'Thanks, yes. Lovely. Well, I must be –'

'If you're free an hour or two sometime drop in for a drink. D'you mind sick visiting?'

Pearl smiled brilliantly. 'Of course not. Perhaps I will –'

'I suspect your husband does. So come without him. Come next Tuesday. To dinner. Can you get away?'

'Oh, yes, but it's not necessary to –'

'I've got two people coming. Miriam, my daughter, – she's about your age – and Salvator the pianist. He's amusing and it would make the four.'

Was that the jade-green car edging its way towards the steps? Wasn't it rude to give a second refusal? Did it matter if one went to dinner, with him in the kitchen? Anyway one could always cancel. Get away now. The important thing was to get away.

'Thank you. I'd love to come. Tuesday Wilfred dines at his club so I could probably manage it. If I –'

'Seven-thirty for eight then. I'll drop you a card to confirm. You know my address? 113 Wilton Crescent.'

'Thanks. Thank you, Lady Vosper.' It *was* the green car. 'Seven-thirty for eight. Goodnight, Lady Vosper.' Goodbye Little God. Merge into the crowd. Why am I so tall? Try to become anonymous. Milling people. The boxing wasn't over but more were leaving. Green car just moving up to the steps.

But she was well away now, hidden by trilby hats, tall upturned collars, umbrellas being raised against a freckle of rain. He hadn't seen her. Would Lady Vosper say anything? Very improbable. Of course her relationship with her chauffeur was over-familiar and she might say: guess who I met on the steps. But still improbable. Much more likely: well done, Little God, well boxed, well fought – well won; beautifully poised olive-skinned body, naked lithe skin but muscular, strong hairy legs; perfectly balanced engine of destruction; black fine hair bouncing with every thrust and blow but never falling in the eyes, petite regular handsome features with full and jutting bottom lip and one flaw on the black eyebrow, one scar like a duelling scar, making the perfection bearable. The will to kill always in his eyes, the intent to hurt or defeat or disable in every co-ordinated thrust of the two deft hands. Well done, Little God, she would say, well done, well killed, now drive me home.

Because, for all their differences, Pearl sensed something vaguely similar between Flora and her chauffeur. Flora was not a killer, but she was a dare-devil, stick-at-nothing kind of woman, the sort who would ride at a five-barred gate knowing she was likely to fall rather than accept defeat by going round it. It was not an attitude Pearl understood but she could recognize its existence.

Several times during the next days she came to the point of mentioning her meeting with Flora Vosper to Wilfred and asking him if he knew why she was ill and what was wrong with her. Once she dropped the name into their conversation but he was preoccupied with his food and did not respond. Always Pearl was afraid of letting out that she had been to watch the boxing.

The little card confirming the invitation arrived. Several times she got as far as the telephone to ring Lady Vosper to cancel the date, but each time she found the excuse she had concocted unconvincing to herself. And perhaps it was unkind to refuse to visit a sick woman. And the company did sound interesting. Since her marriage she had formed no friendship with any young woman of her own age except Veronica Portugal whom she met from time to time – and she saw Hazel once a month. Wilfred's friends were her friends but, except for the Portugals, they were all middle-aged or old. So Miriam might be a good person to meet. And musicians always fascinated her, although she wished Salvator could have been a clarinet player.

Up to the Monday she had not told Wilfred of the invitation out, which created a sensation of deceit where no deceit was necessary. And by Monday it seemed too late to say. She made an appointment for a wash and set and a manicure for four p.m. on the Tuesday, but not at D. H. Evans; she had never been able to force herself into the shop since she left.

And on the Monday night Wilfred went to bed with her.

Tuesday was a windy day, which is always a nuisance when you've had your hair just done.

Pearl took a taxi back, braving Wilfred's displeasure, but she was home before him. He was not in a very good mood because some option agreement he was negotiating with a man in Switzerland was being held up by the sloth of a London solicitor.

'If I could have earned my living in art!' he said. 'Even perhaps by *dealing* in art! I should be a more satisfied man!' He rubbed his finger and thumb together, getting rid of the imaginary crumb. 'To *create* art, of course, is the ultimate in fulfilment.'

'But aren't you satisfied?' she asked. 'You always seem so.'

There was no intended irony in the remark, and he saw none.

'Satisfaction is a relative term. I flatter myself that I have made something of my life, that a degree of distinction attaches to me, that my success is not just a hollow term. But the profession of law is so often stultifying, in the slowness with which it creaks into motion, in the ancestral precedent which determines the motion, in the absence of original and creative thought. Sometimes one yearns for a freer and more bracing air. I have always had a vigorous and inquiring mind, and possibly my late marriage has stimulated that. Like satisfaction, youth is a relative term. Isn't it, my dear. Isn't it?' He patted her head. 'What's the matter?'

'Nothing. Why?'

'You seem to shrink away.'

She laughed. 'I've just had my hair done! Didn't you notice?'

'I saw it was a new style, but I thought you had done it yourself. Isn't it very expensive having it done in the West End?'

'No. Not where I go.'

'I remember a case I was involved in a few years ago. My client was claiming damages against a hairdresser in Bond Street for loss and discolouration of hair following a permanent wave. I think we got £350.'

179

'Do you want anything before you go off to dinner?'

'Food, d'you mean? I thought you were asking me not to eat between meals.'

'Oh, yes, sorry. I forgot.'

'But since you ask, a few biscuits with a glass of sherry would be sustaining.'

'Ryvita?'

'If one must.'

'What time are you leaving?'

'The usual. I shall not be back late. About eleven.'

'I may have gone to bed.'

When he left the house she changed slowly into a black silk dress, a bit longer than the fashion, with sleeves buttoned tight at the wrist and lace covering the low neck. She rang for a taxi at 7.25 and took the fur she had bought last week.

She wondered if he would open the door to her and if he knew she was coming. It didn't matter. His presence was immaterial. He was just a servant in the background. She was there to dine with Lady Vosper and her daughter and Salvator the famous Spanish pianist. The fact of Little God being there was only a tiny flavour of spice added to the dish.

He did open the door. She had paid off the taxi and only touched the bell once, and he was standing there, expression pleasant but non-committal. He was in a good grey suit she had not seen before: no chauffeur's uniform: there was a bruise on his cheekbone from last Thursday's fight, just the one.

'Come in,' he said. 'I'll tell Lady Vosper you've come.'

She followed him into the hall and then into the front room, which was a drawing room. It was a rather dark room; the lights were too darkly shaded, or not enough were on. She took her fur with her but it was warm.

'Lady Vosper'll be down shortly,' he said. 'She said I was to get you a drink.'

'Thank you. I'll have a gin and tonic.'

He poured it, his back to her, then brought it across. 'Lady Vosper'll be right down,' he said as he handed it to her.

'Thank you.'

Their hands brushed, and he moved a foot or two back.

She turned away from him and sipped her drink, knowing he was looking at her. She glanced at her watch. A quarter to eight. It was a bit fast.

He said: 'Lady Vosper told me you was at the fight.'

The drink was pretty strong. When he had gone she would help herself to some more tonic.

'Oh, yes . . . You wrote to me about it. I told Wilfred how pleased you were to get a good fight, so he asked me to go and see how you went on.'

'I went on proper, didn't I?'

'Yes. You won. I told him you won.'

'I always do win.'

'It would be good pay for you.'

'Yes, it was good pay.'

'Have the other guests come yet?'

'No, not yet. They'll be here at eight.'

'Perhaps you'd tell Lady Vosper I'm here.'

'Oh, she knows. But she's not been too well today. It takes her sometimes.'

She walked towards the table where the drinks were set out and looked for the tonic water.

'Can I get you something?' He had come up close behind her.

'This is a bit strong.'

'Sorry. It was a half bottle of tonic water. I'll get another from the kitchen.'

When he was half way to the door, she said: 'Does Lady Vosper have a maid or – or a cook?'

'A woman comes every morning. Then we have a cook when there's people to dinner in the evening, see. If it's just her and me I do the cooking.'

They looked at each other and he suddenly grinned. 'Not to worry, Oyster. I've not done no cooking tonight.'

When she was alone she moved about the room looking at the pictures. After some months of Wilfred's training, she was already fancying herself as a student of painting. These were mostly old works and badly lighted, not like the house in Cadogan Mews where lights were directed tactfully upon the walls. She wondered what Wilfred would make of them. One or two had gilt lettering underneath: John Opie, J. S. Sargent, so that there was no virtue in recognition,

She sipped at her glass and felt the gin going down strongly. By the time Godfrey came back she would nearly have finished it. But that did not matter: she was ill-at-ease and drink would help.

He came back. 'Sorry to be s'long. Couldn't find another bottle of the old tonic. Here we are. Oh, you're half done. Shall I wait till you've finished?'

'No, top it up, please.'

He did so. 'That'll have no taste at all. Here, I'll put a drop of the old stuff in as well.' He took the glass from her and darted over to the table, unstoppered the gin, put some in, brought back the glass.

'Why'd you really go to the Albert Hall? It wasn't to please your old man, was it?'

She looked at him, her eyes an inch or so higher than his. She felt very poised. 'Maybe it was curiosity. I'd seen you fight once. But I don't know *why* you fight. What's the reason?'

'Reason?' His eyes took her in admiringly. 'It's my job. Why not? What other reason d'you need?'

'But d'you like hurting people? Do you like hitting people with your fists, hoping to damage them, make them cry out? Do you go for their eyes hoping to make them swell up, or their noses hoping to make them bleed? I thought in that match last week . . .'

'Yes?'

'I thought the referee was going to stop the fight, but you got in just in time, knocked the other man out. Why couldn't you have waited?'

'*Waited?* . . .' He shrugged. 'I often get swindled. 'Member the fight you went to before – the ref stopped that too soon. This time I made no error – Miller went down on his backside with a real clump. Wham! It was smashing. That's what I'm there for. That's what he's there for too. Don't forget he's trying to do the same to me. It's fabulous when they go down – twice as much fun as a points decision or an r.s.f.'

'Yes, but do you *like* giving pain? Did you – were you a bully as a boy? Did you twist other boys' arms? Did you torture cats and throw stones at dogs? Did you knock down old ladies? Did you –'

He smiled and took her arm above the elbow. 'Listen,

Oyster, it isn't like that—'

She pulled her arm free. 'Remember your promise!'

'O.K., O.K.'

'But even that! . . . You take my arm as if it was a – an iron rail! Why have you always to be so violent?'

'I'm not always so violent. Honest. I know it seemed like it that first time, but it was you taking fright that was half the trouble. I was clutching to stop you running away. Honest, I'm not violent with women. And what you say . . .'

'Well?'

'Maybe you were brought up gentle. I wasn't brought up gentle. I was brought up in a world where things was tough, and the only way not to get trod on was to be tougher than anyone else around. I soon learned that. And other lads – and men! – learned to leave me alone. Soon I could fight anyone. It was fun to fight – lovely! There's nothing like it for making you feel good. But bullying – that's different! I don't twist people's arms or knock down old ladies. Why should I? Me, Little God. I don't bully. I like taking on bigger than myself and beating them! I never was a bully in my life – you don't understand, Oyster, you don't understand.'

Pearl took a longer drink. It was still potent. 'And me? Don't you feel you tried to bully me?'

He fingered the bruise on his cheek. 'I was groovy about you – no mistake. I got it bad. So when I scared you that night I was sorry, real sorry, and I tried to make it up, see. I called with a box of chocolates. I met you on the train. I prowled round in the car and stopped you when you was walking home. But it was only trying to be friends. Why can't we be friends?'

She smiled briefly. 'I *was* scared, you know. Still am a bit.'

'You don't need to be. I played it wrong that night, that's all.'

'Perhaps,' she said, 'I've never been so afraid of you since my marriage. I feel – safer.'

'Yeh. Mrs Angell. It sounds different, don't it. And you're rich now – it all makes a difference.'

'Being rich doesn't make the difference.'

'Tell me, Oyster, just tell me – I've often wondered, like.

It's not me, to worry, but I've often wondered . . .'

'What?'

'This marrying old Mr Angell. You know. Because he *is* old – or getting on anyhow. You didn't marry him because you was scared of me? Did you?'

She smiled at him properly for the first time since their first meeting in the dance hall. 'Good heavens, no! I married him because I was – fond of him, because he was so kind. He's always such a gentleman, so considerate, so . . .'

'All the opposite of me, eh?'

She took another drink and glanced towards the door. 'Isn't it time Lady Vosper was down? If she's not well, perhaps I could go up and see her.'

He went to the window, peered out, pulled the curtains across again. 'Well, I'm sorry, Oyster, but you can't. She's not here. She's in hospital.'

'*What?*' Heart thumped and stopped and restarted.

'In that old clinic place where she went once before. I says to her, stay out of that place, you never been well since you went in before; you stay here where I can look after you proper. But this Matthewson, her doctor, he says she's got to go in and be –'

'*When?* When did she go?'

'Yesterday. I went to see her this morning, but she wasn't looking too good –'

'But there must have been time to let me know –'

'Oh, she wrote. She wrote to you and to this pianist bloke. Her daughter was here so she didn't have to be told.'

'I never got any letter! Aren't the others coming, then? Why didn't you tell me? Why didn't you tell me when I came so that I need not have come in?'

'Well, I thought it funny, Oyster, you coming the way you did. I thought, I wonder why she's come pretending that she knows nothing about it, pretending to ask for Lady Vosper –'

'But I didn't *know*, I tell you! No letter came –'

'So I said to myself, perhaps, seeing she went to watch Little God box, maybe she's come to have a chat with Little God, making the excuse, like –'

'You never posted the letter!' Perfect anger driveth out fear.

'I did. I swear I did! You know what the post is like these days. Why only last month Lady V got a letter from Norfolk that'd taken five days. You'll see if it doesn't come in the morning –'

'Well, you should have told me! When I came to the door you should have told me!'

He ran a hand through his comb of hair. 'You can't blame me, can you, for hoping? Still hoping.'

She stared at him. 'It was a trick, wasn't it. You found I was coming to dinner and when Lady Vosper was taken ill it fitted perfectly. This is what comes of trusting you! This is the way you keep your promise not to – not to –'

'You came to see me box. Nobody made you do that. It made me think things again, hope things, see. That's all. What else have I done? Let you come here and have twenty minutes' talk with me. Why are you so mad at me? I haven't laid a finger on you. Or only one finger, just for a minute. What are you scared of?'

'I'm not scared!'

'Yes, you are, even now. Sit down, Oyster. Let's talk a bit more.'

'I've nothing more to say.'

'Why don't you relax? Why don't you give way a bit – be easy?'

She moved past him and he put his hand on hers. She pulled it away.

'What's the matter with Lady Vosper?'

'It's her kidneys. I'm sorry for her. She's a good old sport.'

'Is she to have an operation?'

'They'll decide tomorrow.'

'Very well, I'll ring up the Clinic later tomorrow.'

'Won't you stop a bit now?'

'No. I'm sorry.' She went to the door, turned the handle. 'This door is locked!'

'Yes. I've got the key. I'll give it you in a minute.'

'Give it me at once! I'll call the police!'

'You're not scared of me, Oyster. Honest you aren't. You're scared of yourself. I wouldn't hurt you. Why don't you let yourself go?'

'Give me the key!'

'I'll give it you if you tell me why you came to see me

box last week.'

'I've told you! Wilfred wanted me to!'

'That's an old falsehood. Truthfully.'

'I was curious myself just to see how it went! We'd arranged it for you. My God, how sorry I am I took the trouble!'

She moved away from the door and walked to the telephone by the fireplace. She picked up the receiver and heard him come behind her. He kissed her neck. She slewed her head away and began to dial. He put his fingers in the dialling holes and made nonsense of the call. She turned and hit him across the face. He smiled and turned the other side of his face. She hit at him again. She was a strong girl and this time she used her fist, but she rocked his head two inches and the blow slid across his forehead. She picked up the telephone and threw it at him. He fended it off with his hands, half catching it, then it fell to the floor with a loud clang.

'Drop your fists, Oyster,' he said. 'That's the end of the round.'

She stared at him with wide angry eyes, out of breath. He looked her over admiringly, with particular interest in the movement of her breasts. Then he looked at his watch.

'Half a minute yet . . . Seconds out of the ring. Time.'

He feinted to put his hands on her throat, and she hit at him again, but he slipped under her guard and took her round the waist and began to kiss her. She beat at his shoulders and the side of his head, but to his relief did not kick his shins. She tried to turn her mouth away but was not too successful.

'This,' he said, breathless himself now, 'is where – in the old movies this is – where the bird always gives in.' His mouth against her cheek, his hard body pressing against hers. 'Give in. Go on. Give in, Oyster. Just for the fun of it. We've always – had this date. Give in.'

She clutched his hair and began to pull at it. He didn't seem to feel normal hurt. His mouth was finding hers more successfully. She thought she should bite him but her mouth didn't want to. Only her hands wanted to go on destroying him. Jees, he thought, it *is* like the old movies, it's *working*. I'm going to get away with it, I'm going to get her. That old sofa bed of Flora's, drag it up to the electric fire, how'm I going to get her clothes off without her going scared on me again? Just go on like this, get her to a state when she won't think any more. Not tear her frock, I got to be gentle, but does she *really* want gentle or can she take it rough? Gentle at first, mustn't scare.

Pain, she thought, pain and pleasure have a frontier where they meet. Do I want to hurt him or be hurt myself or kill him or be killed? Dagger, if I had a dagger, not to kill but to draw blood, his blood. Vile little God, *vile* God, conquering, compelling. Cheap shoddy mind, cheap trick, making me cheap, myself cheap. But what is this to do with what is happening? Fine body, clear, fresh skin, young arms, smooth slim easy muscles, light, strong, beautifully made. Is there cheapness in beauty or beauty in cheapness? Youth in age or age in youth? I can't stand here, I *can't* stand here, half naked, like a prostitute in a brothel, while he pulls a couch which unfolds. How has he got out of his clothes, I never saw him, they seemed to slip away. Wilfred stepping out of his pants, breathing heavily, the roll of fat, the *particular* roll of fat at the base of the abdomen which creases up when he bends, the slow ponderous climb into bed. Slim and light and vital Little God, like Mercury, olive-skinned body gleaming like pewter in the low light. 'Here, let me help you, Oyster, little Pearl, lovely Pearl, oh, lovely Pearl, aren't you fabulous. I'll take your things. Pearl in the oyster. Smooth Pearl, silky Pearl, satin Pearl, velvet Pearl, sleek Pearl, soft Pearl . . . oh, aren't you fabulous, just like that, just like that . . .'

Little God, great God, conquesting, searching, probing, *finding*. Pleasure in pain, pleasure in pain, pleasure in death, pleasure in ecstasy. God, great God, great God, great God, great God.

Chapter Thirteen

Not a single national newspaper had made any comment on Godfrey's victory at the Albert Hall, some had not even bothered to record it. All they were concerned with was the title fight and the controversial decision which had ended it. But the weekly, *Boxing News,* commented: 'Comparative newcomer Godfrey Vosper, called in at short notice to oppose Vic Miller, the amateur champion turned pro from Dundee, provided one of the surprises of the supporting contests by knocking out Miller in the sixth round. The 23-year-old boy from Kensington dominated the fight from the opening round when he rushed in and drove his Scottish opponent to the ropes. Miller fought back but never carried quite the same power of punch or ring-craft. Vosper with his good footwork and his fast fists should go far.'

Jude Davis was not quite of the same opinion. 'That's not boxing, Brown, that's fighting. Oh, I'll grant you it worked; you've got plenty of guts and against someone like Miller it paid dividends. But put you up against real class and that approach'll get you absolutely nowhere. If you had tried that on with someone like Legra or Saldivar . . .'

'Well, you're talking of champs now. I'm not a champ yet.'

'Nor ever will be if you play to the crowd. Remember it's just one man you're fighting – and he happens to be in the ring with you.'

Godfrey grinned. 'It was a bit riling – all them people and none paying any attention. You got to admit it.'

'I'm matching you with Goodfellow at the National Sporting Club on the 18th November. He's nobody's push-over. So it's strict training from now on.'

Godfrey cut out the piece from the *Boxing News* and posted it to Angell. Angell passed it to Pearl. 'Perhaps between us we've fostered a champion after all.'

'Perhaps we have,' said Pearl.

Angell inflated his chest and then blew out the breath through pursed lips. The steam rising from Pearl's coffee wobbled.

'I'm going to Christie's before I go on to the office. There are some Tiepolo drawings on show. One might put in a modest bid.'

'Or jewellery?' Pearl asked.

He winced. 'Not in this sale.'

'I had a thought of buying something for Father. Gold cuff-links perhaps. I haven't seen much of him since our marriage, and I thought I might go and see them this evening.'

'Gold cuff-links are out of date. One can get much more handsome links at half a dozen shops in Bond Street, and at half the price.'

She sipped her coffee.

He said: 'But tonight I'll be home to dinner.'

'Well, would it matter you going to the club for once?'

'Why didn't you go last night?'

'I didn't think of it at the time. And next Tuesday seems a long way off.'

'Are you feeling suddenly homesick?'

'Oh, no. It was just an idea. I'm a woman, so I get ideas.' She rose and patted his shoulder. 'Do you mind for once?'

'Oh, I expect arrangements can be made,' he said shortly.

That morning Miriam McNaughton called at Wilton Crescent. Godfrey let her in. That is to say he opened the door, then half closed it again, and only when she insisted did he just give her room to squeeze past him into the hall.

'Where's Mrs Hodder?'

'Gone shopping.'

'Why are you in, then? My mother said you were training every morning.'

'Not every morning. I don't go Fridays. How's Lady V?'

'I came for some things for Lady Vosper. Allow me to pass.'

She went into the big bedroom at the end of the flat and closed the door in his face. After a minute he opened the door and went in.

'Yes, what is it?' she said.

'Can I help you?'

'No.'

She went to the built-in cupboard and took out a dressing-jacket and a nightdress. Then she stopped.

'Well?'

'I thought you might want help.'

'I don't want help picking out some clothes for my mother! You can go.'

He did not move.

'Will you please go!'

He shifted his balance from one foot to the other. 'Sorry. While Lady V's ill this flat's in my charge, see. She told me so. She told me to look after it.'

'Well, look after it! I won't run away with it.'

'No, but other things might run away, see, and me get blamed.'

Miriam's skin flushed dark red. 'You insolent little swine! How dare you speak to me like that!'

'Because sometimes when you come here something walks that's not got two legs to walk on its own.'

She stared at him viciously. 'I shall tell Lady Vosper exactly what you have said and I shall ask her to discharge you.'

'You already have. It doesn't do no good, does it?'

'For the last time, will you please leave me alone!'

'I'm not interfering with you. I'm just watching.'

She swung away from him, began to open drawers, take out handkerchiefs, underwear, bed-socks. These she dropped into her leather bag while he leaned against the door and watched. Then she swept past him into the dining room, snatched up two clean napkins and a couple of new novels.

'My mother's dangerously ill, you may be interested to know.'

'Yes, I know. I know that.'

'And a lot you care!'

'Oh, I care,' he said. 'I care a lot. But a fat lot you care.'

She said suddenly, viciously: 'You think you're a lady-killer, don't you. You think women fall for the profile. But all you really are is a nasty little bantam cock crowing on a dung-hill. You prey on a sick woman and think you've made a conquest. Poor mother; she must be out of her mind to have sunk so low!'

'All right, all right, spill it all out. What's the matter

with your husband, can't he give it you? You're all sour, Miriam, like a sour grape that's got left on the tree. You're jealous really, aren't you, jealous of your poor old mum. She can get 'em any time. She's got all it takes. But you got *nothing*! I wouldn't lift my hand to you!'

'Don't you *dare* touch me!' she said, as he came towards her. 'If you touch me I'll have you up for assault!'

'Who's touching you? I'm not. I'm just seeing you don't nick anything. That's all.'

She went past him to the door of the dining room and then to the door of the flat. He followed her and saw her out and stood in the open door watching her walk away towards Knightsbridge.

That morning Angell learned from Hollis that the option agreement and the annexed schedule of sale had been posted to Viscount Vosper in Geneva for signature.

Angell had an appointment for lunch with John Square, one of the directors of Christie's. Wilfred had chosen Scott's for the meeting because there one could eat oysters, which were not fattening and which had the reputation of increasing virility. He had had some unusual pains recently in unusual places and he was concerned for his health. His public reason for entertaining Square was that they had not met socially for six months; his private reason was a small Canaletto which was coming up for sale next week and on the authenticity of which some doubts had been expressed. The doubt might bring the price down and no one could know better than Square what the inner, confidential belief of the firm of Christie's was. Angell himself was not interested in the Canaletto, but Sir Francis Hone had his eye on it. Francis Hone knew absolutely nothing about art except its value as a hedge against inflation, and he had often, profitably, taken Angell's advice. One therefore didn't want to advise badly.

John Square was late arriving, so Wilfred had the opportunity to sip a Dry Sack and let his mind drift to considering the shape of Pearl's upper arms and think of the little mole between her shoulder blades and remember how she looked when she smiled. When Square came he apologized but said his brother had been taken ill and had just gone into the London Clinic for an operation. In the course of the meal Wilfred was able to learn that

191

in the opinion of Christie's the Canaletto was genuine. He also learned that in the next room to Arthur Square Lady Vosper, known slightly to them both, was dangerously ill.

After lunch, and still hungry, Angell took a bus back to his office. When he got in he asked for an outside line.

Godfrey's voice. Quite heavy over the telephone.

'This is Mr Angell speaking. I called to ask how Lady Vosper is.'

'Oh, she's not here now, Mr Angell. She went into the Clinic last week.'

'You did not tell me.'

'Sorry. I been busy. I been real busy in training for a fight a week Friday.'

'How is Lady Vosper?'

'I seen her yesterday, Mr Angell. She'd been having a machine or something.'

'A kidney machine?'

'That's it. It didn't suit her. She's real sick.'

His voice was vaguely different. He was trying to talk better, with a drawl, the over-politeness had a suggestion of insolence.

'What do the doctors say?'

'They don't say anything to me, Mr Angell. I'm just the chauffeur.'

Angell grunted.

'She reckons to be out Saturday but I say to her stay in another week. She wants to come to my fight, see, but I say to her she can't even if she gets out because it's men only this time.'

'Men only?'

'At the N.S.C. Café Royal. All posh in dinner jackets. You going to come, Mr Angell?'

'No –'

'It'll be important this. Important. I'm matched with Goodfellow. He went the distance with Wesker last year, so it's top of the milk. Coming to see me win, Mr Angell? I know I'm going to win.'

'I'm not interested in prize-fighting.'

'I'd have liked you to come. I'm ever so grateful for what you done for me, Mr Angell. Honest to God. I'm doing fine now since you just put in that word for me. Doing fine.'

'I'm glad.' Angell hung up. Perhaps he was mistaken, perhaps he misheard, but there had been other times on the telephone in his life when the voice of the speaker at the other end had betrayed nuances that gave hidden feelings away. Insolence, was this? Something slightly more. Or perhaps it was just triumph, the triumph of a little man who thought that at last he was on the road to success.

He returned to the flat at 5.30 but Pearl had already gone. There was a note: *I've made buns. Back about ten. P.* He boiled himself a pot of tea and wolfed five of her buns, then guiltily distributed the others about the dish so that she might not notice how many had been eaten.

Like that time at school Sylvane had caught him eating the cakes; Angell, bend over, you greedy little lump of horse dung. I'll teach you to steal from your betters. Beatings, the terror of pain, the sheer *terror* of pain. Always this consuming fear for the first three years at his public school. The endless beatings, for being two minutes late, for forgetting his pads, for belching in chapel, for having mud on his shoe. After these three years it had been better as he moved up the school and as he grew taller, bigger . . . But even then. He hadn't been fat in spite of his appetite. There had been no Billy Bunter taunts. His name had been the worst thing to endure. Angell. He'd been called Gabriel, Halo, Lucy (for Lucifer). The last had stuck and had been the worst because in the minds of some it implied girlishness. His hatred of games, his lack of physical agility. Come on Lucy, always the last. Now then Lucy, pick up your skirts. Lucy's not too well, it must be one of his periods.

He'd never been a bully at school in the sense of wanting to inflict pain, but in his fourth year when he became a senior a need to dominate and bully had developed from the defensive spasm. It developed suddenly, in a sudden fit of violence against one boy who had tried to continue the old routine of jeering persecution, and the boy had spent two days in the san. Wilfred had needed the two days in bed just as much, but had somehow survived, and no one had split on him. Thereafter he had been on the side of the oppressors, the change having occurred unspoken and in the course of a few days. Nevertheless he blamed most of the hesitancies and fears of his later life on those three formative years at Sherborne. They became a convenient peg on which to hang any inadequacies.

But the inadequacies, most of them, had been successfully hidden for so many years that often he did not recognize the memories of them as belonging to the man he now was. And the inadequacy of his unmarried state, which he had elevated and rationalized into a virtue, and which he had sincerely believed to be no less, was no longer in being. Thanks to his prevision in marrying Pearl.

After his tea he padded into her bedroom for a few minutes and sat on the bed. He would have been embarrassed if Pearl had caught him then, but alone it gave him some satisfaction to gaze round this room and see and smell the evidence of her occupancy. The stockings decorating rather than disfiguring the back of the French Empire bedroom chair, the freckle of powder on the Mansel mirror, the mules kicked off carelessly on the Jushagan carpet, the short flimsy lace nightdress folded on the pillow, the women's magazines on the Regency table beside the bed.

Since he had begun to find Pearl physically attractive, he had sometimes asked himself whether the rational process by which he had picked her out and married her were in fact as rational as they had appeared to him at the time. He had read somewhere that men who married several times often chose women who were alike. What had first struck him about Pearl was her likeness to Anna. And those weeks and months during which he had hesitated – the tentative move and then the withdrawal, the next tentative move and so on – had it all been a deception practised upon his mind by his body? Without these subconscious urges towards Pearl, would he have ever made the moves at all? Looking back on them now, they seemed to have a quiet enormity that surprised him. A growing physical desire masquerading as a cold logical appraisal?

Of course the cold logical appraisal was not altogether dormant even now. He recognized that intellectually she was far his inferior, and he resented that at times because

194

of her looks and because of his desire for her she could at times seem superior to him. Conversation many evenings was a morass of platitudes. And he hated to go out and spend money – as he sometimes found himself doing – in fashionable places merely to satisfy a female desire for display. He despised the people who patronized such places, their fatuous behaviour, their herd instinct for doing what was the thing, their acceptance of mediocre ideas because the equally mediocre arbiters of taste told them to do so. He had little use for a world in which second-rate minds assumed a tinsel coating of fashion which passed for brilliance. Pearl unhappily was all too ready to fall into the rut, to become a victim of the mass hypnotism of the day; but at least when he corrected her she more often than not saw his point of view and came to agree with him. If she could not always judge for herself she willingly accepted his judgment. There was no doubt but that she acknowledged him as her mentor, and this was a pleasure in itself, to feel that she looked up to him and saw him as a man in the prime of life, experienced, wise and kind.

He picked up the nightdress gingerly and smelled it. It had her scent about it, she might have been there, in it, vulnerable, soft, inviting. He rationed his times with her, not wanting to use up all his strength, especially as he had not been accustomed to it, and sometimes afterwards he had heart flutterings. Two days, three days more? Joyous thought. Lying on this bed, her long strong slender legs. The nightdress . . . Oh, dear! He threw it down and then carefully gathered it and folded it as she had left it.

He patted his own stomach. He had lost about seven pounds this month. It already made a difference to the buttons. This suit, six years old, had become tight; now there was comfortable room. It just made a difference. He fancied he even felt better for it. There was a world of difference between seventeen stone nine and eighteen stone two. Perhaps another half stone. It would be incredibly difficult but it might well be worth it. So long as it was done gently. He had seen men looking ravaged after too hasty a course of dieting. Skin sagged, did not contract with the flesh. He might well lose his handsome looks and that would be far more disastrous than a little healthy weight.

He got up and went to the French dressing table, stared at the personal things on it. It gave him a thrill to feel he was invading her privacy: he opened a drawer and with his forefinger stirred the stockings, the handkerchiefs, the scarves. In a box were safety-pins, Kirby-grips, needles, in another box some letters; he slid one out and it smelt old and the ink was faded, signed *Mummy*. A school report, an 'O' level certificate showing that Pearl Friedel had passed in Geography, History and Art. A medical card, a recent photograph of her on skis, a birth certificate.

He shut the drawer and went to the built-in modern wardrobe – a tasteless thing she had had put in but adequate for its purpose. God, what money she must have spent! There were ten or twelve frocks, all apparently new! He was shocked. He could not tell from the labels on them whether they were very expensive but he thought not. Nevertheless they had quality of material and must have cost her altogether two or three hundred pounds. Of *his* money! *Given* to her, thanks to her Jew of a father, but nevertheless his money in the first place, and now she was squandering it. In a good cause perhaps: it was delicious to see her in something new, but this was going beyond reason. And shoes too! He bent to grasp a flimsy pair of high heeled gold slippers and picked up instead a pro-gramme which was lying as it had fallen between them. *'Royal Albert Hall. Welter-weight Championship of the World. Tuesday, 8th October.'*

He turned it over a couple of times and then opened it. In the list of supporting fights was: *'8 (3 min.) Round Featherweight Contest at 9 stone. Godfrey Vosper, Ken-sington, versus Vic Miller, Dundee.'*

Angell carefully put the programme back where it had come from and picked his nose for a moment. Then he closed the door of the wardrobe and rummaged among the scent bottles on the dressing table. Too extravagant. Alto-gether too extravagant. She had told him she could still get all perfumes at wholesale prices. It was natural she would be prodigal in the use of such things as she had once been concerned in the sale of them. Anyway he loved to have the scents about her. But extravagance was still extravagance wherever it was found. What was that thing out of Cato? *Emas non quod non opus est.* How did it go on? Buy not what you want but only what you have need of; what you do not need is dear at a farthing. Couldn't remember the rest of the Latin. Not that she would understand it anyhow. Ten new frocks and eight new pairs of shoes. He would have to reason with her. He would have to scold her for her spendthrift habits when she came in. Gently – but firmly. It could not go on like this or the wardrobe would not hold it all.

'You smell smashing,' said Godfrey. 'I like the smell. What is it?'

'Diorama.'

'It was different last time.'

'Yes, it was different last time.'

'What was it last time?'

'I can't remember. Jacques Fath, I think.'

'Fat! You should keep that for your husband!'

'I don't want you to talk like that. Otherwise I shall go again.'

'Sorry. My little Oyster. No harm meant. I won't say his name again.'

'Every time I think of him I feel vile. We've not been married a year!'

'That's not your fault. That's his fault for marrying a fabulous girl young enough to be his daughter.'

'That's an easy excuse. I went into it entirely of my own free will. I married him with my eyes open.'

'That's just what you didn't do, see.'

'What d'you mean?'

'You didn't have your eyes open. Not like a woman should. You don't mean to tell me that what happens between you and he is anything like what happens between you and I.'

'Why not?'

'Because I know not, see. Already – not the first time when you was all tensed up – but the last three times you been different, you been learning all the time, see. It isn't as if I didn't know.'

'I suppose you think you know everything.'

'Pretty near. In this line of country.'

'I suppose you've had hundreds of women.'

'Not hundreds. Scores maybe.'

'So one's much like another. Why did you persecute me?'

'You're not like the others. And aren't you glad I did?'

'No, I'm sorry. I was perfectly happy until you trapped me –'

'Liar. Oyster's a liar. I opened the oyster and found the pearl. And I'm going to do it again tonight.'

'I'm sorry I ever met you! You've got no respect for *anybody*. You just look on women as playthings –'

'Which they are. I'll show you.'

'Now that you've got me you think I'm no different from other women. Just another one to add to your collection! Just to make you more conceited than ever. Little *God*!'

'You're not sorry you ever met me, Oyster, and you know it. And you show it. So stop being funny, see. Or I'll stop you. That's better, I'll stop you.'

'You're no Little God. You're just a naughty little boy that likes collecting things. Why not caterpillars? Did you ever collect caterpillars?'

'Butterflies,' he said. 'Butterflies. You pin 'em down.'

'You know you're not even as tall as I am. You're just a little boy wanting to hurt people. All this –'

'Do I hurt you?'

'Sometimes. All this –'

'Don't you like it?'

'All this pretence of being in love with me. Don't. Don't. You'll tear it.'

'Then take it off.'

'Why should I? Why should I please you? Why can't you have patience? You've got no manners. You don't love me. Stop!'

'Then take it off.'

'You see? Just the bully. You think you've got me here now and can trample on me any way you want.'

'I'll not trample on you, Oyster. I'm not kinky. Grant me that.'

'Kinky? A bully is kinky. What do they call it?' For a long time then she could not get her mouth free. 'Sadism!' she gasped at last.

'What?'

'Sadism. That's what they call it. That's what you are. A beastly little sadist, wanting to hurt. Oh, Godfrey . . .'

'Stop talking.'

'Oh, dear, oh, dear, oh, darling. I – I want you so much, and you don't care anything for me. Nothing! Nothing! Nothing!'

'Everything!' he said. 'You bet your sweet life. I'm nuts about you.'

'Nuts,' she said. 'That's love talk, isn't it? Nuts. That's what you call love talk. You're a horrible boy. Vile, horrible, beautiful. I hate you, I hate you, I hate you, Godfrey. Stop it, leave me alone, take your hands off me! Be more gentle, be more gentle. I *hate* you. Godfrey. Leave me alone. Leave me alone, oh, darling. You destroy, you always destroy. There's nothing left. Godfrey, I love you, darling. I wish . . . I wish . . . I wish . . .'

No word from Switzerland. Francis Hone fumed, as Parliament was due to reassemble in a couple of weeks, and there would probably be an announcement about the Handley Merrick development. In answer to a parliamentary question probably. That was the way it would come out.

In the meantime Simon Portugal had been putting up the proposition that they should buy a row of houses on the opposite side of the stream from the Vosper property, and he suggested Angell should go down and meet the local solicitor who, although he practised in Sudbury, lived in Handley Merrick and seemed to hold most of the strings of village life in his hands. It would be premature to disclose the size of their plans but perfectly reasonable to meet and get mutually acquainted over this small deal on the side, for his help would be valuable later on. The weather was sunny and warm for late October, so Angell suggested to Pearl that they should go together on the last Saturday. Pearl said unfortunately she had a hair appointment. Wilfred said, what, in the afternoon? Well, it won't be difficult to cancel, ring them up now. For once Pearl looked sulky, but when he was adamant she gave way.

They went down in the Princess, Simon Portugal with them, and carefully talked no business on the way. The width of the car enabled them to sit in some degree of comfort. Wilfred joked about his size and confessed to Simon he was on a diet. Pearl who was sitting between them raised an eyebrow at this, for until now he had made it a condition of his mildly restricted regime that no one, *no one* should be told. At lunch at Chelmsford he refused to eat anything but an apple and some dry toast. He had been in a slightly peculiar mood, Pearl thought, for two or three days.

It was not until they reached Handley Merrick that Pearl realized this was where Lady Vosper had her family home. They passed the grey, porticoed Italianate mansion standing back some fifty yards from the road, and a chord of unease, like something half understood, half premonitory, twisted inside her.

While they called to see the lawyer, Pearl walked through the little village, which was tiny but beautiful. Its nucleus was a score of ancient timbered houses which leaned about in all directions like survivors of an earthquake. There was also a church with a square tower and a curious ornamented spike on the top, a pub called the Admiral's Arms with an inn sign of a sailor with a patch over one eye, and a few village shops. All were gathered about a stream-fed pond which had harshly pollarded elms and willows at its edge. In the church were three monuments to the fighting Vospers. North of this centre were a few bungalows and a score of council houses and a garage, but there had been no new building towards Merrick House which was some five hundred yards away to the south.

She walked back to the house and leaned over the gate looking up at its gloomy façade. Any moment, she fancied, Godfrey would drive round to the front in the jade-green Jensen, and that dark stocky vivid woman would climb in beside him. She did not know what the relationship was between them but the liberties he took suggested it was too close. Godfrey took liberties with everyone. Godfrey took liberties with her. If she thought about them she would not be able to walk back.

Angell and Portugal were about an hour inside, and then they came out and all took tea in the village teashop. Wilfred drank hot water and lemon and refused all food, but continued to be in good spirit and told Simon Portugal all about a hand of bridge he had played on Tuesday night. He had played it, he said, partnering his old colonel, who was now well up in his sixties but in the days when they first met had been one of the youngest full colonels in the British Army.

'I somehow never connect you with war, Wilfred,' Portugal said.

'Nor should you. Nor should you.' Angell lifted an imperious hand to the waitress. 'Our bill, please. Sometimes one is forced into situations which are entirely unnatural and unwelcome; but, being there, one endeavours to make the best of it. D'you know. Of course I was almost too young. But naturally one went. A good case could have been made out for deferment – I was a law student – but naturally one went.'

On the way home Angell, spreading his legs and linking his fingers, had more to say about his war experiences. The essential boredom and inconvenience, the endless organization and difficulties of maintenance behind the lines; the hideous lack of privacy, the shortage of reading matter; the advance to and retreat from Tobruk; the souvenirs he had picked up, the German helmet, the Luftwaffe wings, all of which he still retained as mementoes; the ruined white houses of Mersa Matruh looking out over the blue Mediterranean; the never-ceasing sand, smoking, biting, burning; the corpses, broken tanks, smashed machine guns, half buried in the drifts of Halfaya Pass.

'This would be 1942?' Portugal asked, thinking perhaps as Pearl was thinking that it made Angell older than he admitted.

'I was little more than a boy at the time. Little more than a boy. Later in the war I was sent back to England, worked in Whitehall. But those early days were the days of great hardship, and – if I may say so – great courage. Those were the days when one hardly dared think of victory, only of the avoidance of defeat. This is where I fancy the English spirit is at its best. I sometimes fancy we don't *really* enjoy winning. The wonderful camaraderie of our race shines in adversity. I remember an occasion when an English pilot was shot down in the desert . . .'

So he went on. This isn't quite true, Pearl said to herself; I mean, it may be all true what he says, but there's something not true in the way he says it. Has he seen all these things or has he *heard* some of them? He's talking to impress. This is a gayer, sort of younger, more disarming

Wilfred than the kind, selfish, pompous, stout gentleman I married. Is he talking to impress Mr Portugal or is he talking to impress me? A *braver* Wilfred. But anybody *less* brave than Wilfred . . . that time I had a sore throat, he kept away from me as if he was certain it was diphtheria. He can't *bear* sickness. He's afraid of death (that aeroplane). The thought of pain . . . Is it all something to do with the war? Did he have some terrible experience that he won't talk about? And yet and yet . . . He seems to be putting it on, not playing it down. Why does he suddenly want to appear brave? Is it something between us, something that's happened?

I think he's going to want me tonight. That glance as we got in the car. Quite hot for him. So tonight these heavy uncertain inconclusive caresses. Gentlemanly perhaps even in love. And by coming with him today I had to miss the caresses of the most ungentlemanly man I know. Not that Godfrey is clumsy or – or violent at the wrong time now. Perhaps *he's* learned something. But he's wickedly, overwhelmingly expert. Submitting, one knows. Already he seems to know everything about me, every weakness, vulnerability, response. So it isn't really submission any longer – or it doesn't seem so at the time. Soon he'll be as much mine as I'm his. Bad for his training; he doesn't seem to care. Should I? Cock-sure Godfrey, confident of always being Little God, playing Little God to women. Vital, conquesting; after all the resistance I went down; he must have felt all the time that I should.

Perhaps if I'd been honester, fallen easier and earlier, we should not now all be in this mess. What sort of wife shall I make tonight? *This* will be the submission, now, to Wilfred. The other is partnership. Wild, lustful, seeking, greedy, sweet, sweaty, trance-making. Deeps. Deeps within myself, I go giddy and fall. Godfrey was right, I didn't *know*. I didn't know myself. With Wilfred I never should have.

I am *fond* of Wilfred still; I *like* his weakness, I'm grateful to him and sorry for him. But I should never have encouraged him in love.

I don't know myself and I no longer think. Except to think that I am lost.

BOOK TWO

Chapter One

Flora Vosper came home on the 1st November. She was
very weak and only able to sit up for a couple of hours
a day, so Miriam engaged a nurse to look after her. But
Flora still wanted Godfrey's attention more than anyone
else's, and after three days of friction the nurse left. This
satisfied Flora who said she was quite capable of looking
after herself when Godfrey wasn't in; it didn't suit Godfrey who was training for three hours every morning and
wanted an occasional afternoon off to visit Pearl. They
quarrelled often, Godfrey and Lady Vosper, and shouted
at each other like fishwives, but most of the time there
was no one else in the flat to hear, and it was a surface
abuse that did not go very deep on either side. They
both laughed as easily as they cursed, and often after they
had hurled obscene insults at each other – with Flora the
more inventive – Godfrey would sit on the bed beside her
and coax her to eat something, or hold her head later
while she retched.

Flora's return made dates with Pearl far more difficult.
While Flora was in hospital Pearl could slip over to Wilton
Crescent on Wilfred's two bridge nights and they could be
absolutely safe. The worst that could happen if Wilfred
came home early would be that he found she had gone out.
Each time she wrote a little note and then got back in
time to destroy it. But no such easy meeting now. Flora
was in the flat all the time. Twice Godfrey had slipped
over to Cadogan Mews in the afternoon; but this carried
some risk not only of discovery but of gossip. Wilfred did
not seem to be on more than nodding terms with even his
closest neighbours, but who knew when one would not
perhaps consider it her public duty to send an anonymous

note about the young man who came at two and left at five?

They talked of taking a room somewhere, but with the next fight looming and Flora always demanding, Godfrey had no time to prospect for one, and Pearl had not the hardness of face.

In their after-love conversation there was never any mention on either side of the bigger issues involved. If Wilfred did find out and divorced her, would she want to marry Godfrey? More to the point, would Godfrey want to marry her? Their talk, in fact, seldom got off the ground. It floated around the trivialities of their own immediate existence and the nearest it came to being airborne was when Godfrey talked about his own future. Sometimes he would tell her about his life in the orphanage and his early days as a fighter, but he was no story teller and she had to fill in from her imagination.

She was herself too sunk in the depth of her first love affair to think clearly or to reason closely. She wasn't even quite sure that it *was* a love affair, as she had previously understood the words. In fighting against Godfrey in those early days she had been fighting something in herself.

As for Godfrey, he still crowed like a cockerel over his capture; but events were crowding in on him that made his enjoyment of her just that bit edgy. Flora's grave illness was irritating and a bit of a bind on his good spirits. He told himself that if the old cow died it wasn't his concern. But somehow he'd got saddled with her and while he would have thrown over without a thought any young woman who became a drag, he didn't quite come to the point of throwing over Flora. He comforted himself with the presents she constantly gave him; but in fact he knew these were chicken-feed to what he might be earning at boxing in a year or two if things went right, and it was vitally important to him that things should go right just now.

One morning Pat Prince kept at him about his footwork. 'Look, lad, you can't go for a right cross like you're doing now, that's if you want to keep out of trouble. You got to get your left foot forward when you throw the punch, else you'll be off balance, and you know where that'll land you.'

'I done it dozens of times, Pat,' Godfrey said tetchily. 'Look, you make it all sound like a flaming parade of tin soldiers. I'm too *quick*. I'm in and out and the balance takes care of itself.'

'I know, I know, you're a natural, we get the message. You're quick, granted, but the other bloke can be quick too, and your left leg doesn't come with the punch. If you miss –'

'I don't *miss* with that punch. I save it up.'

'All right, all right, big head, but don't forget you're going up the ladder and you're going to meet little fellers just as clever as you are. Let that other little feller just get his head out of the way by half an inch and you're a sitting target. *Boing!* The bridge you've made with your left hand isn't there any more, and he'll put you on your backside as sure as my name's Prince.'

'I can take care of myself, I tell you! The first time you see me on my backside'll be time to start nagging!'

Nose squashed flat between the pursed, narrowed eyes, Prince peered at him angrily. 'Look, lad, Jude don't like big-mouths in his stable! You come here to learn and I was told to learn you. I'm *paid* to learn you! If you don't like it you can bloody lump it, but so long as you're in this ring you listen to what I say!'

The next time Godfrey saw Jude Davis, Davis said: 'What's this I heard about you rowing with Pat?'

'Oh, it's nothing. But he nags like an old woman. I've got a natural style and he's trying to break it up.'

'He knows more than you'll ever know, Godfrey, I can tell you that. When you joined me you said you wanted to go places.'

'Well, have I let you down yet?'

'No, but it's early days. Goodfellow's a counter-puncher, wins all his fights that way. Your attacking style is just what he feeds on. Pat doesn't want you on the floor in the first round.'

'Nobody's ever had me on the floor in any round.'

'There's got to be a first time for everything. You're getting too uppish on too little, lad. And slack. You're not in top condition. I saw you this morning.'

'I'm fine. Don't worry your head about that.'

'I'm not worrying *my* head. It's you that's got to worry if you let things slide.'

'I'll lay you a fiver I finish Goodfellow inside the distance.'

'I'm not one for laying side stakes with my own boys. But there's plenty'll take you on. Don't think yourself into thinking you're the favourite.'

On the twelfth of November, Angell had lunch with Francis Hone.

'I persuaded Hollis to ring him yesterday,' said Angell, 'just to check that the documents had arrived. He was playing a golf match in Lausanne. His wife confirmed that he had received them safely. Beyond that nothing, no comment, no apology.'

'All these delays,' said Hone. 'It's infuriating. The fellow's been so damned dilatory, all through. D'you think there's anything behind it?'

Angell refused butter. 'I wouldn't think so. He's dilatory by nature; this is his reputation. After all, it's an aristocratic trait. Certainly I cannot see that there is anything more for him to hesitate over. He long ago agreed the broad outline of the deal.'

'If you don't hear tomorrow you'd better go over, see what's holding him up, and stay until it's signed and bring the agreement back.'

'I couldn't do that. Once negotiations have begun, it is unethical of me to approach him except through his own solicitor.'

Francis Hone stared at his fish as if it were a dissatisfied shareholder. 'Parliament reassembles tomorrow. From that moment the news may break at any time. I estimate that there's half a million pounds profit for us in this deal. It would be a disappointment to see it all fall through.'

'No one would be more disappointed than I would.' Angell took a bite of his unembellished sirloin steak. 'But it's completely against the canons of a solicitor's rules of behaviour to approach another solicitor's client.'

'What's the matter with you these days, Wilfred? You're eating nothing. You don't look nearly as well as you used to.'

'I'm extremely well, thank you, Francis. Never felt better. But I was overweight for my time of life. I have simply been reducing.'

'Is it to please your wife?'

'It's to please myself.'

They ate in silence for a while. Francis Hone's well shaven, well lotioned, carefully conditioned, iron-hard face, could have come off a Roman coin.

'It seems a pity.'

'What does?'

'To jeopardize this agreement with Vosper for the sake of an ethical scruple. It shows a lack of judgment on your part that I fancy you wouldn't have shown six months ago.'

'I'm sorry that I ever gave you the impression of a lack of scruple, Francis.'

'No, no, my dear chap, you misunderstand me. I never said that. I am trying to point out what seems to me to be a lack of judgment on your part which results in an *excess* of scruple.'

'I don't understand you.'

'I can hardly make it more plain. We are trying to pull off a successful business deal. In order to do so we have – to put it bluntly – withheld information from Lord Vosper which, were he in possession of it, would almost certainly cause him to call the deal off. This is good business. No more and no less. He will do very well out of the deal, even if not as well as he would if the deal did not go through. But if the vexed problem of ethics is to be considered, it should have been considered *there*, at the very beginning, not at a later stage when the work of months is at stake!'

'Broadly no doubt you are right. But . . .' Angell stopped. 'To put it crudely, since that is the way you wish to consider it, no one can ever know we were in possession of the facts about Flora Vosper's illness. Nor of the intended development scheme for that matter. And if they did, a solicitor, unless he is dealing with a client, is not bound to disclose facts detrimental to his case. But in this later matter everyone – or everyone in the firm of Hollis – would know that I had transgressed by going to see Lord Vosper now.'

'And do you value the opinion of Hollis & Hollis so much?'

'I value my reputation in the profession.'

'More than the very large profit which is at stake?'

Angell rubbed his hands across the looseness of his waistcoat. 'Some things are done, Francis. Some are not done.'

Hone grunted. 'You are the only one who knows Vosper, otherwise I would send someone else . . . if I sent someone else, would you go with them?'

'To see Vosper?'

'Not necessarily. If Simon Portugal went, he could call at the house alone while you stayed in Geneva.'

'What would be the purpose of my going?'

'Portugal knows all about the deal, but if Vosper is quibbling on some legal point, he might not be able to satisfy him. He could tell Vosper that you were in Geneva and call you in – even persuade Vosper to call you in. Would that overcome your scruples?'

'No. You see it would be my duty to inform Vosper that he should consult his own solicitor.'

'But if Portugal went and found himself in some legal difficulty, *he* would presumably be free to consult you if you were in Geneva?'

'Of course. He could consult me in any way he thought fit.'

'Then go.'

They looked at each other a moment, and Angell took another biscuit and an extra scoop of Stilton. One of the few compensations of fasting was that one savoured the precious mouthfuls even more.

'When?'

'Tomorrow morning, if Hollis has received nothing by then.'

'I only consent to go as Simon Portugal's legal adviser. He must make the call on Vosper.'

'I'll fix it that he is able to go.'

Angell picked up the last two crumbs and put them in his mouth. He had established his point and made his protest. That there might be encroachments on this strictly professional attitude when they got to Geneva he did not yet concede. But he knew Sir Francis Hone would expect him to concede something if the need arose.

One could of course always hope that the need would not arise.

'How long will you be away?' Pearl asked.

'If I go on the noon plane tomorrow I may well be back on Thursday evening. But it depends a little on the extent of the business I have to do.'

'Is it the same business like in March when we first met?'

'Similar, my dear. Similar. That's a pretty skirt you're wearing.'

'Oh, d'you like it? I thought you might think it was too short.'

'Well, yes, in a sense it is.'

'Will you ring me if you can't get back on Thursday?'

'From Switzerland? The expense would hardly be justified. Do you mind being alone in the house?'

'Oh, heavens, no. Not in the centre of London.'

'In the centre of London one can be much more at risk than in the country.'

'But one night. How shall I know if you're not coming back Thursday?'

'Well, perhaps I could wire you. Expect me for dinner unless you get a wire to the contrary. Are those those strange long stockings you're wearing?'

'Tights, yes.'

'They seem to go on for ever.'

'Well, not quite ever, Wilfred. Do you want a bag packed?'

'Thank you. Just pyjamas and a change of shirt. I shall not be home for Christie's sale on Thursday. I've put in a bid of £5000 for the Canaletto. You might –'

'Good heavens! Can we possibly afford that? I thought –'

'I put in the bid on my way home tonight on behalf of Francis Hone. I had intended to bid for him on Thursday. You might go, let me know how the bidding runs.'

'All right. Have you the catalogue?'

'On my desk. But take particular care not to catch the eye of the auctioneer. People have been known to buy things without intending to bid at all.'

'That's always the joke. I didn't know it really happened.'

Wilfred's eyes had been following her round. 'Do you know this will be the first night we have spent apart since our marriage?'

'Is it? Yes, I suppose so. Well, we haven't been married very long.'

'Long enough perhaps to take a look in perspective. Do you – regret having married me, Pearl?'

She was startled. 'Why should I?'

'I sometimes wonder. You're so very much younger. Do *you* regret it?'

Wilfred pushed back his hair and dabbed his forehead. 'That was not the point. But of course I do not. Much that I cared about aesthetically has found a new – a new outlet in married life. I didn't expect that to happen.'

'But why didn't you – expect that to happen?'

'Because for so many years I had thought aesthetic appreciation to be all.'

'D'you mean all these years you didn't ever even look at a woman?'

He was still occasionally restive at her lack of subtlety. 'Sometimes, of course. But you have not answered my question.'

'I've forgotten what it was.'

'Whether you regretted having married me.'

There had been a change in him these past two weeks. He was less guarded, less patronizing, slightly less certain of himself, it seemed. Even this evidence of modesty was slightly out of character. She moved across and put her hand on his shoulder. 'How could I? All this . . .'

He fingered the hem of her skirt. 'Good material. Silk? I never know. Very pretty anyhow. That aeroplane . . .'

'What aeroplane?'

'The one to Geneva in March. Has much to answer for.

She would have moved away but he had put his hand round her leg above the knee. 'Wilfred . . .'

'Yes?'

'I have to pack your bag.'

'Pack my bag with five dozen liquor jugs.'

'Pardon?'

'It's an old saying. One learns it in typing schools.'

'Wilfred, I never knew why you travelled by night that night that we met. Was it so urgent?'

'What? Oh, you could call it that. There were reasons.'

She stirred uneasily. 'What time are you leaving?'

'Not till noon. I have to make some telephone calls from here first. I may not yet even have to go.'

'I'll bid at the auction,' Pearl said. 'When you come back you'll find the whole place full of new paintings.'

He didn't appreciate the joke.

'You might watch the gilt on that chair. It could be brought up. It's looking faded.'

'I would if I was as old.'

'But you're not, Pearl, you're not.'

'I'll go and pack your bag,' Pearl said mechanically. 'I'm not sure how you are off for pyjamas. Can I buy you some new pairs while you are away?'

'No. Four pairs are ample. And anyway they have to be made. Control your extravagancies, my dear.'

'Control your hands, Wilfred,' Pearl said. But by now she knew she was fighting a losing battle.

No word from Vosper, so Angell caught the eleven-thirty a.m. plane in company with Simon Portugal. The flight was uneventful and Simon had brought paper work to do on the way, so Angell was free to brood.

The adventures of last night had brought on heart flutterings again, and he wondered whether he should have another check-up from Matthewson. But the prospect of those probing eyes and fingers, the expense, the discussion that was bound to follow, which irritatingly would touch on his marriage; his dislike of being thought to have followed Matthewson's advice – the added annoyance that he also appeared to have heeded Matthewson by reducing his weight, all this together was enough to put him off. He could of course call on his National Health doctor, but the man was always busy and one did not receive the courtesy due to one's position.

Today he was a little depressed. The heady excitements of last night had been fleeting; Pearl had seemed listless, formal, as if performing a duty. He felt he ought to discipline her by disciplining himself. At the moment satiety enabled him to look forward calmly to several weeks in which he abstained altogether from touching her until *she* began to miss his caresses and began to look at him with a puzzled air as if to say 'what have I done?' Indeed, there might come a time when she actually did say that, so that

211

he could reply, 'My dear, nothing at all, nothing at all,' but say it in such a way that she was prompted to question him more. So would come the carefully prepared, ineluctable moment when his caresses could be granted her as a favour, the more exciting for the delay and for the mental processes involved.

His limited intake of food was also a depressant factor. Hunger was a ghastly sensation. Three or four times, when he got mild stomach cramps, he had been on the point of abandoning the whole thing. Here too he knew himself to be imposing a strain on his splendid physique. Last night, after leaving Pearl – in the claustrophobia of his own dark bedroom – there had seemed some extra futility, some extra failure to be admitted, as if his marriage were bounded on either side by chasms of loneliness and failure.

Yet from all *reasonable* points of view his marriage was a success. His loss of weight clearly made him more attractive in her eyes, and it was already advantageous in rendering him less unwieldy in the processes of love. Each morning he carefully examined himself while shaving, and thrice weekly in his baths, and so far there had been no disagreeable wrinkling of the skin or adding of lines. He was a fitter man for it, and younger. Younger for his marriage. Younger for being with the young.

They reached Geneva in time for a light lunch, and Simon, with no regard for expense, hired a car to take him out to the Vosper villa. They had both booked rooms at a hotel overlooking the lake and, since Angell felt tired and had nothing to do here for the present, it seemed a wise precaution to rest. So he went to bed. It was a very rare thing for him to sleep in the afternoon, and perhaps this caused the disordered dreams. They concerned Lady Vosper. Angell found himself in her bedroom and she was sitting stiffly upright in bed, her black hair almost white now and dishevelled, her eyes bloodshot and staring, her face a grey-yellow colour, with blotches of pink that might have been insect bites. She seemed to be staring at him, but he could see that the counterpane which at first he had thought to be grey, was in fact grey with spiders, which seethed and crawled over each other and heaved as if they were feeding on something. She was saying something, whispering something, trying to scream and failing, trying to tell him something. 'I can't hear,' he said. 'They're making too much noise; I can't hear!' Then she suddenly stopped speaking and began to smile. But it was a hideous smile because she seemed to have neither teeth nor lips, and spiders were clinging to the aperture. She beckoned him to come to her. He said, 'I won't, I won't, I can't hear! I can't hear!' Reluctantly, controlled by muscles which did not do his bidding, he began to edge towards Lady Vosper and the spiders and the bed and all the festering infection there.

So the knocking on his door, which began as a noise in the nightmare sick-room and ended in an empty hygienic hotel bedroom with a brass bedstead and lace curtains caught up about the windows with cords, dragged him back gratefully to the fading daylight of a November day and presently, when he had struggled to the door, Simon Portugal.

Simon Portugal smiling. 'It's here. I've got it. No trouble at all.'

'What? What have you got?'

'The option agreement and the contract duly signed. I came straight back.'

Angell tied the cord of his dressing gown. 'I'm sorry. I fell asleep. What's the time? Have you even had time to go?'

Portugal tossed a document on the table. 'He'd already signed it last week before the necessary witnesses. He said he'd intended to post it but had not had the *time*. I thought I'd better grab it right away and bring it straight back.'

Angell fumbled on the table for his glasses, put them on, took up the document.

'Yes. Yes. They're both in order. That's splendid.' His sense of propriety reared its head. 'But, my dear chap, we shouldn't have *these*! These should go direct to Hollis. If he had signed them I wonder what the cause was of the delay.'

'I'd not met him before. Odd chap, isn't he. Francis had wired him telling him I was coming. After he'd established who I was there was absolutely no trouble. I suspect he's one of those chaps who will go so far in taking a vital step and then can't bring themselves to the last one. Also he'd heard Flora Vosper was ill. He looked at me a trifle

213

slyly after he'd given me the agreement and he said "maybe you're on a good wicket after all." '

Angell took off his library spectacles and blinked out at the evening lights beside the lake. 'Of course we can't keep them.'

'What d'you mean? Why ever not?'

'These should go to his solicitors who would inform us and then we should exchange this contract for the one our Company has signed – a counterpart of this – across a table and payment of the option money should take place at the same time.'

'Well, you can do that when you get to London. Take them along to Hollis and go through the ritual just the same.'

'It's most irregular. D'you know. Look, we must post these at once, just as if they came direct from Vosper.'

'I wouldn't answer for Francis's reaction if you let these papers out of your possession now! There might be several days' delay in the post from here.'

'Did you tell Vosper I was with you?'

'No. There was no need.'

'Good. Well, that's all to the good, then. Altogether, Simon, a happy outcome to our visit.' Angell was coming round after his sleep. His cautious legal brain was examining the situation. 'Where is Francis now? I think we should ring him.'

'He's out of town. He's at this directors' meeting in Wolverhampton.'

'When is he due back?'

'Late tomorrow, I believe.'

'Well, we'll have to strike a compromise on this matter of the exchange of contracts. I must have nothing to do with these documents. Nothing at all. I must not even have seen them. But you can take them back to London with you and post them there. There should be absolutely no delay then, and Hollis is not to know Vosper did not give them to some friend to take back.'

Portugal sighed. 'Anyway we've got them. The thing's settled. Whether you strain at the gnat is your concern. But can I leave the papers temporarily in your charge?'

'Yes, I suppose so. But why?'

'Well, there's nothing more for us to do officially and I've a friend I want to call on. I may stay to dinner. You'll be all right this evening on your own?'

'Of course.'

'I'll make a reservation for the noon plane tomorrow. We'll have to have a dinner later in the week to celebrate.'

'Well, I'll go and make a telephone call.'

After he had left Angell pulled up a chair and sat at the table and gingerly and rather guiltily read through the option agreement and the contract of sale, looking at them with a detached eye. He decided that between them he and Montagu had done a very good job.

He slipped the documents into their envelope and then into his briefcase. Now that he was on his own he decided to have a quiet little celebration tonight – a celebration of pure self-indulgence at the successful conclusion of this long Vosper affair. He had fasted too long – one meal could not hurt. There was a restaurant he knew where he had dined two years ago. They made the most perfect *soufflé au fromage*. And then *dorade meunière*. And the steak – you could have cut it with a fish knife. And *pommes bâtonettes* which were quite out of this world . . .

He went into the bathroom and turned the taps on. There was hours of time . . . Then a thought came to him and he turned off the taps. There was hours of time before one dined. But there was also time to catch a flight back tonight. If he left at nine he could be home long before midnight. It would mean that he could have a good night's sleep in his own bed, and be out early in the morning. Also, if he was prepared to overcome his ethical scruples, he could have the documents delivered to Hollis & Hollis by special messenger first thing. Until that was done the deal was not irrevocable. Who was to know who had despatched the messenger? Simon Portugal could well have done it. Any friend of Lord Vosper's. No one in the world that mattered would have any reason to suppose that he, Angell, had ever *been* to Switzerland.

There was another attraction to this idea. They had flown in today first class at the expense of Land Increments. If he could get a seat on the Tourist Night Flight he would receive a substantial rebate on his ticket, and he would be able to keep this for himself. It could easily make a difference of £10.

For a moment longer he thought lingeringly of the *pommes bâtonettes*. Then he came out of the bathroom and began to scribble a note to Simon.

Chapter Two

A seat was available and the plane left punctually to the minute; no fog impeded the landing at London Airport. Resisting the invitations of taxi drivers, Angell took the airport bus and just before midnight collected his bag at West London Air Terminal. There, reluctantly, he used a taxi, and was borne home to Cadogan Mews. Having given the driver six pennies by way of tip and apologized because he said he had no more English money, Angell took out his key and let himself into his house.

Pearl was usually in bed by eleven and there was simply no point in waking her to tell her he was home. It would be amusing when she walked into his bedroom tomorrow morning. Already a good deal of his irritation with her was dying down, and he looked forward to seeing her in the morning. He was still worried about the vital document in his bag. He wished he had not brought it, had refused even to touch it. Yet the urgency of the end on this one occasion just possibly justified the unethical act. Tomorrow he would be rid of it, and no one the wiser. Tomorrow it would be in Hollis's hands.

Still better, tomorrow morning he would be able to go to Christie's as arranged and bid for the Canaletto. Life suddenly seemed warm and cosy, just as the house seemed warm and cosy as he tip-toed into the drawing room and switched on the light. All the beautiful things he owned sprang to view. He had recently rearranged his pictures – an infallible recipe for newly appreciating them – and he stared at them one by one. And there would be others he would be able to buy now. Others. Others from the Vosper deal. He was not tired – after all it was only just twelve-thirty and he was refreshed by his sleep of the afternoon. He thought again of the miracle of the modern jet which put Switzerland within commuting distance.

He was as usual hungry. He had dined at the hotel in Geneva – on the Land Increments bill – and had eaten the sandwiches on the plane. But it was hardly enough, even for his present restricted intake. There had been some good cheese here last night – a sliver of Gorgonzola now on a thin slice of hot buttered toast. And a bottle of beer – cool but not chilled. And the later number of *The Connoisseur* which he had not yet opened. What could be more agreeably self-indulgent? He was *glad* he had come home. He switched on the fire, changed into his slippers and padded into the kitchen. He hoped Pearl had not put the cheese in the fridge. She must know better by now. Refrigeration, he often said, was one of the curses of civilization. It preserved things almost indefinitely, thereby helping the lazy housewife to become more lazy, and whatever it preserved it deprived of juice and flavour. He often thought that the joylessness of American life was due to the joylessness of their eating.

He passed the coat a second time before he noticed it. It was of brown leather with a zip up the front and two zip pockets. It was short and quite small and at first he took it for some sort of apron. Then he assumed it must be an old coat of Pearl's that he had not seen before. Then he concluded it was no such thing.

He picked it up and it did not smell of Pearl. It smelt of masculine things, not quite definable, cigarette smoke, beer, petrol, menthol or something. Not quite any of these but a mixture that might come from all. Angell began to feel a slight stomach cramp and knew it was not hunger. He dropped the coat in the chair and looked round the kitchen. Nothing else.

Two glasses in the sink; knives and forks, plates, too many to be sure. Why had she left them, though? The cheese, rightly, was on the cold slab, covered with a fine muslin cloth. He went back to the coat and unzipped the pockets. The first had a dirty handkerchief in it and a small roll of white gauze, two loose matches and a single stick of chewing gum. The second had two safety-pins and some calculations of money scribbled on the back of a creased envelope. The envelope was empty but had the name Bell & Croydon printed on it and the words *The Prescription*. Written in the centre of the envelope was 'Lady Vosper'.

He went back to the cheese and cut himself a corner, ate it on a dry biscuit. It immediately made him feel sick. He opened a bottle of beer and drank about half. He belched but did not bring anything up. Then he went back into the sitting room, drew up a chair to the fire and opened *The Connoisseur*. After ten minutes, having read nothing, he put it carefully back on the bookcase shelf and switched off the fire and then the light and tip-toed up to bed.

In his bedroom the pyjamas he had had clean on Sunday were folded on the bed, the book he had been reading, *Memoirs of an Art Dealer*, was on the bedside table with his bridge score, in which he had bid and made a grand slam in diamonds, marking his place. Above his bed was the Miro he had moved from downstairs. Beside it . . .

He went to the mirror and fumbled with his tie but did not take it off. The door between this room and Pearl's was closed. This was not unusual, they usually slept isolated from each other. But as he switched on the light in this room he fancied he had seen a chink of light framing the door to Pearl's bedroom. Now, with this light on, he could not tell whether he had been right.

He took out his ring of keys and went to the safe, opened it and put away the briefcase containing the Vosper agreement. Something in the back of the safe registered in his mind but he ignored it, shut the safe, locked it, left the keys dangling. He sat on the bed, kicked off his slippers. His heart was fluttering now, far worse than after his adventures in Pearl's bed. Carefully he leaned back on the pillows, found the light switch, flicked it off. It took about a minute for his eyes to get sufficiently accustomed to the dark to be sure there was a light in Pearl's room. It could not be some light coming in from outside through undrawn curtains; the light was the wrong colour. It might be that she was still reading in bed or had gone to sleep and forgotten the light.

He got up and moved a step or two towards her door. As he did so he vividly remembered his dream of the afternoon when he had thought himself in Flora Vosper's room. He had within himself the same utter reluctance to take one step more, the same nightmare necessity to do so.

He reached the door. His hands were trembling so that it was surprising that he was able to turn the handle without rattling it. He pushed open the door.

Pearl had not gone to sleep with the light on. She had

gone to sleep with the electric fire on, and this gave a subdued pink glow to the whole room. It was a discreet light, but what was to be seen could be seen very clearly. The blonde hair lay over the pillow and strands of it mingled with the black hair of the young man sleeping beside her. One of her arms was flung wide and her breasts almost exposed. The man lay with his face turned towards her and one arm, it could be guessed, probably lay across her body. Their breathing was quiet. It could have been the sleep of exhaustion.

It seemed to Angell that he would never be able to move his muscles again, that he would be forced to stay there until they woke, frozen into a stalagmite of horror and hatred and shock. But at last after some unspecified time that seemed like the turn of a century, he moved one foot back and drew the door to and carefully released the handle so that it should not click.

In his own room it was dark, but some light came in from outside so that he was able to move across to the dressing table without stumbling. Then he switched on a single light and saw himself staring at a stout dishevelled grey-faced old man whom he hardly recognized. His breathing was noisy and he tried to quieten it in case it should wake the sleepers in the next room. He sat down on a chair and put his head in his hands.

So for a time, while a car started up and accelerated away in the quiet street outside. His hands were still trembling when he got up and went back to the safe, reopened the door. He lifted out what he had seen the first time – the Smith & Wesson .45 revolver he had picked up in Mersa Matruh more than a quarter of a century ago. There had been two packets of bullets in the belt when he found it, still wrapped in their original grey paper, and these he had kept. With fumbling fingers he tore open one of the packets and broke the revolver and fitted the heavy bullets into the six chambers. Then he took the piece of oily rag out of the muzzle of the revolver and pulled back the safety catch.

Then with it in his hand he caught sight of himself in another mirror – a beautiful ornate Napoleonic mirror with gilt eagles above the glass. As soon as he saw himself he knew that these last few moments had been a sort of self-dramatization, a fantasy projecting itself into three or four actions that did not have any significance in real life. In a sense it was a desperate seeking after a remnant of self-respect, like someone gathering together the pieces of a broken vase so precious that one has to cling to the illusion for a little while that the shattered thing can be repaired. He knew, of course, that he would never have the courage to use this gun – even if it would still fire – neither on them nor on himself. Least of all on himself. He knew in his bowels that, apart from the corroding bitterness of betrayal, his chief emotion at this moment was fear lest Godfrey should waken and know he had been discovered. He knew that Godfrey the prize-fighter was immensely more dangerous with his fists than he, Angell, could ever be waving an antique revolver.

In any case all his training supported his craven instincts in insisting that no precipitate action must be taken now. Above all he must have time to consider his course of action to weigh the consequences of what he had found and what he did about what he had found.

Carefully he wrapped the revolver in its cheesecloth and put it back in the safe – took out his briefcase – then locked the safe, put the keys back in his pocket. He looked round the room. There was no evidence of his having been in here except the slippers by the bed. He picked these up and tip-toed to the door, switched off the solitary light and went carefully downstairs. Here he picked up his bag, and with his coat over his arm he silently left the house.

He spent the night at the Cadogan Hotel. About five he fell into a troubled sleep but was awake again before eight. He rang for breakfast and a newspaper but he found he could not read. He ate his breakfast – two eggs and four rashers of bacon, four slices of toast and marmalade and coffee with rich cream. At times his big frame was shaken with a tremendous anger, but each time it was a mountain in labour bringing forth a mouse. He could not even cry. This would greatly have relieved him – like blood-letting – but it did not come.

Once or twice he sat up in bed and cursed: cursed Pearl and her beautiful evil body and hoped and prayed it would rot as Anna's had rotted. Sometimes he directed his curses at Little God. It seemed to him that he had been the object of a gigantic conspiracy. Pearl and Godfrey had clearly known each other before; possibly his intervention had been discussed between them and it had been planned that Pearl should agree to marry him just to see what she could get out of him. No doubt a good part of the £5000 settlement had already gone to Godfrey. No doubt the jewellery he had been prevailed upon to buy would go the same way if they could get at it. No doubt they expected that Pearl would be able to twist him round her finger and eventually prise large sums of money out of him. It was a monstrous conspiracy which might have gone on for years but for this unexpected return from Switzerland. Perhaps even her grasping, acquisitive father was in it.

It would have been splendid if he had had the courage of his convictions last night and shot them both as they lay in their lecherous bed. *Crime passionel*. A distinguished solicitor killing to defend his honour. It would go down well in France, but an English judge would regard it coldly and without leniency. He, Wilfred Angell, bachelor of law of London University, would probably have to spend years in prison, whatever the extenuating circumstances. It was far better not. It was better to proceed slowly. It was better to take care. (Apart from the fact that he did not have a licence for the gun. As a memento of some earlier, braver and more heroic life, he had not felt able to part with it. Yet he had never been able to bring himself to pay the licence fee.)

Slowly, shakily, like a man recovering from a serious illness, he rose and washed and shaved. Had this betrayal occurred four months ago he would have felt far less about it. But since August he had committed the cardinal error of falling in love with his wife. This was not just hurt self-esteem; it was a dagger in the back.

He dressed and packed his bag and went downstairs and paid his bill. At some stage today he would have to return home and he had no idea whether he could hide his distress from Pearl or even if he wanted to. Anger surged up in him like lava in an erupting volcano. Even if he did not dare challenge Godfrey Brown he could well challenge *her*, could strike her, could beat her, could whip her naked with a leather belt.

222

But bitter distress followed anger and he saw plainly that if he did any of these things she would leave him and never come back. Fiercely though he hated her, he did not want her out of his life. If there were to be some revenge it must be on a woman who continued to be within reach. So divorce also seemed an unwelcome solution. It did not *punish* her enough. And it branded him as a cuckold. His friends would snigger among themselves and say, 'Poor Wilfred, but what else could he expect?'

He telephoned for a messenger, and when he came he gave the contract and option into his hand for immediate delivery to Hollis & Hollis. Then he left the bag at the hotel and began to walk across the Square and up towards Hyde Park Corner. Something must first be done with the day. Simon Portugal would be home about four. Perhaps it would be all right for him to return home now: if Pearl had recovered sufficiently from her prurient self-indulgence she should be at Christie's attending to the bidding on the Canaletto. But he dared not risk it. He could not risk facing her until he had made up his mind what to do.

He reached Hyde Park Corner and walked on to Green Park. For November it was a pleasant day, mild, with misty gleams of sun. The brown withered leaves scuffed under his feet as he walked. Shelley had described the autumn leaves as 'pestilence-stricken multitudes, yellow and black and pale and hectic red'. But it was people who were pestilence-stricken, sickeningly concupiscent, greedily lecherous, common scum, meanly vilely hypocritical and deceitful. Pictures, revolting pictures floated before his eyes, of Godfrey Brown, thin sharp vulgar midget of a man, crawling over that pale beautiful statuesque body. Like a giant worm, like a spider. Like a great grey spider. There had been something prophetic in the dream in Geneva.

He sat on a bench. At the other end of the bench was a nurse-maid with two little boys. They ran to and fro with shrill cries, sharp with incentive. The rumble of London went past him on the still air. 'I would ne'er have striven As thus with thee in prayer in my sore need. Oh lift me as a wave, a leaf, a cloud! I fall upon the thorns of life! I bleed!'

After about an hour it came to him that he was cold,

223

and he got up and walked down Brook Street to Claridge's, where he had his hair trimmed and a manicure. But his woe-begone expression in the mirror was no reassurance, and the manicurist's soft hands massaging his with cream reminded him unbearably of Pearl.

He went on to his club, but it was still some way from lunch time and there were few members about. The bar was open and he bought himself a stiff whisky and went into the library to read the papers. For a long time he sat staring at a book recording pictorially the latest Park-Bernet sales in New York. They meant nothing to him.

On quieter consideration as the morning progressed, he realized that some of his earlier conclusions were faulty. This could hardly have been a conspiracy from the start. Despite his very scanty personal experience of a woman's anatomy he knew that Pearl had not deceived him when she told him that he was her first man. Indeed he knew only too well that she had remained *virgo intacta* for about three or four times after their first adventure together. They had both been beginners, she no less than he.

There might still have been a lesser conspiracy to deceive, by acquiescing at her marriage to him for the sake of the ultimate profit, but, setting aside jealousy, a critical view wouldn't support the theory. Pearl's early attitude towards Godfrey had been one of dislike. It could have been assumed, but if there had been an understanding between them, why confess to him at all that she had known Godfrey before?

No, everything suggested that his base and vulgar deception was of recent growth, and everything – or almost everything – suggested that not Pearl but Godfrey was to blame. He fancied he knew when it had all begun, quite recently, because of Pearl's changed attitude towards him.

The luncheon gong had gone, and he went into the dining room immediately, the first there. He was not feeling convivial so he asked for a small table and picked up the menu. A waitress came across. He ignored her and went on staring at the menu resentfully. Clear soup, sole colbert, a fresh apple, a glass of white wine. It was as much as he would allow himself.

But why? But *why*? Was it going to make *any* difference now?

'We've some poached mussels, sir,' said the waitress hopefully. 'And the avocado pear's nice. And there's sirloin steak. Or . . .'

'Mussels,' said Angell. 'Yes. Bring me a plate of mussels. Say two dozen to begin.'

'Two dozen, sir? Yes, sir.'

'And I'll have a bottle of Puligny Montrachet with them. The '64.'

'I'll fetch the wine waitress.'

The mussels came and he swallowed them slowly while a few people filtered into the dining room and dotted themselves about the larger tables. Many of them he knew, but he contrived to be staring at something else when they came in. The mussels were excellent. The wine could have been a fraction more chilled. The waitress came across to remove his plate.

'I'll have another plate of mussels,' he said.

'Another plate, sir?'

'Yes. There's nothing in them.'

'Yes, sir. I'll bring them right away.'

Godfrey was to blame. One could see it all now. He was an extraordinary character: sneering, sly, insinuating, sexually mesmeric, with his beautiful hair and clear olive skin, vulgarly virile in his smiling, liberty-taking impudence; indeed with all the characteristics that would appeal to the lowest instincts in a common coarse-grained, unfastidious woman like Pearl. Even one like Flora Vosper who should have known better; but she probably had the jaded, sensation-seeking tastes of a faded courtesan. Possibly Pearl had tried to resist at first. Possibly she might have had that much faint fidelity.

He finished the second plate of mussels. As he did so a man called Chipstead took the chair opposite him. 'Hullo, Wilfred, mind if I join you? You're looking lonely all on your own.'

'Oh?' Angell's stare was not encouraging. 'No, I'm not at all lonely.'

Chipstead was an accountant who had done very well for himself as a result of some mergers, and he spent a good deal of his time out of his office and in the club. He fancied himself as an art collector and a judge of wine, but Wilfred thought little of him in either capacity.

'I see you bought a Canaletto this morning. You ought to be feeling cock-a-hoop, eh? Are those mussels good?'

'Quite good. Waitress, waitress!'

'Yes, sir.'

'Don't leave me all day. I want four lamb cutlets, well done, three potatoes baked in their jackets, and cauliflower. A double helping of cauliflower. And send the wine waitress.'

'Yes, sir.'

When she had taken his order too Chipstead said: 'I suppose it was the doubt cast on its genuineness that depressed the price.'

'What?'

'The Canaletto. I gather you took it to be genuine?'

'I did.'

'Well as I look at it you've paid a betwixt and between price. If it's genuine you've got one of the bargains of the year. If it's a copy, even a contemporary copy, you've paid three times what it's worth.'

Angell finished the last of his bottle of Puligny and ordered a bottle of Cheval Blanc 1961. It was disastrously expensive but what did it matter?

'I gather there's a whole flood of fakes on the market nowadays,' Chipstead said, and repeated his remark when Angell did not reply.

'The Canaletto is not a fake.'

'No. Well, not a deliberate one, I agree. These are deliberate ones I'm speaking of. There's Picassos and Chagalls and what-have-you. It makes one afraid to buy.'

Angell did not have too long to wait before his cutlets came.

'It's an extraordinary thing,' said Chipstead, 'the price one has to pay nowadays for almost any old junk so long as it's genuine. When my grandmother died in the thirties she had a lot of undistinguished Victorian paintings – a couple of dozen at least – and we sold 'em off to a dealer. I doubt if we got more than a fiver each for them.'

Angell split open his potatoes with a knife and put butter and salt and pepper in. The steam rose through his fingers. Godfrey was the one to blame. You could guess what had occurred by the change in his manner. Those first visits – obsequious, polite, the servant, then the gradual change with the glint of conspiracy in the eye, the dropping of the 'sir', the calling round when he wasn't at home; then the neglect, the near insolence in his voice when Angell had rung him that last time. The near insolence and the *triumph*. The insufferable triumph.

'I doubt if we got more than a fiver each for them, which wasn't nearly the value of the *frames*. Today – probably not one of those painters is anything like well known, but I'd guess the least they'd fetch in an auction room would be a couple of hundred guineas each. It just shows.'

Angell belched behind his hand and began to eat. He was miserable, sore, jealous, enraged; his mind's eye provided vividly obscene pictures that might have come from a postcard seller in Montmartre; they goaded him and would not let him rest; yet what he was eating and drinking was somehow becoming a defence against the worst that his imagination could do. Every mouthful that went down added something to the barrier against hurt, to the poultice on the sore place. His very hunger and emptiness over the last weeks contributed by contrast. Each gulp of wine helped in the anaesthesis.

The club made a splendid bread and butter pudding, a moist, creamy pudding full of sultanas that was far removed from what its name suggested; and after the chops he had this. As the tightness of his waistcoat increased, as the packing-in process neared its limit, Angell began to feel less hostile towards the brash intrusive fellow sitting opposite, a fellow who in the last ten minutes had been intimidated into silence. He began to talk a little, grudgingly, and they rose from the table together and had brandy and coffee and cigars together downstairs. By the time they separated it was 3.30 and, although Angell was still very unhappy, he was not as unhappy as he had been before. He felt very angry, rather confident of himself and sleepy. Outside the club there was a taxi waiting, and against the instincts of a lifetime he hailed it. In no time at all he was paying it off outside his home.

'Hullo!' Pearl called from the kitchen as he came in. 'That you, Wilfred? Safely back?'

'Yes, thank you. Safely back.'

She came out, looking cool and beautiful and completely unchanged. She put her hands on his shoulders and kissed

227

his cheek. Soft lips. Perfume. Lying lips. Common clay.

'Guess what?'

'What?'

'You got it.'

'What – the Canaletto?'

'Yes. It went to you at four thousand one hundred pounds. That was quite a bit less than you were prepared to pay, wasn't it?'

'Than Sir Francis was prepared to pay.'

'The bidding was very quick. I could hardly follow it. And then suddenly it stopped – like turning off a tap – and the auctioneer hit down with his knuckle thing and said: "Sold at four thousand one hundred pounds. Angell." Just like that.'

'Very good.'

'Did you have a good trip? Everything successful?'

'Very successful, thank you.'

'No fog this time? No diversion to Zurich?'

'No diversion.' Angell put his hand to his mouth and hiccuped.

There was no obvious embarrassment now they had met. The secret that each held bore no betraying stamp on their faces. Deception seemed as easy to wear as an extra coat.

'You look tired, Wilfred.'

'I am a little. One never sleeps as well in a strange bed. D'you know.'

'Are you going back to the office? Or shall I make you tea?'

'I had a meal. On the plane. A meal on the plane.' He took off his hat and coat. 'I think I'll go and lie down for an hour. I think I need the rest.'

'Of course,' she said. 'You do that. You look as if you need a rest.'

Flora Vosper said: 'Did you buy yourself a new dressing gown?'

'Yes,' said Godfrey. 'Like you said. Name on and all.'

'Well, that thing you wore at the Albert Hall. So loud and showy.'

'You bought me that too.'

'Nonsense. Maybe you bought it with my money.'

'Maybe. Anyway, this is much more luxe. I'd best be going.'

'Damn it, I'm here in bed and can't watch my little man.'

'You couldn't anyhow, Lady V. I told you. It's strictly for the cock birds.'

'Well, T.V. then. Why the hell haven't they put it on T.V.? Have you got all your kit?'

'My bag's in the hall. I think I got the lot. Towels, jock strap, foul cup, shower slippers. I only got one gum shield, but I've never needed more than one.'

'Borrow some cologne if you want it. Freddy Teasdale sent me a mammoth bottle while I was in the Clinic. Can't think why, I never use the stuff.'

'Thanks, I got some.'

'Any brandy?'

'No, never need it.'

'This man heavier than you, Godfrey?'

He sighed patiently. 'Three pounds at the weigh-in, that's all. I told you it won't do him no good because he's had to sweat it out to get under the limit. Much better to be eight-ten like me. No effort. I'd best be going.'

'What's he like, Goodfellow? You saw him?'

'Yeh, just to glance at. Oh, he's like any other man. Taller than me. Short hair. Eyes close together. Not tight built. *Long* muscles.'

'The paper says he has never been beaten.'

'Well, there's got to be a first time, hasn't there. And he's only had ten pro-bouts.'

'Don't let him spoil your looks, little man. That would be a pity just now. As I may have not much longer to enjoy them.'

'Lay off that talk, will you! It's bad luck before a fight.'

'Think I bring you bad luck?'

'Course you do. That's why I stick with you.'

'Give me a kiss before you go.'

'I'd give you something more if I'd time.'

He kissed her. She held his face a moment. 'Do I smell?'

'What? What's got into you now?'

'Sick people often smell. In the old days doctors would diagnose an illness that way. Will you tell me if I ever do?'

He pulled his face away. 'Horrible old bag,' he said. 'You know you are. Now tuck yourself in and be quiet. And think of Little God up in that there ring fighting for your life and honour.'

'Making a bad fellow out of a Goodfellow?'

He grinned and patted her cheek. 'That's it. You've got it, duchess. Back soon. Ta-ta.'

He caught a taxi in the crescent and was soon in Piccadilly. This was a lot different from fighting in Bethnal Green, or even the Albert Hall. Thick plush wall-to-wall carpet, posh waiters floating about, smell of food and cigars, murmur of conversation, a general air of luxury that you didn't expect in boxing; the clatter of plates as he went silently up to the fourth floor, chandeliers everywhere even in the dressing-rooms. The set-up was apparently that all the god-damn audience dressed in evening dress and had a slap-up meal with drink and the lot, and then when they'd had all they could carry they drifted down to the boxing ring and sat around and watched the fights and drank themselves insensible.

All the same he was impressed, as he saw the other fighters and trainers were, so that there wasn't the same noise as usual. Maybe this wasn't nearly so big an audience as the Albert Hall – or even Manor Place Baths – but it was more choosey, more select; there were people whose names you knew, T.V. stars and other jerks. Godfrey had never known what it was to be nervous but he could see Goodfellow was a bit on edge and this was a good sign for him.

Riling him a bit was the fact that he and Goodfellow were listed to come on second, which meant they were still one of the unimportant bouts, and maybe half the audience would still be not properly settled. He'd have thought after his Albert Hall showing he would have rated a better spot. And there was nothing much in the way of talent in the rest of the bill.

Pat Prince was there of course, peering at Godfrey through his thickened eyelids and uttering last minute words of advice. Soon it was time to strip and put on your trunks and have your hands taped. Then the two men who'd had the first bout were back and you were pushing your way out into this hot smoky arena where there were more chandeliers and a packed audience of men in black jackets and black ties, and then you were grasping the ropes and climbing up, trying to cough because the cigar smoke caught at your throat, and the ref was coming up to you, and in a minute the announcement was going to be made; but before it was made you noticed that it was a lot quieter than an ordinary hall and there was the clink of glasses and this pall of smoke and everybody watching attentively. At least you couldn't complain that the audience hadn't settled into their seats.

Even Angell had settled into his. It had taken some arranging at short notice but when he wanted something very badly he usually knew the right strings to pull.

The guest of Mr Berkeley Neill, the owner of a restaurant chain. Messrs Carey, Angell & Kingston had acted for him last year in litigation over the renewal of the St Martin's Lane lease. Mr Wilfred Angell, the guest of Mr Berkeley Neill, taking up a new interest, watching the new white hopes of the British boxing world.

They had had dinner on the sixth floor – some two hundred dinner-jacketed men – a modest meal by Angell's standards: four courses which would put him on for an hour or two – with some passable Chablis and Chateauneuf and banal, noisy conversation. Mr Neill had a table for eight, and Angell thought the company commonplace and over-hearty. He avoided taking a 10/- raffle ticket on the grounds that he could not possibly predict any of the results.

Eventually they rose and went down two floors to the room where the tournament was held; similarly elaborate in its decorations, with the ring raised in the middle. Mr Berkeley Neill's party had seats reserved at the side. While the first fight was taking place a half bottle of whisky and some soda were put unobtrusively on the table beside Angell, and he helped himself to a stiff drink as the bout proceeded.

This was the first tourney Angell had ever been to, and like his wife at the beginning of the year it was to watch Little God. If it had not been for this preoccupation, which gripped at his bowels like mild enteritis, he would have had leisure to feel a full and satisfying intellectual contempt for this atavistic primitive entertainment. Grown men, adult men, supposedly cultured, dressed themselves in dinner jackets, wined themselves and dined, and then, stomachs filled and cigars going, they took their seats to watch these bizarre bouts in which young men attempted to beat each other down with their fists. It was cock-fighting on a licensed, twentieth-century, supposedly civil-ized basis. It was the bully-in-the-dormitory still coming out, the university rags, the fox-hunting, the duck-shooting, the inbred desire to hurt or see hurt, the uncouthness of man, a schoolboy brutishness, neatly packaged and pretending to take dignity from its smart surroundings.

So he just had time to think. Just time and leisure to despise the entertainment before the entertainment for which he had been waiting gripped at him. Peter Good-fellow of Walsall. Godfrey Vosper of Kensington. Climb-ing into the ring, two small men. That was he: take a good look at him again. At first he was hidden by his seconds, then he took off his dressing gown and stepped into the middle. Very smart. Vivid scarlet silk trunks, scarlet socks and boots to match. Quite the dandy. (On whose money?) Referee talking, back to their corners. The bell.

In the first round Little God made all the running. His opponent was for ever backing away, side stepping, using the ring, getting out of trouble rather than initiating any-thing for himself. Goodfellow was a tall young man with a slight stoop and a shuffling stance. Compared to him little Godfrey was perfectly built for his size, muscular but slight, balanced, quick as light and so good-looking.

Seeing him now nearly naked Angell realized more than ever his attraction for women; even, one would imagine, his attraction for some men. Angell felt that attraction. which to him was like the reverse side of hate. In the boxing ring Little God was nearly beautiful, but it was with the effortless grace and poise of true evil, Angell thought. If Angell had been a praying man he would at that moment have begun to pray for the other side.

At the end of the second round he was surprised to hear Neill say to his other neighbour: 'Goodfellow's well ahead so far.'

'Why d'you say that?' Angell asked, gulping his whisky. 'What makes you say that? It seems to me that the other man, Vosper, is attacking all the time.'

'So he is, and it's getting him nowhere. You're not attending. This little fellow Vosper is pushing ahead all the time and doing all the leading but mostly he doesn't even connect. Goodfellow brings up a counter about a dozen times in a round and he scores every time. He's way ahead.'

This view was put to Godfrey by Pat Prince. 'Box him,' he urged. 'Try to get him to come to you. And if you do have to follow him try to get inside. His reach is too long for you.'

'O.K., O.K.,' Godfrey said, as Prince slipped in his gum shield just before the bell.

He had realized as clearly as anyone that his present tactics were giving Goodfellow the contest on a plate. Goodfellow was a brilliant *boxer*. He had made Godfrey miss more often than he had ever done before. By just shifting fractionally he wasn't there. His shambling footwork was deceptive. His low guard, almost casual, was deceptive. Half the time you'd think he was coasting along. Like someone doing the twist. Watching his opponent thoughtfully and every now and then putting through a little jab that sent Godfrey's head back. It made you mad. But with this sort of character it didn't pay to get mad. You'd got to match cunning with cunning.

Goodfellow in a corner. Godfrey aimed two lefts at him and a vicious right, all as fast as a snake. Not one of them touched Goodfellow. Without ever raising his gloves he avoided them, and then quickly slipped away into the centre of the ring. Like Trappist monks breaking their vow of silence, the audience applauded.

'Gentlemen, please,' said a voice reprovingly over the microphone.

Godfrey followed like a bull being goaded with a red cloak. As he partly rode a counter-punch that caught him on the side of the jaw, some words of Prince's came back: 'If you do have to follow him try to get inside.' Godfrey feinted twice with his left, took the counter-punch high up on his forehead and then went left, right, left for Goodfellow's body. Only one of them got through that low guard, but he heard his opponent's grunt and suspected that he had found a weak spot. He cursed himself for not having seen this weakness before. Goodfellow, with his supreme timing and sense of balance let his jaw and face take care of themselves. His low guard was not a casual pose, it was deliberately kept low to guard his long thin rib casing.

By the end of that round, Godfrey knew he had as much chance of outpointing Goodfellow as of being elected to the Athenaeum. So it was now all a question of time. Time and stamina. If he could wear Goodfellow down in the next three rounds with a heavy persistent attack to the body he might get a K.O. in the eighth. But it was not going to be easy, for it was he who had been rushing in and using up his vitality; Goodfellow had been pacing himself for the full half hour: Godfrey's gloves were beginning to feel heavy: he was not in the condition he ought to have been. Too many sick-room vigils and too much Pearl.

'You done better that round, boy,' said Pat Prince, giving him the bottle to rinse his mouth. '*Box* him. Try to get him to do the work.'

Fifth round began like a continuation of the fourth. Feinting to the face and the jaw did not bring that guard up. The only way you got that guard up was by inviting the counter-punch. And if you invited it you usually *got* it. That was the trouble; you swapped; and on the whole you were the gainer; but you'd wasted four rounds and the energy of four rounds.

'I'll hand it you, he's a game cock, your man,' said Berkeley Neill. 'He never stops or lets up, does he.'

'He's not my man,' snapped Angell, mopping his brow. It was very hot in here. 'Goodfellow deserves to win.'

'Ah!' said Neill, 'that hurt Goodfellow. He's in trouble. *He's in trouble!* Watch that. Your little fellow has the guts of the devil.'

Goodfellow was in trouble because for once Godfrey had really got through his guard and had landed two punches near the solar-plexus. The gong came just in time. Godfrey was bleeding at the mouth, and there was a nick over his bad eyebrow, but these were superficial things, while Goodfellow was grunting and blowing in the other corner.

'Bore in,' urged Prince. 'Go after him, but watch his left. He'll keep scoring with that and it can still be dangerous.'

The sixth round was Goodfellow's all the way. Weakened by those jabs to the body, he retreated all through the three minutes yet scored persistently with counters, sharp crisp

234

jabs with no weight behind them but every one a score in any referee's book. It was beautiful boxing, with Little God throwing punch after punch and finding only the air a skin-breadth away from his opponent's face and body. Godfrey's gloves, for almost the first time in his life, felt like lead. At the end of the round he sat back with his eyes closed taking slow deep breaths. He'd got sixty seconds to recover. He ignored Prince's whispers and let himself go completely limp. When the bell went he opened his eyes, got up slowly, then moved after Goodfellow in continuance of the old pursuit.

But if he was tired so was his gangling opponent. It was tired science against tired brute stamina, and in the second minute Godfrey got in two punches with his fully balanced weight behind them. He saw Goodfellow's eyes go glassy, he threw everything into the next sixty seconds, aiming for the body, punch after punch that Goodfellow only partly blocked. Then with sudden inspiration he saw that Goodfellow's guard was low for the wrong reasons and switched his attack to the face. That did it. Click, click to the jaw, the young man's knees sagged. He half lolled against the ropes, straightened up, Godfrey went in for the kill, but the referee was in the way. The referee had put his arm up, was pushing Godfrey back. Reluctantly, angrily, Godfrey stopped fighting. The bell went, the bell for the end of the seventh round. But it was a cheat, he'd been cheated of a fair K.O. The blasted referee . . .

The blasted referee had come across and was holding up Godfrey's hand. There was applause. Goodfellow was sitting on his stool and his second was sponging his face. So it was the end of the fight. The referee had awarded Godfrey victory on a technical K.O. It was all right then. But it would have been better to have seen Goodfellow on the floor.

'Go across and shake his hand!' Prince hissed in his ear.

'What?'

'Man, it was a great fight! Go across and shake his hand!'

So Godfrey went across and reluctantly shook Goodfellow's hand.

Chapter Three

'My dear Wilfred, it's not as easy as you appear to think,' Vincent Birman said, smiling his fallen-cherub smile reprovingly at the law books; Button on Libel, Wilshere's Leading Cases. 'Not easy at all.'

'You gave me the impression. You said that in the boxing world most things could – be arranged.'

'Did I? Well, hardly. Of course it's true in a way. Where there's big money involved there are always pressures. Boxing doesn't escape.'

'Well, then.'

'But you mistake the ends to which the pressure may be directed. I –'

'Last time you spoke of it you said the organization of the profession was directed by one or two men.'

'That's true enough. But I was shooting my big mouth in a general way. The boxing world, like some others, runs as a closed shop. Intruders in that closed shop are *not* welcomed. Far from it. But if you accept that, and most people do accept that, then the works run smoothly and without interference. There *is* no interference from outside – not the way you want it – the way your client wants it. Pressures, if or when they are applied, are not used to help somebody to even up an old score.'

'My client,' said Angell sourly, and tapped the end of his spectacles against his teeth. 'Well, I've told you what he wants.'

'He's certainly changed his opinions, hasn't he? Different from a few months ago when he wanted him helped.'

'I attempted to reason with him. He was not reasonable.' Birman transferred his smile to his finger nails. 'But you're still acting for him?'

'Well –' Angell shifted in his chair and swallowed some spittle like a bitter medicine. 'He's an old client. Er – long and very substantial connections. This – clearly this is not the sort of business one would wish normally to – er transact. I was on the point of refusal, but I consulted my partners. They thought, in view of what you had told me, we might continue to . . .'

'Can't he wait? Getting beaten in the ring – soundly thrashed as you call it – is bound to happen to Brown sooner or later without any interference. It's an occupational risk. It happens all the time.'

'Unfortunately no. He did not seem willing to wait.'

Birman allowed himself a curious glance. He was no student of human nature; he was not sufficiently interested in other people; to him they drifted by as casually as twigs down a stream. Neither psychiatrist nor priest, he offered the impersonalness of the couch and the anonymity of the confessional, so perhaps to him more than to most, people betrayed themselves. Over the last six months an old school friend and a distinguished solicitor had been stepping out of character. Angell perhaps had never been the typical lawyer: after his slow emergence from the timid youth and the reluctant, inept soldier, there had always been a degree of flamboyance about him, and this had grown with the years: his size, his walk, his talk, his large gestures, even his meannesses. But lately he had become tight drawn, more imperative, less cautious in his judgments.

Experimentally Birman said: 'This could cost your client a lot of money.'

'He seems,' said Angell, closing his eyes, 'to be prepared to pay for this. To pay for his whim. Within reason, of course.'

'Look, Wilfred, I don't think he knows quite what he's asking. Or you either. I don't even believe it's possible. Fighters aren't matched out of their class. That's why there are divisions, eight divisions. You might get this Brown character matched with a light-weight, that's the most you could do: but you don't often do that. And even then it might not work. You ever heard of the *Boxing News*?'

'A paper, is it?'

'Right. Well, the *Boxing News* publishes ratings. Your lad appeared in them for the first time this week, because he beat Goodfellow. He's rated seventh in British featherweights and Goodfellow is now rated eighth. Well, Jude Davis's next job is to get him matched with the next above him – or the next one above that. That's the sort of match he'll expect – and everyone else will expect him to have – next. Even if Davis could get a matchmaker to line him up against Boy Anderson, who rates top in England, I doubt if Anderson could be persuaded to sign! And if they *did* fight, and your lad got badly beaten – which isn't such a foregone conclusion after his bout with Goodfellow – it would be a bad mark against Davis, who would be blamed for spoiling a good fighter by pushing him on too fast.'

Silence fell. Angell still tapped his teeth. 'It *could* spoil him, such a match?'

'Oh, it does indeed sometimes. Even a hard slogging fight can take something out of a fighter that he never gets back. It doesn't *end* his career, but he starts going downhill instead of going up . . . It's a question of *degree*, of course. Being beaten a few times in a normal way does no one any harm. Maybe it even helps if it cures a swelled head . . . Goodfellow, for instance, came to no physical harm for being beaten by Brown. But it did underline his lack of stamina. What a wonderful boxer! If he only had stamina he'd be world champion in eighteen months . . .'

Angell was not interested in Goodfellow. 'Our client instructs us.' He put his hand on two volumes of the Law Reports for 1936, seeking extra authority. 'He instructs us. We only interpret his instructions.'

Vincent Birman lit a cigarette. 'Well, I can *try*. But I could only try by the direct approach and by talking big money. A thousand in cash, say.'

'As much as *that*? . . .' Angell rubbed startled fingers. 'Oh, I don't think that. It could surely . . . be done for *much* less.'

'Have you your client's sanction to talk in those terms?'

'No, no. Impossible! It's a monstrous cost.'

'It's a monstrous thing you're asking. Frankly with less than a thousand to offer I don't think I'm prepared to make the approach.'

The telephone buzzed. Angell picked it up and after a moment snapped: 'Tell him I'll ring him back,' and slammed down the receiver. '*Well?*'

'Well, you heard what I said, old man.'

'Could you not try someone higher up?'

'You'd be wasting your time. Who is there? Eli Margam? He wouldn't raise a finger. Boxing has its crooks but they're not crooks in this way.'

Silence fell. It was the more noticeable for Angell's sudden violence over the telephone.

'You'll of course exercise every discretion,' he said. 'This firm, the name of this firm, mustn't be mentioned.'

'D'you think you'd like to sleep on this for a day or two more?' Birman flicked ash off his MCC tie. 'Maybe some other idea . . .'

Angell shifted his legs where his trousers were tight. 'The thing – it's been looked at all round. For more than a week. My client is not in a, well, a charitable frame of mind. Of course if you're unable to do anything . . .'

'It wouldn't be sense to go with a smaller offer.'

'If you're unable to do anything I shall tell him so and that will finish it. His other business – extensive – we might lose it. But, well. If you see Davis, see what his reaction is. If it is entirely negative that will end it.'

Jude Davis said: 'Look, Mr Birman, if that's your name, I suppose you know that by rights I should have you thrown out of this office.'

Birman's bright blue eyes were slightly bloodshot, like stained innocence. 'Much what I've been thinking myself. But few things go by rights these days, Mr Davis. Don't be offended, please. Y'see I'm only the go-between and I put a proposition to you that was put to me. Frankly I only saw this lad box for the first time at the N.S.C. last week and I don't know how you rate him. It's really whether you rate him worth a thousand pounds.'

'It's also how I rate my licence with the British Boxing Board of Control.'

'Well, I don't know. Is it? Of course, if it ever came out. But it never could. Could it? You're Brown's manager. You match him as best you can. If you match him too high it's an error of judgment. How good *is* he, by the way?'

'What's it to you?'

'Well, I only asked.'

Jude Davis scowled. 'He *enjoys* fighting. He's a natural. May go a long way.'

'So will a thousand pounds.'

'The door's behind you, Mr Birman.'

'You think he may go a long way but you won't back your fancy, is that it?'

'What d'you mean?'

'Suppose you could match him with Flodden. He's number two, isn't he? Flodden might knock your lad out in three rounds. But on the other hand he might not. That's what I call backing one's fancy. After all, if you take this offer you can't *guarantee* that Brown will be beaten. You only guarantee to match him out of his class. I would call it easy money looked at that way.'

Jude Davis said wearily, 'Look, Mr Birman do me a favour and go away. I'm being very patient with you. I'm a manager. Does that mean anything to you? I look after my boys and Brown is one of them – *now*, thanks to you or your client. What's got into him, your client? You acting for a lunatic?'

'No, just someone who's changed his mind and has money to waste.'

'Well, tell him to go waste it somewhere else. Tell him to go jump in the river. What sort of a reputation does he think I have, eh? What sort? Who was it coached Llewellyn Thomas all the way from a butcher's shop to European Light Heavy-weight Champion? D'you think I did that by selling him down the line to the first crooked punter who came along? And I've got a good group of boys now. Tom Bushey is the best spade in England: in two years he'll be challenging for the title. Tabard's another. Little God might be a third. I don't know yet. I don't know.'

'I thought the other night he was more a fighter than a boxer.'

'He's a *natural* fighter but he boxes too. He's uppish and he's got too much spunk, but if I bring him on right a thousand pounds may be nothing to what he'll earn me. What sort of a manager d'you suppose I am to arrange that he shall be hammered by one of the top boys?'

'So you think he might be British champion?'

'I think he just might be British champion. It depends how he develops, whether he's quick enough and ready enough to learn.'

'My friend might go up to two thousand pounds.'

'What's got into him? He ought to be certified. Why this vendetta? You're a man of the world, Birman,' Davis said petulantly. 'Maybe you know some of the snakes wriggling in the undergrowth. For two thousand pounds you don't *need* to arrange a hammering in the ring. For that kind of money you can hire a couple of thugs from Birmingham or Liverpool who'll come down and knock Brown off and drop his body in the river. You don't want me to tell you that.'

'I know. It just happens that my friend is a respectable citizen and –'

'*Respectable?*'

'*Very*, but losing out . . . Anyway, dear boy, he's not looking for that sort of blood. He's a law-abiding citizen, too cautious to step far off the track but wanting to see Brown defeated for personal reasons of his own.'

Jude Davis twisted with his little finger at the wax in his ear. 'He'd not make *anything* out of this, you know, however it was planned. However you fixed it, the other fellow would be so much the favourite that you wouldn't get any odds at all. He'd never get back two thousand pounds, not in this world. He needs to go to a skull-scraper.'

Birman rubbed his hand along the threadbare arm of the chair. He detected the first weakening of Jude Davis's completely adamant attitude. A move from hostility to curiosity, the way temptation comes.

'Shall I leave the suggestion with you for a day or two?'

'You can leave it where you want – put it where you want.'

'Really it's a question of rationalizing it, Mr Davis, isn't it? Look at it from my point of view. I think my friend is nuts wanting to spend his money this way. But it's his money and why should I refuse to let him spend it? Why should you?'

'Because I have to do a lot more for it.'

'Well you get paid a lot more for it.'

Their eyes met and Jude Davis shook his head. 'It certainly takes all sorts.'

'Let me give you my card,' said Birman.

'Drop it in the waste-paper basket.'

'No, no, certainly not.' Birman got up, and the unshaded light glinted on his hairless head as if it had a laminated cover. 'I'll leave it here. Think it over. Just think it over,

Mr Davis. It's a big sum. You can't lose.'

'Brown can,' said Davis.

'Oh yes, that's the point, isn't it. Brown can. But what can he lose? A single fight? I've no doubt my friend would like to see him really punched up, but who is to say it would happen? No one can predict exactly what is going to take place in any ring once the gong goes. What are good referees for but to stop a contest when one boy is getting the worst of it, before he gets too badly hurt. My friend is in no position to stipulate what has to happen. He can only pay for a set of circumstances and then watch them work out. You would get well paid for providing the circumstances, that's all. If they don't work out as he wants them to he can only complain. If he complains you don't have to listen.'

Jude Davis took off his gold-rimmed glasses. 'Whose side are you on, Birman?'

'Nobody's, my dear chap. I only do the job of work that is put before me.'

'I'm in the ratings now,' Godfrey said, 'that means something. It means I'm on the ladder! It means I'm one of the named ones. One of the feathers in this country! I'd have been kicking my heels for another year with Rob Robins and nothing like this. I'm on the way up, Oyster. Don't make no mistake.'

'Godfrey,' she said. 'Godfrey, I don't think we can go on meeting like this.'

'What? Why not?'

'It's not safe. I'm scared.'

'Scared of Wilfred? Oh, come off it!'

'No, it's *true*. You think he's nothing to be afraid of – and maybe he isn't, physically. But I'm his *wife*. He's my husband. I don't *want* him to find out, at least not yet, not this way. I couldn't bear it if he came back for something one afternoon and found us. I *hate* the feeling of betraying him. All the time. Truly.'

'But you don't hate being with me.'

'Of course I don't hate it. Not now. I don't know what's happened to me. Not now. You ought to know . . .'

'Yes, I know. I know. So that's the important thing, isn't it?'

'Well, yes. But is there nothing – no other place safer than this? You did say about taking a room somewhere.'

'I been thinking.' Godfrey ran a hand restlessly all over his head so that when it was done his hair stood up like the crest of a cockatoo. 'How would it be if you came round to our place?'

'What, Wilton Crescent? Lady Vosper is there.'

'I know that. As if I didn't know that. But she never gets out of bed now. Not except to go to the bathroom. We'd be safe enough in my room. She's never been in there in six months.'

'I *couldn't*! I couldn't begin to relax, to enjoy anything.'

'I'd make you relax. You know that.'

'No. Not ever. Even if I could, I wouldn't. It would be far worse even than here. I don't know how you can suggest it!'

'O.K., O.K., it was just a thought. Forget it. Not to worry.'

'What's the time?'

'Only just four. There's plenty of time. Slip that pillow from under your head.'

Presently the telephone began to ring in the next room. They lay in silence while it went on and on. Pearl made a movement to get up but he gripped her and held her down.

'You're hurting me.'

'Relax. You went to the post at four. Remember? Pity you was out.'

'You see what I mean,' she said. 'Now I'm all tensed up; I *can't* go on like this.'

'Well, we're going on like this now.'

At half past four he got up to go, pulled back a curtain and peered at himself in the mirror. 'My lip's still swelled at the side. It's taken a long time this time. Kissing doesn't help, mind.'

She lifted herself on her elbow, stared at the young man she had thought she hated. Even now she could not understand. It was as if for months she had been shoring up a dam, patching the tiny leaks, dreading the menace on the other side. Now it had happened, she was swept away, sometimes swimming ecstatically, sometimes drowning.

'Your next fight doesn't have to be for a long time yet, does it?'

'Nothing's lined up, but I've got to keep in trim. I want one more fight this year. I'd like to meet Pat O'Hare. One fight before Christmas and three after, I'd like. That'd put me one off the top before next summer.'

'D'you never *think* of being beaten, Godfrey? Doesn't it – don't you ever consider it at all?'

'Oh, I could maybe have bad luck, slip at the wrong moment, or get a bad decision. But not else. I *know* I'm good, see. That makes all the difference.'

'And the week we never saw each other – it was just because of your face that you didn't come?'

'Hey, hold on, what's all this "just because" of my face. I'm attached to my face. I got to take care of it. I don't like it when it's mussed up. And I don't like you to see it either. Maybe you'd go cold on me. Maybe you'd start handing me off again. Like before.'

'You know that won't happen.'

He pulled on his jacket, zipped it up.

'Godfrey. It can't go on like this for ever, can it. Between us, I mean.'

'Why not?'

'It's too sordid. You coming to see me in the afternoons or when Wilfred's away. Meeting at the movies. Hole in corner arrangements. You must see it can't go on like this.'

'You just said you didn't want Wilfred to find out.'

'I don't, this way. I'd *hate* it. If he has to know then I want to *tell* him, not any other way. So that it could be a complete break. So that I could give him back his money, as much as I have left.'

'What money?'

'He made me a settlement when we married. Dad insisted on it.'

'Good for him. How much?'

'How much? It was £5,000. I've spent about a thousand of it – or nearly that.'

Godfrey came across and patted her cheek. 'You'd be strictly birds to give him any of that back. Why, stone me, an old gent like that's already had his money's worth. You keep it, Oyster. Keep it for a rainy day.'

'And us?'

'Give it a bit of time. We're all snarled up right now. Look, I've got Flora on my plate still. She's had her chips

244

– it's only a question of time. But I've got to stay with her. As for me – I'm on the up and up. Give me another six months and who knows where I'll be. Let's float around like we are for the present, eh?'

'Have you *got* to stay with her?'

He wrinkled his scarred eyebrow, observing his own expression in the mirror. 'When an old girl like that is dying, there's always pickings to be had. Why should I push off now and leave it to her daughter or some toffee-nosed nurse?'

Pearl shivered. 'I don't *want* you to talk that way . . .'

'Can't please you anyhow, can I?'

'Are you by any chance *fond* of her?'

'God Almighty, haven't you seen her?'

'Yes. Yes, I have.'

'She's nearly old enough to be my grandmother, and she was no oil painting to begin. But she's a poor old wreck now. Dead but won't lie down. So Little God stays on to see what he can get. I'm not pinching what don't belong to me. I'm just staying around and seeing her off. When she's gone maybe we can start thinking again, eh? How's that? That please you?'

'I never know,' she said. 'I never know if you mean what you say.'

'Where the hell have you been, you bloody little twerp?' Lady Vosper demanded.

'Oh, flip off. You can't have me hanging around your neck twenty-four hours a day. For crying out loud! Chauffeurs' Union won't allow it anyway. What's wrong with you? What's biting you?'

'Twenty-four hours a day! You dirty little undersized jerk! I've not seen you since eight this morning. It's five now! Nine blasted bloody hours! What d'you think you are, little Lord Fauntleroy parading up and down Picca-dilly in a frock coat and spats? Jesus wept! You're my chauffeur, my servant, you insolent conceited little runt! Nothing else! A paid employee, nothing else! You strut off like a bantam cock at eight in the morning, spend nine hours crowing on some stinking dung-hill and then come strutting back expecting welcome written on the mat! Well, this is the last time. I tell you, it's the last time!'

'Oh, go chase yourself! I'm not a flaming nurse-maid. What d'you want me to do, hold your hand all day long? I don't owe you nothing. And that's what you'll get if you go on like this, nothing from me!'

'It wouldn't be any less than I've had! And you pretend you don't owe me anything, when every last thing you stand up in has been bought by me over and above your wages. *And* you drive about in my car as if it belonged to you! Half the time you don't bother to ask. You just *take* it. You've lived a soft comfortable life with me for up-wards of eighteen months and nothing's been denied you. Bloody nothing! And you know it. You've had a nice easy berth, but now because I'm dying you think you can throw your weight about just as you like! I'll bet you've been off with some tart this afternoon! Some tart with a blonde rinse and three-inch heels and a roll of fat flopping over the top of her girdle. Some blowsy big-breasted bird-brained tart that you fancy you can prove you're a man with . . .'

Godfrey came over to the bed and glared down at the sick woman who strained off her pillows to shout at him. He raised his hand. She did not flinch.

'That's right – that's another way you can prove you're a man!'

'I don't need to prove nothing with you,' he hissed. 'God, why I stay with you! Why don't you go in a home? You're no good here. Go back to your clinic and stay there!'

As he turned away and went to the door she picked up a glass and threw it at him. It missed by a yard and smashed to pieces on the silk damask wallpaper. He didn't even look round but went out with a slam of the door that shook the house.

In the kitchen he banged a kettle on the stove, whistled furiously but soundlessly through pressed lips. He had had enough. For crying out loud, he'd had enough. He was sick to his tonsils of this arrogant old cow. Bawling at him, him, Little God, seventh in the fly-weight ratings. What the hell and who the hell did she think she was? Because she'd got a bloody label in front of her name. He could have killed her, saying that about him being with a tart. He'd tart her. He *could* kill her, stone him he could. A grip round the neck and a sharp twist and she'd stop her screeching.

She'd be quiet for ever. Like doing an old hen in. It would be a mercy to her, put her out of her misery. Doing a good turn. Why didn't she ask him to do it? Maybe that was what she wanted. Maybe she thought that way she could get him had for murder.

The kettle boiled and he put tea in the pot, slopped water in, got milk from the fridge, clattered two cups and saucers on the tray. Bit of cake. Two flaming biscuits. Sugar basin. Bloody lackey. Bloody footman. Bloody nurse. Male nurse. Little God, seventh in the ratings, male nurse.

He carried the tray, kicked open the door to the bedroom. She was lying back on the pillow wiping her eyes.

'What the hell do you want?' she shouted.

'Brought you tea. Thought you could throw cups next time.'

'Don't want any tea. It's too damned late. Anyway, I can't keep it down. I shall only sick it up.'

'Suit yourself.' He banged the tray on the table, slopped milk in the cups, poured out the tea, put in sugar, took up his cup, spooned it round, sat on the corner of the bed.

'You don't know *how* to drink tea,' she said. 'You still look as if you're in an all night café.'

'So what?'

'Well, for God's sake, look as if you *like* having a saucer! After all those months with me.'

'Being with you only means I get blackguarded all the time.'

'Well, you ought to look to your manners. If you're going to be a champion boxer you might try to look as if you're house-trained.'

'Good manners I'm taught here. Lady Vosper, the great teacher of manners, chucks a glass at my head. Wonder you don't start a school for etiquette.'

'Shut up, you little runt. Anyway I aimed it to miss you.'

'That's a fine tale.'

'You little ass, d'you think I can't throw better than that, even in bed?'

'Drink your tea. It's going cold.'

'God,' she said. 'I've been feeling terrible all day. Miriam said she was coming but she's never been near.'

'Miriam won't come because I'm here. You know that. You know she hates my guts.'

'Well, I'm damned if I'll be dictated to; not by her, not even by you.'

'Well, no, but it means if I'm here she stops away and you don't see her. Want a biscuit?'

'No. You know I can't eat.'

'You'll be a shadow soon.'

'Feather-weight. To match you.'

'Cor!' He nodded his head in acknowledgement. 'You'll be down to paper-weight. Champion paper-weight and glass thrower.'

She sipped her tea. 'Where the hell have you been all afternoon?'

'I was training all morning, then Jude Davis wanted to see me. Then I had a date with an old mate of mine.'

'Male or female?'

He looked at her. 'Female. I suppose you want the truth, do you?'

'So I was right.'

'No, you wasn't. She wasn't any – what was that you said? I must say you're the world champion slanger when it comes to that – what did you say: bird-brained, big-bummed blonde – was that it?'

'I can't remember.' She sipped more tea and sighed. 'Well, I'd rather you were honest. I suppose the way I am now I can't exactly expect you to stay celibate.'

'What the hell does that mean?'

'Was she nice, little man?'

'Oh . . . so-so. Nice in a way. Young.'

'That's not very kind to me.'

'Well, I don't mean it that way, see. You've got something she hasn't got, that's what I meant.'

'I *had* something perhaps. D'you mean that?'

'You told me to be honest. I'm being honest. She's a right ornament, this girl. A smasheroo. Tall, big, a honey of a figure, long legs, twenty or twenty-one, *nice*, see, not a tart, not a *bit* of a tart, brought up genteel, all that. A dream girl. O.K., O.K. But . . . when you've climbed in the hay, that's it, that always is it. No worse than most others. Better than some. She's learning fast. She *likes* it. *I* like it. So that's fine. But you ask me, and it's funny, I don't see why, but she hasn't got what you've got, so help me.'

248

'You little bastard,' said Flora.

'Well, ta very much. That's all the thanks I get.'

'I'm *sorry* for her. I'm sorry for anyone that tangles with you. I wish I'd hit you with that glass.'

'Here you are. Take my cup.'

'Oh, Godfrey, I do hate you and yet . . . Even when you're confessing to having been in bed with some honey blonde, yet you're still a sort of – stimulus. You keep me alive.'

'Yeah, Flora. Maybe. I'm not a winner at it, though, am I?'

'Not a winner with me. Nobody can be a winner. I'm on the way out. D'you know what I shall regret most of all? Not seeing you as feather-weight champion of England.'

Godfrey munched a piece of biscuit. 'Maybe I shall miss that too. Not miss being champ, but miss you being there.'

'I wish you meant that.'

' 'Course I mean it, you old fool.'

There was silence. Flora had no energy left to raise her head from the pillow. Her frail but still capable hands plucked at the bed jacket, pulled out a packet of cigarettes, a lighter. She flicked the lighter and blew out the first smoke.

'Godfrey, you know I've no money. No personal money.'

'What?'

'All my marriages . . . I was too careless. Lived too well and enjoyed myself and didn't worry about wills or settlements. So when I married Julian I had practically nothing of my own. He'd quite a lot and while he was alive we burned it up. Then when he died he left money and property to me, but it was in trust for his children by former marriages. There's Claude, his eldest son, who lives in Geneva, and Lettice and Arthur. I was left with the income for life. When *I* die the money will go to them. I've got sweet nothing – practically. Nor has Miriam. When I die Miriam will get about six thousand pounds, that's all. And I'm going to leave a thousand pounds to you. That's all there is. Everything at Merrick House – even the furniture in this flat – belongs to the trustees. So . . . if a few things have disappeared these last months with Miriam, a few things people won't notice, don't blame her too much. It's only her helping herself to a few bits and pieces. I feel she's entitled to them.'

'You knew all the time then?'

'Not at the beginning. Until you told me about it. I didn't think then I was going to die. Evidently Miriam did. Maybe the doctors said something to her, I don't know. But when a few other things went, I knew about it then but I said nothing. Miriam's *my* daughter, you know, and although she isn't everybody's light and joy, blood is thicker than water. I don't begrudge her anything she's had. But I want to ask you. When I'm dead *don't* make a fuss about these things she's taken. If you don't, nobody else will notice, nobody will care. If you don't tell them the trustees won't know. It's a small thing – they're small things, but she prizes them and they have value. For my sake, if you care anything at all for me, say nothing to anybody.'

'O.K.,' said Godfrey. 'If that's how you want it, I'll muzzle myself. But it'll be against the grain.'

'It's against the grain for me to leave you no more, little man,' Flora said. 'You've made a difference to this last year.'

He said: 'It's funny with women. You get them and then that's it. This one, this blonde, I'd nearly have done murder to get her. First off she didn't want me, wouldn't touch me with a barge-pole, thought herself too good, too pure; but that made me all the keener. What you can't get you want more. I even thought I'd like to marry her.' He stirred his tea reflectively. 'Could still, I suppose. She'd be O.K. to come home to, a smashing piece. She'd be a smashing piece at the ringside, and you could *introduce* her to people. You know. But in bed she's like any other. And after a while I'd maybe want others more than I'd want her. There are *too many* birds in the world. They all look different and they all turn out the same.'

'Why these soulful confessions, you stinking little beast?'

'You're the only one I ever talked to – or ever would talk to – see. You're an old bitch but that's the way it is. Maybe living with you this long.'

'You've been softened by the pure influence of an understanding woman.'

'Go and stuff yourself.'

Silence fell. Lady Vosper's eyes closed and she fell into a light doze. It seemed as if sleep were always stealing up on her now, and shortly it would become a sleep from which she would not waken. Godfrey got up and began to sneak out.

'Where the hell are you going?'

'I'm going to pack my bags and go, seeing as you've left me no money in your will. I'm going to shake the dust of the house off my feet.'

'You ungrateful louse. All I've done for you!'

'All I've done for *you*, you mean. It's time for your dope. You like it in soda, don't you?'

'Is there another cup of tea?'

'Maybe.' He came back and poured her one. 'Yes, it's not bad. Where's your pills?'

'I put them in the drawer.'

He took them out. She said. 'Before you leave for ever, have you time for a game of rummy?'

'What's got into you? You don't think you can win, do you?'

'I can beat the pants off you any day of the week.'

'Oh, yes, like you did Wednesday. Like you did Monday. Like you did last Sunday week.'

'I let you win then. You get so downhearted, so bloody-minded when you lose. Sort of cry-baby.'

'Like you was when I come back just now. If I had all the money I'd won from you at rummy, I'd be a rich man.'

'Stop speaking so badly! And get the cards.'

'Two minutes ago you was going to sleep.'

'Well, this will keep me awake. I've got a long enough sleep ahead.'

He went to a drawer, took out a pack of cards, pulled over the invalid table that slid over the bed in front of her. He began to deal.

She said: 'You know that bureau in the drawing room? The bottom drawer's locked.'

'Six-six, seven-seven,' he counted and turned up the next card.

'When I'm dead,' she said, 'you'll find my keys in my purse. Unlock the bottom drawer and in the corner there's an attaché case. Queen, King, Ace of Spades.'

'For Chrissake,' he said, 'I've not started yet! That's thirty-five you've scored before I've even started! Talk about a crook.'

'I've told you. It's *you* that's going to sleep. Not sorted your cards yet?'

'I'm thinking,' he snarled. He discarded and she picked up.

'In the attaché case,' she said, 'there's two hundred pounds in tenners. I want you to have that.'

'What you been doing, robbing the poor box? I don't want any more of your lousy money.'

'Have you got a bank account?'

'Bank account, me? Like hell. I got a few quid in the post office.'

'Well, maybe tomorrow you'd better take the money and pay it in. If I die there'll be people about, and you might be accused of taking it.'

'I would if your Miriam got half a chance.'

'Leave her out of it, Godfrey, leave her out of it.'

The game went peacefully on.

Chapter Four

Angell had not been so unhappy for twenty years. In the two decades since the death of Anna he had more and more retreated into himself, barricaded behind his law books, insulated by a careful passion for the arts, comfortable within a slow growing mountain of flesh. From within this protective bastion he had made careful limited sorties which had enabled him to keep in touch with the rest of humanity, and to patronize it, without ever being in danger of losing his foothold and being swept into the crowd. But this year madness had fallen on him. Prodded by a half dozen accumulative circumstances, prompted, he thought, by a casual likeness, impelled by some middle-aged urge not to let life slip quite away before it was too late, he had left his defensive position and deliberately stepped into the thick of the throng. Even his decision to reduce his weight seemed to have a symbolic significance, a stripping off of a protective layer.

So for a while he had lived more vividly, breathed deeper, known what it was to be young.

Now came the penalty. Life had lured him out, now it had betrayed him. And he found to his grief and his chagrin that there was no way back. If Pearl had died like Anna, perhaps the new-grown tentacles would have been cut away. Love, lust, jealousy, hate, the emotional ferment, would have been amputated by death, and after an injured, wounded spell gasping on the edge, he might have been able to crawl back behind his ramparts again. Not so now. Pearl still shared his house and board. Beautiful, statuesque, impassive, commonplace, soft-fleshed, gentle, her presence constantly speared him afresh.

All his life, deep down, had been a knowledge of his own weakness, a weakness of the flesh and of the spirit, but in two successful decades he had built a front that had deceived everyone, even himself. Now his weakness was exposed – most of all to himself. He *wanted* Pearl, and in spite of his hatred of her, he still enjoyed her from time to time. He did not have the resolution to turn her out.

Even his attempted reprisal on Godfrey had so far come to nothing. Birman had reported back that he had raised the offer to Jude Davis to £2000 but that, although Davis had seemed to waver at the last, he had turned it down. Angell had been horribly shocked that Birman had advanced the offer so far, and when Birman had said he thought another thousand, or possibly even five hundred, might be enough to turn the scale, Wilfred had rejected it with the vehemence of sea-sickness. His client, he said, would *never* pay more than had already been offered.

But the memory of this failure nagged like a sore tooth. Nothing would have given him greater delight than to see this ignorant, insolent, undersized jackanapes soundly beaten in the ring, preferably with Pearl watching; but even revenge could be priced too high. Sometimes he looked at his pictures and his furniture and thought: I don't *need* to buy anything more for months, if necessary I could even *sell* something: that Minaux, for instance, or the rather dull Dufy, that would bring me in ample without my ever feeling it. But he could not quite goad himself to squander the money in such a way.

He could not tell whether the love scene he had surprised was an isolated incident which had blown up while he was away, or whether it was only the one observed act of a sequence. Several times he had telephoned his home in the afternoon and twice there had been no reply. That of course proved nothing. He had been tempted to come home unexpectedly either in an afternoon or on one of his bridge evenings, but he had not dared to because he did not *want* to discover them together. He had put off the exposure the first time in order to avoid a precipitate move he would later regret. Now he knew if it happened again he would behave in exactly the same way.

Twice when she was out he searched her bedroom. This always gave him a sort of sexual excitement, and now jealousy had become a bitter element in it. He searched among her underclothes and her frocks, sniffed her brassières, looked in her bag and the pockets of her coats and frocks, expecting to find he knew not what. Nothing came to light.

He thought he was successful in disguising his feelings from her, behaving just as he had done before she went away; but this relationship had subtly altered. A certain kindliness had gone. When he made love he was like a man searching for something on a dissecting table.

He knew some men would kill her – or still better kill Godfrey: the idea he had briefly contemplated on the night, and the classic way out for a wronged husband. But this was a pipe dream, entertained only in the drowsy hours while reality lost its grip. He would never summon the strength to pull a trigger or raise a knife. In Egypt he had not even been able to shoot a rat; they had laughed at him.

Failing that, he should divorce her; the civilized solution. But by divorcing her he lost her, and he knew too well that any brief periods of loneliness he had endured before his marriage would be as nothing to what he would suffer if she left him now. What you have not had you do not miss. But there is no way of putting the clock back. Even if he hated her he wanted her around.

The third solution was to do as he was doing: pretend that he knew nothing, hope that the affair would break up of its own accord, and take what steps he could, if there were other steps to be taken, to break it up from without. Repeatedly he debated whether to throw another five hundred pounds into the balance to suborn Jude Davis. It was just too much for him to bear, the thought of all that money. And with no *sure* result. He thought, he *believed,* that Pearl was taken by Godfrey's physical beauty and undersized dominance. Break that image and you might break the whole illusion which led his beautiful stupid wife into an affair with a common vulgar little stable boy. But women were unpredictable. You could not be sure.

Of course it would be worth a fortune to see him so beaten, taken down a peg, his bantam cockiness destroyed, his insufferable insolence humbled . . .

Nor did the successes of the rest of his life in any way compensate. Contracts had been exchanged, a cheque for £10,000 passed across a table; Lord Vosper, enjoying the proceeds in Lausanne, was now as legally bound as human ingenuity could make him to sell Merrick House and all that went with it, to Land Increments Ltd, for a further £80,000, if or when it became his property. Sir Francis Hone was very pleased there had been no announcement in the House during the debate on the Queen's speech. Things were going quietly ahead, and he knew that a firm of consultants was about to be approached by the Ministry to advise on the development plan . . .

Sir Francis was also pleased about the purchase of the Canaletto. As soon as he got possession of it he had called in independent experts, who had substantiated Christie's opinion. The picture now occupied a place of honour over Sir Francis's Adam fireplace.

To Wilfred it was all ashes in the mouth, dust underfoot. The only zest he found in life was at the table, and he brought a perverse enjoyment to making up the weight he had lost. He kept up the pretence of dieting at home, but his meals out were gargantuan. His club was not a gourmet's paradise; members went there for conversation rather than food; so even on his bridge evenings he more often took to one of the notable eating restaurants in Soho. One Tuesday at the end of November, he dined in St Martin's Lane, off pastry turnovers with Roquefort cheese, followed by Sole Bercy, and a whole small roast chicken with chicken liver canapés and mushrooms, then a fillet steak with fresh *foie gras* and truffles and Madeira sauce. Following this was a vanilla soufflé and coffee; and he drank two bottles of wine.

When he arrived at his club and settled to bridge he had heartburn, which worried and surprised him. He had drawn as his partner an old man called Maurice who had been one of the noted male courtesans of the twenties. Poets and peers had quarrelled over his Greek profile, there had been bitter jealousies about his favours in the Bloomsbury set, he had been a noted figure in one of the great scandals of the time. Now he was a withered old man with furrowed cheeks, receding grey hair and a droop to the corner of his mouth. One had to make an effort even to begin to perceive that there had ever been beauty there.

He was a kindly enough old boy, fussy and old-maidish; but his presence irritated Angell tonight. He seemed to Angell to be a reminder of his own mortality and what all youth and beauty must come to in a short time. They were a niggling reminder of the youth and beauty at home in 26 Cadogan Mews, succulent and yielding and fresh, that might even now be prey to another man who was invading his property and stealing his happiness and pleasure.

They played one rubber and lost, then cut together again. Maurice had been a good player in his day but the slight stroke had made him absent-minded. They somehow got into a three no-trump call without a single guard in clubs, but thanks to a bad lead Angell just made his contract. In the next hand, because they were vulnerable and because he was not sure how reliable his partner was, Angell allowed himself to be jockeyed out of a game call in spades and justifiably doubled his opponents' five diamonds. In the course of the play their opponents took two tricks in hearts, on which Maurice dropped first the knave and then the three. As soon as trumps were led Angell played his ace and led a heart. Maurice had the ten. The contract was made.

Angell said: 'What were you thinking of, man? You signalled a doubleton in hearts. We could have just got them down.'

'Did I, Wilfred?' Maurice lisped. 'Oh, that's so, old boy, I remember. I was bluffing them, d'you see. I thought they'd make their contract by cross-ruffing, so I thought I'd bluff them into getting their trumps out.' He chuckled at his own subtlety. 'One never knows, of course, when one is going to deceive one's partner, what?'

The next hand, the other side bid and made a small slam in diamonds. Angell declined a further rubber. It was only nine-thirty but he was tired and wanted to go home. A sense of fatalism and doom had come on him. If he was going home to discover them together, then this was his fate. He could not evade it for ever. He drank two stiff whiskies and went out and hailed a cab. In the cab he felt sick.

He got home and went in without any pretence at stealth, shut the front door with a bang, dragged off his coat. There was a light in the hall and under the drawing room door, but nobody called. He went lumberingly in. Pearl was sitting there mending the hem of a skirt. Alone.

'Wilfred,' she said, 'you're early. Is anything wrong?'

'I don't feel well,' he said. 'I feel – very peculiar.' He sat down with a thump on a chair and nearly broke it.

'What is it? Can I get you a brandy?'

'It's my heart, I think.' He had felt a pain when he

arrived at the house. 'I think I'll just rest here for a while.'

She went out to the kitchen where Wilfred insisted all drink should be kept. (The cocktail cabinet or the miniature bar were vulgarities beyond *all* redemption.) While she poured it she thought, what an escape, Godfrey only putting it off at six. Lady Vosper sick unto death, he could not get away, what an escape.

She brought the drink and stood over him solicitously while he drank it. 'Have you been doing too much? What happened? Were you taken ill at the club?'

'Not taken ill, but I felt unwell and came home. I'm glad you are in, Pearl.'

'But of course. Shall I call the doctor?'

'Not yet.' Was this genuine concern on her part or did she hover about him already speculating on his death and its advantages to her? The pain was hovering too, like an evil thought, not quite there, not quite dismissed. 'A busy day. I felt tired when I left the office. I should have come straight home.'

He finished his drink and took another. Presently he allowed her to help him into the bedroom. His head was swimming. He allowed her to help him to undress, but when she would have gone he asked her to stay, to sit by the bed for a while. All the food and drink he had taken was beating in his head.

She sat by the bed and he put out his hand and held one of hers. He needed comfort. Whether it was sham comfort or genuine, he still needed it. Once as a child his mother had slapped him hard across the face, and immediately he had fallen into her arms seeking solace from the blow.

Presently with a third brandy the pain went away and he was left only with a feeling of fullness and distension. But he was still emotionally demanding. It was on his tongue to pour forth all his distress, to confide in her as if she were not one of the participants, to fall into the arms of the one who had struck him. Only a small eroded core of common sense warned him that that way he would lose her.

Instead he suddenly began to talk about Anna. It was an inspiration; he could transfer all his present distress to that old tragedy; he could pour out the whole tale and demand sympathy and *receive* sympathy. He told her of their

258

first meeting and of the later ones. He did not explain that he had met Anna soon after the end of the war when his years of discomfort and humiliation in the army had just come to an end and when, in comparison to the rough and tumble of service life, civilian life and civilians had seemed less intimidating than they were ever to do again. He had a brief spell of physical confidence, and during it had met and wooed Anna. Her death had killed more than their love affair.

'The last time I saw her,' he said. 'It's something I try not to think of, something I can forget for months, and then, suddenly – D'you know. Perhaps marriage to you has made it more vivid. It's as if she came alive again in you.'

Pearl hunched her shoulders in discomfort. 'I don't want to be anybody's reincarnation.'

'No, you're not. But perhaps it's true that I'd never fallen out of love with her, and so being in love with you . . .'

It was one of the first times in their association that he had ever mentioned love. It fell strangely from his lips like someone experimenting with a foreign quotation in a language they did not know too well.

'That must have been why you spoke to me on the plane.'

He sipped the last of his brandy, dried his lips with his fingers. 'That last visit I paid her . . . She had been ill for only a month – noticeably ill, that is – off her food, her beautiful complexion fading, like a lily with a worm at the root. D'you know. There were doctors, consultations, tests, then she wrote me to go and see her. I went and was worried, but chiefly at her loss of looks. I thought it was jaundice or something – at 22 one does not *die,* one is ill but recovers. I – well, men are attracted by looks, I hoped she would not lose hers. I was still having sensual thoughts about how we should meet when she was well. Then a week later I called again. I have told you that her father was something of a recluse; they lived alone in that big house except for one woman. This time the door was opened by a nurse. She said, "Oh, yes, you're Mr Angell, Miss Tyrrell is expecting you. Come this way." So I went up to her bedroom and she looked much better. Or so it seemed. I suppose I did not realize how much of it was due to make-up. She had had time to prepare. The nurse left us and we talked for half an hour. Anna let me kiss her. We chatted cheerfully and made plans. I thought she was tense, on edge. Suddenly she said she thought it was time for me to go. I got up, a trifle offended. I kissed her again, saying I'd be in again next week, and she said good-bye.

'As I came out of the bedroom there was no sign of the nurse and the house was very silent, just as if there were no one else in it. I thought of trying to find the nurse, but instead I went downstairs. Then – for even then I was something of a connoisseur – I stopped to look at a painting, wondering if it were genuine. She must have thought I had left.' Wilfred put down the glass and his hand was shaking. 'She began to scream. She began to scream at the top of her voice as if she were being tortured to death – as indeed I suppose she was. Her voice echoed round and round that empty house. On and on and on and on. I shall *never* forget it. It all came back this week. I cannot tell you why, but it did. It all came back tonight.'

'What did you do?' Pearl asked, quietly, talking into the silence. 'I mean then. Was she really alone?'

'No. After what seemed an hour I heard the nurse running up the stairs. I turned and let myself out and *I* ran, as if the devil and all hell were after me. When I got home I was sick as if I had taken an emetic. Then I went to bed. I was ill the following day. D'you know, I was ill all the following day.'

'How long did Anna – live after this?' Pearl said presently.

'About seven weeks. It was very rapid. From complete health – or apparently complete health – to death was less than three months.'

Pearl got up and switched off a bar of the electric fire. Then she went to the window and peered out. She glanced back quickly at the bed in which her husband lay, the mountain of his bulk, his handsome woe-begone face, the thick faded fair hair falling. On the table were his heavy spectacles, the empty glass, a bottle of aspirin, a handkerchief, a bunch of keys, three half crowns, four florins, three sixpences, three pennies, all in columns; a crumpled bridge score.

'You didn't go to see her again in those seven weeks?'

'My father was concerned for my health, sent me to

Austria. When I came back she was dead.'

'You went to Austria for seven weeks?'

'For five. I – at the last I felt I could not intrude.'

Rattling your knacks. That's what Godfrey called it. When you died you 'rattled your knacks.'

Godfrey might have been here and then they would have been discovered. It couldn't go on like this. There had to be a change. Suppose she said tonight: 'Wilfred, I have to tell you something. I'm not going to leave you as Anna did, but I'm going to leave you all the same . . .'

Yet she felt affection for Wilfred, and sympathy. The story he had just told her stuck in her mind like a small poisonous limpet. She could understand its remaining with him for twenty-five years. It was the only memory Anna had left him, the memory of her pain. By speaking now he had at last transferred some of the memory.

'How is Lady Vosper?' she asked suddenly, the words just coming out.

She was looking out of the window so she did not see his face. 'Lady Vosper? Very ill, I believe. It's only a question of time.'

'Is it the same with her as it was with Anna?'

'No. It's the result of some accident she had many years ago. Godfrey Brown hasn't been here, has he?'

'What? What d'you mean?'

'With some message about her. I wondered, as you asked.'

'Oh, Oh, no. No, nobody's been.'

He said sharply: 'He hasn't been to see me recently. Brown, I mean. Last time I spoke to him he was cheaply insolent. He betrayed all the limitations of a commonplace vulgar mind. One wonders if it was worth helping him.'

'Well, it's done now.'

'Yes, it's done now.' Like a crime committed. But perhaps it could be undone. If only one could unwind these last months, recover them, set them off again on another track like a clockwork toy. 'I can well understand why you did not like him.'

'When?'

'Before we were married.' He peered at her. 'When you first knew him.'

'Yes. Oh, yes . . . Are you feeling better?'

261

'A little. But I'm still not at all well.'

'Did you eat something that disagreed with you?'

'You know I eat very little nowadays.'

'You've put on weight again recently.'

'I can't tell. I never weigh myself now.'

'I'm sleepy,' she said. 'If you're feeling better I'll go to bed.'

She kissed him and went into her room and slowly undressed. Her body felt unused, neglected, deprived. It needed the attention that Godfrey would have given it — more the attention perhaps than Godfrey himself. Her mind was filled with complex emotions that she couldn't separate. Her perverse passion for Godfrey, her sympathy for Wilfred, were both newly interlaced with apprehension. It was an apprehension that derived almost solely from this evening, from Wilfred's indisposition, from things he had said, from things he had left unsaid. It was as if her mind recognized but could not identify events that were portending, events deriving from a situation and moving towards a crisis that none of them could avoid.

Godfrey was matched against a light-weight called Sheffield in a catch contest at the Shoreditch Town Hall on December 5.

'It'll keep your hand in,' said Jude Davis. 'I want to get you matched with Mickey Johns, but he's fighting in Denmark next week and there's no chance of a contest before Christmas. Alf Sheffield will be a useful stop-gap. He'll be ten pounds heavier than you and two inches taller, but if you lose it'll do you no harm prestige-wise, and if you win Fred Armitage will sign you up with Johns all the more readily.'

The girl was in the gym this morning, the one Godfrey had only seen twice since that first meeting in the Thomas à Becket. She was dressed in a dark silk blouse and something that looked like harness for a skirt; at least it was all buckles and belts and it stopped short. To Godfrey it looked pretty kinky and her legs kept showing through it in a kinky way. It made you think of dungeons and mediaeval orgies. Her name he had discovered was Sally Beck. She was smoking from the usual long cigarette holder, and only a glance every now and then from under the artificial fronds of her lashes made you realize she wasn't indifferent to the company.

After Godfrey had done his usual skipping and shadow boxing and punch-ball work, and after Davis had gone out, he saw Sally Beck was sitting at the solitary table in the corner making her face up. He walked over and sat at the table and looked her over.

She did not lift her head. 'Sit down,' she said. 'Please don't mind me.'

'I thought maybe you had a fag,' he said. 'I thought maybe you might offer me one.'

Still staring in her compact mirror she pushed the packet across the table. Then with a little finger she began to modify the lipstick at the corners of her lips.

He said: 'How is it, then?'

'How's what?'

'Things.'

'Oh – so-so.'

He took out a cigarette and then carefully replaced it. 'Maybe I better not . . . I've seen you three or four times around, but I never had the chance of speaking to you before.'

'Fancy.'

'You – a friend of Jude Davis's?'

'What's it to you?'

'I was just wondering.'

'Anything else you wonder?'

'Maybe. When I see a smashing girl like you it's not surprising, is it? I just wonder. You must have lots of boy friends.'

'Yes, lots.'

'Can I ask another question?'

'Nobody's stopping you.'

'No, maybe I'd better not.'

At that, as he'd expected, she stopped making up her face and looked at him. He smiled back. Coolly her gaze went over his face and hair, his bare shoulders and chest.

'Are you boxing next week?'

'Yes. Will you be there?'

'No. I don't like it. I'll be at the dogs.'

'Maybe we could go together sometime. To the dogs, I mean.'

'What makes you think I want to go with you?'

'You like the dogs. So do I. It just seemed natural we might go together.'

'Why natural?'

He smiled at the peeling wall behind her. 'It seems natural to me. How about next Saturday?'

'What will you see with?'

'What d'you mean?'

'After Sheffield has blacked your eyes.'

'Look,' he said gently, 'nobody has ever hit me that hard. This feller won't. Take it from me. Care to bet?'

'What sort of a bet?'

'If I can see out of both eyes next Saturday, you come with me to the dogs.'

'Seems to me I lose anyhow.'

'You'll win, dear. I promise you. Little God's honour.'

They stared at each other a minute. 'Little God,' she said. 'What a groovy name. D'you think people ought to burn joss-sticks to you?'

'Dead right,' he said. 'You ought. Sitting cross-legged in that skirt.'

She smoothed the skirt with long red-speared fingers. 'Fresh, aren't you?'

'Kind of. But I like it. I think it's great. I think you're great.'

'Thanks, I'm sure.'

'So will you come?'

'I'll think about it.'

'Be a chick. I'm O.K. really. You'll like me. House-trained. Good watch-dog. Only need exercising once a day.'

She raised her carefully depilated eyebrows. 'How fresh can you get . . . Blow now.'

'Is that a promise?'

'Blow now.'

'A bet anyway.'

'O.K., O.K. But blow.'

As he moved back to the punch-ball Godfrey saw that Jude Davis had come back into the gym.

Godfrey's fight with Alf Sheffield on the Thursday was unexpectedly easy. Sheffield, a west Indian of 30, was slightly on his way down; but he was still a man with a good name and a following among the coloured population of Whitechapel and Hoxton. But, as happens once in a while in the life of most boxers, he was mentally and physically unfit on the night. Somebody said he was having wife trouble. At any rate he was sluggish and without stamina and made no use of his extra height and weight. He was down on one knee in the first round, down for a count of five in the second, and down twice in the third, from the second of which he was counted out. The suspicious might have thought it fixed, seeing this lithe well built Negro going down before the thin white man, and there were some boos. Godfrey did not take his win modestly and Jude Davis, watching him shake double hands to the crowd, took off his glasses to polish them and avoid the sight.

On the Saturday Godfrey, who had seen Pearl and told her all about his win on the Friday, escaped from the Vosper flat in time to take Sally Beck to the White City. It wasn't that he was all that keen but she was a bit of fresh and she had a look in her eye. Afterwards they drove back in the Jensen to Sally's flat, where Godfrey found out all about her belt and buckle skirt.

Afterwards, when he got back, he looked in and at first thought Flora was asleep but her colour was so bad that he telephoned for the doctor. Her breathing was funny, too, deep with an occasional snore. Protheroe, Matthewson's partner, came and said Lady Vosper was in a coma. Miriam was sent for but had gone out of London for the week-end. Protheroe said he would make arrangements for Lady Vosper to go into hospital in the morning, but Godfrey reminded him that she had wanted to stay at home and said he could manage. Protheroe left, saying he would arrange for a nurse to come in first thing in the morning.

Godfrey sat out the night, nodding by the electric fire, memories and fantasies passing through his brain like smoke. That left hook that took Sheffield on the side of the chin: a real honey which had bruised his fingers, Sheffield was only sitting up when Godfrey left the ring; Sally's naked body arching under him, much smaller and slighter than Pearl's, the bones of her hips standing out, more avid than Pearl, more practised, but coming quicker;

the smell of her scent still on his hands; old Flora, really on her last legs now; but different from the others; a bit of class, that was it, a bit of subtlety and polish, like driving an old Rolls. Another victory in the ring; it wouldn't alter his ratings but it would do him no harm. The short jab on the button in the second round, a lolly-pop, a classic, the weight, the footwork, the timing; Sheffield had looked glassy even when he got up. What would happen to the Jensen; be sold probably; driving the Jensen had been a valuable prop, impressed them all; soft, he'd lived soft with Lady V, soon it would be harder; but he was making good money; free soon, *free,* when this old bag rattled off; get a place for Pearl to come to – and Sally; or maybe not Sally, don't get in wrong with Davis. That day at Norwich; God, the old girl could drive; rummy, how many games of rummy he'd played with her these last two months. Funny how much he'd wanted Pearl. Still did, though not the urgency. You can never tell. Little bastard, get the potatoes out of here, else you get no supper; there's twelve sacks to go and not a bite till you've done! Foster-father Arnold, back in the days at Yarmouth. Nine years ago. Someday go and settle with the old bully. The British Boxing Board of Control suspends Godfrey Brown for a period of twelve months, suspension to date from . . . Temper, temper, his one failing. Take the money, Flora said, two hundred pounds in tenners; he'd taken it, it was in the P.O. in his name, little nest egg, along with another hundred he'd put by; but it wouldn't buy a Jensen. Not even a Mini; he'd need a car. Get something hot from one of the yards, something they wanted to get rid of for a hundred or so. Brown, G., for stealing, six strokes of the cane. Funny, you could take it on your chin without minding, not on your backside. Pearl was lovely in spite of her size – all over, shaped well right through, better shaped than Sally.

He woke with a jerk. Flora had moved or muttered something. Her breathing had changed, become easier. One good thing about an electric fire, it didn't lose heat or need stoking. He got up, staggered with sleep on his way to the bed. She was awake or had come out of her coma or whatever it was.

'Godfrey,' she said.

'Yes, ducks?'

'You've been a pal. Stuck by me. Made this last year. Can't say more than that.'

'Like something to drink, luv?'

'No,' she said. 'Can't say more than that.'

And then she died.

Chapter Five

Miriam arrived from Eastbourne on the Sunday morning, and her husband in the afternoon. They gave Godfrey until midnight to get out. Everything he took with him they scrutinized to see if it was his. He moved to a bed-sitter in Lavender Hill. There it took him best part of a day to sort out all the belongings he had accumulated through Flora's generosity. He reckoned he had four or five hundred pounds' worth of stuff without counting watches or cuff-links. Then there were quite a few odds and ends in his room at Merrick House. He reckoned he hadn't done badly out of the old girl, all things considered.

He went to the cremation at Golders Green, and it was quite a turn-out. A bunch of people with titles and fancy names. Even Angell, but not Mrs Angell. It was the first time he had seen Pearl's husband since heaven knew when. They had had that talk over the blower one day in November and he had been sassy and Angell had been pretty sharp – that had been the last communication. Angell looked as pompous and as bloated as ever; no wonder Pearl wanted to leave him. But it was a pity to lose the meal ticket. All that cash. Maybe she would see sense – stay on with fat Wilfred and take her pleasure with Little God. When he really got in the big money, Godfrey thought, it might be different. Pearl would be one of his most prized possessions.

It wasn't really until about the Thursday that something hit him. He had been having a casual work-out in the gym, and he glanced at the clock thinking he ought to be back before Flora got in a tizzy. Then he realized there was no Flora to go back to. Of course it was not Flora he was missing, it was the luxury car and the luxury flat; but all the same there was a gap in his belly and after changing he went into L. C. House in Piccadilly and tried to fill it. He stuffed himself on steak and chips and bread and butter pudding – instinctively copying Angell to allay hurt – but the food didn't go to the right hole. He came out and mooched along to Leicester Square and went to the pictures. When it was over it was dark and the hole was worse. Christmas was near, and the traffic was jammed solid up Regent Street with cars coming to see the lights.

Last Christmas Flora had had Miriam and her husband to dinner, but on Boxing Day she had gone with him to a Jacques Tati film, and afterwards they had had coffee and sandwiches and had talked for upwards of two hours about cars and boxing and hunting. One of the things he would miss was the talking. He'd never talked to anyone like he'd talked to her and he'd never listened to anyone neither. He'd learned a hell of a lot from her. It was like having a sort of sporting aunt that you could argue with about all sorts of things. He'd never had an aunt, or an uncle for that matter. Only a lot of lousy officials and a God-damned foster-father.

He didn't fancy Sally somehow, he didn't all that much fancy Pearl. He wanted something new to help to cut out the memories, so he went to the Lyceum and picked up a girl who was willing enough afterwards. But in the end she didn't help much more than the steak and chips. He got home to his bed-sitter about three and threw himself down in his clothes and went straight off to sleep.

Just before Christmas the news filtered out of the intended development of another satellite town to be sited in West Suffolk north of the river Stour, covering an area bounded by Delpham Brook, Brockley Hall, Witherham-by-Stour and Handley Merrick. In the country as a whole the information created less stir than 1d on the price of sugar; most people had never even heard of the places, and for goodness sake overspill population had to go somewhere. The only ones upset were those directly concerned, and with the backing of the West Suffolk County Council, the C.P.R.E. and various other bodies, protest meetings were called and the long process began of attempting to stay the hand of the desecrator.

Wilfred, having done his part, sat back in his solicitor's office and rather nervously waited for some reaction from Lord Vosper, but none came. In the meantime he was convinced that Pearl's affair with Godfrey was in some measure continuing. Godfrey, he heard, had been immediately sacked, and this would clearly leave him free to hang about Cadogan Mews at all hours. No one so far as he could find knew where he had gone or how he was living. But pretty certainly Pearl did. The situation fretted him even when he was in the auction rooms; it disturbed his concentration at the office, and Esslin twice had to correct mistakes he made; it went with him into the bridge room so that even a grand slam bid and made only temporarily distracted him; and needless to say it was at its most abrasive during every moment he spent with Pearl.

Then one bitterly cold and deceptively sunny morning in early January, Miss Lock spoke through the intercom to say that a Mr G. Brown had called and would like an interview. Angell never arranged to see clients before 11 a.m., the first hour being devoted to the post and any matters oustanding, so he was free.

But what was he free to say, how was he free to act? After Miss Lock's message he sat for nearly ten minutes trying to concentrate on his post, trying to stay the quickened pulse, trying to rationalize the cold hate knotting in his stomach. It wouldn't move, nothing would change if he sat there all day. He had to see him – or refuse to see him. At last he pressed the switch.

'Show him in.'

Godfrey came in in a brown shirt with white tie, a russet jacket without lapels, and light grey flannel trousers with flared bottoms. He nodded good morning in his usual over-familiar way, and Angell stared back, nourishing secretions of hatred.

Godfrey waited carefully until the secretary had gone. Then he said: 'I thought I'd come and see you, Mr Angell.' He put his hands in his pockets, standing loosely like a man used to being on his feet. He waited. Angell did not speak. 'Because of this Lady Vosper, her will.'

'Oh?' Breathe slightly easier now, and despise yourself for so doing; hate him for the relief.

'Lady Vosper, she left me some money in her will, but I've heard nothing about it since and I want to know what was in the will. It's only fair to be told, isn't it. I mean only fair. Lady V says she left me this thousand pounds but these characters McNaughton and his wife, they shut the door in my face every time I go there and it's not good

270

enough. You're a lawyer . . .'

'I'm a solicitor, Brown. But I am not your solicitor. Nor was I Lady Vosper's. So I can't help you.'

Godfrey licked cracked lips. There was a pinched look about him as he came forward, like a memory of his days back in the orphanage before he became important. 'I've my rights,' he said.

Angell said: 'I'm not interested in your rights,' and pretended to make a note on the pad in front of him.

Godfrey sat down. 'Mean you can't help me or you won't?'

'Whichever way you care to look at it.'

The hostility was so obvious that in that moment Godfrey guessed that his secret affair with Pearl was somehow no longer a secret from Angell.

'There's another thing,' he said, 'I got stuff up at the house in Suffolk. My togs. Suits, shirts, boxing togs. I go down there day before yesterday to get 'em. Not allowed in! Some clerk opened the door. Instructions, he says. No one to be let in. Well, what do I do? It's robbery. Thieving lot. I want my rights.'

With his little finger Angell picked at a tooth where a filling felt rough. 'Your rights, Brown, are not my concern, and they never will be. Perhaps you will find some less particular member of my profession to act for you.' The brutal ingratitude of Pearl welled up in him again as he spoke, the commonness, the vulgarity of this situation in which he found himself. Like a delicately nurtured man flung into a cell full of thieves. One could smell the coarseness of flesh, the sweatiness of lust, the rank odour of the human animal.

Controlling his voice he added: 'In case you are not aware of this, Brown – and I gather you are not aware of it – when an individual dies a closure is put upon all his or her affairs until such time as Probate has been granted. If Lady Vosper has been so ill-advised as to leave you some money, you will be informed then. Your personal effects, if there is a proper assumption that they are yours, will be returned to you in due course. No good will come of hammering on doors and demanding rights which do not exist. Lady Vosper's solicitors are Messrs Ogden & Whitley of 9 New Square. That's all I have to say to you.'

271

Godfrey hitched up his tight trousers so that he should not stretch them. He sat taking Angell in. 'I don't see what right McNaughton and his wife have to throw their weight about. Lady V told me that they don't get much; all the property, etc., etc., goes to somebody in Switzerland. So if I'm turned out, why shouldn't they be turned out? They'll be nicking things right and left, you can bet your boots on that. Who's to stop 'em nicking things that belong to me?'

Angell took his finger away from the tooth. He pressed the intercom.

'Miss Lock, will you ring up Mr Denhurst and see if you can get an appointment for me any time after three this afternoon or before eleven in the morning. Tell him I think a small piece of filling has chipped off.'

'Yes, sir.'

Godfrey said: 'You weren't like this when I called a few months back, were you. Wanted to know things about Lady V, you said. All that.'

Angell pulled his appointments book towards him. 'And Miss Lock, bring me in the Mitchell Thomas file. And let me know as soon as Mr Thomas arrives.' He switched off the box. 'I'm not interested in this conversation, Brown. I don't think we have anything more to say to each other.'

'Did me a smashing good turn once, though,' said Godfrey between his teeth. 'I'll not deny you that. I'm doing well with Jude Davis. I'm ranked now among the feathers. How's your wife? How's Mrs Angell?'

Angell took off his glasses to polish them. This enabled him to keep his eyes down, but it did not prevent his fingers from trembling. Out of the corner of his eyes he could see Godfrey crossing his brown suède boots. He could guess the sort of expression there would be on that hated face. Leering, sneering, lying, lecherous little rat. Damn him in all hell. Might he rot, fade, fall, break his back. If one could kill a man like this, *kill* him, even hire a killer . . .

He switched down the lever again. 'Miss Lock, Mr Brown is now ready to leave.'

Miss Lock came in with the Mitchell Thomas file and stood there waiting for Godfrey to get up. Godfrey got up. He stared at Miss Lock, grey hair, grey suit, neat, withdrawn, on her dig., typical middle-aged secretary. He stared at her wondering if she'd ever been laid and what she would be like. His expression was not hard to read and Miss Lock flushed. Angell had taken the file and was thumbing through it, ignoring his visitor, waiting for the moment to pass.

'So long, Grandpa,' Godfrey said, and went out.

A terrible silence lay over the office after he had gone. Miss Lock followed him to see if he was really through the outer door, shut it, and returned through her own office to Wilfred's.

'Mr Angell.'

'Not *now*, Miss Lock. I want ten minutes' peace, *please*, to study this correspondence.' Angell glanced up and she was startled at his face. Like a man with a bad heart who has climbed too many stairs. 'Whatever it is will wait.'

'Actually, it's Mr Birman, sir. He's waiting to see you, but I didn't announce him while that – that fellow was here.'

'Mr Birman . . .' Angell closed the file. 'Did he say what? . . . Show him in.'

Vincent Birman was also surprised at Angell's colour when he entered. The whole situation was getting even more complex, for he had recognized Godfrey Brown as he passed through the outer office on his way out. But it was his business never to know more than he was told.

'*Well?*' said Angell harshly.

'You all right, old boy?'

'Why shouldn't I be all right?'

'Oh, sorry, yes. I thought I'd ask. There's a lot of 'flu about just at the moment.'

'What is it you want to see me about? My next client is due.'

'I came,' said Birman, 'to ask you for a cheque made payable to cash for £2,000.'

A car started outside, revved up violently. It jagged at the nerves. Birman folded his gloves and stuffed them in his pocket and blew on his fingers. 'It's pretty cold this morning.'

'Two thousand pounds?'

'From your client,' said Birman, not quite able to keep

the irony out of his voice.

Angell detected it, but blood was beating so thickly in his ears that caution could hardly be heard. Possibly the fiction that he was acting on behalf of a client had outlived its usefulness.

'What am I to assume from that?'

Birman shrugged. 'You are to assume that human nature is as nasty as we all supposed.'

The colour was coming back to Angell's face. He cleared his throat.

'I thought Jude Davis had refused. Refused.'

'So did I. But he's had time to think and he's changed his mind. There's no righteousness in the world.'

Angell's trousers were sticking to the chair. He shifted. At the last, now that revenge was almost on his tongue to be tasted, like a suspect wine, he drew back for a moment, aghast.

'Do you mean . . . What guarantee do we have that, once the money is paid, the agreement will be followed?'

Vincent Birman smiled thinly. 'None, old boy. Absolutely none. You've got to face the fact, I'm afraid, that once you step off the path and start walking on the grass you may get your feet wet. But I only give Davis a thousand now, and the second thousand when it's all over. At the worst you can only be cheated of half.'

Angell stared out of the window at the false sunshine which from here gave the same illusion of warmth as Birman's smile. Almost to his own surprise, a twinge of conscience, an echo of old training and beliefs. They legitimized the objections which arose from his hatred of squandering money. He hesitated and felt the roughened filling with his tongue. Then he thought of Godfrey – the man who had made him a cuckold, that derisory figure of all farce. The world was black at this moment, when the prospect of revenge opened up, blacker and more hopeless than it had ever been.

'Unless,' said Birman, 'your client has gone cold on the idea and wants to withdraw.'

'No,' said Angell. 'When last I spoke to him he was quite decided that this was what he wanted. I'm empowered to pay out the money on his behalf. A thousand pounds now?'

'Two thousand pounds now. I have to guarantee that the

second thousand is in my possession when the first is paid.'

The following week Godfrey was skipping in the gym when Jude Davis beckoned to him and they sat down in a corner together. Davis had been distant recently, so Godfrey was glad to find him in a confidential mood.

'Look, boy, I've got a big possibility for you. You know Tokio Kio?'

'Who doesn't?'

'Well, you know he's booked for ten rounds at York Hall next month with Kevin O'Shea, the Irish champion?'

'I ought to. I was hoping to get on the same bill.'

'Well, maybe you will . . .'

'Oh? That's what I like to hear.'

'O'Shea's manager rang up last week. O'Shea's twisted his ankle in training and is out.'

Godfrey ran a hand through his springing hair. 'What you trying to say?'

'Take it easy. You know Tokio Kio's main job in coming to Europe is to meet Karl Heist in Hamburg at the end of Feb. for the World title. He wanted a fight before it to get used to things over here. He's never been to Europe before. This ten-round bout with O'Shea was just intended to be a limber up. It was going to be a break for O'Shea as well.'

'How d'you make that out? Kio would have eaten O'Shea. Everybody says so.'

'Yes . . . Yes.' Jude Davis stared at the gold signet ring on his wedding finger. 'Go and put your robe on; you've been sweating.'

'No, this towel's O.K. What're you driving at, Jude?'

'O'Shea has had a bad deal recently. We all feel that. He got that decision – in Dublin of all places! – then he broke his hand in Liverpool and was out of the game for six months. He needed a come-back. Now he's ruined the works by spraining his ankle.'

Godfrey grunted. 'What sort of a come-back was he going to make against a feller with the heaviest fists in his class?' He stared at his manager. 'D'you mean it was going to be fixed for him to win?'

Jude Davis smiled at his fingers. 'You have romantic ideas, boy. Tokio Kio wouldn't spoil his reputation. But

275

Kio's manager wanted him to have a full work-out with all the trappings of a real fight but without too much pressure on him, as you might say. Training isn't the same. And an exhibition bout doesn't have the build-up of tension. Kio's manager had agreed that Kio should let O'Shea go the full ten rounds, and Kio would obviously win on points. That way O'Shea gets a good write-up – man who went the distance with the probable new world champ. Kio gets his full work-out and the German fans are encouraged to buy tickets for the title fight thinking their man will most likely win.'

Godfrey pulled his towel thoughtfully backwards and forwards across his shoulders.

'What's on your mind?'

'I thought for a bright boy you could probably guess.'

Two young boxers were thumping away at each other in the ring. The bell went and they immediately broke and like Zombies began shadow boxing until they could start again.

Godfrey whistled faintly. 'What a break. But why me?'

'It is not decided yet, but I thought I'd let you know. Keep it under your hat. Nobody knows yet that O'Shea is going to withdraw. He withdrew last week, and ever since Sam Windermere the promoter has been looking around for a sub. But Boy Anderson is fighting in Australia. Len Flodden has just had an operation on his eyebrows. There's others who'd give a lot for the chance but I don't believe they'd do as well on the night. You're ready for a quick step up. But it's a question whether you'd pull in the paying customers.'

'Kio will. Kio would against anybody. He's the big draw. He's never been seen in England before. *I'd* pay to see him!'

'You'll see him all right. If this goes through. Anyway you can't lose.'

'You mean I can't win.'

'Just tell me if you don't want it. Windermere can get Sanchez over from Madrid.'

'No, it was me joking, see. 'Course I want it. Both hands and feet. Smashing. But will Kio play?'

'How play?'

'Well, at least he was fighting the champion of Ireland –

276

even though it was a bit of a joke. Now he's only fighting the champion of Kensington, a bloke with only sixteen professional fights under his belt. Won't it be beneath his dig?'

'I don't think so. He's a stranger over here. The Japanese are very polite. They'll consider it ungentlemanly to complain about the quality of a substitute. And on the night you'll do as well as O'Shea would have done.'

'You can bury me if I don't do better.'

'The man I still have to get round is Sam Windermere. He's half there. Of course he knows it's meant as a rehearsal for Hamburg, but he can't afford to let it be generally known. It's got to be a good show and it's got to *look* like a good show on the bills.'

'Soften him up,' said Godfrey. 'Needle him, get to him, bribe him, put the screw on.'

There was a glint of dislike in Jude Davis's eye as he took out his notebook and made an entry in it. 'Leave me to manage my own business, Godfrey. You see to your end. I take it you're willing to fight Kio if I can arrange it?'

'You bet!'

'It's a big chance. If we fix it up it will mean strict training from now on.'

It meant strict training from then on. And for once Godfrey was prepared to lay off the women. On his second visit to Sally's flat they had bickered afterwards, scratchily, edgily, more like people getting near the end of an affair than at the beginning; she had flung his clothes off a chair she wanted to sit on, he had sulkily ignored her chatter; when he left there was no suggestion of another meeting. As for Pearl, she was too close to him, and he was too edgy and mixed up inside to want her just now. It was obviously nothing to do with Flora, it was just that he was used to having the old girl around, someone to *row* with, someone to sharpen his wits on.

When he got home one day to his bed-sitter, in the ten-year-old Vauxhall Velox he now drove, Pearl was waiting for him on the doorstep.

'Oyster!' he said, slamming the door of the car and jumping up the steps. 'Well, stone me! I didn't reckon to find you slumming it out in Clapham. Come on in! Come on up! I'm third floor, and it's crummy, but it's just somewhere to hole out till I find something better.' While he talked and showed her up, his mind flickered casually over the fact that nine months ago he had had to wait outside *her* house, time after time after time, because he'd got it bad then. Now she'd got it bad, and that pleased him.

He admired her legs all the way up the dark and dirty stairs. Then when he unlocked the door and showed her in he pushed her back against the door and began kissing her.

She was in a cream top-coat and he began undoing the buttons. She weakly tried to push his hands away. 'Godfrey, we've got to talk.'

'What about, Oyster? Talking's a waste of time . . .'

'I haven't seen you for over a week. A week yesterday. You haven't telephoned or –'

'You told me not to –'

'Well, you could have tried in the afternoon. What is it? Lady Vosper's been dead for three weeks and now you don't come. Have you found a new girl?'

He laughed, dark eyes staring steadily into blue ones that were themselves darkening with the sensation of having his hands upon her.

'Have a bit of common. Where could I find another girl like you? Think you find 'em two a penny in the boxing ring? Have a bit of common, Oyster.'

'How am I to know if you don't come?'

'I'll tell you,' he said. 'But a bit later on. Later on I'll tell you.'

'Godfrey. I want to know *now*.' With a great effort she pushed his hands away and slid along the wall.

He dropped his own hands, petulance, annoyance in his face. 'What's biting you? What's wrong, then?'

She said: 'When – when Lady Vosper died I thought it would be better. But it's been worse. You've only been near me once. You've *changed*. In yourself. I want to know why. Have I done something?'

Normally he could have taken this in his stride, have jollied her along, laughing and – if necessary – lying, but all the time good-tempered, confident that his good looks, his own particular way with women would do the trick and overcome her doubts. But somehow things weren't quite like that nowadays. You pressed the usual stops: hearty self-confidence, cheerful easy manner, inquiring practised hands, but they didn't quite work, even for him. They'd got a false note to them, as if he didn't believe in them himself, as if bad temper or annoyance or grief or the thought of bloody Flora had put a curse on him – and when you didn't believe what you were saying to a bird how could you expect *her* to believe it? And his anger at his failure transferred from himself to her. He remembered, with resentment now, how difficult she had been at the beginning, how her restraint and choosiness had given her a special attraction – all the pains he had been at to break it down. Now it was broken down but she was *still* difficult. He didn't want her to be difficult. He had no *patience* with her. He wanted sex – the appetite was there just the same – but he had no patience with any woman. Any tart would have done, and yet no one did.

He said: 'Look, what the hell . . . I've got this fight. It's the biggest ever. I got less than three weeks to be in absolute peak. You got to get out of my hair – stop needling. Everyone has. Not you but – everybody.'

'All your other women.'

'O.K., O.K., if you think that. I'm a sultan. This pad looks like a harem, doesn't it? I can't help your worries. Go back to your old man if you don't like me. He'll be a treat for you. Does he take his law books to bed with him?'

'Shut up! You're horrible! When you sneer I see you all over again. Like last spring. Sometimes I think I'm mad to – to . . .'

He was surprised to see the unexpected temper in her; it struck a responding chord, and he shouted at her, shouting her down. She glared voicelessly back at him, eyes really blazing, and suddenly hit him across the face. It was like hitting a piece of stone, but her fingers left red marks. He grabbed her hand and twisted it; not hard but his grip hurt. She tried to wrench it free. He put his free hand greedily down into her blouse. She bit him.

He lurched away from her so that she stumbled and nearly fell.

'You – you great bitch!' he shouted, out of breath with his own rage, nursing his forearm through his jacket sleeve.

'I won't be taken for granted!' she gasped. 'I won't, I

won't, I *won't*!'

'One of these days, little Oyster, you'll get what's coming to you.'

'One of these days,' she said, 'I'll be *done* with you! And I shall thank God when I am!'

'But you're not yet, Oyster, and you know it. You want me and I want you, and that's the way it's going to be. So keep your teeth to yourself or one of these days I'll give 'em a tap and knock 'em out. Nothing easier, see.'

He raised his fist as if to hit her. She stared at him wildly, expecting to be hit, but he did not bring his fist forward. She turned to hide the sudden tears in her eyes, grabbed the door handle, got it open and stumbled down the stairs.

When she had gone he took off his coat and rolled up his shirt. She had drawn blood in two places and he dabbed it with a handkerchief and then put on some sticking plaster. While he was doing this and using all the curses a hard life had taught, he was sufficiently occupied to think no further. But when he had done what he had to do he sat on the bed and kicked off his rubber shoes and lay back against the bed-head with his arm on his forehead and stared at the old fight posters he had stuck on the opposite wall.

If he'd played it differently she would be with him now and it would all be coming along fine. She had come for it and she had gone away without it. That was his fault, and for the life of him he did not know what had gone wrong. Even worse, it would take time to make up a row like this, he knew her.

Somehow Flora had still got him. Maybe he'd cared more for the old girl than he'd thought; but it wasn't just that. While Flora was alive and he was living with her he had gone gaily all through the pursuit of Pearl, and three or four other affairs which had come along so easy you couldn't call them pursuits at all. He had gone back to Flora all the time, getting fun out of her even though she was so much older. She was his employer, a viscountess, someone not on the ordinary production lines. Yet at the time it hadn't seemed anything more. She wasn't his special bit of tail; she wasn't his mother. Now she was dead she was hard to shake off – that was all.

But while it was like this he put his foot wrong everywhere. He was bloody miserable. He didn't want his own company and he didn't want anyone else's.

He turned his face to the wall. Anyway this mood should make him an even better fighter. Maybe he'd take this Tokio Kio apart.

Chapter Six

Godfrey got his belongings sent on from Merrick House. They were short of a few things, but what the hell. He didn't understand the law. A seedy lawyer he went to see confirmed what Angell had told him, said he'd probably have to wait months for his money.

The property of Merrick House, not being a subject concerned in Lady Vosper's will, was handed over without delay to the fourth Viscount Vosper by the trustees administering the third Viscount Vosper's will.

At this stage Angell tried to prevent Land Increments from immediately exercising their option to purchase the property. He argued that it was an unfortunate coincidence that Flora Vosper should die almost at the same time as the announcement of the development scheme. Had the two events been separated by even a few months it would not have looked such a suspicious case of pre-knowledge; and he felt that if the option to buy were exercised immediately it would look too calculated a manoeuvre.

Francis Hone would have none of this. 'Of course it was a calculated manoeuvre: this is what business is about. Vosper is bound to be annoyed but he can do nothing. A perfectly straightforward legal proposition was put to him and he accepted it.'

'My position is a shade delicate . . .'

'Nothing of the kind, Wilfred. You know better than I do that the purchaser's solicitor is in no way bound to disclose information to the vendor's solicitor. It is the job of the vendor's solicitor to find out all he can. That's why you were so wise in putting Vosper off employing a Swiss solicitor, in which case the ethics, you tell me, would have been different. We live in a tough commercial world, not the world of the kindergarten. If Vosper has a complaint, let him complain to Hollis for not exercising sufficient vigilance.'

Claude Vosper had a complaint. He flew to London, something he realized he should have done long ago; and

282

Hollis, soundly – though quite unfairly – upbraided, took him for a long conference with Counsel. Counsel studied the option agreement at some length and informed them that in his opinion nothing could be done to break it. Conveyances must be delivered, as stipulated, within 28 days of the notice being given. They still had 21 days' grace in which to seek further advice if they so wished.

The following day Viscount Vosper called on Angell – without an appointment. At first Angell refused to see him, sheltering behind the ethical point that he could only properly deal with Lord Vosper through Mr Hollis. Vosper sent in a message that Mr Hollis was no longer his solicitor. After some further hesitation Angell consented to see Vosper, and it was a thoroughly unpleasant interview. It ended by Vosper threatening to send a full report to the Law Society.

Angell put on an impressive show but in fact felt extremely uncomfortable. He was particularly susceptible to anything impinging on his professional behaviour, and while he knew he had nothing really to fear he nevertheless feared it. With great relief he heard a week later that Vosper had gone back to Switzerland. It seemed that everything was going to be all right.

On that front. The domestic front was still in disarray. For the first time in their life together Pearl was moody and listless. To help her out of it, to charm her on her way, to give her a new interest, he had prepared a special surprise for her. An evening out. He had, he told her, bought two ring-side tickets for a boxing match at York Hall, Bethnal Green on the following Tuesday. Their friend Godfrey Brown was topping the bill.

Pearl stared: 'What made you do that?'

'Do what? Buy the tickets? I thought it would be a nice surprise for you.'

'I don't like boxing. I never have.'

'But you went once to the Albert Hall – on your own. Do you remember? Last October, was it?' Angell smiled and puffed and looped back his hair, the better to scrutinize her. 'You thought I didn't know, but you left the seat ticket and the programme in your room. It's *quite* unimportant of course. I'm not trying to attach any importance to it.'

'It was – a championship fight. I had nothing to do and went out of curiosity.'

'Well, I'm going to this out of curiosity, my dear. To see how far – with our help – our little champion has progressed.'

'I thought you didn't like him – had lost interest in him.'

'I never had an interest. The interest was yours.'

'He called here to see *you* in the first place.'

'Yes . . . Yes. That was a temporary convenience . . . But he is so ill-mannered; an oafish creature. A true product of the slums. I suppose one cannot expect too much of such a person.'

'Then why go to see him fight?'

'We launched him. This is his first important bout. I thought it would be – interesting.'

Pearl stared at her finger nails, which she had just re-varnished. 'I don't want to go, Wilfred.'

'But my dear, I've bought the tickets. They cost the ridiculous price of five guineas each. It's really outrageous, almost three times the price of a theatre stall.'

Pearl screwed on the top of the varnish bottle. The pear-drop smell was unpleasant to her. Something in Wilfred's tone was also unpleasant. Five guineas. This was the pointer to something, but she did not know what. The expenditure of so much money indicated some harping persistence of interest.

'How did you know about it?' she asked.

'About what?'

'The fight? You never read sporting papers.'

'He told me about it. I forgot to tell you he came to see me in my office recently. He wanted to consult me about a legacy he expected from Lady Vosper. How did *you* know about it?'

'I didn't know – you've just told me. What fight is it?'

'Against a man called, I believe, Tokio Kio. He's champion of Japan. Quite a big affair.'

'Is he likely to win? Godfrey, I mean. Against a man like that.'

'He seems very confident. D'you know.' Angell gave a grunt of satisfaction. 'He seems very confident indeed. We shall see, shan't we.'

'I'd rather not go.'

'Brown said he would like us both to be there.'

'He *did*?'

'Yes. He did.'

To give herself time to think, Pearl got up and waved her outstretched fingers about, drying the varnish.

She said: '*Has* she left him a legacy?'

'I don't know. I declined to deal with the matter. It can't be very much anyhow, as she had very little to leave.'

'Is he still boxing under her name?'

'I believe so . . . I think there was something deeper, more intimate between those two than one would have supposed.'

'What makes you say so?'

'Well, I think she may well have been his mistress,' Angell said, watching her face.

'Oh, that,' said Pearl.

Boxing News ran a profile that week of 'Godfrey Vosper, formerly Godfrey Brown, 23-year-old almost unknown feather-weight, who after only 16 professional bouts has been surprisingly chosen by Promoter Sam Windermere to replace accident-prone Kevin O'Shea to meet Tokio Kio, Champion of Japan, over 10 rounds at York Hall next Tuesday. Vosper who has won all but one of his professional fights became a pro four years ago after a successful run as an amateur.' (The *News* charitably did not attempt to explain how a man came to have had only sixteen fights in four years.) 'Vosper, brought up in an orphanage, changed his name from Brown earlier this year in gratitude to ex-racing driver and sporting benefactor Lady Vosper who died recently and who never wavered in her belief that he would become one of the leading boxing names of today. Bringing along a young fighter who shows great potential is, of course, no easy task. Too often we have seen a youngster fed on a string of soft touches, racking up victory after victory, then being tossed in over his head and found wanting. Yet this certainly looks like Vosper's big chance, for Kio comes to Europe for the first time with a reputation as a fast man and a deadly puncher. Of forty-three fights to date he has won thirty-nine, twenty-one of his opponents not lasting the distance. One drawn bout, two adverse points decisions, and stopped only once fours years ago by the then world champion Saldivar; this adds up to a formidable record. Karl Heist will have to work hard to defend his new-won crown. In the meantime British fans will have a chance of seeing Tokio Kio in action on February 4.'

Tokio Kio said in soft Japanese: 'Who is this man I am to fight? How is it that he is rated seventh only among the fighters of England? Is this not a reflection on my own position? Is it intended as an insult?'

'When the cable arrived I knew nothing of this,' said his manager. 'The cable stated merely that the Irishman was injured and this Vosper was the best substitute they could get. Windermere I relied on as a gentleman. Ratings were not discussed. Windermere has agreed to pay you three thousand pounds in American dollars. There is no insult in that.'

'Sam was sorry he couldn't come to meet the plane himself,' Ed Marks said, through his cigar. 'But this charity show tonight, he couldn't skip it. He sends his salaams and says he wants us all to meet up later this evening.'

'What is it he says?' Kio asked.

His manager translated. 'That's all right,' he said to Ed Marks, smiling. 'We understand. That's all right.'

'How small the automobiles are here,' said Kio. 'After the States, I mean. In a sense it is more like Japan. But the houses are ugly and old. You will see Windermere this evening about it? Perhaps I shall refuse this fight.'

'And lose the purse?'

'I could make an exhibition match –'

'It would break the contract. There is no need to act hastily. This Vosper may be much better than his rating.'

'Talking about Vosper?' said Ed Marks through his cigar. 'He's a good boy. He'll make a good showing, you can stand on me for that.'

'What is it he says?' Kio asked.

His manager translated. 'That's all right,' he said to Ed Marks, smiling. 'We understand.'

'Seventh among the fighters of England,' said Kio. 'I did not imagine there could be seven worse than that Scotsman – what's his name?'

'Look, Kio,' said his manager, 'this is a warm-up for

your fight with Heist. Fares and hotel expenses are paid. This is all sheer profit. If you want to fight an exhibition, fight it with Vosper. There will be no loss of face.'

'And what will the papers in Japan say? Kio matched with a seventh-rate. That will show them how Kio is esteemed in England.'

'I'll talk to Windermere tonight. But I think it will be too late to do anything. And we can't postpone.'

'The women look interesting – and display a lot of themselves. There will be time to see what they are like?'

'After Tuesday,' said Kio's manager nervously. 'After Tuesday.'

There was silence for a time as the taxi was blocked in a traffic jam.

Ed Marks coughed through his cigar, and ash floated down on to his coat. 'Sam says let's all meet up tonight at the Colony. Say about eleven, he says. His show'll be over by then, he says, and we can have a slap-up meal. How about that?'

'What does he say?' Kio asked.

'He says I am to meet Windermere tonight after his show, in his office. There we can talk business.' To Ed Marks, Kio's manager said, smiling: 'That's all right. I shall be honoured to come. But for Kio it must be an early night. Bed at ten. I shall be honoured to dine with you.'

'Seventh only among the fighters of England,' said Kio, putting a sweet in his mouth and crunching it. 'I think it has been done to insult me because I am a Japanese. The English still hate the Japanese. They hate us for the beating we gave them in the last war. My father died from the hardships he suffered in that war.'

'A lot of people died,' said the manager. 'Many people suffered. Why don't you relax. I'll ask Windermere tonight. There may be very good reasons why he has chosen this man.'

'Oh, very good reasons, yes!'

'I have heard that O'Shea would have been too easy for you. He's on the downgrade. This young man, though he is unknown, may give you more to do.'

'He will perhaps have more to do himself, picking himself up off the floor.'

'That's the way I like to hear you talk. Remember this is not the important bout, the next is.'

'Every fight is important,' said Kio. 'Especially against an Englishman. But I have not decided to fight yet. You will see what Windermere says. I do not like this man who has come to meet us. He is of no account and his cigar is cheap.'

'Take it easy,' said his manager. 'Windermere can't be in two places at once.'

'Tell him we got him a sparring session tomorrow at eleven. A couple of good boys,' said Ed Marks through the smoke. 'That is at the B.B.B.C. gym at Haverstock Hill. Eleven o'clock tomorrow.'

'What does he say?' asked Kio.

Kio's manager translated. 'That's all right,' he said, smiling at Ed Marks. 'That's all right.' To Kio he added, 'If these boys are not good enough I'll get you better over the week-end. There isn't much time to get settled in.'

'I don't want to get settled in,' said Tokio Kio, flexing his hands. 'I am ready to fight now, tonight. But not with the seventh-rated fighter in England. I will not put up with that chosen insult.'

'Relax. You may have to.'

'Then I will be sorry for him.'

On the Thursday morning Angell found in his post a letter from the secretary to the Professional Purposes Committee of the Law Society. It enclosed a photocopy of a 'letter of complaint' from Viscount Vosper of four pages in length, and it invited his comments.

Anxious as never before about his own rectitude, Angell immediately began his reply. First he thought that as there was initially nothing to answer in Vosper's letter of complaint he would write a single sheet of dignified denial and leave it at that. Then he suddenly felt the need to comment at length on every part of the letter, scrapped the first attempt, and ended up with a scribbled draft which would have filled eight pages. This too did not satisfy him and he took the matter to Esslin, who was astonished at all the fuss necessary to explain a matter of basic legal pragmatism. Angell returned to his office and began again. By lunchtime, when he was feeling very hungry indeed, he had made a third draft which seemed to him to embody the virtues of both the others. He dictated it to Miss Lock and then walked up to Holborn and had sole veronique, with six veal cutlets to follow, a rather good Christmas pudding and some perfectly ripened Camembert.

There are times in the lives of most people when difficulties, anxieties, problems seem to crowd on top of each other, and the solution or the removal of the most pressing only means there is room for the next one to take its place.

This week he had to come to a decision whether to let young Whittaker leave or give him the extra 5% of the profits that would keep him. All winter he had been stalling off this painful decision; yet it had been submerged today, when he had hoped to give it full thought, by Vosper's letter. Now that the Vosper letter was answered, instead of turning to Whittaker, his mind obstinately moved towards Pearl.

It seemed to him that this preoccupation with and worry over the Vosper business had been a thoroughly dangerous one from the beginning. To further it he had allowed Godfrey to make excuses to call at his house; in its encouragement he had gone to Switzerland and allowed Godfrey to sneak into his bed. In the very *first* place, long, long ago, nearly twelve months ago, his first flight to Vosper had introduced him to Pearl. Without it he would never have met her. Happy, happy time before he met her, when he had lived in his tightly cocooned world and had had nothing to think about but his food and his pictures and his furniture.

He nourished illogical expectations about the events of next Tuesday. The whole idea of this very appropriate revenge would never for a second have come to his mind except for Pearl prompting him to help Godfrey in the first place. It would be a fitting retribution – a wholly fitting retribution – if only one could be *sure*.

At times he could not bear to think how much hung on the outcome. If anything went wrong it was money thrown away, wasted, torn up. Two thousand pounds on the outcome of a few rounds of fighting. Two thousand pounds given away to this man Jude Davis, who was perhaps preparing to double-cross him and laugh in his face afterwards. There was no redress. One paid up and took a chance. The thought made him ill.

Soon after lunch, Miss Lock brought in the typed letter to the Law Society and Wilfred read it through carefully and signed it. Immediately afterwards he rang Pearl. There was no reply. Wilfred worried his way through another hour of the afternoon before he remembered it was the day for Pearl's monthly lunch with that egregious friend of hers Hazel Timpson. This relieved him for a few minutes until he realized that Pearl's appointment was probably only a blind for a secret meeting with Godfrey. Today, even at this very moment, they might be . . . He told Miss Lock to ring again; again there was no reply.

'But I keep telling you,' said Hazel. 'You *have* changed. Not just in looks, I mean, though of course you're *thinner*. It's not just that. You seem to have *changed*, dear. This last two months, mostly.'

'I've grown up,' said Pearl. 'It happens.'

Hazel eyed her with satisfaction. She thought Pearl looked restless, unhappy, her eyes were darker, older. She didn't wish Pearl any harm but there was a grim compensation in observing a situation in which her friend, having so obviously married for money, wasn't finding life a bed of roses. The first few meetings had been very hard to take: Pearl's expensive clothes, Pearl's ring, Pearl's hair-do, the glittering restaurant, the gloves, the handbag with the nice little bunch of notes, the lizard shoes. In the time it took the leaves to fall she had changed from a rather ambitious shop-girl into a dignified, quietly sophisticated West End beauty.

Then before Christmas she had become absent-minded, more excitable than she had ever been before, eager to finish lunch and be gone, happy in a strained way, but almost *rude*, Hazel thought.

Now this third change, in which Hazel was welcome again, a new interest shown in the old scenes, all the time in the world to stay and talk, almost wanting to sit on and on. She had brought up that visit to the Trad Hall when she had thrown over Ned McCrea for that awful little man with the good looks who had taken her home. It was an occurrence that most girls would have wanted to forget, but Pearl insisted on talking about it today and about Godfrey Vosper as he was called. She seemed to want to go on talking about him. Apparently they had met several times – even met since her marriage. It was all very odd, Hazel thought, and suspicious. Yet it would be stretching it too far to suspect that Pearl, who had married for money and who even in the old days had really been too snooty for Hazel's friends, should be having it off with a shabby little boxer. You couldn't swallow that.

. . . And Pearl, feeling herself more and more separated from Hazel, more and more detached from the life she had led before her marriage, less and less interested in the doings of that world with its Saturday night hops and its fumblings in the back row of the flicks, its Ned McCreas and its Chris Cokes, listened to herself, *heard* herself talking on and on, bringing Godfrey's name in every now and then because she had to talk about him to *somebody* and Hazel was the only confidante she had, the only one who had even *met* him. She tried to stop and yet went on with growing incredulity, knowing she had already said too much and watching the speculation grow in Hazel's eyes. It was all so pent-up inside her that talking to Hazel, skirting round the essentials, never touching them with words but touching them in her own mind, was the only alternative to a hysterical outburst. Even so she had to watch her voice to make sure it was level, to keep the tears out of it.

She despised herself all the more because, not merely was her life with Wilfred so much superior to the way she had lived before, but even Godfrey, *even* Godfrey's life with its tawdry gym and its brutal climaxes seemed to her far superior to any sort of life Hazel's friends led. All right, she thought, you can't get much lower than fighting for a living; and yet it had a vitality, a courage, a sincerity that most other ways of life lacked. You could cheat and figure the angle in most jobs and professions, but there was no show you could put on in the ring that didn't have to be backed by guts and stamina and ability. There were no easy berths, there was no avoiding the issue, no way of passing the harsh responsibilities to somebody else. The weaklings were soon weeded out.

She had not seen Godfrey since the meeting in his bed-sitter. Something had gone wrong between them, and she knew that if they met again now it would not come right. She was offended by his casualness, hated him *always* for taking her for granted, was glad she had bitten him and would do so again. But she wanted to *see* him, she wanted the argument, the quarrel, the talk to go on and on. And at the end perhaps there would be agreement again and love. But she did not *see* him; he never called, rang, wrote. She might have dropped out of his life. Though she knew he was in strict training for his fight, she was racked with jealousy at the thought of the other women he most probably had.

Nothing, nothing, nothing would induce her to risk the first move again, to be the asker instead of the asked. She had been wrong-footed last time by the knowledge that she came to him instead of he to her. But she desperately needed to see him and to talk to him. So instead she talked *about* him to Hazel, with bitterness grinding deep.

Sometimes she wished Flora Vosper was still alive. It had been better then. Coincidentally or significantly there had been a sourness in him since Flora died. She had been a centre for his life, a stabilizer. And if he wasn't with you, you knew at least where he was likely to be. Now no one had any idea where he was likely to be. Pearl only knew that if she accepted Wilfred's invitation she would see him next Tuesday.

Where Godfrey was that afternoon Pearl would never have guessed. Yesterday he had jarred his hand taking his frustrations out on the punch-ball, and Pat Prince had said: 'Take a day off, boy. You've been going at it all week. You don't want to be over the hill by Tuesday.'

So Godfrey took the day off, and after lying in bed most of the morning reading the strips in some American mags he suddenly dragged on his clothes and ran out to his Velox and drove off. He kept south of the river for a time and then crossed and soon joined the A 12 north of Ilford. From there it was all familiar driving, bypassing Brentwood and Chelmsford and striking north. It was a good enough day for the end of January with heavy clouds but gleams of wintry sun, and the roads were not wet. He had a sandwich and a Coke at a lorry driver's pull-in and reached Handley Merrick soon after three.

He was careful not to park his car outside the gates of Merrick House but backed into a lane near by and strolled up to look at the old house. The gates were shut and there seemed no sign of life. He wondered if Mr and Mrs Forms were still in occupation. It didn't look like it because last week's snow hadn't quite melted, and you could see it had never been cleared off the steps.

He climbed over the low wall and sidled round the house, whistling silently to himself. All quiet. He went up to the windows of one of the kitchens and peered in. The place was completely unchanged from when he had lived there; furniture, table, cooking pans, ancient Aga, cupboards, crockery. He walked round to the front and climbed on the sill of a window to look into the hall. This great gaunt room was just the same too: refectory table, tall-backed chairs, armour on walls, suits of armour at foot of stairs, battle flags, the two cannon.

He went on to the wing where Flora had lived. She might only just have left it. Except that a curtain hung loose from a window – that she would never have stood for – and there was dust. The declining sun fell on this window and showed up the dust.

He slouched round to the next window and found as he expected that nobody had repaired the defective catch. He pushed it up with his penknife, opened the window, climbed in.

It was cold. That was the first difference. It wasn't too bad outside, but inside it was as cold as the tomb. It had been impossible ever to heat the whole house without a completely new system which would have been vastly expensive, so Flora had had pipes and an oil-fired boiler put in just to heat the eight rooms she lived in. Flora was always one for comfort, so these rooms normally had been pretty warm. Going out of them in winter to the rest of the house had been like going out of doors. You put on a coat or you ducked rapidly back.

Now this heated part was as cold as all the rest. Like Flora. It had lost its heat.

Whistling through his teeth, Godfrey sat in his favourite chair and looked at the empty chair opposite him. You only had to imagine a little and there she was opposite you, dark haired and sallow skinned and sardonic and middle-aged and witty and irritable and a dare-devil. Smoking and drinking all the more because she wasn't supposed to.

293

Poking fun at him. Learning him things. One jump ahead. You never knew when you had her. Even in bed. Old bitch. Old bitch.

Godfrey got up and looked around the room. Everything was just as they'd left it last time they had been here. It was all locked up, preserved in aspic till the will was proved or until some lawyer, some fat stupid lawyer like Angell, decided something. Until then here it all was. You could nick things and nobody'd be the wiser. All that malarkey about getting a few of his own things sent on, and then they left the whole lot for anybody to nick who came along and could force a window.

He wandered into her bedroom, and here some things had been taken. Miriam, he supposed, claiming personal belongings of her mother. He went into his old bedroom, and from there passed into the long corridor that led to the big hall and the great house proper.

It was still light when he got to the hall. The setting sun was staining the windows but in a few minutes it would be going dark. What was that fool thing Flora often said? 'Life is too short for cynic peep or critic bark, quarrel or reprimand; 'twill soon be dark.' She usually said it just after she'd had a row with someone, for God's sake! Well it had gone dark for her now.

When you come to think of it, and looking round this hollow gaunt room, maybe there wasn't all that much to nick. Who'd want a cannon? Who'd want a flag that'd been waved at some goddam place called Malplaquet? Who'd want a suit of armour?

Godfrey had always thought the main house a bit of a mausoleum, and now and then in the dark days of winter his hair had pricked as he went up and down the stairs and poked about in one or other of the main bedrooms with their fourposters and their tapestries and their crests. Well, it was soon going to be a dark day of winter now. Even while he stood there the sun plunged behind the trees and left the hall clammy and shadowy and chill.

One day last winter he had walked through the house with Flora while she had told him all about the Vospers. Not that she was a Vosper herself; he reckoned she came from something better than a line of bloody generals; but anyhow she had told him about them. And he had said, what was the use of it, all this crap about swords and shields and flags and who fought against who and when? And she had said: 'Little man, little man, if you ask that, nothing's any use, any time, any more. We're chaff on a floor that the wind blows away. But wouldn't you prize the Lonsdale belt if your father or your grandfather had won it?'

He walked out into the library; and here somebody had been at the books. They weren't so much disturbed as fewer in number. Miriam again, pawing them over, wondering which she could sell without it being noticed. Mostly they were musty old books of battles and collected editions of the classics; but you never knew what would fetch money these days.

As he walked round the shelves he thought he heard a footstep in the hall. *That* made his hair prickle. He turned and went back to the door.

The light was fading quickly, and there were a lot of shadows where there had been no shadows five minutes ago. The two suits of armour at the foot of the stairs glinted in the dusk. There might have been men in them. Maybe now the house was empty all the flaming Vospers had come back to live in it. Champing their jaws, flaunting their medals and rattling their bones.

Then he thought he saw a figure move from behind the stairs and slip towards the corridor to the west wing. It was just a trick of the light but it looked like Flora. Sturdy figure, dark heavy hair, brisk mannish step.

'Flora!' he said. And then he stopped, and rubbed his hand through his hair and sniggered. Silly twerp. There was no Flora here. Flora had been turned into best ash. Aristocratic cinders. Blue-blooded urn fodder. She was off the market for good.

He went to the foot of the stairs.

'Flora!' he called softly.

He couldn't see properly now, and he flicked the light switch. Of course the current was off.

He went up the stairs. 'Flora!' he shouted into the echoing passage at the top.

A tattered flag. A steel engraving of some battle scene

with guns blazing and horses snorting. A table with a model of a Sherman tank on it. A Chinese screen. A hole in the carpet.

'Flora!' he shouted.

The bedrooms along this first passage were the principal bedrooms, furnished in a mixture of heavy Jacobean and Victorian. They were, as always, draped in sheets, and the doors and sills were thick with dust. These bedrooms faced north.

'Flora!' he shouted. 'Flora!'

He went in and out of the gloomy rooms, opening doors and slamming them, while the dark crept round him and followed him everywhere.

'Flora!' he screamed, half laughing at himself, half serious. *'Flora!'*

The bloody woman was dead, rotten, burned, and the episode was over. Nothing would ever be quite the same again.

'Flora!' he shouted, having looked in ten bedrooms and drawn blank. 'You old cow! where are you? Flora!' If anyone heard him they'd think him off his trolley. For God's sake. 'Flora!'

He clattered down the stairs again, and in the dark barged into one of the suits of armour. It clattered its metal bones, and he steadied himself and went off towards the door that led to the occupied – or formerly occupied – rooms. His nose and eyes were wet with laughing at himself and he wiped them on his sleeve.

At the door he looked back into the misty angles of the dark hall. It was all dead, long ago dead and best burned like Flora and forgotten. He slammed the door behind him and groped his way into the drawing room that Flora had used. But there was nothing there for him. It was empty, sour, stale, and neglected, like all the rest. He did not know why the hell he had bothered to come.

He opened the window and climbed through it, shut it behind him, and tramped off through the overgrown garden to find his car.

Chapter Seven

Godfrey and Tokio Kio did not meet until the weigh in on the Tuesday at 1 p.m.

It was the usual gathering; the boxers, their managers or trainers, the Board of Control doctor, the matchmaker, a few old pugs and hangers on. They drifted in one by one as the time drew near. It was all shabby and casual and in a low key. The two Japanese were the last to come, and with them was Sam Windermere the promoter, a small grey-haired man with a red cheerful face. He introduced Godfrey, but instead of shaking hands Kio bowed from the waist like a dummy. Kio's manager said, smiling: 'Hullo, Vosper. Glad to know you.' Godfrey nodded distantly. He was strictly against fraternizing.

They all went inside to get undressed. As the chief fighters of the evening they were given first turn on the scales. Godfrey was eight stone nine and a half pounds, Kio eight stone eleven. They looked much the same height, but Kio had heavier shoulder muscles.

Then the doctor. Sound your heart, look in your throat, prod here and there. 'Take a breath. Let it go.' 'Are you feeling well?' 'Any dizziness?' 'Any sickness?' 'Any headaches?' 'When was your last fight?' 'Stand up straight. Stand steady.' 'O.K.'

Kio understood some of the questions, but his manager stood beside him to interpret the others. When he was passed he bowed in the same way to the doctor and went in to dress. For God's sake, Godfrey thought; the manager'd better be in the ring too tonight. To Godfrey a man who couldn't speak English was a savage from outer space.

All the same you could see he might be a tough nut. Somebody'd flattened his flat nose, and one of his ears wasn't so good. A tough nut to be cracked.

Jude Davis wasn't there this morning; Pat Prince had come along. Jude, he said, had a touch of 'flu. But he'd be there tonight.

He'd be there tonight. Godfrey felt there was something

297

odd about things. Davis had been cool, unwelcoming thes
last weeks; yet he'd arranged this fight which was the sor
of chance any boxer would jump at but almost never go
A ten-round work-out with a champion who was onl
concerned to win on points, principal bout, all notoriet
to Godfrey after for lasting ten rounds, and £600 as hi
purse into the bargain.

Well, don't look a gift horse . . .

After the weigh in Godfrey drove Pat Prince back, an
Hay Tabard who was fighting on the same bill, and Ton
Bushey the coloured heavy. Young Tabard was eating a
home, and Pat Prince got off at Oxford Circus, so Godfre
drove Bushey to one of the Angus places and they had a
big juicy rare sirloin each.

Bushey was a queer case, Godfrey thought; a classy
African from the West Coast, son of one of the chiefs
who'd come over to England to read Law, failed his finals
done odd jobs for a year or so and then after some amateu
bouts had turned pro nine months ago. He'd won all hi
five pro fights but was still a long way from the top, –
further than Godfrey, maybe because there was more
competition in the top weights. Godfrey had been on two
bills with him, and in so far as Godfrey had any friend in
his new stable, Bushey qualified.

They talked over the meal. Bushey wasn't fighting tonight
but had been up at the gym sparring with Billy Oscar who
was fighting at Wembley in two weeks. Just before they
separated Bushey said: 'Well, good luck for tonight, man.
I'll be there watching. You've got a tough assignment.'

'I'll deal with him,' said Godfrey.

'Watch out for his right. He's a spoiler. I saw him work
out in the gym yesterday. He doesn't make the best use of
his reach, but he's going to be very difficult. He's not pretty
to look at.'

'I'll see what I can do to make him not pretty to look at
afterwards.'

They both laughed. Bushey said: 'By the way, what was
that man Birman doing at the weigh in?'

'What man Birman?'

'That bald headed little man with the sharp eyes.'

'I don't know him. So what?' Then some memory clicked
in Godfrey of seeing such a man watching him curiously

t the weigh in.

'Birman's Agency,' said Bushey.

'What is it, a sports' agency?'

'Yes, they *have* their sports side. They're *arrangers*. They do everything: divorce, the lot. Birman's the head. You see, man, I worked for him for a while, though he didn't cotton on this morning.'

'Doing what? Fighting?'

'No. I was on my beam ends – didn't want to go back home – looking around. I met him in a bar. He wanted some private inquiries made and reckoned a Negro would be less noticeable than a white man. I said O.K. Then I did other jobs. Then I didn't like his outfit so I got me another job.'

'So what's it all about then? What am I supposed to do? Tell the B.B.B.C. who they can let in to the weigh ins?'

They came out into the street. It was a nasty February day with a strong searching north-east wind. Odds and ends of paper blew before it along the pavements. Dogs walked slightly sideways, their fur ruffled.

'I reckon I'm seeing things,' said Bushey, 'so it means nothing at all. But I just don't like the Birman outfit, and I don't know why he should be interested in us. And, man, I don't like Birman. He's a feller that knows a thousand people but doesn't have a friend.'

Godfrey was hardly attending. It occurred to him that he had five hours to pass before he needed to be at York Hall and he didn't know how to pass it. It wasn't the time to get himself a bird. Most boxers went home after the weigh in – had a good meal and a rest. But his bed-sitter and strip-cartoons wasn't much of a home. Before his last fight he'd had that silly cow Flora Vosper to talk to.

'How about you and me going and seeing a flick?' he said. 'You doing anything?'

'No . . .' said Bushey, and looked at him. 'Maybe you'd be better taking a sleep.'

'Who says I'll be better?'

'Well, it was just a thought. But O.K., if you feel like it, I'll go along.'

Pearl had known Wilfred less than a year, but she already knew him too well for him to be able to hide his moods.

She saw that he came home early tonight with an appear
ance of casualness put on to deceive her. Under the calm
tension was running, like a dynamo that you could feel but
not hear. He got her to cut sandwiches and when she had
done them he wolfed them down as if he had an urgent
appointment. He told her twice how they would go: York
Hall, he said, was just near Bethnal Green tube station;
there was simply no point in hiring a car; they could catch
a 137 bus in Sloane Street to Marble Arch, and then a
direct tube all the way to Bethnal Green. The total cost of
the journey this way would not be more than 3/6 for the
two of them. It was a fine night, though cold; a little walk
would do them both good. Not to dress up, of course; the
most casual clothes, one would not want to be conspicuous
in the East End. He did not realize, Pearl thought, that
however he dressed his size and manner would make him
so.

There was something greedy about his looks tonight. She
caught him looking at her sidelong the way she had noticed
him doing when he wanted to sleep with her. Yet he had
achieved that only four days ago and it was too soon for
him to want her again, or if not too soon to want her too
soon to yield, because he thought his health suffered.
Anyway, they were going *out*; one did not know how late
they would be; and they were going to see Little God.
Somehow Little God was involved.

She almost feigned sickness and called the whole thing
off, just to measure the degree of his disappointment. Yet
her need to see Godfrey was great. She wondered why
Wilfred's need was great.

Leave at 7.15. The contest did not begin until eight, and
then there would be two or three bouts before the main
one. But one did not quite know how long it would take
to get there. So the bus and the tube. It was cold out but
hot in the underground, and Wilfred mopped his brow like
a nervous applicant for a job. They climbed out of the
earth at ten minutes to eight. In Bethnal Green the frost
was crisp in the air. They were directed across the traffic
lights to a big grey building, up the steps, tickets and a
programme, into the hall. The M.C. was just climbing into
the ring.

It was like a big gymnasium, the central ring raised above the body of the hall. Very full. Promoter Sam Winermere had a sell out.

'Ladies and gentlemen, may I ask you to please take your seats, as the first contest is about to begin . . .'

They took theirs, in the first row of the seats proper – not ringside but very near. Little iron seats with canvas bottoms and backs fixed together in rows. Wilfred pushed his way in, treading on toes and shuffling through. When they sat down it at first seemed quite impossible. Wilfred sat on his arm chair and overflowed onto the next. Pearl could hardly take her seat; the man on the other side was insulting: 'If you want two seats, Guv., why don't you pay for em?' Wilfred was full of indignation at the discomfort of the seats, and the commonness of the people around him who in a Welfare State could afford such a price.

The first bout was half through before they relaxed; gradually there was a shifting and a settling, an easing of position. Angell took out his glasses, breathed on them, polished them; Pearl let out a breath and took one in; it was just possible; at the first interval she would get her coat off, it made for less bulk.

The first fight ended in a cut eye and the referee stopping it in the third round. Programme. There it was, Godfrey Vosper (Little God) of Kensington versus Tokio Kio of Kobe in a feather-weight contest of ten three-minute rounds.

There were few women here, and Pearl was glad of her head scarf which hid part of her blonde hair and made her, she thought, less noticeable. But a number of men glanced at her, and when one of them cursed, a neighbour chuckled and nudged him: 'Careful, Joe; we got ladies present.' It was like an old world courtesy. The West End might be swinging; the East End still believed in these things.

The next two fights went past in a dream, the sweat of the fighters spraying like iridescent fans, the squeak and stretch of their boots on the canvas, the thump of one when he fell, the isolated shouts of supporters, the growl or applause of the crowd. Seconds ducking in and out of the ring, sweatered, pug-featured, white trousered men, fanning, massaging, whispering, urging, patching, the clang of the bell, the only word the referee apparently ever uttered:

'*Break!*' The strange unbelievable way some of the fighte
embraced at the end, affectionately, after *all* those blo
exchanged, all that brutal striving. And then it was tin
for the principal bout.

Godfrey had been waiting for this calmly enough, sitti
in his little private cubicle which was like a Victoria
bathing hut in design but in fact was much more mode
and cheerful than the Albert Hall. The Whip had calle
out the order of bouts almost as soon as he arrived. It w:
the first time ever Godfrey had been anything but a
unimportant fighter on the undercard. He liked it this wa
He meant to keep it this way.

He was tensed up but not really nervous. He didn't hav
nerves because he had perfect confidence in being able t
take care of himself. Even if he hadn't been told it was a
fixed to go the ten rounds he would have had just th
same confidence. In fact he'd never been told to pull h
punches. What would happen, he wondered, if he knocke
Kio out? Better not try. Davis had given him this chanc
and it would be dangerous not to play it his way.

Pat Prince was bustling in and out a lot, seeing he'd g
everything, offering last minute advice.

'Where's Jude?' Godfrey asked.

'I doubt 'e'll be here. He's got 'flu; I told you this morn
ing, and you can't monkey with that. He said he wa
hoping to come but I doubt 'e'll make it.'

Godfrey grunted. 'It's funny him not being here.
thought he'd be here tonight.'

'You think what you're doing,' said Prince. 'You watc
this lad. You watch his right. He's not a south-paw bu
he's got a square stance and his right's fast as a snake. You
remember what I told you, see. You box him. If you tr
to mix it he'll leather you. Use the ring. Use your feet. He':
not so fast on his feet as you. If you see your way
through ten rounds you'll be on your way up real and
proper.'

All along it had been clear that Prince was not in the
secret.

The British Board of Control inspector came in with the
bandages and Prince stuck lengths of tape to the wall, began
to tape Godfrey's hands. After his hands were bandaged.

he inspector signed across them, so that nothing could be added. The third fight had three more rounds to go, but one or the other of the fighters might be stopped, so they'd better be ready. Through the open door Godfrey saw Kio's manager open the opposite changing booth and go in. Three or four other people were drifting about the narrow passage. Two coloured fighters were lying stretched out on a trestle with closed eyes as if they had already been knocked out. They were relaxing before *their* fight, which came on after.

The scurry of feet and voices. You were too far away to hear the crowd but you could tell. Sure enough the other two came in. One was complaining to his manager: 'It's ri-*dic*-ulous. Ri-*dic*-ulous. I was just waiting there on me knee, waiting for the count of nine!'

'Ready?' said the Whip at the door. 'It's time. Come on.'

Out into the narrow corridor, along the passage towards the indoor baths, through the double doors and into the noise and light of the arena. He hardly noticed the squat little figure on ahead of him wearing the robe with the rising sun on its back. It didn't worry him that this was a champion in his own country. He listened to the spatter of applause as he climbed into the ring; knew he would get a good round when he was introduced. He was popular already because of his last few fights – the real fight fans travelled from one hall to another – and he was the British lad against the foreigner.

The ref was a bloke called Waterford. Godfrey hadn't had him before but knew he'd had a lot of experience: a great big character in black tie and trousers and white shirt; they always seemed to choose the big refs for the small fighters and the little refs for the heavies. In his corner Pat Prince whispered some last dead-beat advice; now into the middle. Yes, he held his hands up and the crowd really gave him a welcome. This was living. There were only two sorts of living for Godfrey, sex and fighting. This was the peak. Sex afterwards, maybe, but this was the peak.

Introduced, ref talking, usual guff, clean fight and the rest; what did Kio understand anyway? squat face nodding politely, cold walnut eyes, black hair cut very short, black silk pants, red gloves. Touch the gloves, now return to the corner. Just then with his back to the ring, holding the ropes, waiting ready for the bell: Holy Jesus, in the front row, *Pearl*. Pearl and her fat ox of a husband. Both of them. Holy Moses! Well, well, well, so he hadn't lost his fans after all! A little grin turned at the corners of his mouth; he nodded at Pearl, who seemed too fascinated, too riveted with attention to nod back. And that old ox, that fat old mountain of lard, fairly wedged in his seat.

The bell. He turned and there was no one in the ring, no one in the world, but the big white-shirted ref and the small olive-skinned figure of the featherweight champion of Japan.

First round much as you'd expect it, whether it was exhibition or dead serious. No fireworks; you circled round each other, dogs on a lead, sizing each other up, looking for openings, testing out the replies, mixing it now and then but not committing yourself too far. Godfrey saw soon enough what they'd meant about Kio. He had a hunched up way of fighting, shoulders pushed forward like a man sheltering from a cold wind; with gloves raised and held in front of the chin it didn't offer much target; you hit his shoulders or his gloves or the top of his head. Of course this two-fisted defensive stance limited his own reach: it took a good three inches off the length of his punch; but when the punches came they were absolutely stiff and straight, like pistons thrust from the shoulders and almost always with feet solidly on the ground. He was probably a bit flat-footed; his footwork wasn't good by western standards. He'd got an ugly mug, Godfrey thought, spiteful and nasty, and there wasn't any brotherly love in his eyes. It'd be good to flatten that flat nose, give him a few lumps where there weren't lumps already.

So in the first round Kio mainly occupied the centre of the ring, circling in a small area, while Godfrey came in for forays and a flurry of punches, moving out and round again, landing a good deal more often than the Jap but with no effect except to score a few points. As the bell went there was a smattering of applause, no more; it looked like being a routine encounter, perhaps a bit dull, and as for points there was nothing in it so far; the ref might *just* have put Godfrey ahead; he certainly didn't look out-classed.

He didn't *feel* out-classed. As he relaxed and rinsed his mouth round with water and spat it in the bucket he could hear Prince giving the usual corny advice. 'Fight your own fight. Take it easy. Watch for that right. Don't go in to him. Let him come to you . . .'

'Seconds out.' Both boxers stood up off their little swing stools, advanced, the ref kept them apart with outstretched hands, then closed them as the bell rang.

Godfrey had never been short of confidence and he was brim full of it now, dancing in, landing a flurry of blows – all falling uselessly on arms or gloves except one that got through and caught Kio above the eyebrow – dancing away, two counter punches in the ribs he came away with, hard but unimportant; in again, tempting Kio with a slightly dropped guard, back came the counter punches aimed at his heart, but Godfrey leaned away from them. Kio fol-lowed this time, taking Godfrey into a corner; three vicious punches and one got through, hurt his ribs, if the other two had landed he might have been in trouble. Good, Kio wasn't pulling anything. Godfrey stepped away, leaning this way and that like a dancer so that three more ramrod blows missed altogether. He heard applause. Clapping not shouting. From the real fans, who knew. Applause for his boxing. It was music. Just music. It was something he couldn't have done twelve months ago – box like this. Fight, yes, but not this classy stuff. Weaving, feinting, he came again, like a master, two on Kio's nose, not weighty but beautifully balanced, sending Kio's head back an inch; Kio hadn't ridden them; away again, untouched that time. Holy smoke, he'd show them.

A sledge hammer hit him on the side of the jaw, brought him up sharp as if he had walked into a wall; blinking stars he covered up, staggered back, blocking the follow up. Knees groggy, head singing, both gloves to his head, and head down to weather this storm in the corner. Kio was hitting him almost at will, one, two, three, four, almost down. He leaned on Kio, working at Kio's ribs, both men working. *'Break!'* said the ref. Kio pushed him away. Godfrey tried to clear his head. His jaw felt as if all his back teeth were loose. He kept out of trouble by retreating, dodging, retreating. The bell . . .

In his corner Pat Prince was sponging his face, someone was rubbing the muscles of his calves. 'Now, God, take it easy. I told you, watch out for that right. You was doing fine till you walked into it. He's an old hand and he knows just when to throw it. Box him. You was doing fine. Try to keep your distance. Don't mix it – above all, don't mix it. You was doing fine – maybe with a bit of luck you can ride it out.'

Godfrey, recovering, looked across at the squat, black haired man in the other corner. Jees, he thought, if this is supposed to last ten rounds, maybe he'll ease up this next one. It was just bad luck I walked into that one. I never seen it coming at all. I'll watch the yellow bastard this time.

Seconds out . . . The third round. Godfrey had not even heard whether there had been any applause at the end of the second.

If this was a fight arranged to last the distance Kio seemed to have got rather absent-minded about the arrangement. He came out ready for the kill. He came on like a small warship, still covering himself but aiming lefts and rights like gun fire at Godfrey's face and body. Godfrey covered well, slipping away each time Kio tried to pin him against the ropes, and then, when he was eventually cornered, leaning on Kio until they were told to break. No more thunderbolts landed. They came near, but each time Godfrey just saw them. A half dozen times he landed himself, and one of these blows again hit Kio above the eyebrow where a red swelling was growing. Thwarted of an immediate K.O., Kio began to work on Godfrey's body, trying hard to reach him for the big punch. It was a long three minutes. Godfrey wondered if the flaming time-keeper had gone to have his supper. In spite of everything he could do, the little yellow bastard kept edging in, pistons going, feet moving but moving almost flat-footed, rock-solid, never off balance. Another flurry and he got out of trouble only by taking two vicious punches on the ribs.

Bell. Godfrey went to his corner. There was a lot of applause this time, and all for him. Maybe they were just clapping because he was still standing up.

'*That*'s better,' said Pat Prince, rubbing his legs. '*That*'s better. You really kept your distance. He's a hard man. Just keep out of trouble.' (The flaming fool, the ring wasn't a mile wide.) 'Watch his right and use your feet. You're doing fine, boy.'

Actually his knees were feeling better and his head clearer. But his jaw was aching like it was cracked. Several of his teeth felt loose. He took water in and spat it out and saw that it was still red. As his head was turned towards the bucket he glanced behind his second and saw Angell and Pearl. Pearl wasn't looking at him; she was staring down at her hands as if they were the only things in the world. But Angell was looking at him. Angell was looking at him hungrily, evilly. It was like a time once in the orphanage. There was this lousy master who would never beat kids or give them a cuff behind the ear-hole like the others; he'd never *touch* them, but he'd try to make the older kids beat the younger, and sometimes when they did he'd stand there watching and you'd see a *look* on his face. *This* look. Sweet Moses . . . *this* look. That fat old ox. He was *enjoying* it. He was enjoying seeing him take a knocking.

'If you get a chance work on that there eyebrow,' said Prince. 'It's the one that let him down against Saldivar. If you could open it up . . . But watch it. Play safe as much as you can.'

Godfrey stood up for the fourth round. That fat old crud-face. He'd heard he was outmatched and come to watch him beaten. But how had he *heard*? . . . And *she* was here, pretending she wasn't interested, pretending not to look, hiding behind that great bladder of lard. Give *him* one left hook in his guts and he'd burst, spilling his liver and lights like a gutted chicken.

Circle round Kio. What about the arrangement? What about the ten goddam practice rounds? Let this yellow perisher bring one of his rights up and the fight would be rolled up in four. Curtains for Little God. For crying out loud. He thought maybe Prince was talking sense for once, and he kept shooting out his left as Kio came on, aiming for that eyebrow. The yellow bastard had got no footwork so he should be easy to hit, and he *was* easy to hit, but he was all shoulders and elbows and gloves and hard black head, and if you once got within reach of his fists . . .

A lot of the round had gone and no harm done except this ache in the jaw and your gloves were getting heavy when Kio feinted to get Godfrey into a corner and side-stepped to meet Godfrey's side step and aimed a vicious upper cut that Godfrey saw just in time. It missed his bruised jaw and landed on his cheek. When they separated Godfrey felt the blood running down his cheek. It was the first time he'd been really cut in the ring since that eyebrow four years ago. It annoyed him. It riled him to think someone was spilling his blood. If this is what you get with science, let's try a little scrapping. He went for Kio like a madman.

If nothing else the sudden attack put Kio right off his stride. In the main Godfrey's blows hit the protective barrier, but Kio was hustled out of his rhythm, harried by the pressure and forced to retreat, which he always did badly because he was not used to it. His flat-footed foot-work could not get him out of trouble quickly enough. He found himself against the ropes, and his piston punches not landing as hard as they should on a wild man who was throwing everything at him.

They fought it out then against the ropes, and the noise in Godfrey's ears made him think he was in a mad house. The bell . . . And the screaming didn't change at all: it went on all the way back to his seat and after. There wasn't enough air to get his breath and he needed a pump to shove it in. *Flop* on his stool, legs straight out, arms dang-ling; the crowd had gone really wild, was still simmering, murmuring like a pot only just off the boil.

'*Great,* boy! *Great,* boy! You're coming up roses!' Dab-bing his cheek, stopping the blood. The ref had come to peer but passed on. 'Only a graze you've got, nicked the skin, I can fix that. You know me, one of the best cuts men in the business. Take a breather this next round. You really got him rattled, no faking.' Breather – as if he could get his goddam breath back even lying on his stool. The little yellow bastard had been denting his ribs all through that last blow up; taken its toll. Face dabbed, Vaseline smeared, bottle upended, spit out, massage; oh, to hell, he was ready, the yellow peril couldn't be feeling in the first flush after what he'd soaked up. Spit the bit of tooth that was on his tongue. Fat Angell still staring. Fat Bloody

308

Angel. Big Pearl. Settle with her after this. In with the rubber gum shield. Bell . . . Wow, his legs were groggy, someone had put lead in his gloves. Take a breather. What about the little Japanese warship? He was coming on just the same.

They circled, both wary, Kio in command but not wanting to walk into a madman again. He had another much more important fight in three weeks; the bruise on his eyebrow had been treated in the corner but one wanted to avoid any real damage there. It was this round or the next that he would put the upstart out, but this was only number five, there was plenty of time. It all helped him to practise pace and staying power and the way to destroy. Methodically he moved in, shouldering away the punches, nudging them off his body, weaving with his head till he got within range. Godfrey ducked away from the ropes but caught a right hook in the throat that made him choke and splutter. Following up, Kio caught him again, then his head clicked back as one of Godfrey's lefts got through. It didn't matter; you took it, you exchanged it; inside at last and quick as light left, right, left to ribs; right, left, right, and again. Upstart was hitting back now; screaming, the crowd was screaming but not for him; British crowd screamed for British boxer. In a minute now they would have nothing more to scream about; Upstart would be out cold. *Just* missed with that killer right, but two lefts home nicely; Upstart was sagging, back-pedalling across ring; no need to hurry, there were only four corners. Catch him this time, feint with your left and feint again, then *in* with the right, the way he'd finished off Kim See Ko and Matabishi and Joe Oscar and Fernandez Loos. It didn't work this time. Upstart had stepped inside it, was leaning, not hitting, but leaning. 'Break.' Kio pushed him away with both gloves, brushed the thumb glove across his nose, weaved in, boring, shoulders hunched, chin tucked away; a flailing left caught him dead on the nose and stopped him; crowd screamed; in again. Upstart leaning, weight on weight; both trying for ribs. 'Break.' Push away, bore in again. One, two, three. A nice right, almost spent, but telling all the same, knocked out Upstart's gum shield. Lean again, a vicious uppercut just missing; *that* would have finished the fight. Leaning. 'Break.' Upstart, side-stepping, got in two quick lefts; made the crowd happy, but mer taps, there was no strength in them. Lean again. Bell . . .

Godfrey just had the strength to get back to his corne while one of his seconds dashed across and picked up the mouth-piece. Pat Prince went to work on him.

'He's finished,' said the man next to Angell. 'Always a sign when you lose your gum shield. Kaput. Doubt if the ref'll let it go on. There, what'd I tell you.'

Waterford was coming across to Godfrey's corner, peering at him, at the cut on his cheek, which had been treated and had stopped bleeding. He could hardly get at Godfrey because Prince was dabbing witch hazel on a swelling on his other cheek bone.

'What?' said Angell. 'They may stop the fight? Ridiculous! Why, he's not *beaten*! Nobody has won. Why should they stop the fight now?'

'It isn't good for a man to soak up too much,' said Angell's neighbour. 'You try it yourself, mate. That finking Jap's been sinking 'em wrist deep in Vosper's ribs.'

'I want to *go*, Wilfred!' Pearl whispered. 'I've *told* you! If you don't come with me I shall go alone!'

'One more round,' Wilfred said. 'Or perhaps the fight is over. Perhaps it's already over. It's better to wait till it is over.'

But the fight wasn't over. Waterford had come away from the Vosper corner satisfied that Godfrey's eyes weren't glassy and that the cut on his cheek wasn't serious. As soon as the ref had turned his back Godfrey spat more blood into the bucket. 'D'you *want* to go on, boy?' Prince asked. 'Nobody's making you. You shown you got plenty of iron.'

'I'm O.K.,' said Godfrey. 'I pushed his knob back last punch I give that round. It near broke his neck. I'm O.K. I never been beat yet. This ain't going to be the first time.'

'Take a drink of this.'

'I don't wannit.'

'Go on, boy, it'll brace you.'

Brandy burning his throat. Shades of Flora. *She* should've been here instead of those two. That Angell gloating. Why had he come? What did he know? That bald headed bloke that he'd first seen in Angell's office waiting, and then t the weigh in. What had Bushey said? 'They're *arrangers*.' What had been 'arranged'? Angell had helped him into the ude Davis stable. Was he helping him out?

In went the gum shield, tasting of Vaseline, seconds out, tand up, stool swivels out of the ring . . . Bell.

Feeling better again, and angry, blazing angry. Some-ody'd sold him down the river. Jude Davis spilling out his soothing syrup about the practice rounds. Jude Davis ot here tonight. 'Flu. Something smelled bad. And the nly way to make it smell sweet again was to lay out this ellow bastard. That way you thumbed your nose at them ll. But laying Kio out was a nice ambition: standing on our feet long enough even to hit him back was the first hing.

He blocked a murderous right beautifully, picking it off n mid-air and just in that second scored with two sharp efts to Kio's jaw. If there'd only been the weight in them f the early rounds. He ducked under another right, and ould almost smell the glove as it went past. Then they clinched. He was getting used to the look of that square allow face, the walnut eyes like sunken buttons, the sweaty lippery feel of the hard muscular body, the hissing of breath, the angry pushing and grunting. They were lovers nating like rodents, the crowd screaming obscene encour-agement. *'Break!'*

The brandy was helping, giving him a last chance. He lanced around Kio, tormenting him with sharp, flicking efts that Kio shook off like a dog shaking water. In Kio came, perfectly confident, watching his chance, edging God-rey towards a corner; when he escaped, beginning all over again. Perhaps it was the eyebrow that changed the se-quence. With the round half spent Godfrey thought he saw a chance of landing on it, and quick as a flash moved in and delivered two lefts, the second getting exactly on its target, Kio countered with a tremendous uppercut which glanced off Godfrey's injured jaw, then brought his left through Godfrey's guard to the other cheek bone. Blood welled and Godfrey stood with his back almost to the ropes ex-changing blow for blow. Kio's eyebrow was bleeding as he pounded into Godfrey's ribs.

It was Little God's end. Lashing out wildly, his sight

blurring, he caught Kio again and again. The crowd was on its feet and screaming. Kio gave ground and then came back, hitting twice into Godfrey's face and then bringing a terrific right to the nose. Blood spurted from it as the referee caught Kio's arm. Godfrey was sagging on the ropes, half in, half out of the ring, the screaming of the crowd now only in his ears as he fought to see, to breathe to stand. Someone was holding his arm, helping him to his feet, he tried to shake it off, to look for Kio, the pain in his nose above all the rest. He had no legs, only sticks that gave at every joint; two men helping now. The round was over, get him back to his corner, finish the yellow bastard, just a chance yet. Yellow Peril's eyebrow was opened, that he'd done good and proper.

He was on a stool, someone giving him smelling salts someone dabbing his nose that ran blood. The ref was in the middle of the ring with Kio. Applause and booing What the hell. Anyway he was the wrong way round looking towards the back of the hall. He was sitting in *Kio's* corner.

He tried to get up but could not. Blood was in the back of his throat and he hawked and spat in the bucket. Jees he was bushed. As never before. Something was wrong; he hadn't heard the bell.

'O.K., boy?' Pat Prince was saying. 'Take it easy. Relax You done a *great* job! You couldn't be expected to win A smashing job you done! We got to get that nose seen to. See, let me plug it, will yer. There, that's better. The doc'll have a look at you in the dressing room.'

Someone else. The ref. And Yellow Peril.

'Good fight,' said Kio. 'Eh? Good fight. Fight well Good fight.'

Now Kio was going out of the ring. So it was all over Jees, his nose.

'All right now?' said Waterford. 'How are you feeling?'

Another man, with a beard, wanted to touch his nose 'Leave me alone!'

'Afraid so,' said beard. 'We'll get him to hospital. He'll be more comfortable. A couple of days there will see him all right. Can you stand, Vosper? Let's look at your eyes.'

Godfrey stood up and swayed, hands steadied him.

'And a big hand for the gallant loser,' said the M.C.

They raised the roof. They bloody near took the roof off. It did him good to hear. It was better than brandy. He lifted his hands and they cheered him again. Then with help he somehow got himself down out of the ring, and the crowd cheered him all the way to the dressing room.

In the dressing room they carefully didn't let him look at his face.

Chapter Eight

'I tell you we shall never get a taxi here,' said Wilfred. 'It's impossible.'

'Well, *ring* for one! I'll wait here till one comes!'

'You'll be home much quicker by tube. If you like we could very easily obtain a taxi at Marble Arch. But the direct tube from here only takes about –'

'Ring for a *taxi*!' Pearl said. 'I'm not going into that tube tonight!'

By luck they found a booth and Wilfred telephoned and Pearl, careless of her clothes, sat on the stone steps of the hall in the icy wind while they waited. People glanced at her curiously, but not many had yet left the hall as there were still two bouts to come. Two officers in a police car passed and stared, but Wilfred stood, a mountainous figure, on guard over her. His size was impressive, so long as one did not challenge it. In about ten minutes a taxi came. While he helped her into it Angell could not but glance at the clock and see that 4/6 was already on it before their journey began.

They drove home in silence. Down Whitechapel and Leadenhall Street and Cornhill and Queen Victoria Street and along the Embankment, where all London glittered about the river in the frosty night, they sat in silence. Up Northumberland Avenue and along the Mall and Constitution Hill to Knightsbridge and down Sloane Street, they sat in silence. As they drew up outside their door Pearl said: 'I'll pay for this.'

'Don't be absurd, my dear.'

'*I'll* pay for this!' said Pearl taking out her note case.

He went and opened the door and switched on the light and waited for her. She came in and swept past him and dropped her coat off and went into the drawing room and switched on the lights. Then she switched on the electric fire and crouched shivering over it.

He came in and stood at the door a moment, picking at one of his teeth, staring at her, trying to assess her mood by the curve of her back. Fear stirred in him of what he had done.

'Let me get you a warm drink,' he said. 'It was a great mistake to stand about waiting in that cold wind.'

'When do you want me to leave you?' Pearl asked.

The fear had become a reality, no longer treacherously creeping but knife sharp.

'Whatever do you mean?'

'It must be plain what *I* mean. You've made it plain what *you* mean.'

'I don't understand. The fight must have upset you.'

'It *upset* me – as it was meant to upset me! Wasn't it? *Wasn't* it?' She turned on him with blazing eyes, all the natural sedateness of her nature melted in this crucible of anger. 'It was planned! You planned it, didn't you? You planned it – somehow – and got seats and took me there to *watch* it! You knew he'd be beaten, you *knew* it all, you fixed it, you planned it, you must have bribed somebody!' Conviction became certainty as she watched his face. 'I wondered; all evening I wondered – you were so excited, like someone looking forward to a treat. Well, you've had your treat, and you've had it at my expense! I'd like to pay for the tickets before I leave and then it will have cost you *nothing* – nothing except what it cost you in your soul to stoop so low! –'

'You saw your young man beaten,' said Wilfred harshly. 'He's a boxer. At some time or another boxers are *always* beaten. It's part of their profession. If you're upset, that's what comes of getting – involved with one.'

There was silence. She pulled off her scarf and her hair fell free. It was dropping the last subterfuge. 'Well, that's what I thought. I thought it must be that. You know about him and me.'

'Yes. Yes, I know about him and you.'

She half turned, shivered again though the heat from the fire was growing. 'I think I'm going to be sick.'

'I know you've been sleeping together,' he said with malice. 'Is that nothing? You married me because you *wanted* to. Nobody compelled you. I gave you everything – everything I could. Five thousand pounds settled on you. Five *thousand*! And living in luxury after being just a shop-girl –'

'You can have your money back.'

'Oh, yes. But a fine time you've had with it! Spending it right and left. I know all the clothes you've bought, the spending sprees. And no doubt a lot of it's gone to him –'

'Not a *penny*.'

'I give you all this.' He waved his arm at the room as if to include all the luxury, the wealth, the culture, he had offered her: Impressionist paintings, French furniture, dining at the best restaurants . . . 'And within a few months – *a few months only* – you betray me with a cheap scullery boy! Here in this house, in my house, in our house, you let him come here with his dirty pawing hands, his dirty hard common hands, pawing you naked . . .' Wilfred choked as if a hand held his throat.

'So this was the way you got back at us,' she said. 'You weren't man enough to face him . . .'

'*Man* enough! He's *half* my age! I'm a man of intellect, an aesthete. What could I do against a pugilist?'

'You paid to have him beaten up! Is there anything lower than that? You think you're civilized! You're only a gangster in a city suit. Al Capone up to date . . .' Rage and anguish were giving Pearl eloquence.

He came over to her, face distorted, mottled. 'What *was* I to do? What did you expect me to do? Can you tell me that?' He stared at her, not masking his horror. 'Start divorce proceedings after only six months of marriage – make myself a laughing stock and show you up for a cheap little whore? You tell me what I ought to have done! *You tell me!*'

She went out into the kitchen and vomited in the sink. He followed her angrily, on the attack now.

'*All* that I thought you were – a decent charming girl, decently brought up. A sense of *loyalty*, of *honour*. This cheap little boxer with his smart-alec ways, his voice like a – a costermonger, his vulgarity, his lack of intellect . . . Just a *brute*.'

She turned, wiping her face on a towel, make-up streaked. 'So he's a brute! So that's the way people are made. He happens to be a *man*. Didn't you know? You can't make love with beautiful pictures!'

He stared at her with hate. 'I loved you. God knows I indulged you, to – to the detriment of my health. I – I made

316

love to you at *frequent* intervals. Are you trying to say you were deprived?'

'Yes!' she said. '*Yes, yes, yes. Of course* I was deprived! Your *love* . . . Oh, God, what's the good of *talking*!' She dropped the towel in the sink and turned on the water. 'I married you, yes. I was unfaithful, yes. Now you've got your revenge – isn't that it? My little boxer is laid up, going to hospital, may never box again. *Look* at his face? Smashed up. And you're responsible – just as much as if you'd done it yourself! That's the vilest revenge you could have taken. Why didn't you take it out on me? *Why* not? Why didn't you take it out on me? You couldn't fight a boxer but you could fight me. You could have knocked me about, couldn't you. Were you afraid even of that?'

They remained silent, like two people with no weapons left. The armoury had all been discharged in profligate broadsides. Then Wilfred said: 'I could not have knocked you about. I couldn't have harmed your looks. Because I love you. Hasn't that ever – ever been plain?' He put his hands up to his face and began to cry.

It looked very silly: a mountainous middle-aged fat man blubbering into his hands. But there was no one there to laugh. Pearl stared at him for a few seconds, the bitter desolation in her too complete to admit either contempt or pity. Then she pushed past him and ran out, into the drawing room, through to the hall, and upstairs to her room. In it she looked blindly round, trying to think why she had come. Then she dragged out her old suitcase from under the bed. She opened it, began pushing in a few personal things. Several times she rejected what she had picked up because they were not belongings she had brought to this house. All the great agglomeration of pretty frocks and shoes and hats and gloves and scarves must be left behind. She would take nothing, nothing but what she had brought with her that day in June last year. He could *sell* them, *sell* them for what they would *fetch*. That way he might cut his losses. And there was over four thousand of his money still in the bank; he could have it all back. She would go tonight; first she would go home and then later she would join Godfrey. She'd see him in hospital and then go to his room in Lavender Hill and clean it and make it tidy and home-like for his return. He would need some looking after to begin with until he got on his feet again, until he was fit again, until—

Wilfred was standing at the door.

'What are you doing, Pearl?'

'Packing.'

'Don't be over-hasty.'

She ignored his remark, threw in a pair of shoes.

'It's over-hasty, I tell you. What right have you to leave me like this?'

'What right have you to expect me to stay?'

'You're my wife. Does that mean nothing?'

'Nothing at all. Nothing any more.'

His face was streaked worse than hers; it was blotched pink and white as if his fingers had been pressed too hard against it. 'Where can you go tonight?'

'To a hotel.' That was better than going home, waking them all.

'Stay till morning. It can make no difference.'

'It does to me.'

He came into the room and sat on the bed. The springs squeaked. He suddenly looked like a beaten child. The last combativeness had gone out of him.

'Don't leave me, Pearl.'

'Oh, stop *talking* to me!'

'It was a fair fight. He was beaten in fair fight. It's nothing. He'll be all right in a day or two.'

'He was out-matched, and somehow you made sure it was going to happen!'

'Please don't go. I am *asking* you.'

'You should have thought of that before.'

'Are you blameless? Tell me that—do you consider yourself blameless?'

'Of *course* not! Of course I'm not! I've told you, I'm to blame as much as anyone. But I don't go in for this vile way of planning to—to destroy someone. I don't—' She had been going to say she did not do things in this underhand way; but what difference—at least in method—between his way and hers? The stolen meetings in the bedroom . . .

Wilfred took out his handkerchief and mopped his face.

'Do you—love this man?'

'Yes!' Did she? Was it love she felt when she was with

318

Godfrey or a mixture of attraction and lust?

'And you don't love me?'

'*No!*'

'But you're my *wife*, Pearl. We're married.' His legal mind still clung to this, like a drowning man to a rope which at its other end was attached to nothing.

'Well, we're going to end it now.'

'In the morning. You're worn-out, exhausted, chilled. Sleep here.'

She looked at him. His face was still blotchy, uneven, like a child's. But how did it compare with Godfrey's? In those closing seconds before the referee stepped in it had become a mask of blood.

Wilfred said: 'What is there you see in him?'

'I've told you. He's a man . . .'

'He's a brute, nothing more. His brutality appeals to your baser instincts.'

'You dare to talk about baser instincts tonight!'

He sat there in a sort of backwash of passion, half accusative, half in retreat. 'I need you more than he does, Pearl – even though he is superficially injured. He will have many women. I have only you. If I have done something wrong, unethical . . . But there has been wrong on both sides. You're all I have, Pearl. I don't believe now that without you I can go on living.'

She closed the lid of her case. 'Why should you?' she said.

At this direst of all blows, Wilfred put his hands to his face again. 'Oh, Pearl. Oh, Pearl . . .'

She went to the cupboard, dragged out her old coat from among all the smart new ones, dropped it on top of the bag. She felt so faint and sick with emotion that it needed all her anger to drive her to leave tonight. She needed to inject herself all the time with memories of the fight, like adrenalin, to keep up the anger.

As she passed him Wilfred grabbed her hand. 'Pearl, don't leave me. You promised . . .'

She pulled her hand away. 'Promised *what*?'

He said: 'I suppose I fell in love with you on that aeroplane. I deluded myself, provided myself with all the other reasons why I should marry you, to avoid admitting that. Only these last two months I've come to realize. There wasn't any other reason for marrying you, there isn't any other reason why I did what I did tonight. There isn't any other reason – as I know that you've been unfaithful to me – why I ask you now to stay.'

A sort of cramp descended on her. She stood there. 'I'm sorry.'

He said: 'In marriage a – a contract was entered into. It is for better or for worse. If I have done you harm tonight, think of the good times we have had, the – the companionship. There *has* been the better . . . Don't deny it. We have much in common – you have a love of the good things in life – good wine, good scent, a cultured way of existing, pretty clothes, intelligent conversation, all the rest. Even if I can't give you all the love you want, there's all the rest. Must you throw it all away?'

'Yes, I must.'

He went on talking, pleading, took her hand again and held it in spite of her efforts to get free. In the end she wrenched her hand away and almost fell with the effort.

'Don't you *see*?' she cried. 'Can't you even *begin* to see! After tonight . . .' She burst into tears.

There was no conversation between them for a time. She was weeping, silently, bitterly, hideously unable to stop. He had his hands before his face, hair falling over his hands, rocking a little on the bed. She tried to gather her last few things, but in a defeated way, as if every movement weighed a ton. At last she was ready and moved to the door. He fell on his knees and took her hand again, talking to her almost incoherently, muttering endearments that had no place in his ordered, careful, legal life before. It was a painful, embarrassing few minutes that always remained as incoherent in Pearl's memory, the sentences, the postures, clear in meaning but imprecise in detail, as if the embarrassed mind developed astigmatism as a defence. At some stage she found she too was sitting on the bed conceding that she would not leave until the morning.

If she stayed tonight it was certainly no victory for Wilfred but only for a consummate weariness that told her she had no strength left to go through the last processes of departure. The walk downstairs, out into the bitter February night, the walk to the Cadogan Hotel, with the probability that they would be full, then if she were lucky a taxi to some hotel where there was room, signing, the covert stares, the lift to the bedroom, the porter and the tip and the cold cheerless bed.

At some stage Wilfred, half reassured, half forlorn, was pushed out and she was alone in her own room – her own room for one more night.

She was determined to leave early in the morning. After what had happened tonight, and with his knowledge of her unfaithfulness, there just wasn't a basis for a relationship any more. She could not understand how he supposed there was. Whatever else, her marriage to Wilfred was ended.

Chapter Nine

They took Godfrey to Bethnal Green Hospital and put eight stitches in his cheek and two in his eyebrow, and they set his broken nose. He was dazed for some hours after the fight, and the next morning they took an encephalograph. They also X-rayed his ribs where they were so badly bruised, just to be on the safe side. The doctor said he could go home at the end of the week but would have to come back as an out-patient through the following week.

Godfrey did not make a good patient. His nose was still plugged and his body ached, and he lay simmering, thinking over the defeat, the double-cross, the humiliation, the terrible destruction of the last two rounds, glaring down the long ward, expecting more attention than he got. In the afternoon they let him have a mirror and a safety razor and he glowered at this bruised and bandaged freak and wanted to know what the hell he'd look like when the bandages came off. The doctor said he'd be all right, except that he might need plastic treatment for his nose which had had a nasty fracture, and they hadn't the facilities for a lengthy treatment here.

Later in the afternoon Pat Prince came to see him, bringing the press cuttings about the fight and a bottle of Pol Roger from Jude Davis. Godfrey hadn't a wide vocabulary but he used it all in telling Prince what Jude Davis could do with the Pol Roger. Prince snuffled and blinked uneasily.

'Hey, boy, it isn't no good getting sore. The fight was made for you. You agreed for it, O.K.? If you didn't expect to be beat you was a blamed fool. You haven't got no complaint against Jude.'

'Got no complaint?' Godfrey snarled through his bruised mouth. 'You can tell Jude that the next time he wants to cross somebody it won't be me.'

'Get off it, boy, there wasn't no crossing.'

'So you say. Well, you can tell Jude I've finished with him and his management, see. Tell the filthy little crud that dogs that mess in their own kennels ought to be destroyed.

One day – maybe soon – somebody'll *do* for him!'

Pat Prince rubbed the scar tissue around his eyes. 'Look, boy, let me give you a word of advice, see. It won't be no good taking your beating that way. You were beat in a fair fight, as any bloody fool knowed you'd be, taking on the Jap champion – and if you're too big-headed to take a beating you'll be no good in the ring, not to Jude nor me, nor any other manager who's fool enough to take you on!'

Godfrey tried to sit up, but his nose throbbed. All his head throbbed for a minute, and he could hardly concentrate on what the old pug was saying.

'When the fight was made,' Prince said, 'when it was made I knew you'd be out-matched and I said so to Jude, but he said it was a great chance for you and you'd get more glory going down to Kio than in a dozen ordinary matches he could make for you. And be-God, I believe he's right if you read these press boys. You ain't *read* your press yet. It's a rave. Go on, read your cuttings!'

Godfrey screwed up his eyes to read his cuttings. They all praised him: from the local papers up to three national dailies that thought fit to mention it. *'Brave Showing by London Boy.' 'Crowd-raising fight in Bethnal Green.' 'Jap Champion nearly meets his match.'* While he was reading them he was half listening to what Prince was saying, his still not lucid brain tackling the problem of diplomacy and cunning self-interest, considerations which never came easy to him at the best of times.

'So when I go back, boy, I'm not going to say not a word to Jude about what you've just said to me. I'm just going to pretend I haven't never heard a word of it. See. Because – even if he made a mistake this time – and I'm not saying he did, mind, I'm not saying he did – he's still your manager and you'd be hard put to find another if you gets on the wrong side of *him.* And if you stays with him you're in the *money,* soon as you mend. Soon as you mend you're in the *big money,* boy. That's where you want to be, isn't it?'

'Tell Jude I want to see him,' said Godfrey. 'And see him quick. Tell him to bring his 'flu along – and his bed. Maybe he'll need it.'

'I'll tell him you want to see him – won't say nothing more. If you want him to cut you off where you hang that's your concern, boy, not any of mine!'

When Prince had gone Godfrey lay back on his pillow and dozed till supper came. He swallowed it with a sore mouth and took his sleeping pill and fell asleep with the problem not resolved. It was against all his temperament to stay with Davis. It was against his temperament even to pretend to stay with him while looking around. His natural instincts were to wait outside his gym until Davis came out alone and there go about disfiguring him for life. (He knew that if he did this, with his record, it would finish his boxing career.) His second alternative was to go to the B.B.B. of C. and lay a formal complaint, hoping Davis would lose his licence. (But where it was simply one man's suspicion against another's word, it was an unlikely outcome that he would be believed and a fairly prominent and esteemed manager called a liar. There was no proof, not an atom – only guesswork. Pat Prince had known nothing, he was sure.) If Prince kept his promise and passed on nothing of what had been said, there was the third alternative of meeting guile with guile and deceit with deceit. Next morning when his head was beginning to clear he decided to let the thing run on and see if Davis came.

Davis came, but not until the afternoon. Thursday was visiting day. He came down the long ward, looking thin and dark and distinctive in his own peculiar way. Godfrey had always thought him a natty dresser, in his invariable dark suit and white shirt with its prominent cuffs, and the diamond tie pin and the opal cuff-links. But today, looking at him with different eyes, Godfrey saw an air of shabbiness about the gentility, a shaky seediness in his walk; his eyes were evasive behind their glasses as he said: 'Well, well, how is it? Not too badly, I hope?'

'I'll live to get my own back,' said Godfrey through his swollen lips.

'Ah, I doubt if I'll match you again with Kio, the bastard. I only hope he gets what he deserves in Hamburg.'

'He fought fair enough,' said Godfrey. 'Which is more'n you can say for some filthy Micks.'

Davis bent and opened a bag he was carrying. For the moment he was prepared to misunderstand Godfrey's replies. 'Another bottle of champagne. Thought you might like it. Did you know Kio's fight with Heist has been postponed three weeks?'

'So what?'

'It was your doing. You opened up his eyebrow. I wish I'd been well enough to see the fight. All the writers are raving about you.'

'I was raving about it too,' said Godfrey.

'No wonder. No wonder.' Davis coolly put the champagne on the table, then some dirt in the nail of his index finger attracted his attention and he cleaned it with the nail of his other thumb. 'Kio and his manager let me down. I was annoyed when I heard, when Pat came over later that night. But Kio I couldn't talk to. I've seen his manager since and we've had a row but his manager says it was Kio's doing, breaking the arrangement. He thought we'd insulted him by not putting him on in a bigger hall, so it was a question of "face". So all the original plan went overboard and he was out for your blood. If I'd been there on the night I could maybe have intervened. But as it was you had to face it out yourself. And a red hot job you made of it. A red hot job. It's going to do you a power of good, you can stand on me for that.'

'It's done me a flaming lot of good,' said Godfrey.

'Reputation wise it has. Reputation wise it's as good as a gold brick. Now you're a *name*. Soon as you get over these bruises we can talk *big* for your next fight. That's going to mean a lot to you, Godfrey. You're a big wheel now. Oh, by the bye, I've got the cheque here for the fight. Six hundred less commission.'

'Thanks for nothing,' said Godfrey taking the cheque and sneering at it.

Jude Davis leaned on his umbrella and put the handle against his teeth. This was the turning point. He had gone as far as he could to paper over the cracks. Whether Godfrey believed him or not he didn't much care. What he did care was whether Godfrey appeared to believe him. If he made no effort to do so they couldn't go on. That would be a pity, because if Godfrey survived this beating, he would now be a valuable property. If Godfrey survived the beating and *took* it right, everybody would profit.

'Well, it's not nothing, Godfrey. You carry it to a bank and see. But I've got something more for you here. It's a hundred pounds in tenners. When you get out of hospital I want you to go away and have a good holiday before we consider your next fight, see. This is a bit of extra to take care of the expense and because I wasn't there on Tuesday to see it worked to plan. I want you to take this and have a good time. Have a good time on me and come back fighting fit.'

Godfrey hesitated and then put out his hand for the envelope. 'Thanks.'

Davis did not put the envelope in it.

'No hard feelings. That's what we have to be sure of. No hard feelings, see. Manager and fighter can't ever get on if there's hard feelings between them.'

There was another pause. Then Godfrey tried to move his lips into a smile. 'No hard feelings,' he lied. You bastard, you muck face, you jerk, you punk.

He took the money and put it under his pillow. 'Thanks Jude,' he said. 'I'll remember this.'

Godfrey's third guest missed Jude Davis by only ten minutes. She was as much in white as Davis had been in black, and he recognized her tall figure coming down the ward. He swallowed a mouthful of venom and lust as he saw her. She hesitated and licked her lips and smiled, then came on and held out her hand.

'Godfrey, how are you? I was so sorry. I thought I'd come and see.'

Even her voice had changed since her marriage, he thought. How *are* you? *So* sorry. He looked her up and down with bruised bloodshot eyes but did not take her hand.

'Sorry I can't touch me forelock. That's what you expect when you visit the peasants, isn't it?' Deliberately he pitched his own voice at its worst.

She sat on the stool beside the bed. Kid shoes and nylon legs and fine wool skirt under the white straight-cut coat. 'I didn't come to quarrel – to go on with our quarrel. I came to see how you were.'

'Well, you can see now, can't you. Labelled pug at last. I said this'd never happen, didn't I. Little God with his looks rubbed out. That's what. Pig-Face wanted it, didn't he? That's why Pig-Face fixed my wagon.'

She was startled at this; the things she had intended to say were stopped. She licked her lips again. 'Wilfred took

me to watch the fight, but . . . I don't know if you were –
I'm only sorry the fight ever happened.'

'So'll your fat pig of a husband be when I get around
to him. You can tell him that from me.'

She began to say something and then checked herself
again.

'Have some champagne,' he said sarcastically. 'It's just
come. Compliments of the management.'

'Godfrey,' she said. 'I was so upset on Tuesday; I don't
know how we got home. I – felt so sick, so sorry. When
that Jap – It was horrible. I never want to see another boxing match . . . Your face will heal, won't it? You put up a
wonderful fight. It must make your reputation.'

He turned over and grunted; his ribs were now at their
most painful. 'I'll still be able to lay you if that's what's
fretting you.'

She flushed. 'Do you hate me all that much?'

He grunted again and sighed. 'Who knows? Who cares?'
He was bitter at her for coming and seeing him like this.
It rasped at his vanity, his manhood. And this girl, this girl
was *married* to . . . 'What d'you *expect*? I'm not a mud pie.
When somebody treads on my face I tread back.'

Shrinking into herself but still seeking some reassurance,
she said: 'Are you like this with me just because of Wilfred
or is there some other reason?'

'Just because of Wilfred,' he mimicked. 'Isn't that good
enough?'

'It may be good enough, but I want to know.'

With clumsy fingers he touched his cheek, and the sharp
ends of the stitches brushed his hand. 'Oh, what's the odds?
What does it matter?'

'It matters to me. I still don't understand.'

'How could you?'

'Well, then d'you want me to go now? To leave you
alone?'

'Please yourself.'

She sat there hesitantly, with the drone of other people's
voices around her.

He said: 'Go on. Have some champagne.'

'Godfrey, are you trying to say Wilfred had some hand
in arranging what happened on Tuesday? How could he?
You've got a manager –'

'He fixed me up with Davis – remember that? So he –'

'Because you asked him. Or asked me to ask him –'

'So he fixed me up with Davis. So he fixed this too.'

She glanced round the big ward, at the old people and the sick people in the beds, at the visitors, some genuinely concerned, others here out of duty, exchanging platitudes, waiting for the time to go.

'When will you be able to leave hospital?'

'Next Monday, the body-slicers says.'

'Where will you go – back to that room in Lavender Hill?'

'To begin.'

'If you tell me the time you expect to be home I'll be there. I'll try to make it a bit more comfortable for you.'

'Slum visitor. That'll be smashing.'

She shrugged helplessly. 'Do you want me to leave Wilfred?'

'Jees, I don't know how you stay with the old crud!'

'And you want me to come and live with you?'

'How can you? You're too much in love with Mayfair and posh restaurants.'

'That isn't the point.'

'Isn't it? I thought it was.'

After a minute she said: 'Do you love me, Godfrey?'

He fiddled with the bandage on his nose and grimaced with pain. It was the last thing to ask him now, when his nature was bunched up, muscle-bound with resentment. He knew she was watching him and that he looked like something out of a leper colony.

'I mean truly,' she persisted. 'Apart from sex. Enough to marry me.'

'What's love?' he said. 'Never heard of it. I'm a pug. Maybe you haven't noticed.'

'You never let me forget it,' she said.

'Why should you want to?'

'Why should I? Maybe because I'm a woman. I don't mind you being a fighter, but I don't want you to be *only* a fighter.'

'So what sort of a set-up is that? Some love nest.'

'I can work. I always used to work. I can perhaps get my old job back.'

'You'd love that, wouldn't you.'

'It was an easy enough job. I didn't like the travelling before.'

They seemed to have nothing more to say. His sarcasm, his mimicry had wrong-footed her, dried her up. She had said all the wrong things in all the wrong ways. His first words had made her feel self-conscious, over-formal, priggish. Now she sat beside him like a paid sick-visitor. But how else should she have come? Run up to the bed, arms round him. 'Godfrey!' Sobs. You couldn't have. Not with him. Anyway a public ward was not the right place to meet. (And the last time they had met in private she had bitten him.)

A spark was lacking, his crudeness offended her. He wanted her, you could see that, but did he want her more than he did a lot of other women? If only he had been different this afternoon, if he had been receptive to sympathy. Instead he snarled like a maimed wolf, ready to fight to the last.

So the talk dropped between them. She stayed to the very last minute, wanting more resolution that she could not find, needing him but resenting within herself the existence of the need. She tried to encourage him to talk about his boxing future, but that led quickly back to the old hate. Soon as he was out of here he'd take a rest to get fit again. Then he had a job to do.

'A job to do?'

'Yes, I've been fixed. Remember that? By your Pig-Face. Next time I see him I'm going to lean on him. I'm going to knock the stuff out of his guts.'

'Oh, Godfrey, that's *hopeless*. Can't you realize it? How can you prove anything?'

'Prove? Who wants proof? Last time I called on him – your old man – at his office, that time I called at his office, I could tell then that he knew about us. Just the way he sat there – sweating his guts out with hate. He'd have give me poison if he could. There was a bloke called Birman there that day – in the office, in the outside office. You can stand on it: he did the fixing for Angell, he did the dirty work. I'll settle with him one day. But it's Pig-Face first. Then Jude . . .'

She hesitated, on the edge of indiscretion, wanting to talk but fearing to talk.

'Even if something *was* arranged – and really I can't believe –'

'I'm dead sure, so save your breath.'

'But it's your *future* you've got to start thinking of – not what's over, done with. What about your reputation? For Heaven's sake. You're a name for the first time! Someone who stood up to the champion of Japan for six wonderful rounds –'

'You try it. You try six wonderful flaming rounds with three teeth knocked out and a broken nose and eight stitches and ribs like they've been beaten in with hammers. You try it, Oyster, and see how it feels!'

She said miserably: 'Everything I say you turn against me. If I didn't feel for you, why should I have come? All I am trying to say is –'

'All you're trying to say is, let your old man off.'

'Not because I admire him. Not because I care anything for him at all any more. You know that. But if you try some – some sort of revenge it can only get *you* in trouble. You *can't* box Wilfred – he's old and unfit. You can't even box this man Davis. So why ruin your own life, your own prospects *now*, when you've got a big chance to succeed?'

The second bell had gone while she was speaking. He was eyeing her up and down.

'It sounds all right the way you say it. You might even be thinking of me.'

She picked up her bag.

He said: 'Anyway you'll be there on Monday when I get back to my room?'

She said without hesitation: 'If you want me to.'

'That's a date. Here, you take the key of the room. I expect I'll be home about twelve. Eleven's the time they jet people out of here. So I should be there by twelve. I got a spare key if I'm early. You can cook me dinner.'

Their eyes clashed. 'All right,' she said.

They had stayed together through Wednesday, Thursday and Friday in a silent arid desert of enmity. After a lot of hesitation she had decided not to make the final break until after she had seen Godfrey; then when she saw him he had never given her the sort of encouragement she wanted. She so much wanted to be able to say to Wilfred: 'I am going to Godfrey,' instead of 'I am going home.' So again the break was postponed, this time until Monday.

As for Wilfred, each time he came home and found her still there he breathed a sigh of relief, though he was careful not to show it. His supplications of Tuesday evening humiliated him to remember and he tried to forget they had ever happened. If she told him she was leaving him now, he persuaded himself he would be able to bear it, and each hour that passed without an announcement gave him a fraction more confidence. In a month he would be persuading himself that his abject surrender of Tuesday had hardly happened. Also the light of day, of several days, had convinced him that she had out-manoeuvred him on the night by pressing her accusations and disregarding his own. A woman caught in adultery is not a particularly admirable sight even in these permissive days. He had every right to divorce her and turn her off without a penny. His own retaliatory act was the merest justice, a fit retribution. He was bitterly angry with himself and with her that a woman half his age should have been able, by sheer nerve, to get the better in open conflict of a man like himself.

All these thoughts he thought more convincingly when in his office surrounded by his pink- and green-taped documents. When confronted by her, sight of her weighted the scales of justice alarmingly by reminding him of what he might lose. Those beautiful legs, of which she showed so much, those long elegant arms, the fine skin of brow and cheek and neck and breast, the glinting blue eyes and the long fair hair. It was utterly unfair that she should be so capable of undermining the rational process.

Since Tuesday he had not dined at home, but on the Friday he came back and clearly expected something, so she cooked him a shoulder of pork, and they had a selection of cheeses to follow. Like all the breakfasts, it was a silent meal, punctuated only by the clink of knife and fork and the sound of his breathing. Afterwards he sat in front of the fire with a cigar and a glass of port while she cleared away. When she came back into the drawing room she saw he was reading the *Boxing News* she had bought that day. He glanced up and saw her look and rashly spoke.

'Well, they speak highly of Brown – or Vosper – they speak highly of him in this boxing paper that you have. It cannot have done him all that much harm, this defeat. He should be grateful for having had the chance to shine.'

Echoing Godfrey, she said: 'A broken nose, eight stitches in his cheek, two in his eyebrow, concussion. I'm sure that's something to be grateful for.'

He dropped the paper on the floor and sipped his port. He should have known that the longer the subject was avoided the better. *Keep off it*. Talk of anything else. Compliment her on her frock, her cooking, her hair. He must not gamble with his future. But now the subject, like a vein, was irrevocably opened. Now his frail cause might bleed to death.

'I saw him yesterday,' she said.

He nursed his fear and his enmity, keeping them close, trying not to let them show.

'He's in Bethnal Green Hospital,' she said.

'I suppose I should have expected it.'

'Expected what?'

'That you would go to see him.'

She poured herself a glass of his port. She didn't like it, it was over-sweet, cloying, like a moneyed existence.

'He knows all about it. All about the arrangement between yourself and Jude Davis.'

It was so quiet that you could hear the 18th century French Ormolu clock in the bathroom striking ten.

'I don't understand. You are imagining things. What have you been telling him?'

'I told him nothing. I pretended *I* didn't understand. But he knew all about it – or he'd guessed – as I did. He said he was going to get even with you both.'

Angell put his port down. His cigar smouldered in the ashtray. 'I've never even met Davis, wouldn't know what he looks like. It's a persecution complex Brown's got. Anyway, how could he possibly – get even, as you call it?'

'I think he means in the way you arranged it for him,' Pearl said with malice.

Angell's face quite noticeably paled. It was as if the blood had suddenly remembered another appointment and gone elsewhere. He stayed quite still.

'I've never heard anything so absurd,' he said boldly. 'This is a law-abiding society.'

'Is it?'

'Why, a man can be convicted merely for uttering threats. In some cases he can be sent to prison for uttering threats. Brown had better be careful.'

'That's what I said.'

'You told him to be careful?'

'Yes.'

'What did he say?'

'He wouldn't take any notice of me. No notice at all.'

A further silence endured, until the clock in here also struck ten. Angell wanted to ask her if she were seeing Godfrey again, but this other sudden danger which had arisen impeded his tongue. Physical danger to his body, not just danger to his possessions. Inconceivable.

'Of course it means nothing,' he said with conviction. 'Just empty words.'

'Yes. I expect so.'

'But empty words that show his vicious nature.'

'Aren't we all vicious?' said Pearl.

On the Sunday they had booked for a concert at the Albert Hall, but she would not go with him. He went along half an hour before the performance and tried to sell the tickets. He failed in this so went to the concert by himself in order that only one ticket should be wasted. When he came out it was dark and he took a taxi home. He was not sure what day Godfrey came out of hospital. He realized that for quite a long time perhaps he would have to take taxis home.

He was an hour late reaching his office on Monday morning, but as soon as he got in he rang Vincent Birman. Birman was out but rang back at twelve and they arranged to have lunch.

When he heard what was on Birman said: 'Well, I've been as tight as a clam. You know me. I don't spill. And the only other feller in the know is Jude Davis; and you can bet he wouldn't say. He's got a licence to lose. Brown can only guess, and how he has guessed is your problem not mine. How d'you know he blames you?'

'I happen to know. And he's threatening some sort of reprisal.'

'On you? Or on your client?'

Angell bit his lip. 'On me apparently. Though I have only

been the go-between.'

'Like me. I believe he did see me in your office one day. Maybe that's the link. But you surely don't take it seriously. A little broken-down pug. He's got no influence, no money. And no vestige of proof. What could he do?'

Angell said to the waiter: 'More soup. And bring the grated cheese.' Because he was paying for this meal they were eating at an inexpensive luncheon café in Fleet Street. 'One does not know what a vicious little prize-fighter like that might attempt if he brooded on his grievance . . . Did you say "broken-down" pug?'

'No, thanks,' said Birman to the waiter, and watched Angell swallowing the soup. 'Well, he did take a terrific beating, didn't he?'

'You were there?' Wilfred was startled.

'Yes, I went along, old man. I'd agreed to hand over the other thousand pounds that evening. It was part of the bargain.'

To hide his pain Wilfred broke a roll and stuffed a piece of it in his mouth.

'Davis wasn't there,' Birman said. 'He was ill, or pretended to be, so I had to go to his house. That's another ten shillings for a taxi on your expenses.'

Angell said: 'My client must have been out of his mind to spend so much. Brown was certainly well beaten, but one wonders . . . Beyond some temporary disfigurement . . . Beyond that . . .' He spooned up the last of the soup and looked at Birman hopefully.

'Beyond that is anybody's guess. Boxing's a funny game, as I've told you before. Boxers come into the ring with their tails up. It's a psychological thing. When they get stopped the way your man got stopped last Tuesday something happens to them. Their bodies have got to recover – and that can take a time: that Kio had one of the most vicious right hooks I've ever seen. That's a physical thing. But their *minds* have got to recover too. Before this they've always gone into the ring *knowing* they're going to win. They always have won – or if they lose on a cut eye it's just bad luck, or a points decision they can con themselves the ref was wrong. They never admit they're beaten: there's always some *excuse*: it's the way they go on fighting. But when you get beaten all over the guts and brains

334

like your man on Tuesday, there's no excuse they can dream up for that. They know there's stronger, cleverer fists in the world than theirs, and it may be they'll never quite go into a fight with the same zest again. That's mental. Then they're over the hill. Even at twenty-one you can be over the hill. So it's just a matter of luck with Godfrey Vosper. We'll just have to wait and see.'

'In the meantime . . .'

'In the meantime I hope your client's satisfied.'

'In the meantime I am considering these threats . . .'

'Oh, those. Forget 'em, old man. That'll be his excuse, no doubt. He was framed, it wasn't a fair fight. *That*'ll help him to recover. But as for reprisals. If he was one of the big boys who could pay to have a couple of thugs look after you, there might be a bit of danger. But not from a little down-at-heel feather-weight.'

This was much in line with Angell's reasonable thinking: but reasoning is not all. 'Nevertheless I'd like to know something of his movements. I'd like you to keep an eye on him for a few weeks.'

Birman sighed. 'I'll assign one of my men if you *like*, but it will cost you more than it will be worth. I'll forecast Brown's movements for you. He'll have made a nice little packet out of this fight and he'll probably take it easy for a while – even go for a holiday to Brighton or somewhere where he can pick up a girl or two and play the slot machines. But as soon as ever he feels fit he'll tire of that and come back to the gyms and start hanging around waiting to pick up a few pounds sparring until his manager arranges the next fight. He'll be far too busy thinking about himself to think of taking it out on you.'

'He's a very *peculiar* man,' said Wilfred. 'What little I've seen of him . . .' He knew that if he insisted, the results of this order to Birman would be likely to be double-edged and would probably expose his wife's perfidy to another's gaze. He did not like this, but he saw no way out. For the moment fear was the dominant emotion, over-riding all the others. Fear and hunger. Fear and hunger. They seemed to have a common frontier. Fear and hunger, worry and hunger, jealousy and hunger. They met in a psychosomatic no-man's-land between the countries of the body and the mind.

'I want him watched,' Wilfred said, and waited impatiently for the steak and kidney pie.

Pearl left her house at 11.30 and took a taxi to Lavender Hill. No one answered the door so she went in, climbed the two floors without meeting anyone and let herself into Godfrey's room. She had brought food for a midday meal, and she prepared this before setting about clearing up the mess. There was only a gas-ring and tiny oven, and the grease on them suggested they hadn't been wiped over for a month. The bed was roughly made, but the imprint of his body still marked the tattered counterpane, and comic papers were strewn on the floor. As she picked up the papers and glanced through them she shivered slightly: they emphasized the paradox of her passion, which all through her maturing mind, her ambition, her fastidiousness, had fought against.

An old pair of boxing boots were under the bed along with two pairs of hand-made brogues and two other pairs of expensive shoes. She rubbed these over and put them in the wardrobe, which she was startled to find stacked with almost new clothes: sweaters, jackets, suits, silk shirts. All from Lady Vosper, no doubt. She shivered again. It was as if she again detected something parallel in her life and Godfrey's. They had both lived with older people, who doted on them, and from this association were loaded down with the small profits of their servitude. She had *married* Wilfred. Was that the only difference?

By one o'clock the flat was looking a different place. (The outside of the window was still filthy but she did not fancy leaning out and trying to clean it.) The furniture was free of dust, the threadbare rug reversed so that the worn end hardly showed. She had waited to put the steak in, but the potatoes and cauliflower were nearly ready and she thought he was sure to be here any minute now. (It was strange to be cooking for someone who only cared for food as a secondary consideration.) She had brought a bottle of Wilfred's best wine, and although there was no decanter it was at the right temperature. The deal table was covered with a check cloth, and the old bone-handled knives and the drunken-pronged forks were laid. There was nothing more for her to do, so she washed her hands again and rinsed her face and powdered it and re-fixed her lips. She knew he didn't like her hair too tidy, so she did not comb it. He preferred his steak rare, so she took his out and allowed hers to sizzle for another few minutes. When that was done she turned down the gas and left the dish on the top of the oven and hoped it would not spoil.

She sat by the window and began to watch the traffic. She had only seen his grey Velox once but she fancied she would recognize it again. Every three or four minutes she got up and went to examine her meal, which clearly was not going to improve if it were left much longer. At one-thirty she felt angry, at two she grew anxious. She left the food where it was and went downstairs and out. There was a telephone box down the next street, but it was occupied and a man was waiting. She walked back to the door of his place and ran up to see if he had come while she was away. Then she went down again and back to the telephone. After a five-minute wait she was able to use it.

The hospital was not helpful and seemed to know nothing about him. Eventually they told her that G. Vosper had been discharged this morning and had left about eleven.

Back to the flat. The food was drying and cooling. She tried to eat something but had no appetite. She drank two glasses of wine. At three-thirty she threw all the food in the waste bin and washed up. At four-thirty she went home, wondering if there would be some message left there.

There was no message and he did not come.

Having heard nothing at all from the Law Society, Angell rang up the secretary, who had forwarded Lord Vosper's complaint to him. The secretary said that he had written to Lord Vosper informing him that the matter he had raised was not one on which the Law Society could take any action. In relief at this – though perhaps he should have known better than to feel anxiety – Angell reluctantly admitted Jonathan Whittaker, 32 years old and a bright young man of law, to an extra 5% of the profits of the firm, such percentage to be debited from the senior partner's share.

The deal for the purchase of Merrick House and its accompanying lands finally went through. The Minister of Housing at Question Time stated that every consideration should be given to objectors and objections raised agains the South Suffolk Development Scheme. Replying to supplementary question he assured his questioner that ever possible care would be taken to preserve the beauty and the country amenities of the villages involved.

The furniture and all the furnishings of Merrick House still belonged to Lord Vosper, and through Hollis a suggestion came that it would be more convenient to auction the contents on the premises than to have them brought to London. Land Increments Ltd could afford to be magnanimous and agreed that all facilities should be provided to enable the sale to take place provided this occurred before the 31st March. The sale was fixed for the 21st and 22nd March and was to be widely advertised.

Pearl daily expected some note or letter or even a visit from Godfrey. On the following Monday she went again to his room and let herself in. Some of the things had gone from his wardrobe but there was no sign of his having slept there. The half-used bottle of wine was where she had left it, the tea towel folded on the chair back, the dustpan and brush unmoved, the salt and pepper on the table. When she got home she looked up Jude Davis's telephone number and rang him. She gave her name as Hazel Boynton.

'Godfrey's out of town, Miss Boynton. I can't tell you where he is because he didn't leave an address, but I did suggest he should take a holiday after him being beaten by the Japanese champion, like. I expect he'll be back in a week or so and looking us up.'

'He was supposed to go back to the hospital to have his stitches out, and also for attention to his nose. Did he do that?'

'I would think so, but I expect you could check with the hospital. I haven't seen him since the Thursday after the fight. I've been very busy and rather poorly myself – so I have left it to him to look after these things.'

'I thought you might have been concerned about *his* health and whether he was recovering after the fight.'

There was a pause, and the voice at the other end hardened. 'We do what we can, Miss – er – Boynton. Godfrey Vosper is not the easiest person to control, as perhaps you know. Even a manager can only advise.'

338

'And make money out of getting him beaten,' said Pearl, and hung up, breathing hard. It was a foolish thing to say, but it had come out.

Birman made his weekly report to Angell over the telephone.

'He's definitely not in London. He left hospital last Monday morning, picked up his car off a parking lot and drove to his room in Battersea. He was there only about ten minutes and then he left again. He came back a couple of days later and stayed about two hours; but he hasn't been back since then. A young woman called on the Monday after he left and stayed four hours. Part of the time she was in his room because my man saw her at the window. But we don't know who she was. Quite obviously my prediction about Brown has come true. He's off for a holiday, or maybe visiting his family, if he's got one. We also checked with the Davis gym, but no one has seen him there. No one was *expecting* him there – yet.'

Angell grunted. 'Couldn't your man have followed him? For all we know he may be staying round the corner.'

'He could have followed him but I didn't know you wanted that sort of coverage. And think it out, old man. If Brown is in London he isn't paying to hire somewhere else and letting his own bed-sitter go to waste. It doesn't make sense.'

'Ah,' said Angell. 'Perhaps you are right. But tell your man to continue to check, will you, and let me know as soon as he returns.'

After two weeks Pearl tried his room again and then went to find the gym Godfrey had often spoken of off Cranbourne Street. She found Pat Prince there and, stared at curiously by rough young men in track suits or boxing shorts, she put her questions. Prince was more forthcoming than Davis but the substance of his answers was the same.

It was lunch time and she ate at a restaurant in St Martin's Lane. While she was having lunch a good-looking man of about thirty with an Italian accent came to sit at her table and tried to pick her up. She froze him off instantly, instinctively, and left as soon as she could, leaving him looking hurt.

She walked for quite a while, embarrassed and slightly angry and slightly amused. Of course she was not unaccustomed to approaches, and she was used to being able to brush them off and forget them in a couple of minutes. This time for some reason it went a little deeper, as if the protective varnish she had developed had for once been dented. She thought perhaps it was because he was a handsome man and, after his own lights, good-mannered. She allowed herself to speculate what would have happened if she had been a different sort of woman, and what it would be like to be a different sort of woman. Would she have ended the afternoon taking tea at the Ritz or in some bed-sitter in Bayswater? And would it have given her pleasure and release or merely a fleeting satisfaction and a renewal of the empty need?

It was all speculation, which she would never allow to become reality because it was against her nature to do so. But it was a little surprising to herself that the speculation, with all its detailed and possible developments, should linger so long in her mind after she had tried to dismiss it.

Imagination for her now had so very much more factual experience to build on than it had in the past.

Chapter Ten

Mr Friedel was an infrequent correspondent and a rare caller, but she had a letter from him that afternoon telling her that Rachel had gone into hospital for the removal of a cyst in her back and would be gone a week. She showed the letter to Wilfred and said coldly:

'I think I'll go and spend a week at home. Dad says they have this woman but she's only afternoons, and getting everyone off to school must be a nightmare to him.'

Angell looked at her out of suspicious bloodshot eyes. Was this some trick to meet Godfrey? But she no longer, alas, needed an excuse. He could not stop her walking out at any time.

'And who will look after me?' he asked, conscious that physically he felt very frail this morning. He had had some pain during the night and feared it might be gall stones.

'Well, Mrs Jamieson comes in.'

'She doesn't cook.'

'You could eat at your club.'

The indifference to his welfare was plain in her voice, and he winced. She had no heart, no thought for him any more. It was the harshness of youth, almost more like a daughter casting off her own father. He would have preferred enmity to this cold non-interest. His marriage was lost.

And yet she only said a week. Perhaps she would come back.

'When would you want to go?'

'If I'm to be any use I should go soon. Tomorrow.'

So Pearl returned to her old haunts, and Wilfred went to stay at the Hanover Club. It was better, he thought, than sampling the loneliness that might soon become permanently his. He buried himself in work at the office and in bridge at the club. He had a remarkable run of luck, so that in five evenings he made £40, even at the very moderate stakes allowed by the club. Twice, leaving the office after dark, he hailed a taxi instead of walking for a bus.

On the Friday he went down with Francis Hone and Simon Portugal to look over the land in Suffolk they had bought. Sir Francis was anxious to buy other small properties in the vicinity, even at the now inflated prices, and the development plan seemed to be even larger than they had at first supposed.

Going home, Pearl realized, was the ideal temporary solution. It would give her time to breathe, to draw back from events, to reflect. And Rachel's illness was the ideal excuse because she could return without comment. It was with a marvellous sense of release that she shut the door of No 26 Cadogan Mews and made for Selsdon.

Mr Friedel welcomed her gratefully, with open arms, allowing for once the warmth of his Jewish blood to overflow the restraints of his adopted country. She fitted in quickly, easily, back into her old life, slept in her old bedroom.

She found she was able to buy them lots of things she had never before been able to afford: fillet steaks, farm eggs, Devon butter, peaches and oranges, cartons of fresh cream, a Stilton for Mr Friedel and some hock, new football boots for the boys. It was all enormously enjoyable on that level; she was like a rich aunt come to stay. One morning after being back five days she woke early just as it was coming light and almost believed that nothing in the last year had ever happened and that she was a girl living at home again.

It was not difficult to believe: it had all been an unpleasant dream; you rubbed your eyes and you woke. She lay for a long time thinking about it. In spite of everything, in spite of the bitter disappointments of the year, the frustrations and the harsh experiences, would it be a welcome thought, to know that she was a girl living at home again?

She looked around the room that had been hers for so long. She looked at the walnut veneer dressing table with the wing mirrors, one of which would not move because the hinge was sprained. She looked at the chest of drawers with the glass top and the tall, too narrow wardrobe with the tall, too narrow doors so that coat-hangers had to be turned to hang diagonally in it. She looked at the two thin Wilton rugs that Mr Friedel had bought second hand in a sale, or top of the brown inlaid linoleum, and at the wicker chair that she had painted white and which needed repainting. The rose pink patterned candlewick bedspread, the pink striped cotton curtains already letting in the day, the bedside light with the plastic shade. She had always instinctively wanted something better than these, yet in her life in this house had taken them for granted. Now they all looked terrible. Even the district looked grey and conventional, isolated from the centre of life, the houses regimented and small, the people in them dull suburbanites. Her marriage to Wilfred, with all its drawbacks, had lifted her out of this milieu. Settling back into it, if she ever had to, would be like trying to put a plant back into its restricted seed bed.

The boys when they came home at night seemed not only noisy but common; their attitudes were wrong, they sniggered at what was unamusing, they laughed too long at small jokes, their accents had a south London whine. Julia, grown pert and two inches in a year, was worse. Even her father seemed to have changed, shrunk, become less impressive. For him she felt a greater affection because of this. In spite of their good relations before, she had always been slightly in awe of this slow-speaking, bearded, important little man. Now she was on equal terms with him and love welled up in her. She was more than once on the point of confiding in him, but she knew that she would find no understanding in him of her case. She found little understanding of it in herself. If she were a snob, and feeling the way she did that could hardly be denied, Little God represented someone whom it would be impossible to love or to marry or to go and live with. Yet there were times when she ached for him, longed for his vitality, his crudeness, his hardness, his male dominance, his near cruelty. It was endless weeks now since they had been together. Only twice since Lady Vosper's death. He had changed, changed towards her. Sometimes she felt she could hardly go on without him.

The problem had no solution, or none that she could see. Each alternative was distasteful to her and none was better than the others.

Rachel eventually came out of hospital, looking thinner and a poor colour. Pearl hoped it was only a cyst. She stayed four days extra to see her step-mother safely installed and then had to make the choice either to return to Cadogan Mews or begin to explain to her family why she was not returning. Nine days was as much as one could respectably absent oneself.

She left, but before going back she called at Godfrey's room. No one was there. All that had been added was another layer of dust.

Mrs Jamieson was in the house when she got to Cadogan Mews, and everything here was looking bright and well-cared-for. For twenty minutes she wandered round the house looking at the pictures and the furniture, then she changed into a new outfit she had bought in the January sales and went out. The weather for early March was balmy, the icy winds had gone and a pale sunlight filtered through the tall trees of Cadogan Place, promising spring. She thought, in a week or two the daffodils will be out.

She walked down Sloane Street, stopping here and there to look at attractive window displays. Then she went into Peter Jones and wandered through department after department. She had opened an account some months ago, but she did not really intend to spend any money today. It was a form of pleasure walking among the fine linen and the glass, the elegant garden furniture, the Italian trays and chairs, the sunshades, the hats, the dresses, the underwear, the lamps, the bedspreads, the rich carpets, the chandeliers. It all smelt and looked good. It was the way a lady spent an afternoon. She was the client, not the assistant; she was young and rather beautiful and people looked at her. Men looked at her. Some looked at her face, some looked at her legs, but not many were without admiration.

She thought of ringing up Veronica Portugal but by now it was too late. In the lengthening shades of the afternoon she walked back to Cadogan Mews.

Wilfred was there before her. It looked as if he had left Mrs Jamieson instructions to ring him, for quite clearly he had cut his day at the office short. The meeting was strained and without any obvious improvement on their parting; but they had tea together and he tried to be friendly and interested about Rachel. He was obviously relieved that she had come back at all, and for a while her power and influence over him gave her pleasure. She saw that if she stayed – though staying permanently was almost unthinkable – she would have an ascendancy over him that she had never had before. The fact that she had been unfaithful had somehow got overlooked by him in his determination to keep her. He was fighting, in his own way and in the only way open to him; he was fighting Godfrey's influence and still hoping against hope that he would win. Their marriage and the earlier relationship of rich solicitor and poor shop-girl, was still too close to be entirely forgotten by her, and she could not help but be astonished at the change and get a certain not very nice satisfaction out of it.

Tea ended with an exchange of information and at least without obvious enmity. But when he had gone upstairs a weight of depression fell on her. In spite of all this, in spite of what she came back to and what material gain she might have from it, coming home to him had become a return to the gilded cage.

On the Friday Wilfred mentioned the sale at Merrick House which was to take place in two weeks' time. The first viewing day would be Monday the 17th, and all the previous week the auctioneer would be in itemizing the stuff to be sold. This week-end, therefore, would be the last chance of a private look at the contents without interference from anyone, and as he now had his own key he thought of going down tomorrow. Would Pearl like to come? Pearl listlessly agreed. She had nothing better to do, and the thought of seeing inside the house where Godfrey had lived with Lady Vosper interested her.

On the way down on the Saturday, seeking common ground, Angell mentioned the few things he thought might interest him: he gathered that most of the furniture and paintings were junk; they hadn't bothered to go in when they were down last week. It hadn't even been decided yet what to do with the house; it was of little architectural merit and Sir Francis wanted to bring the bulldozers in. But it had sentimental connections for the neighbourhood, and so as not to offend the locals it probably would be left for a time as it was. Wilfred's real interest was in some Persian rugs he had heard were there, and a natural tendency to like snooping round old houses to see if he could pick up a bargain. Though his discoveries had never been sensational, he was always hoping that one day he would find an undiscovered Claude or Chardin or Canaletto in a neglected attic.

The fine spring-like weather of earlier in the week was over, and it was a grey day with flecks of rain constant but solitary in the wind, and heavy cloud drifting over the land. In their hired car they made good time and were there by eleven-thirty. They drove up the pebbly drive and Angell told the chauffeur, a little man called Heath, to be back at 12.45. They would lunch on the way home. When the car had gone they did not immediately go in, but Angell stood on the steps telling Pearl of the development plans.

'It is almost certain that when this road is widened the main shopping centre for the new area will be over to your right. About three-quarters of the land is ours, but the other quarter belongs to a man called Jenkins, a farmer, who will make a fortune if he plays his cards properly. Of course all this will take a long time, but it's the intention of our Company that it shall all be done very well, with two supermarkets and parking space for a hundred cars. The housing development should mainly begin in those woods to your left, but of course in time it will spread north as well to envelop the village.'

Rooks flew low overhead, their wings creaking like paper.

'And what will become of the village?' Pearl said.

'It will stay exactly as it is. In fact one of the features of the scheme is that the existing village will remain completely untouched and will become an offshoot of the development, yet a centre in itself.'

'But if you surround it with a new town, put supermarkets and all that, and smother it in brick and cement, mightn't you just as well pull it down? It will have lost all its beauty, all its quietness, all its dignity. It might as well be dead.'

'My dear, I know many unattractive things are done in the name of progress, and possibly this is one of them. But it is not we who conceived this scheme, it is the Government of the day, a government faced with a pullulating electorate who demand decent new houses in decent new towns so that they can reproduce their kind in ever greater

346

numbers. Someone must serve such developments. If Land Increments did not, there would be another company anxious to step in. Eager and anxious!'

He unlocked the front door, and they walked into the big hall.

'Of course all towns have developed this way,' he said. 'It is only that now we have to *create* new towns, out of almost nothing, and this gives a greater impression of vandalism. Some cities have gradually removed all the evidences of their village origins, some preserve them. Even an industrial town like Wigan, surrounded by gaunt factories and coal mines, has some beautiful timbered houses in the centre. Wigan, like many others, was a victim of the Industrial Revolution. Handley Merrick in its small way is to be a victim of the social revolution of this century. Better to preserve what we can than try to fight the inevitable.'

Unconvinced, Pearl walked round the hall with him. She did not understand Wilfred's exact position in the Land Increments empire, but she instinctively distrusted arguments based on profit.

She said: 'This perhaps. It's – not much to look at. It could go. But to destroy all the village . . . And the peace and the quietness.'

Angell stared disparagingly at a suit of armour. 'Taste is not the perquisite of one class. Everyone knows the common man lacks it. One forgets how unforgivably some of these old landed families were equally lacking.'

Pearl went towards the great double doors on the right. 'It doesn't look as if it's been lived in for ages.'

The door creaked and she went in. Wilfred followed her but found it dark inside, as all the shutters were closed. He couldn't see Pearl, but chinks of light showed it to be a ballroom or a very large reception room. Such furniture as there was was swathed in dust sheets. He clicked the light switch.

'I've tried that,' said Pearl from the darkness. 'I suppose we're not *trespassing* here, are we?'

'Of course not,' said Angell, colliding with a chair. 'The property is ours.'

'But not the furniture. Well, I certainly wouldn't like to buy it. But Lady Vosper *couldn't* have lived here, Wilfred.

347

It's like a tomb.'

'She lived in some rooms. She hadn't the money or the staff to keep it all up.' He took out a slab of chocolate, broke off a piece and began to eat it.

Pearl was at one of the tall windows. 'I wouldn't think these shutters have been opened for years.' She rattled them.

Wilfred struck a match and the feeble smoky flame cast a jumpy light over the dust sheets and the iron work. 'I wonder where the master switch is for the electricity.' The match went out.

'There's a door at the further end,' Pearl said. 'If this is the dining room it might lead to the kitchens.' She went on towards it.

'No, this isn't the dining room!' Wilfred said in irritation, putting another piece of chocolate in his mouth. 'How could it be? Let's go back to the hall.'

But she was moving down the room, her eyes growing more used to the darkness. She avoided the chairs and the two shrouded statues and reached the other end. Impatiently he waited where he was, like a parent with a disobedient child. She opened the door at the end.

'There's another passage,' she said. 'It's only curtains.' She disappeared.

The soft milky flavour on his tongue, he groped his way down the chamber and reached the further door. He could hear her but she had gone on. The light was better, and after a moment he caught up with her. She was in a small hall with stairs leading up. They were narrow stairs, but it was daylight for she had pulled back the faded velvet curtains.

'There's pictures here,' she said.

'Engravings. Not even good ones. I think this may be the staff staircase.' Chewing, Angell threw away a piece of silver paper. 'I'm not interested in the staff quarters.'

'It'll all lead the same way in the end.' She looked in another door but the room was quite empty. A second door led into what might have been a sitting-room.

'We'll go back to the hall,' Wilfred said.

'Let's try this way . . .' She went up the stairs and after a moment, deciding that he must humour her, he followed.

But half way up they stopped at the sound of a door being slammed somewhere. On the narrow stair Pearl peered down at Wilfred's face.

'Did you leave the front door open?'

'Yes,' he said. 'Of course.'

'I didn't think there was that much wind.'

'Well, there must be. In a house like this, the draughts . . .'

On the landing above were three doors. Two led into small bedrooms. The third had green baize on its further side and led to a long passage with doors off either way and two shuttered windows. They went in each room in turn.

'I don't think this is leading us back at all.'

'Look,' Pearl said. 'Look.' There was a small unshuttered window and they peered out towards the back of the house, at the overgrown lawn, the tree, the rotted apples, the broken wheelbarrow, the clouds lowering.

Angell said irritably: 'You've led me completely wrong. There *must* be better furniture at the front of the house.'

They turned back and found a door they had missed in the dark. It led to a wider passage. Pearl gave a sharp exclamation as a flag hanging from the wall brushed her hair.

'What is it? What is it?' said Wilfred. 'Oh, the third Dragoon Guards. I wonder when that was used . . . Ah,' he added, moving on, 'this is one of the rugs. Open that door.'

She opened a door onto a bedroom. There were no shutters here, and the light helped Wilfred in the passage to examine the rug he had found on the wall. She waited by the door, aware that her hands were dirty and that there was a smear on her coat. She was vaguely uneasy. The slamming front door had disturbed her, and the house was like a giant sarcophagus. She thought of Flora Vosper and her friendship with Godfrey. She thought of Godfrey's disappearance. She wondered where he had gone. She was not happy about it.

'It's not first-class,' said Angell, rubbing his glasses and slipping them back in the breast pocket of his suit. 'It might fetch four or five hundred pounds. But I don't want it. The colours are not good. There isn't the usual taste in *choice* of colour . . .'

'Let's go, Wilfred,' Pearl said. 'If there's nothing here. It's so *dirty*.'

'There's much more to the house than this. There's a big library, and also a gallery, though I tremble to think what horrors of Victorian art there may be in there. And Flora Vosper converted a wing, which may have a few tolerable things.'

They looked in the rest of the rooms and then came out at the top of the main staircase which more properly they should have come up. From here the hall looked like a museum that had been closed to the public for a year. Two crossed tattered flags hung above a coat of arms. A cannon on a pedestal, swords, muskets, and the two knights in armour silently waiting. The front door was shut.

They went down the stairs together, not speaking now. Through the windows Pearl could see the slim poplars at the edge of the road. Their tops were not waving.

As they got to the bottom Wilfred rested his hand on one of the armoured shoulders. 'This time if we go the other way, there are probably two comparable rooms on the other side . . .' He went off to the right, but Pearl stayed where she was, looking at the front door.

Wilfred opened the door he had chosen and said: 'Yes, this is the library.' He went in.

Pearl's heart was trying to beat a little harder than usual. She was cold and getting colder. She went to the front door and turned the knob and pulled. It did not move. It was a very big door, of course, but it should have opened. Then she looked up and saw that the top bolt was across.

Her head went swimmy. She leaned against the door. The bolt was too high to reach without standing on a chair. She did not feel up to standing on a chair. Like a sick woman she walked across the hall to the library. It was a long room but Wilfred was not there. The door beyond was ajar. She opened her mouth to call but changed her mind.

She made her way down between the long dusty shelves which were heavy with old books grinning in faded gilt. She stumbled over a pile on the floor. Rain was freckling the windows. She reached the other end and found Wilfred in the next room holding a picture he had taken down from the wall.

'Look at this,' he said. 'It's not an old master but –'

'Wilfred, somebody's bolted the front door!'

'The trouble with these genuinely old – What?' He stared at her over his library spectacles. 'What d'you mean, bolted the door?'

'From the inside. Since we came in.'

He frowned down at the picture again, reluctant to divert his attention. 'Oh, impossible, Pearl. There's no one here but ourselves.' He looked up again, her alarm communicating at last. 'I expect the door is heavy and hard to move.'

'The bolt's across. I've seen it. It's the top bolt.'

He put the picture down. 'Perhaps the auctioneers have left a caretaker. In that case perhaps we should make ourselves known.'

'Why didn't he?'

Neither of them moved. He said, almost absently: 'This way leads to the part of the house she occupied. You see the new central heating pipes . . . A caretaker . . . He might have thought the door blew open.'

'I think we should go,' said Pearl.

'Yes . . . yes. There should be a way out this way, shouldn't there?'

'Let's go back, Wilfred.'

He had been slow to catch any idea of the fear that was in her mind. Now his colour changed. He said with an assumption of calm: 'Oh, very well. If you think so.'

He led the way past her, almost pushed past her, and walked down the library. Half way he stopped and she caught him up. They had both heard something. It was a movement in the hall. They listened. There was no further sound. Angell rubbed a moist hand down the side of his coat. Then he straightened up and walked into the hall. Little God was waiting for them.

He was on the first step of the stairs so that his head was level with the suit of armour. He had not shaved since leaving hospital and the rough black beard was an inch long. The stitches had been taken out but his face was still lumpy. His nose was bent.

It was the first time in all their association that they had confronted each other together, and for a few seconds they were all quite still, existing in an unlucid incredulous border

351

world between the imagined and the actual. Outside the rooks cawed and water dripped from the rain-wet branches of the trees. Then Godfrey laughed.

The sound stiffened Angell, who had looked as if he was going to fall. He cleared his throat, swallowing down panic like a morning sickness.

'What business have you here, Brown? You're trespassing.'

'I'm trespassing,' said Godfrey. 'So're you. You're trespassing on your luck, and it's going to let you down.'

'Godfrey!' Pearl said.

'Shut up! I'm just going to even with your fat husband, that's all.'

Angell's knees were threatening to give way. 'You must be insane, man.'

'I'm going to fight you, see. Kio made a mess of my face, didn't he. I'll see what I can do to yours.'

'If you touch me it will be a police matter! I'll see you in prison!'

'Maybe afterwards you'll see me in prison.' He stepped down into the hall.

'Godfrey –'

'Get lost!' he snarled.

Angell grabbed Pearl by the arm and pulled her back into the library: with trembling fingers he slammed the library door: by chance there was a key. He turned it as Godfrey reached the other side and rattled the handle and then thumped on the door.

'Quick,' Angell panted. 'Help me!'

Together they pushed a glass-fronted bookcase across the door. When it was there Angell leaned against it, hands vibrating with fear. They listened. Godfrey began to laugh. He laughed unpleasantly for about fifteen seconds. Then there was silence.

Angell collapsed on the nearest chair, took out a handkerchief and mopped his face. He could not stop sweating from every pore. It was as if the ducts were emptying, losing the juices of a lifetime. A car passed along the main road outside; a cow lowed in a nearby field; a dog barked. In the hall there was silence. Pearl was horribly reminded of her second meeting with Godfrey.

She put her face close to Wilfred's and whispered: 'We'd

352

better try to find our way out this way. It's better not to stay here.'

Angell levered himself up, instantly on the move again. Trying to make no noise they stole back through the library, opened the door into the next room. The picture standing against the wall was now of as much interest to Wilfred as a looted necklace to a soldier lost in the desert. They moved through into the next room, which was a well furnished sitting-room with an electric fire switched on and the remains of a meal on the table. A coat hung over a chair-back; a newspaper lay on the floor opened at the strip-cartoons. A pair of slippers, a white dressing-gown with red letters on the back, a transistor radio.

Pearl, slightly ahead of Wilfred now, opened the further door into another and smaller hall. Little God was waiting for her as she stepped out.

Angell fell back into the sitting-room, fumbled his way round the table, backed towards the other door. Pearl stood her ground, taller than Little God.

'Out of my way, Oyster.'

'Godfrey, I don't know how –'

'Out of my way!'

'– I can tell you that –'

He put his hands on her shoulders, and shoved her. She reeled back into the centre of the room, upset a chair. He ran round her after Angell who had already gone.

Angell blundered panting back the way he had come, through into the library. In despair he saw the bookcase he and Pearl had pulled across the further door. By the time he . . .

He reached it, scrabbled at it, half got it away; footsteps behind him; he turned like a baited rabbit, not even his hands up, waiting to be killed.

Godfrey hit him a glancing blow on the side of the head and then a right to the stomach. Angell collapsed across the bookcase and retched. Godfrey tried to haul him upright, but even his distended strength could hardly manage seventeen stone of dead weight.

'Godfrey!' Pearl behind him. 'You'll *kill* him! You –'

'Stand up!' Godfrey screamed at Wilfred, and then turned on Pearl. 'Look at him! Call this a man! This foul-up? He ain't got the spunk of a fat canary, so he fixes it

so I shall get beaten up! This . . . Call this a husband?
Why don't you sweep him under the carpet –'

'Stop it, Godfrey! You *fool*! The police –'

Angell incautiously straightened up, and Godfrey turned
on him again, punched him in the eye; Angell's flailing
defensive fists blocked two blows and then Godfrey hit him
once more in the soft part of the belly. The great figure
slowly collapsed like a deflated balloon and thumped down
upon the floor.

Chapter Eleven

When Heath the chauffeur drove up twenty minutes later the front door was open and Pearl came to the door urgently signalling him to enter. He went in and found Angell lying on a settee in the hall, conscious but with a heavy bruise on his face and groaning with pain.

'There was a man in the house, stealing things! He tried to get away and my husband tried to stop him! There was a fight . . .'

'That man I just saw turn out of the drive in a grey car? Little man with black hair and a wild sort of face.'

'Yes,' said Pearl, doubtfully. Recognition would be inconvenient. 'Yes, that's the man.'

'Breaking and entering,' groaned Angell, with his hand to his stomach. 'Breaking and entering and grievous bodily harm . . .'

'Shall I go fetch the police?'

'I think we should get my husband straight back to London. I don't think he's seriously hurt but it's been a nasty shock—'

'You're going to have a black eye, sir. And your cheek's swelling. D'you think if we ran him into Sudbury?'

'He wants to go home. Do you think you could get up, Wilfred . . . walk to the car?'

'I don't at all think so. I feel very ill indeed . . .'

'It's only at the bottom of the steps. We can stop at the first hotel and buy some brandy. Take his other arm, Heath.'

Wilfred had been felled and was not easily got on his feet again. All the bulk had collapsed, and his frame no longer had the strength to reanimate it. Somehow they got him down the steps and into the car. He fell back in the seat, sighing heavily and Pearl dabbed at a smear of blood on his cheek. Then she ran up and pulled the door of the house shut as Heath re-started the car and turned. She climbed in and gingerly he drove off.

They stopped in the next village and she bought a double

brandy for Wilfred and one for herself. They drank this i̇
silence. She bought him a second and then went across the
street to a chemist and got some witch hazel and sticking
plaster. Presently they were off again.

After that they scarcely spoke.

It had been a terrible moment in the house when Wilfred
fell. The weight, all that weight might alone cause him
injury. Godfrey had stood over him fairly shaking with
anger.

'Look at him, look at him! I hardly touched him yet!
What can you do? Look what he done to me! Look at my
face! Look at my nose! I haven't *touched* him hardly.
You'd think I'd beaten his brains out! You'd think I'd
killed him! You can't get back at a slob like this!'

'*Go* on, *go!*' urged Pearl, pulling at his arm. She could
hardly speak. Her hair was coming loose; she felt the
sweat of faintness. 'You fool, you fool, you crazy fool!
He'll have you in prison! You're out of your mind doing
this. Go on, Godfrey!'

'I'll kick his guts out! Look, I done nothing yet. He's
not taken enough to kill a bleeding canary. Leave go my
arm or I'll fix you next!'

'*Go*, Godfrey! I tell you! Look, he's coming round. If
you're still here there's *nothing* I can do to help you! The
chauffeur'll be back any minute. This is just your one
chance *now* to get away!'

He was so angry, so ready to be violent again, that her
voice never seemed to penetrate to him at all. Only her
hand clutching his sleeve and shaking him had any effect.
Twice he tried to throw her off but she clung to his arm,
dragging him towards the habitable part of the house
where his things were scattered. It was minutes before
common sense came back into his eyes, and minutes more
before he could be persuaded that what she urged was
best. Eventually she pushed him out through the further
door as her husband began to try to sit up, and she ran
back the length of the library to help Wilfred and to get
his head into her lap. From there they somehow crawled
together to the settee.

As soon as she saw that Wilfred had not banged his heȧ
in the fall she knew his injuries were not likely to be ser

ious and her sick alarm turned to calculation. A fall down the stairs had been her first thought as an excuse to tell Heath – but no one would believe it. So it had to be an unknown intruder, and luck brought Wilfred back to coherence before the chauffeur came.

'Keep it *quiet*! by Heaven! He shall be – shall be in prison for this if it's the last thing I –'

'If you bring in the police, Wilfred, I'll leave you tonight!'

'Damn you and curse him! I wish I'd never set eyes on either of you . . . Sluts! Whores! Savages!'

'I mean it. I mean it, Wilfred. I swear it! This is the end. If you tell the police I'll leave you tonight!'

'How can you *expect* me to feel about this? You clearly agree with him! You think a young thug like that is entitled. My own wife –'

'I don't agree with him! Of course not. But what did *you* do?'

'What did *I* do? When my own wife –'

'Oh, don't talk such rubbish. It's too late to think of rights and wrongs. I'm only trying to stop all this, stop it, stop it, *stop it!* before it all begins again. If you bring in the police it will all begin again . . .'

So until Heath came. Angell did not contradict her story to Heath but it lay like an unexploded bomb between them all the way to London. Silence was the only hope. At any minute it might go up.

'Thank you, Heath. If you'd help me to get him upstairs. I'll undress him and then telephone for a doctor. Would you like to rest, Wilfred, on this chair while I put the kettle on for a hot-water bottle? Thank you, Heath. It's only another half flight. (Do I pay him, Wilfred, or is it on account? All right, I'll just tip, then.) Thank you, Heath, it's awfully kind of you. We're going to ring the doctor now and then make a full report to the police . . .'

Even in his distress Wilfred showed extra displeasure at the pound note changing hands.

'Who would you like to see? Dr Matthewson?'

'No . . . Wait until morning. There's a man I go to on the Health Service.'

She made him some scrambled eggs and he ate these

with thin bread and butter and a half bottle of Chablis. Then he took a pill and read *The Law Society's Gazette* for about an hour before dropping off to sleep. She went to her own room and spent a restless night impregnated with the most horrifying dreams. One of them was that Wilfred and Godfrey had become friends in the old cold tomb of Merrick House and had turned against her. They would not let her out of the hall, blocking her exit whichever way she turned, and when she stood at bay they whispered together plotting obscene enormities against her which she did not understand but which were half sexual and half surgical. When she tried to run up the stairs Lady Vosper was waiting at the top . . .

In the morning Wilfred's eye had gone blue-black but the split skin on his cheek was scarcely noticeable. Although he was sore and could hardly move his left leg because of some sort of delayed strain, he had changed his mind and wanted no doctor. If there were to be no retribution, the less publicity the better. This was tacit between them, never given voice. Indeed that day was a full return to the arid silences following the Kio fight.

But in the evening he was still in some pain so she rang his National Health doctor who came and said: 'There's no damage at all that I can find beyond a few bruises. If you continue to have pain we'll take some X-rays; but my view is that it's mainly shock and a couple of days in bed is the answer. It's a very unpleasant incident, though. The police haven't found the man?'

'No,' said Pearl.

'Not yet,' said Wilfred, his injustice simmering, the bitterness, the loneliness, the resentment.

He stayed in bed for two days. Pearl waited on him and conversation remained at a minimum. Sometimes she wondered at herself. She had always thought of herself as a straightforward, uncomplicated person, and she wondered at the ready lies that had come to her lips in this crisis, the cool words slipping out, evading, concealing, explaining. It was a new talent, all born of her affair with Godfrey . . . and it came so easily . . . But one couldn't go through life cheating, deceiving, making up pictures to fit inconvenient frames.

Wilfred clearly blamed her for the assault as well as for the forced deception afterwards. On the Wednesday he got up and spent the day rearranging his paintings. For this he needed her help and once or twice her advice: nails had to be knocked in the wall and taken out, judgments had to be made regarding height and situation. Talk began. Because it concerned a common interest it was not quite strangled with constraint. They took tea and dinner, and afterwards he claimed his conjugal rights.

It was the first time he had dared to do so since the Kio fight, and it was an astute move for, however much she might tell herself different, the assault of Saturday had left her feeling in the wrong. So, although surprised and affronted, she still did not refuse him. But it was a meeting giving little satisfaction to either of them. Physical love without the infusion of either affection or passion is flesh without spirit, and as dead. She clasped him limply, for form's sake, and he took what he could, claiming the un-claimable.

Afterwards, without being explicit, she made it plain to him that it signified no change on her part, no change of heart towards him, no decision to stay. So long as she did stay, it could be that she would fulfil her undertakings, just as she would continue to order his house and sit at his table. But what had happened now implied no extra commitment for the future.

Yet his chief comfort from the event, however comfort-less the event itself, lay in the fact that it had happened. Without Brown's vile attack on him, it would not have occurred, so whatever she might imply to the contrary it was a move in his favour.

On the Thursday afternoon, Pearl was shopping in Knightsbridge when someone came up beside her and said: 'Well, is he dead yet?'

She felt as if she had fallen off a step. His face was still a mess but he had shaved since Saturday. The lone wolf. The wolf looking for its mate.

'How *can* you kill a man like that?' he said. 'Honest to God. It's like socking a feather bed. You have to hold it up with one hand while you thump with the other.'

'He's better,' she said. 'No thanks to you. If he had stood

up to you, you *would* have killed him.'

'Tell him I'll kill him next time. Tell him if he lies down next time I'll kick his guts out of his ears.'

'The police haven't been told, Godfrey,' she said. 'The only thing anyone knows is that a thief attacked him. So you're free.' She breathed out her distress, her perplexity; they made her look older, like a weight of experience. 'This time. But I promise you that if you ever attack him again I'll go straight to the police myself and I'll tell them about the first attack too!'

'You really love him, don't you. Old money-bags.'

'You know I don't!'

'You pretend you still think something about me?'

'Why else d'you think I've persuaded him not to report what you'd done? If I didn't care something, what would I care?'

'What d'you do to persuade him? Come on, tell me what you did. Something special?'

'I didn't persuade him. I threatened I'd leave him.'

Godfrey sneered into her shopping basket. 'I see he isn't off his food. So now you're stuck, aren't you?'

'Stuck?'

'With him. You say you'll leave him if he tells the dicks. So if you do leave him he will. Eh? So you're stuck.'

'Does it matter to you?' she said.

'Well, maybe it could, see. Maybe when I get over this it could.'

'Like when you left hospital and I went to your room and cleaned it up and cooked you a meal and you never came!'

He gripped her arm. 'Look, Oyster, you stupid kook, what d'you think I looked like when I got out that day? Flaming stitches standing out on my face like pig's bristles. Nose swelled like a big toe with a bunion. Gums with holes in 'em where the teeth had come out. D'you think I was going to face you looking like that?'

She eased her arm away. 'Isn't there ever anything else I can do for you but get into bed? Is that all you want? Couldn't we have talked, had a meal, made plans?'

'Oh, talked . . . Yes, when we talk you always get snotty. You've always thought yourself too good for me, haven't you. It's always been an effort to work your way down to my level. Well, I'll tell you one thing: Flora Vosper never felt that way. That's because she was a real lady, not an imitation one. She –'

'It's a pity you ever lost her, isn't it! I suppose that's why you went down there, isn't it. I suppose –'

'Yes, that's why I went down there.' His face suddenly contorted. 'That's why I went down there. Because I could get a bit of peace and quiet and time to think. About how I been let down by everybody. When you coming to see me, Pearl?'

They stood there like jammed logs in a stream, neither physically nor mentally able to make the decision to separate or to join, while the indifferent crowd moved past.

'I can't, Godfrey, we're no good for each other. You – we do nothing but quarrel. I've brought enough trouble to you – we've brought enough to each other. Leave me alone.'

'D'you want me to do that?'

'Yes . . . I don't know. Sometimes I feel I'm in a trap.'

'I'll ring you,' he said.

'No – don't do that. Leave me alone.'

'I make your flesh creep, don't I?' he said.

She took out her shopping list and studied it. 'I haven't bought the meat yet. I shall be late back.'

'I'll ring you,' he said, 'but not yet. I'll choose me time – not when he's at home. Now I know I'm in the clear I'll go and see Jude Davis, see when I can get back into training. I'll ring you maybe next week.'

'Don't do that,' she said.

They were all glad to see him in the gym. Jude Davis and Pat Prince and the other boxers in the stable and hangers on. He found he was quite a hero. How was he feeling now; and the stitches would hardly show in a couple of weeks and had he seen the ratings; he'd gone up two places since the fight with Kio.

Jude said take it easy for another three weeks, then light training; if he wanted to see a plastic surgeon about his nose he had only to say, but actually you'd hardly notice, the kink was so slight. There'd be a couple of easy pitches lined up for him in April. You didn't need to match him with one of the top boys just yet; *he* was the draw now. Put him on anywhere in London.

He was in the gym about an hour and then left wondering how he could get his own back on Jude. Jude had played it easy, him coming back. Just as if nothing had happened. Maybe Pat had never told him anything of what had been said in the hospital, but in a way that made it worse if it meant Jude really thought him such a stupid pus-head that he didn't know he'd been led to the slaughter. The resentment of his defeat, and more particularly of having his looks spoiled, had festered during his two weeks in Merrick House. The tiny revenge on Wilfred had hardly soothed it at all. Sometimes during those days in Suffolk he had wandered through that gaunt dark building making plans to destroy them all. They were wild irrational plans; but someday, somehow, one would crop up that would work.

At present he had money to spend and not much to spend it on. He rang up Sally Beck but a man answered and said she was out of town. One thing that worried him was that at night he still couldn't breathe properly through his nose, and sometimes during the day it stopped up with catarrh as if someone had plugged it.

Eventually, bored with hanging about, he got a job on a building site helping to clear rubble after the bulldozers had done their work. It rained most of the first day, and the place was a morass of mud; but he came home with his muscles tightened up and for the first time for a month had a night's sleep without dreams. He worked the next four days and on Saturday morning rang Tom Bushey and they spent the week-end together in Brighton. It seemed to Godfrey that there was no colour bar nor an injury bar in Brighton: they had no difficulty about girls, and the one he took up with said she liked a man with a few bumps on his face.

But it all added up to nothing much, and he began to think more and more about Pearl. He'd been pretty mixed up so far as she was concerned right from the start. And for a time Flora's death had knocked him right out of the ring. There had been no real time to get his sights fixed or his mind made up.

Well, it was two months now since Pearl, and distance lent enchantment. And revenge lent enchantment. You couldn't get even with a man who fell down like a jelly at the first poke. But you could maybe make him suffer his other way. You could enjoy his wife. You could make the old man suffer by letting him know what was going on and how unfaithful his dear beloved really was. Godfrey didn't doubt his ability to have Pearl come to him. She was hooked.

Another month went by before Godfrey's next fight. It was an easy one, as Jude had promised: a man called Ferry, from Nigeria. Godfrey got a big hand when he went into the ring and he won inside the distance, but it was not a convincing win. Little God's confidence was not as complete as it had been and he was too concerned to cover up his face. Ferry got a cut eye and that stopped it, but Jude made an expressive face to Prince after the fight. 'Give 'im time,' said Pat. ' 'E wants three cushy bouts before 'e'll begin to look good again.'

Godfrey knew just as well as they did that he hadn't done right, and the kindly write-ups didn't deceive him. He nursed his resentment and spent his money on a girl called Mickey who attached herself to him and finally came to live with him. He didn't know what the hell was wrong with him in the ring: he wasn't turning yellow, that was for certain. But his reflexes were different from what they had been: it was something he couldn't at present control: he had set out to beat the punk in the other corner but his reflexes had been more concerned that the punk shouldn't beat him.

He would grow out of it. It was just a question of time.

Just before his second fight he got rid of Mickey – or Mickey walked out on him – according to which side you heard. Godfrey said he never had asked the little yard-cat to come, she'd slid in where it was warm and the money was good. He was glad to be shut of her. *She* said she'd had enough of his moods and his tantrums and his sulks. As for him being good in bed, he was good in bed if you counted orang-utans.

For his second fight Jude had chosen a man called Ephraim. This time they had been moved down to second on the undercard; but as it turned out it was a better fight than the first and Godfrey out-fought and out-boxed his man. Everyone thought it good and Godfrey was pleased with their congratulations. But somewhere inside him there was a little cold coin of the realm which told him he still had his personal battle to overcome. He had won because he was much better than Ephraim, but his reactions weren't fast enough or sure enough, and he knew he was being fed easy meat. And his nose was troubling him. He had catarrh every morning and sometimes in the ring it got blocked. Although he was fourth in the ratings he wasn't sure he could beat any of the first three yet. Yet. How long before the next fall?

He rang Pearl. She agreed to meet him, but only for a meal. He said O.K. and they met in the Grill at the Cumberland, and he told her his doubts. For once they talked like reasonable human beings without obvious conflict. It was almost the first time. Always before passion and revulsion had been so strong between them, colours too violent to give a chance to any of the pastel shades. Now temporarily, so temporarily, they talked like companions. It was only when they were separating that he asked her to come back with him. She refused. He said if she came back it would make him feel better, feel he was really himself again. As he'd just told her, he'd had the confidence knocked out of him: this would help, her coming, it might even put him right on top of the world, back in the groove as a feather-weight, undo all the damage that knock-out had done. It would be doing him a favour. Besides, he wanted her. Remember what it was like those last few times?

Blood thumping, she refused. But she agreed to meet him next week same time, same place. Godfrey was reasonably satisfied. He thought next week would fix it. And it did.

The bitter knowledge that the connection had not broken came to Angell slowly. Not a particularly perceptive man except where his own feelings were involved, he had hoped that the terrible affair in Suffolk with its injuries to himself, had put Pearl off Godfrey for good. Like Godfrey he had been quick to see that her threat to leave him if he told the police carried with it an implied promise to stay with him if he didn't. And her attention to him during his convalescence and her acceptance of his later claims had given him cause for hope.

The slow unease was much later, a month or more later. It crept on him like a chill you have caught from being out in an east wind without an overcoat. You just can't pick out the moment when you first know it's there. Then a few little clues. Then a realization.

Again, then, all over again, suffocatingly again, the agonies of deciding whether to pretend not to know. The humiliation within yourself for so pretending. But the bleak alternative. To live with her on these terms or to live without her. He had long since called Birman off Godfrey.

If only Godfrey would be run over by a bus, or die or commit suicide. In the night sometimes he even vindictively toyed with Birman's earlier suggestion that to get Godfrey beaten up out of the ring was much easier than to get him beaten up in. But the step into crime was something that he just could never contemplate seriously. Ethically the two acts might not be very different, but the gap for Angell was unbridgeable. And any new revenge would almost certainly bring a new reprisal in its wake.

This really put it out. Not since those early days at his public school had Angell felt anything resembling the terror he had felt running through the library towards the blocked door. And never since then either – and not even then – had he known the physical pain of being struck hard, the hideous grinding shock of knuckle on bone, the pain, the hurt, the bruising, the *injury* inflicted on one's own person by another person standing there whom one could not *stop*. The not knowing where the next terrible blow would fall. To fight was useless, to cry for mercy equally useless, the blind oblivion of collapse the only escape.

And it had come soon. But those moments had left an indelible mark. If Angell had feared Godfrey before, now he was terrified. The only true safety would be to see Godfrey in prison for a long term, or emigrated to Australia.

In the meantime Godfrey helped himself to his wife, and there was no better alternative than to pretend one didn't know. It was insupportable, unbearable, intolerable. The worry, the jealousy, the fear, were destroying his life.

But the present situation could continue only on the basis of this pretence. So long as everyone pretended it was not happening, life could just be lived. There were even times when it had its pleasures, and those pleasures could be heightened, like a banquet in war-time. Break the pretence and you broke the bandages on the wound.

Chapter Twelve

Godfrey got his third cushy fight at the Anglo-American Sporting Club in June. It was against a man called Roy Owen, who had won well in the lists a few years ago and had then gone to America. He had made big money there, but he had had too many hammerings in the process. He was a pawky fighter, not in the least interested in stopping his opponent, only in avoiding being stopped, and garnering the points on the way so that he stood a fair chance of a decision. He was the right sort of opponent for Little God, who for the first time since the Kio fight began to open up in his old style. Owen scored a fair number of times on Godfrey's nose, but there was no dynamite in the glove, it scarcely hurt, it was just a tick in the referee's book: it was good boxing but arid, unambitious, the sort Godfrey had always despised. In going for a knock-out now he showed his contempt and found some of the confidence he had lost.

He did not get his knock-out but it was a narrow points decision in his favour, and the members at the dining tables clearly liked him. The fight did him more good psychologically than either of the other two.

He left the Hilton just as soon as he could get away and drove back to Battersea where Pearl was waiting for him.

As always after a fight his impulses were more than ever arrogant, conquesting, had elements in them of a continuing wish to destroy. Pearl bore it because sometimes in her now was a wish to be destroyed.

When she at last said she must go he rubbed his chin and said: 'Why not spend the night here?'

'I *can't*! You must know that. I'm supposed to be visiting my family.'

'D'you think he believes it?'

'Well, of course! But not if I stay any longer.'

'He only has to check. Just once he has to check.'

Pearl was silent; then she slid out of bed, began hurriedly to dress. He watched her lazily.

'Isn't it right? He only has to do that.'

'Yes. I suppose so. But if he doesn't, if he still believes what I tell him –'

'Why should he? I'd like to tell him to his face.'

'That would be a way of getting back at me, wouldn't it. You'd really like that.'

'He wouldn't have the guts to divorce you even then. I'd take a bet on it.'

'Why do you still hate him so much? It's over now, and you've recovered. You've only gained, in a way, by that fight – in reputation, I mean. And you've got me – as much as you want me . . .' She stopped but he did not answer. 'You don't want me for keeps, only when the fancy takes you.'

'Who says I don't want you for keeps?'

'Well, for marriage.'

'Oh, marriage. What's that? A ball and chain.'

She zipped up her skirt, opened her bag and took out a comb, began to tug at her hair. 'Yes,' she said. 'I suppose that's how you see it. What's the good of marriage when you only have to crook your finger . . . Isn't that enough revenge on Wilfred?'

He sat up in bed and licked a swelling on his lip. 'Every time I look at myself in the mirror, Oyster. Every time.'

'It might have happened in any fight.'

'But it didn't. And it wouldn't. Know what a girl said to me the other day – girl I hadn't seen for a year or more? "For crying out loud, Godfrey," she says, "who bent your hooter?"'

Pearl struggled into her coat. 'Did it make her any less loving?'

He smiled, but did not speak.

She had got to the door. 'Sometimes I think you hate me as much as you do Wilfred.'

'I don't hate anybody,' he said. 'I feel real good.'

'Despise, then,' she said. 'Perhaps that's the word. Despise.'

It was a sultry July, the hottest in London, the papers said, since some time or other. The three fine days and a thunderstorm of a typical English summer were repeated at intervals all through the month. St Swithin's day, significantly, was the hottest of all.

On it Pearl deliberately cut an appointment with Godfrey and went with Veronica Portugal to a swimming pool in Roehampton. She lay in the sun or the water all afternoon letting the impersonal warmth seep into her and the dark desire drain away. When she was away from him her blind mind stared into the dark, comprehending and recognizing nothing reasonable in her behaviour. When she was with him only the need and the fulfilment of the need existed; love was a forgotten word, hatred nearer to the root of her submission.

This time, this time only she had broken free, exercised a puny independence, stretched damp wings, knowing that she was no freer for doing it but was only postponing; some part of her subconscious already busy in horrid fascination with the price she'd have to pay. And yet resenting it. Resenting it.

Veronica Portugal had problems of her own with Simon, and it was clear presently that she had invited Pearl for the afternoon to use her as a confidante. Pearl didn't mind. She listened to Veronica with a quiet, lazy detachment, asking a question here, putting in a comment there; all that was needed. Veronica's problems seemed so simple compared with her own, so surface-borne, so upper-class, so resolvable within a limited code of behaviour. She felt she had become a savage, without roots or guidance, existing in this polite civilized matter-of-fact world but not belonging to it. Wilfred belonged to it. Godfrey sang tribal songs that only her blood understood.

In the early evening, warm and tired and refreshed she drove home, Veronica leaving her on her doorstep. Wilfred, who had been in two hours and imagining the worst, was just in time to see Veronica driving away. The lines of petulance and distrust which so often settled on his face nowadays cleared on the instant and he brushed aside Pearl's mild apologies and would not have her cooking at this late hour. They went out to dinner to a little place in Draycott Avenue – within walking distance; no need for a taxi – where he had heard the escargots were specially plentiful and good. Knowing his moods and his glances to the last shade, Pearl felt her contentment ebbing away into little shallow gullies of new emotion. She saw immediately ahead an event in which she would be the destroyer instead of the destroyed.

A couple of days later Wilfred was unwell in the morning and had only just left for the office when Godfrey called. Pearl tried to prevent him from coming in but he came.

'Ssh! The woman's upstairs!'

'Where was you on Wednesday?'

'I – went out . . . with a friend, a woman friend. It was so hot.'

'So you let me down.'

'Yes . . .' She steeled her eyes at him. 'You've done it to me.'

He took her arm, fingering the arm through the thin silk. 'Well, don't do it to me again! I waited near on an hour.'

'It was just the way I felt . . . When I waited for you I waited four hours.'

'Don't do it again. I warn you. It's a dirty trick. When next?'

Pearl listened for Mrs Jamieson's footsteps.

'Tuesday.'

'Not before then?'

'Not before then.'

'What time?'

'Usual. Three-thirty. Please go.'

'O.K., O.K. Only please don't let me down.'

'I'll please myself,' Pearl said challengingly, just before she closed the door. But she knew this time she would go.

Sam Windermere, the promoter, was putting on a big show at Belle Vue, Manchester, with the main fight a return contest for the Middle-weight Championship of Great Britain. Second on the bill, and nearly as big a draw, was Manchester's own Billy Biddle against the rising new star Hay Tabard, in the Welter-weight division. Tabard was at present Jude Davis's most precious possession. He was a tall blond young man, son of a German prisoner of war, and he looked like being the best welter-weight – or later middle-weight – prospect of his generation. He was not yet 19, and he drew crowds of admirers everywhere he went for his looks and for his fine promise. Jude had had splen-

id offers for him from two bigger managers but he was
ot interested in selling. He was too valuable a potential.
ude had been bringing him along cautiously. Because of
is youth, two-minute rounds instead of three-minute
ounds had been imposed by the B.B.B. of C., and his oppo-
ents had been carefully selected to gain him useful ex-
erience without imperilling his confidence. This was his
irst important fight, and it was the only one Jude had on
his bill.

Godfrey was not involved except as a sparring mate for
Tabard. Nearly all Jude's stable had been utilized from
ime to time: Tom Bushey, two stone heavier, and God-
rey, a stone and a half lighter, among them: Bushey for
is weight, Godfrey for his speed. It gave variety to the
ractice rounds and all added to Tabard's knowledge of
ing-craft.

Two or three days before a fight the sparring ended, so
he Tuesday session was the last that Tabard undertook.
After that it would be the bags or the ball with light shadow
oxing. Godfrey had watched the blond boy a good deal
nd knew his merits and his weaknesses. So of course did
Prince, and while Hay was a tremendous puncher for his
weight, and a beautiful mover, he had defensive faults
vhich Prince was working hard on. Hay was still vulner-
ble to in-fighting, and at times allowed his natural aggres-
iveness to lead him into trouble. Often Godfrey, who to
is credit had learned a lot from his defeat, was able to
and lightly on Hay's jaw and nose from an inside position.

On the Tuesday Davis came down to the gym in the
afternoon and watched Tabard box a couple of rounds
vith a man of his own weight. Godfrey, who had his
appointment with Pearl at 3.30, was to follow the other
spar mate. For the last few days he had been carefully
vorking something out.

Davis watched the first round between them and then
was called to the telephone. This was the moment.

Godfrey dodged round his big opponent, trying a few left
jabs and picking off some fairly hearty lefts in return.
Then he invited the manoeuvre that he knew Tabard
would not resist: head-feinting, a dummy move to the left
and a circle to the right. It was like waving a rag at a bull,
you knew it would come at you because this was what it

had done before. Hay came at him, hitting him high o
the forehead, and Godfrey was just going backward
enough to take the bite out of it. A fierce right he slippe
over his shoulder so that Hay's two fists were just outsid
the line of his body, then he uppercut him with his righ

He'd done this before at half power, registering the poin
without aiming to damage. (When he landed like this Ha
got a lecture from Prince.) This time he put all the powe
of his body and the balance of his feet and the resentmen
of his mind into the one blow. Hay half saw it, though hi
own left arm hid sight of it until too late; he jerked awa
and the uppercut missed his chin and caught him unde
the nose.

Even with the heavy practice gloves it seemed to lift hi
nose half off his face. He staggered back, sagged at th
knees, hit the ropes and slid into a sitting position on th
canvas.

He was not down for a moment before he was struggling
to get up, but by then Prince had leapt into the ring and
was bending over him and pulling off his head guard
Two other boxers were in the ring. Hay was standing up
blood flooding from his nose, crimsoning his gloves and hi
chest. He looked dazed and kept shaking his head, so tha
Prince's efforts to plug his nose were not successful.

Godfrey went over and began to say he was sorry. Pa
Prince turned on him and told him he was a clumsy vicious
little rat. Then Jude Davis came in.

'It's O.K.,' said Tabard. 'I'll be O.K. in a minute. It jus
shook me up. I'm O.K.'

'Sorry, Hay,' said Godfrey. 'I didn't mean it like that:
you just walked into it.'

'It's O.K., I tell you. We was sparring fair enough. Yeh,
I walked into it. I'll be O.K.'

'Let me see,' said Davis. 'Bring a chair, Martin. Sit down,
Hay. Let me see.'

'Keep your head still, for Pete's sake,' snarled Prince,
trying to get the swab up Hay's nostril. 'You little louse,
you,' he said to Godfrey, 'get out of my light!'

'Well, stone me!' said Godfrey, all injured innocence, 'I
was supposed to be boxing, wasn't I? He walked into me
like you walk into a wall.'

'Get Doc Wright,' Jude Davis said quietly.

'He was too little and too quick,' Tabard said. 'If he'd been my own size, I'd not have been open the way I was. See.'

'Sorry, Hay.'

'O.K., God, you wasn't to know.'

Tom Bushey had gone in to telephone the doctor. Jude Davis looked across at Godfrey, but the light on his glasses hid his expression. Pat Prince had at last managed to get plugs in the injured nose, but it was already swollen and he was in a good deal of pain. Bushey came out and said the doctor would be along in a quarter of an hour. Godfrey got Bushey to untie his gloves for him, then he put a towel round his shoulders and stood watching the scene.

Though careful to keep his face expressionless, his heart was seething with joy. He didn't know whether Hay's nose was broken, but anyway he would not be fighting on Friday night. There were ways after all of getting back at Jude Davis without fighting Jude himself. And more than that, who could blame a spar mate for injuring a man twenty-two pounds heavier? It would do Hay no good when it got out, and that was a pity because he was not a bad kid. But it would do him, Godfrey, good with everyone except Jude and Pat. And they could stuff it. Jude would miss his big match on Friday and his darling boy would have a nose like an electric bulb by then. And Godfrey's name, for all Jude might do, would be talked about in the circles where it mattered.

The doctor came but couldn't pronounce till he'd had an X-ray. Godfrey wanted to slip off but Jude made him stay till the very end, so that it was four o'clock before he could get away. During it all Jude had only spoken three sentences to Godfrey. The first was: 'Stay around.' The second was: 'Give him air, you've done enough.' The third was: 'You can clear out now.'

Godfrey 'cleared'. He slid into his Velox and gunned the engine and forced his way out into the traffic, so that the taxi drivers swore at him. He made the V-sign back. He was feeling good. This had done him more good than anything since the Kio fight. He was feeling wonderful, as good as after a top win in the ring. The last effects of the defeat were gone. He knew he was on his way up again and on his way up for keeps this time. The Kio defeat had not destroyed him, it had tempered him, taught him, matured him. He knew all there was to know now. If Jude Davis did not get him the right fights he'd make a fuss and change stables. Little God would be known everywhere as an awkward customer but a coming champion. Managers would swallow a lot to handle a winner. Even his face didn't matter so much now.

It was great. And he wanted Pearl. He wanted her two ways, because he wanted her as a woman and because afterwards he wanted to tell her all he'd done and all he planned to do. It was the way he used to talk to Flora, and now for the first time he wanted to talk this way to Pearl. If she got quit of this old doddler he would even marry her as he'd once planned. She was learning fast and was the classiest-looking girl he would ever have, and it might be good to have her for keeps. She was hooked firm enough now to stand him having a few other interests on the side.

For the first time he even felt almost free of Flora. Not free so that you could forget her but free so that remembering her didn't poison everything you were trying to enjoy.

He parked his car, using his bumper to shove another locked car forward, and then ran upstairs to his room. Pearl wasn't there. There was a scribbled note on the paper covering his table. 'Waited half an hour. Why don't you find somebody else who will wait longer?'

It was like a blow in the face, as if Kio had suddenly come back. It was like an insult to his manhood. He stood in the middle of the room and cursed her aloud for three minutes. The fury kept volcanoing up in him. All his feeling good turned into feeling angry. He'd been let down again. Today of all days. Let down! It was the worst insult he'd ever suffered at the hands of a woman. He'd show her.

He went out of the door, and plaster floated from the slam as he skittered down three flights of stairs and out to his car. More goods-wagon shunting got him out of the small space he'd just got in; and then he was off down Latimer Road and across Battersea Bridge. When he came to Cadogan Mews he did not park in there but round the corner out of sight. When he rang the bell he carefully took shelter in the overhang of the door so that no one looking

ut of the window should see him. When the door opened
he was round the corner with his foot in the way before
he could shut the door again.

'Godfrey! Go *away*! I've had enough –'

He put his whole weight against the door and it jerked
open, nearly knocking her over.

'You stupid kook, standing me up again!'

She was in an apron, green turtle neck jumper, short
linen skirt; she stared at him, ice and fire flashing, then she
looked down at her hand, sucked the knuckles.

'You hurt me, lurching against the door. Will you please
go!'

'Standing me up! No woman can do that! It's the
second time –'

'What d'you think I am, some sort of slavey to be at
your beck and call! –'

'I couldn't get away! I tell you! D'you think I did it on
purpose?'

'What does it *matter*! You were late! I couldn't wait any
longer! –'

'So you couldn't wait. So I came on here.'

She looked past him, at the warm windy street, feeling
old, as if she had lived years in the last month. 'Please go.
You're making a scene.'

'I'll make more of a scene before I'm done.'

'Some other time.'

'Now.'

'You must be crazy.'

'So I'm crazy.'

She leaned against the banister, breathing out despair at
the futility of it all. 'Oh, Godfrey, I wish I could finish
with you for ever. You haven't *any* idea . . . How d'you
suppose I feel when you come bullying your way in like
this?'

'Now,' he said.

'It's a quarter to five. Wilfred might be back in half
an hour.'

'So what does it matter if he is?'

Her eyes lit up with anger and fright. '*No!* I tell you it's
impossible! Haven't you any sense? I'll – we'll make another date. Perhaps –'

'Now.' He kicked the door to behind him.

375

She said: 'If you come any nearer I'll phone the police.'

'Phone away.'

'*Godfrey!* Haven't you *any* sense? What's come over you? Tomorrow perhaps.'

'Now,' he said.

She made a move towards the telephone which was in the hall, but he blocked the way. She turned and ran up the stairs where the other telephone was. He went after her. She tried to lock the door but he burst it open. He reached her as she grabbed the telephone and caught her under the arms; they fell together, heavily, but he under and his hard body suffered no hurt. He began to kiss her hungrily, wickedly, like a wild man short of food. She knelt up and hit at him and he laughed at her and pushed her back on the floor, his hands grasping her expertly, creating the sensations in her that undermined her will. She tried to get up again and this time he let her because he had the sense to see she was struggling less violently. They stood up together and he pushed her towards her bedroom.

She struggled all the way but no longer with the violence of the first moment. He began to murmur what passed with him for endearments, because he knew now that this was another fight he couldn't lose.

Angell had not been feeling well all week. He had had peculiar pains of a sort he was beginning to become familiar with, and also he was anxious about his heart and his blood pressure. He had been sick with worry for months, and now he had been overdoing it in other ways. It was a commonplace history for an older man to marry a young girl and die comparatively early as a consequence – everyone knew that. He thought angrily of Matthewson's little lecture a year or more ago when he had suggested that the human character was healthier for being outward looking and for having a little worry to contend with. What criminal nonsense doctors talked! They flashed advice about like touts on a race-course, and with as little sense of responsibility. He would have liked to go to Matthewson and say to him: 'Look, I took your advice, and see the mess it has landed me in! You ought to be in prison!'

He had kept himself at work, but his work suffered and he was a trial to Miss Lock and to everyone in the office.

The fact that his business prospered as never before was little consolation. Even a first round defeat of the objectors in the Handley Merrick satellite development plan did little to cheer him. The body and mind, once they are linked on a downward spiral, seem each intent on pulling the other deeper into the abyss.

Even his appetite was a little affected, in that it seemed to demand more personal dainties, and before his workday was fully out he was considering going to his club, but he passed this thought over for what Pearl could make him when he got home: hot buttered toast with strawberry jam and probably cakes to follow. He felt in need of comfort. With luck, if Pearl was in, he would get it.

Even in his present frail state he would not take a taxi, so it was half-past five before he walked slowly round the corner into Cadogan Mews.

The first thing he noticed was that the front door was ajar. This sometimes happened when it was slammed, and was caused by a faulty catch – it was very dangerous and he must remember to get it repaired and to warn Pearl not to be so careless. Did it mean she was out?

Then in the hall the small table lamp by the telephone was overturned. Burglars? His heart froze. The police. Dial 999. But he must be reasonably sure. 'Pearl,' he called in a soft voice.

He peered cautiously through into the drawing-room, where all seemed undisturbed. The kitchen . . . This showed recent use. Flour and pastry on the table; the electric oven on; nothing inside. He switched it off. Unlike Pearl to waste . . .

A thump upstairs. Her bedroom was over the kitchen. Perhaps she had slipped up for something. Must not be unduly hasty. He switched the oven on again. It took an effort of will to connive at possible waste; but she would be annoyed if the oven were being heated for –

Somebody was talking. Was it upstairs or perhaps next door? He did not remember ever hearing voices from next door.

Outside a dog barked. It emphasized the silence. All his appetites, the need of his palate for butter and sweet jam, were drying, souring, as in an east wind. He picked his way carefully across his ornate drawing-room, reached the hall, put the lamp upright, picked up the telephone book and smoothed its ruffled pages. A-D had been dropped or knocked over. A-D. He mounted the stairs.

Like all big men he could move very quietly, even when as now he was beginning to sweat and tremble. That dog. It belonged across at No. 35. No discipline. He went into his bedroom. The intervening door was shut but there were movements in the next room. Not voices but movements. Just Pearl. Why did he suppose otherwise? It was at the root of all his malaise.

Without noticing he had carried his briefcase upstairs, and this he now put on a chair. He had brought some work home with him tonight. It was a matter of material misrepresentation when entering into a contract. He wanted to refresh his mind on Rawlins v Wickham and relevant cases. He pursed his lips to blow out a breath. And then Godfrey laughed.

Angell stumbled and half fell. His stomach revolted as if he had taken poison. A recurrence of the nightmare of Merrick House. He could not *stand* it. It would drive him out of his mind or bring on a stroke. To be assaulted in his *own* house . . . Blows in the face, in the chest . . .

He clutched the end of the bed while the attack of nausea slowly moved away. Pearl's voice. He could not hear what she said, for the blood was pounding in his ears. And she was speaking low, anxiously, almost on a note of complaint.

Where a person has been induced to enter into a contract by a material misrepresentation of the other party, he is entitled to have the contract set aside, and not merely to have the representations made good. That was it. Rawlins v Wickham. Life. His own life. Law. Law and order. This was what all his own life meant. Interpretations of the precedents of England, by which men could live peacefully with their neighbours. One lived in a state of contractual harmony. Groping, he fumbled in his pocket, with clumsy fingers took out his key ring, went over the keys like a man reading Braille. The long thin, double-toothed one. He found it at last, slid it into its lock, opened the safe. He groped again at the back, among the documents, the price lists, the wills, discovered the revolver, unwrapped the cheese-cloth, knowing the gun was loaded from last time. Then he slumped in a chair, the revolver dangling from his hand like a broken stick. He could not defend his honour – he had no courage for that – but at least he could defend his life. Another assault like last time would kill him – the shock would kill him. If he had the strength to pull the trigger he would defend his life.

But if he sat here perfectly quiet until Godfrey left there was little chance of having to do that. Sit perfectly still. Neither of them would come in here. Let them have their lewd play. Let them spawn and copulate on his Hepple-white bed. It would be the last time. There could never be anything more now. When Godfrey had gone he would confront Pearl. Confront her for the last time and turn her out tonight. It was the only way. He must steel himself. Even loneliness was better than this. He must return to books and paintings and the quiet of the law. *Anything* was better than this . . .

Pearl's voice on a note of complaint again – antagonism almost. Had Godfrey *imposed* himself, then, forced himself on her? Oh delusion! No more delusion. No woman would allow herself – she would call for help, ring the police, scream. It was useless, even to *begin* to pretend to one-self . . .

Except the open front door, the overturned lamp, the interrupted cooking. And Little God. For ever damned, dominant Little God. Capable of over-ruling all other wills, of transgressing all civilized behaviour. The savage at large. The savage in a civilized society, de-civilizing all he came in contact with.

That dog, it was on again. It ought to be shot. Suddenly the dog stopped and Godfrey laughed again. Wilfred shuddered like a man in a fever. Like a man in a fever, sweat was dripping from his forehead. Whatever the rights or wrongs he could make no move to correct them. To steal downstairs, to telephone the police. He knew how long *they*'d take to come. Godfrey would hear the bell and it would spark off the confrontation Wilfred feared above all others.

Concentrate, think of something else, take a deep breath, steady oneself, bold heart, don't thump, relax, think of blood pressure. My Lord, under the Trades Disputes and

Trades Unions Act of 1927 any strike or lock-out which has any object other than . . . Under the Solicitors' Remuneration Act 1881 . . . remuneration for business done in lieu of ordinary charges . . . Sell the Dufy. Prices for him were high, might not rise beyond this peak for 10 years. He was tired of it. Buy that Kokoschka. Peace and quiet among his lovely furniture. The end of love, the end of fighting. He would grow into an –

'So *what*!' he heard Godfrey say. 'Let him go and – mm . . . mm . . . mm . . .'

'Godfrey, if there's to be anything ever between –'

'Well, you brought it on yourself, Oyster. mm . . . mm . . . mm . . .'

'Whatever I say you – Not that way.'

The communicating door swung open and Godfrey came in. He had opened the wrong door. He was fully dressed, ready to go. His eyes took in the mistake and then they saw the fat collapsed waxen figure sitting in the chair staring at him.

At first he looked startled, slightly alarmed, then he let out a hoot.

'Oyster! Come here. I got a surprise for you!'

He came a couple of paces into the room, his mop of black hair flailing and flaunting. He was the savage in the civilized world. He looked out of the tops of his eyes just as he did when he was in the ring.

'So he's come to fight me, eh? Just like he did last time. In a sick trembling haze Wilfred raised the gun. It wavered all over the place like an insect looking for food. 'Don't come near me. I'm telling you! I'm warning you!'

Pearl's face and naked shoulder came round the door: Wilfred saw this through the haze: her expression was horror, her colour like dirty paper. Godfrey's face also took on a change. Staring at the revolver he suddenly looked scared, afraid for himself, the bombast and the arrogance gone: he was the little chauffeur. Then something in Wilfred; the same convulsion as that time at school: the utter revolt, the panic revolt against oppression, the bullied become the bullier, the terror turned inside out. He pulled the trigger. Twice.

The revolver clicked emptily on the old dead cartridges. Godfrey's face changed again. The alarm was gone in a lash, he began to laugh. He laughed in utter derision. Contempt and triumph. He laughed and Angell pulled the rigger again and there was a great explosion. His hand erked up as if it had been kicked and Godfrey's face disappeared. The noise seemed to split the mind. The smell and the smoke hung over the scene like fog in a hollow. When it thinned Godfrey had disappeared. Angell dropped the gun and stared at Pearl who was staring at something on the floor. She came into the room, a frock clutched in front of her, gasped, gave a choked scream. 'Godfrey . . . *Godfrey* . . . *Godfrey!* . . .'

He hadn't disappeared; he was lying on the floor. He was lying like a parachutist who has fallen from a great height, and part of his neck had gone. Angell's Aubusson rug was becoming stained with a new dye.

Chapter Thirteen

Detective Chief Inspector Morrison said: 'Can you tell u
again briefly what happened, Mrs Angell? In your own
words. Take your time. It would be a help to us all.'

'If my husband . . .'

'Dr Dawson is with him. We shall be told as soon as he
comes round.'

'It's been a terrible shock.'

'I quite understand . . . You say you knew this man?'

'Yes. Godfrey Brown. He was a boxer. We – got to know
him through a Lady Vosper who was a friend of my hus
band's. Godfrey Brown worked as a chauffeur for her.'

'But you said he was a boxer.'

'Yes. He didn't make enough to live on, and he acted
as her chauffeur. Lady Vosper befriended him in all sorts
of ways – almost adopted him. In the end he took her
name, began to box as Godfrey Vosper, to call himself
that.'

'Is he still with her?'

'No, she died last year. Since then he's been on his own
at a loose end. I think that was the beginning of the
trouble.'

'How do you mean?'

Pearl wiped her lips. They tasted as if she had been
sucking copper. 'I think he expected a legacy from Lady
Vosper and it was delayed. Probate or something. He
thought he'd been cheated of it and for some reason
blamed my husband.'

'Is he – was he her solicitor?'

'He wasn't the family solicitor. But he acted for her
sometimes. He advised her.'

They were in the drawing-room. Upstairs there was the
sound of movement, the discreet, solemn, decent move
ment of professional men about an unpleasant business.
Photographs were being taken, measurements, the rest. It
would soon be time to move Godfrey out to the waiting
ambulance. Little God, the undefeatable, the untameable

the irresistible, had disappeared, like a demon king in a puff of smoke; resisted, tamed, defeated for ever by a piece of lead and a whiff of cordite and the hysterical reflexes of a terrified middle-aged man. Tears flooded into Pearl's eyes at the thought, and she dabbed at them with a fine cambric handkerchief. She was wearing a green turtle neck sweater and a short linen skirt. Morrison's eyes went over her politely but speculatively. He noted that she was not wearing a brassière under her sweater.

'Well now, how did this trouble begin?'

'Godfrey – Godfrey Brown accused my husband of poisoning Lady Vosper's mind against him and so losing him his legacy. He threatened Wilfred.'

'When?'

'Oh . . . in February it began. When he thought he wasn't going to get the legacy.'

'Were these threats made before witnesses?'

'I was there.'

'Other witnesses?'

'Not then.'

'What did he say exactly?'

'Well.' Her lips gave a nervous quiver. 'I can't remember exactly. Something about getting even. "I'll do you for this."'

' "I'll do you for this." I see.' Morrison rubbed his long nose. 'Was there any reason for Brown's belief that your husband had turned Lady Vosper against him?'

'Wilfred may have thought Lady Vosper was being taken in by Godfrey Brown. Other people did. He may have said something to her at some time, I don't know. But it became a sort of obsession with Godfrey Brown. He kept calling here, asking to see Mr Angell.'

'Did he see him?'

'Not if we could help it.'

Godfrey was being brought down the stairs now. It was a slow and clumsy process. Pearl's lips were still quivering under their blurred lip-stick. But it was the quivering of a taut wire. Inside she was stretched, alert, raw.

Godfrey. Little God. Great God. Cruel God. She had responded at the last this afternoon but in an intensely masochistic way. At heart she was a conventional girl with a respectable background, and one could offend against that background too far. He *had* gone too far. At the time it was acceptable but to think of it after was intolerable. But Godfrey . . . Gone. It was impossible in so short a time. Destroyed. Disappeared. Sweet and bitter Godfrey.

'And then? Coming to this afternoon . . .'

'Before this afternoon,' said Pearl, crying for she knew not what. 'Some months ago, my husband had to go to Merrick House, which was the Vosper family seat. It was on business to do with the sale of the contents. I went with him. When he got there Godfrey Brown was there.'

'Was this after Lady Vosper's death?'

'Oh, yes . . .' she added: 'He had no right there. But he'd been living there, camping out in the country house. When we surprised him he attacked my husband.'

'Attacked him? Physically?'

'Yes. Knocked him down. Cut his eye. Bruised his ribs. He had to have the doctor.'

'Was a charge brought against Brown?'

'No. My husband didn't want all the fuss and bother. I tried to persuade him but he wouldn't call the police.'

'Always a mistake, Mrs Angell. Was anybody witness to this assault?'

'I was. And also the chauffeur.'

'This was some months ago, you say?'

'Yes. In . . . it would be March.'

'And since then, have you seen anything of him?'

Pearl shivered and tried to hide it. Underneath she was still unclothed. She had noticed the inspector's earlier glance and she fancied that everyone could detect her nakedness. She still bore the marks of Godfrey's hands. If they were to examine her . . .

'Since then?' prompted Inspector Morrison.

'He came to the house twice when Wilfred wasn't here, but I wouldn't let him in.'

They had got him out of the door. A crowd of people staring were being moved on by the police. An hour ago. All that life.

'What did Brown *want*, Mrs Angell?'

'Want?'

'Yes. There must have been some reason for him calling. It surely wasn't just to threaten and bully.'

'He wanted money – the money that he thought Mr

Angell had cheated him of.'

'He demanded money in your hearing?'

'Oh, yes.' She hesitated. 'Several times. But he often seemed just to want to threaten and – and bully, as you say. Perhaps my husband when he comes round will be able to tell you . . .'

'Of course. And to your knowledge did he ever give him any?'

'No. He told me he never had.'

Morrison stretched his legs. This chair he was sitting in: it had been designed for an 18th-century dandy. 'Now could you just tell me in detail what happened this evening?'

'What, again?'

'Yes, please. If you wouldn't mind.'

The doors of the ambulance slammed, the engine started up. A shadow moved across the window as the ambulance turned the corner. Good-bye, Little God. Good-bye now for ever. Those vilely grasping hands, the glinting impudent smile, the coxcomb hair, the courage, the sheer fighting guts, the cruelty, the energy, the strength. Above all the courage, the utter lack of fear. They at least shone out. And all destroyed by a flabby old man. She put her hands up to her face and burst into tears.

Morrison waited patiently. After a while Pearl blew her nose, wiped her eyes, dabbed at her streaked face. 'Sorry.'

'Take your time. I know it's been a great shock.'

'Yes . . . He came while I was baking a cake. I went to the door. I was – upset when I saw him and tried to shut it. But he got his foot in. Then he pushed me back, forced his way in.' Pearl showed her bruised knuckles. 'He did that, pushing so violently.'

Morrison nodded. 'What did he say?'

'Well, it was then he took this huge revolver out of his pocket, started waving it at me. He seemed very excited. He said where was Mr Angell? he wanted to see him. I said he was out. He ranted at me, saying he'd just knocked out a man he had been sparring with and he'd knock me out if I – if I tried to call for help. He –'

'Pardon me, did he threaten you with the revolver?'

'To hit me with it, not to shoot. He said he didn't know if it *would* shoot because it was a relic he'd brought from

Merrick House – the Vospers' place – but he was waiting to try it on my husband. He – he went through the ground floor rooms, seemed to think Wilfred was hiding from him. Then he went upstairs.'

'Yes.'

Pearl crossed her legs, and then, catching Morrison's involuntary glance, carefully uncrossed them. 'After a minute or so I followed him. He had gone from Mr Angell's bedroom through to mine. He was pulling things about, as if he wanted to – to destroy . . . just then Wilfred must have come in. I didn't hear him because I was trying to telephone for the police, but Godfrey – Godfrey Brown pulled me away. I've got – I expect I have bruises on my arms and shoulders . . .'

'Just so. Er – where was the revolver during all this?'

'I think he must have put it on the dressing table. I don't really remember.' She cleared her throat, plunged on. 'All I remember was that we were in my room there and I heard Wilfred come upstairs. I was terrified what was going to happen. Brown had stormed through into my bathroom and then he must have heard too because he came back and pushed past me into my husband's bedroom and when I followed him he was holding the revolver and threatening Wilfred, who had backed against the door. And my husband said: "I am going to telephone the police, Brown. And don't attempt to stop me." And Brown laughed out loud, he laughed and said: "If you do I'll try my old revolver on you." So *I* rushed for the telephone again, and Godfrey tried to grab me and Wilfred joined in and somehow he got hold of the revolver. And the next thing I knew he was backing against the door and saying: "Keep your distance, I warn you, keep your distance." And Brown was still laughing, and he said – or shouted – "The thing's too old to work! I got it off the wall at Flora's." That is Lady Vosper's. "But I'm going to *do* for you, Angell, I'm going to *do* for you!" And – and he took a couple of steps towards my husband and there was this terrible explosion, and then Brown was lying on the floor . . .'

This much true. The terrible explosion and Godfrey lying bleeding on the floor. Horror, horror, I had to pick up his hand. My heel got in the blood, I had to wash it off:

386

it's sticky, not like blood, like thin jam. And Wilfred helplessly fainting on his bed, vomit on his chin; and the thin spread-eagled, strangled, little boy-corpse of Godfrey with half his neck gone and terrible blood oozing; and the great revolver blue and polished shining between them. Only me, only me left with any consciousness, any working mind between us, only me left to think, to plan, to scheme, to try to salvage. Perhaps that's justice because I'm the cause of it all . . .

'What time was this, Mrs Angell?'

'Time? . . . I don't know. About half-past six, I suppose. What time is it now?'

'Seven-twenty. Just seven-twenty. It would be about fifty-five minutes since this happened?'

'I suppose so. I've lost touch. How long have you been here?'

'Let's see. Thirty-five minutes. It was at six twenty-five that Scotland Yard received your call. A patrol car reached you at six-thirty and I arrived at a quarter to seven.'

Pearl lifted her hair away from her face. 'Yes. Yes, if you say so. Why?'

'One always likes to pinpoint the time if one can.' A perfunctory frown crossed his long face. 'According to the police surgeon who examined the body at seven, his estimate was that Brown had *then* been dead about an hour.'

'Does it matter?'

'Well, yes, Mrs Angell, it does rather.'

Pearl had seen the pitfall but there had been no way to avoid it. All that time. Those first minutes that had ticked away in frozen fear. A lonely midnight of the soul. Then sudden action like some galvanized robot. Shaking Wilfred into a semblance of consciousness; removing one impression of her bedroom, creating another. 'The same *story,* Wilfred, if you can think, we must tell the same story.' 'I shall go to prison for this: several years. No licence for the gun, even.' 'No *licence,* then who knows you've got it?' The sick horror of getting Godfrey's fingerprints on it without getting her own; the deliberate wrecking of Wilfred's bedroom . . .

'I rang you as soon as I could, Inspector, but I can't tell you how long it took. When – when I saw all that blood I felt so sick. I crawled back into my own room. I think

387

I was trying to get water – I wasn't sure if Wilfred was shot too – but I lay on the floor of my room and couldn't get any further. I must have passed out.' She shivered again. It was all right to shiver there. 'When I came to, my first thought was for Wilfred, and I went back and found him lying across the bed. I thought perhaps he was dead, but I found he was breathing – in fact he seemed half to recognize me – and I got his head on the pillow and his feet up . . .'

'Where was the revolver at this time?'

'Where you found it – where the police found it.'

'You didn't touch it at all?'

'No.' I wiped it clean and then used gloves. It can't have left –

'And when did you telephone?'

'As soon as I'd made sure Wilfred was alive I went to it, but just then he began to moan so I went back to him and was with him three or four minutes more. Then – then I dialled 999. Then I sat there by the telephone not moving at all until your patrol man rang the bell . . .'

Morrison nodded and made a note in his book. It all looked plain and straightforward. Yet in cases where the wife is young and blonde and pretty and has a flared, wild wide-awake look . . . And he had a slight uneasy feeling that although her evidence was very convincing, her second telling of events had been just a fraction too similar to the first.

'Did Brown ever attempt to attack you, Mrs Angell?'

'Me?' She opened her clear eyes from which the tears had now almost gone. 'No, he wasn't that bad. Except in the way I've said – pushing me away from the door, stopping me from getting at the telephone.'

'Has he used that sort of violence to you before – for instance at this house where he assaulted your husband?'

'No. Never before.'

'And at no time – his aims were never sexual?'

His gaze was very direct and she met it. 'Oh, no. Certainly not. It was my husband he came to see, not me. The only thing he had against me was if I got in the way.'

Morrison closed his notebook and snapped the elastic round it. Brown must have been blind then, he thought. 'Do you happen to know his present address?'

'Brown's? Not since Lady Vosper died. But I think he worked for a man called Davis. Davis was his trainer or manager or something – arranged his fights.'

'And d'you know Davis's address?'

'It was in Shaftesbury Avenue. Wilfred might know.'

'Did Brown have any relatives in London?'

'I've really no idea, Inspector. We didn't know him well. You don't get to know somebody else's chauffeur well, do you. It's very unfortunate that we ever met.'

'Too true. Can you remember the date when you actually did first meet him?'

'Oh, about a year last March.'

'Before you married or after?'

'Before. I met my husband about the same time.'

'How did you first meet Brown?'

'Well, I got to know Lady Vosper through Mr Angell, and Brown was her chauffeur. As I've told you. Oh, and there was a dance I went to with some friends. It was just a local dance, like a tennis dance, and Brown happened to be there. Everybody was very friendly, and he asked me to dance and I danced with him and he offered me a lift home in Lady Vosper's car.'

'Did you accept?'

She hesitated, on the brink of the wrong lie. 'There were a lot of us and it happened to be more convenient. He just dropped me off at my house.'

'So you were quite on friendly terms then?'

'Casually, yes.'

'Enough to dance with him?'

'Well, yes. He asked me. It would have seemed snobbish to have refused.'

'You didn't mind him asking you?'

'I was a bit surprised. But there seemed no harm in it.'

'He was not – over-familiar then in any way?'

'Oh, no. While Lady Vosper was alive he seemed perfectly normal in every way.'

'Was that your only contact with him, apart from when you were with your husband?'

'Well, I saw him with Lady Vosper. And he called at my parents' home a couple of times with messages from her.'

'Messages?'

'Invitations. We were not on the telephone.'

'Did your husband know about this?'

'Know about what?' There was a slight chill in her eyes.

'I mean you knowing Brown before you were married.'

'But of course. It was through Mr Angell that I *met* Lady Vosper.'

Well, she had all the answers. Morrison nodded gently to himself. 'Did you know, by the way, that your husband appears to have pulled the trigger three times?'

She frowned. 'I didn't know. I only heard one shot.'

'There was only one shot. The other two cartridges did not fire.'

'I see . . . Well, you said it was an old revolver.'

'Thirty years old, probably. Did you see Brown with it before?'

'No.'

'You never saw it in this Lady – er Vosper's house?'

'Lady Vosper's house is *enormous*, Inspector. And it's full of old armour and old guns . . . Er – how do you know my husband pulled the trigger three times? Brown may have tried it before he came. He said – I told you he said: "It's too old to work." '

'You did.' They looked at each other and it was Morrison who looked down to put his notebook away. Just then there was a tap on the door and a constable came in.

'Excuse me, sir, the doctor says Mr Angell is coming round.'

'Get Mumford,' Wilfred had whispered in that terrible twenty-odd minutes before the police were called; but to avoid what might have seemed like too much forethought she did not ring him until after seven. He arrived just as Wilfred had finished giving his first account of what had happened. Wilfred had chosen Mumford because although he was not as clever as Esslin he was eminently English and solidly respectable. Wilfred needed above everything respectability at this time. They were closeted together with Inspector Morrison and a sergeant for upwards of an hour.

Thereafter the routine processes of the law. Mumford protested at Angell's having to go to the police station, arguing that his client was too unwell. But Morrison was politely pressing and Angell went. The horrors of a night here. Something ingrained for ever afterwards in the soul. As if he were a *criminal*. He who had lived all his life so scrupulously within the law and by the law. To be regarded as a criminal, to spend the night in a room in a police station. And with the horrifying prospect that in the lunatic world in which he now lived he might have to spend many other such nights. Mumford was reassuring but Angell was not reassured.

And in the early morning it was all too true. The police charged Mr Wilfred Angell with manslaughter. Detective Chief Inspector Morrison had found sufficient elements of dissatisfaction in the case. A Mrs Howard Leverett at No. 24 Cadogan Mews had heard the shot. She had been taking a bath and had her transistor radio in the bathroom with her and had just switched on the six o'clock news. It confirmed the surgeon's estimate and left a gap of almost twenty-five minutes before Mrs Angell called the police. Twenty-five minutes was a long time for a swoon. It was the only evidence so far to put in doubt the story the Angells told. Yet there were other straws in the wind . . .

The inquest was opened and, after formal evidence had been given, was adjourned indefinitely. This was almost immediately followed by the hearing in the magistrate's court. After a discussion which lasted nearly as long as the hearing, bail was allowed on a surety of £500. Angell was free to go home.

On the way home Mumford was furious with the police. It came to something, he said, when a householder of the greatest respectability, attacked in his own home and in defence of his own life, caused the death of a brutal intruder, and the police were so stupid as to bring a case. It was a monstrous piece of officialdom and should be brought to the notice of the Chief Commissioner. Of course, said Mumford, heartily, there was still no need to worry. The outcome, if even now it ever came to trial, was a foregone conclusion. Self-defence. Justifiable homicide. Just the same, it was as well to get the best man, one supposed. Whom did Angell fancy? There was Nigel John, a good solid chap with a long history of defence successes in the criminal court. Or there was Bergson. Or young Honiton; they were talking about him.

When they got home Mumford said, should he come in

but Angell said, thank you, no, I'll just get to bed.

After the car had driven away Pearl stood for a moment on the step, before following Wilfred into the house. A beautiful afternoon with thundery peach-bloom clouds drifting overhead. It was the day of one of the Royal Garden Parties: they had seen the toppered men and flowered women coming away as they drove home. The warm air of London was almost flowery after the police station and the court.

It was a lovely day but now for her everything was changed, everything had to be adjusted, nothing would ever be the same again. There had been reporters as they came out of court: lucky none was here to welcome them home.

She shivered and went in. Angell was sitting crouched in his coat in the drawing-room, his shoulders hunched. Since those frantic twenty minutes after the shot, while Godfrey cooled between them on the floor, they had had no private conversation. Since those phrenetic moments when she had taken charge.

She said: 'Let me get you to bed.'

He did not reply, might not have heard. His thick hair was over his brow.

After a minute she came and sat down opposite him. 'Wilfred, what do you want me to do?'

He looked at her, and it was as if Godfrey's brief angry presence was still in the house.

'Until the trial,' she said. 'What will you do?'

He shrugged. 'I shall go in the Clinic for a week or so. I'm on the verge of complete breakdown.'

'Shall I get you tea now or a drink?'

'I'll never forgive you,' he said, the words coming thickly in a froth to his lips. 'Never as long as I live.'

She folded her hands. Her features were wan, shadowed by the afternoon light, a firm-cut, austere mask. 'Do you want me to leave you right away or to stay on until after the trial?'

Before he could answer the telephone rang. She went into the hall and lifted the receiver. Presently she came back. 'The Sunday Gazette.'

'You didn't speak to them?'

'No.'

392

'The scavengers of the press. The jackals. The carrion. They only foregather at such times. Sitting round howling to the moon . . .'

There were things in the room needed tidying. After a sleepless night she had not been able to concentrate this morning. Upstairs, the rug had been taken away, and Mrs Jamieson had said she would try to get the stains off the wood of the floor. Godfrey. It had all happened in a few seconds. Feather-weight. Blown like a feather out of the world.

She said suddenly: 'If you think I invited him here yesterday you're mistaken. That was all true, what I told the police. I can show you the scratches and bruises on my arms.'

'I shall never forgive you,' he whispered with hate and horror. 'All this. I can't ever forgive you for what you've done.'

She paused in the mindless occupation of picking up a used ashtray. 'Tell me, Wilfred. Just say. I'll do whatever you say. Do you want me to leave at once, tonight?'

He hesitated on the brink of assent: it wouldn't do: his personal safety was at stake. 'No.'

'Then what?'

'It would give the wrong impression. It would be wrong until after the trial.'

'All right. Whatever you say.'

'There's no other way. Now that you've . . .'

'Now that I've what?'

'Told this story. *Imposed* this story on me.'

'Wasn't it the best? You didn't want it to come out that you'd killed him as a betrayed husband, did you? And with your own gun.'

'What did you do with the other packet of bullets for the Smith & Wesson?'

'I pushed them down the toilet. I dropped them in and then pushed them out of sight with the brush.'

'Do you realize what would have happened to your story if the police had found them?'

'But they didn't, did they.'

He listened to this as to the voice of deception, the voice of the serpent.

'And anyway,' she said, 'it's not true – it wouldn't have

393

been true that you shot him because you were a – a betrayed husband. You *did* kill him in self-defence, because you thought he was going to attack you.'

He levered himself out of the chair, lumbered like an old man into the kitchen, poured himself half a tumbler of whisky, splashed it with soda. At this moment he hated her almost as much for the way she had acted after Godfrey's death as for the rest. Reeling as he was, fainting and retching with horror and nausea, she had come at him, dominating him, directing him, demanding information of him, telling him what to do, while he lay inert and only half conscious on the bed. *Whose* revolver was it? *Who* knew he'd got it? *Where* had he bought it? *How* did you put fingerprints on it?

Today his acute legal brain had partly regained its equilibrium, and all day it had been busy finding variants of justification and defence; but *all, all* were restricted, circumscribed by the story she had told and insisted that he tell. All must conform to that. It might be, at least it might seem, that she had had the idea of saying that the revolver was Godfrey's in order to save him, Wilfred, from infinitely worse trouble. If she succeeded, if they succeeded, and the police were proceeding on this assumption, it was indeed a brilliant idea which might save him from a prison sentence. But he could not appreciate it. She had had no *right* to have that idea. It was a criminal idea and a criminal deception, and if it were found out the consequence would be infinitely worse, even worse yet.

He, the lawyer, should have taken control last night, not she, the guilty wife.

When he went back into the drawing-room she was standing at the window looking out. For someone who usually stood so well, her dejected stance was like a confession of defeat. Youth had decayed in her heart.

He said: 'That story. This story you forced me to accept while I was in – in shock, that you imposed on me. Even if in your view at the time it was the best, it's so *weak*, so shot full of holes. If the police find out the truth, as they will, it will be the worse for you as well as for me.'

'I don't see any reason why they should.'

'You don't know the police.' He drank again, and the whisky went down like hope. 'It was your reputation you

394

were thinking of, not mine. Wasn't it?'

'I don't know.'

'For instance, how many people knew of your friendship with him before your marriage?'

'It wasn't a friendship. What I told the police was nearly true.'

'How many?'

'A girl called Hazel Boynton. Two young men.'

'Your family?'

'No. He called twice when I was out.'

'So if the police ask. These others, this girl, these young men, of course they will talk.'

'They can only say I met him. I told the police I met him. It's so near the truth that you could see it either way. There's nothing to disprove at all!'

'Were there letters? Before or after marriage?'

'No.' That note . . . But she had not signed it.

'Did Lady Vosper know anything? So that she might have gossiped before she died?'

'He said not. He wouldn't want to make her – jealous.'

He put his empty glass down. 'I suspected as much. But you. Even then you . . . God, you make me feel sick! And his visits here? How many?'

'Recently none. Until yesterday.'

'And before that?'

'I can't remember. Three or four.'

'Your visits to him?'

She turned away from the window, her eyes stony, moving as if to get away.

'Tell me, please.'

'Three or four. But it was just a room he had. Not flats. You just walked up the stairs. I never saw a caretaker or a janitor.'

'And what did you leave there? How many things? Handkerchiefs, shoes, a comb?'

'Nothing. Nothing at all.'

He did not immediately go to bed. She made some soup and opened a tin of tongue and baked four potatoes in their jackets and there was some cheese. All this time he had never been upstairs. They ate at the same table, separated by Godfrey. Twice they had telephone calls and once there was a ring at the bell, but each time it was the news-papers and they would give no satisfaction. When they spoke to each other it was of the only subject. At the end of the meal she asked him when he thought the trial would be.

He said: 'Not until October at the earliest.'

'Oh, my God!' She was horrified. 'Not until . . . But why?'

'It is the cross one has to bear. The next Law Term does not begin until October.'

'Oh, my God.'

'Yes,' he said drily. 'My God.'

She moved restlessly, her mind busy with all the implications. And he watched her with contained horror. Her white glinting teeth bit into a biscuit. Her red lips moved gently. A tip of tongue came out to take in a crumb. Her bare arms were like beautiful snakes. 'Mr Mumford didn't tell me that. But he said it will be just a formality when it does come off.'

'Nothing is a formality. We do not yet know what the prosecution's case will be.'

'Three months or more.' Must she stay with him like this for three months or more?

'In the meantime,' he said, 'I remain with this deep and terrible accusation hanging over me. The head of one of the most respected firms in the Fields. Until then the cal-umny will ruin our business. At the end of that time, even if I am acquitted, it will ruin me. Aren't you happy about that?'

'No, I'm *not* happy about that. I never wanted to ruin you. What good does it do to ruin you? My own life is ruined anyway.'

'*Your* life,' he said with contempt.

'Do you think I'm not entitled to one?'

'Not at the expense of people with whom you have – ties of loyalty and honour.' He had been going to say 'contractual obligations'.

She got up, pushing her chair back so that it screeched on the parquet floor. 'You forced him on me,' she said.

'*What!*' He was outraged.

'Oh yes, I'd *met* him before my marriage, I know, but I'd always choked him off – he was too crude and brutal –

would never have anything to do with him.' Pearl moved tearfully to the door, but came back again. 'It's *true*! I told him if he wouldn't leave me alone I'd call the police. So he did leave me alone. In the end he left me alone! Then when I married you, you *insisted* that he should call here at our house. You invited him! I asked you not to but you invited him! You had some reason. Heaven knows what it was. But you forced him on me. Don't imagine the fault is all on one side.'

He was so indignant he was speechless. He stared at her, leaning back in his chair, consumed with anger that he could not off-load.

'I did not know I had a wife who would go with any servant who called at the door.'

She said: 'I didn't know I was a wife who would.'

Just as her previous remark had contorted him with anger, this took the weapon out of his hands. He stared at her dumbly. She always surprised him. Perhaps he was unused to women, perhaps she was unique.

He said: 'How am I to believe you?'

'You don't have to any more.'

She put the plates together, again an involuntary action. It was Coalport china, King pattern Georgian silver, Waterford glass.

'I'm *glad* I killed him,' Angell said with sudden venom. 'I'm *glad* I shot him down.'

'Don't ever say that!'

'Why? Because you loved him. That's it, isn't it. You still loved him in spite of it all. All his coarseness, his brutality . . .'

She put her hands to her face, as if about to cry, but withdrew them. 'I don't know. How can I answer you when I can't answer myself?'

On the Friday Hazel rang.

'How awful for you, dear, how awful. Really. Tell me how it happened.'

'Just like it said in the papers,' Pearl said. 'It's been terrible. We've been quite distracted.'

'And your husband, Mr Angell? Is he – d'you think he'll . . .?'

'Oh, he'll be all right. It was plain self-defence. This

man had broken in and –'

'This man? You mean Godfrey Vosper?'

'Godfrey Brown. He only took the other name for his boxing.'

'Well, it's the same man, isn't it? The one you went out with that night at the Trad Hall?'

'I didn't *go out* with him. I danced a few times and he drove me home. But that's nothing to do with it.'

'Well, I thought it might have, dear. The papers always get hold of the wrong end of the stick, and it says –'

'It says he broke in with menaces and threats and demanded money. That's it, dear. That's all. It was Wilfred he was threatening, not me. Sorry. I just happened to be there.'

'Oh, well, I see . . . It must have been absolutely awful for you, Pearl. I mean, did you see it all?'

'Oh, yes. Look, Hazel, when were we going to meet again; was it this month or next?'

'We didn't actually fix a day –'

'Well, I'd rather tell you all about it then. It's difficult over the phone. There's a few things I'd like to tell you, but just at the moment I feel so dazed and sick, and the telephone keeps going, and Wilfred is upstairs in bed with shock and I have to look after him, and Dad came to see me last night, and Rachel came this morning, for Heaven's sake, I can't think why, and the newspapers won't leave us alone. I really don't know whether I'm coming or going.'

'Would you like me to come one evening?'

'No, honestly, Hazel, by evening I've just about had as much as I can take. I just want to go to bed and forget it all. But in a week or two –'

'When is the – er, trial?'

'I haven't heard yet,' said Pearl. 'But do let's meet. It would be fabulous to have somebody really to talk to. And I could tell you *all* there is to know then.'

'I thought you might have liked me to come with you to the trial. Perhaps you could ring me if you hear the date. I could take a day off work, say I was sick, and then I could sit by you all through. I thought it would be nice if you had someone of your own there.'

'Well, it's super of you, Hazel, but Dad's offered, and I suppose he's my nearest. Anyway they don't think it will be much – I mean they don't think it will last long, and I honestly don't know when it will come up.'

'Your husband – he's free then while he's waiting?'

'Oh, yes, of course, he's not a *criminal*. It's just that the law has to take its course.'

In the end, after another two sixpences in the box, Hazel rang off, with a promise to meet Pearl on the 12th August for lunch.

Chapter Fourteen

August passed, and September. Detective Chief Inspector Morrison was still not satisfied, but on the whole he kept his dissatisfaction to himself. In the first place it had been a borderline choice whether to charge Angell at all, and then, later, another narrow decision whether or not to proceed with the case. Morrison and his superintendent had seen the Director of Public Prosecutions and they had considered at length the flimsiness of Morrison's dissatisfaction. (a) A delay of twenty-five minutes in calling the police. How had it been filled? Did one faint and hesitate for as long as that before taking the simple action of dialling 999? If not, why not? (b) Morrison had a hunch that there had been a closer association between Brown and Mrs Angell than she would admit, but there was only the suspicion. Her friend, Hazel Boynton, implied as much, but under further questioning Mrs Angell was unshakable. And no other evidence had come to light. (c) Why should a boxer, with all his trained aggression in his fists, bring an old revolver to the house, wave it threateningly around, and yet at the crucial moment allow himself to be dispossessed of it by a man twice his age and then contrive to be killed by it?

Yet if the revolver were Angell's, there was no evidence of his having recently bought it, and it seemed highly unlikely that a law-abiding solicitor of impeccable repute should have owned one for years without bothering to apply for a licence.

And the fingerprints on the revolver were only Angell's and Brown's. If Mrs Angell had somehow come by the revolver and murdered Brown, and her husband was taking the responsibility, there was no way of proving it. Failing such proof, one could only accept the defence as it stood and at its face value.

It was touch and go whether the case should be referred back to the coroner's inquest with the intimation that the police were not proceeding with the charge. But in order to drop a charge, once it has been made, one has to be utterly sure. In the end the Director said: 'Let it go on. Let it be publicly heard. It's the best way. Angell's profession is a disadvantage to him in this case. One must bend over backwards to remove any suspicion that the law is protecting the law.'

. . . There is nothing induces a solidarity among people more than a feeling of danger from without. Wilfred and Pearl living together in a slow-slackening hate, were yet held by the long-delayed trial, were forced into consultation, discussion and connivance by the suspicions of the police. You can live in enmity but it cannot be in silent enmity if one of you has just had another interview with the police and been asked new questions that may affect the trial.

It was a hot summer and a trying one. Having survived the worst of the shock, Angell felt he must remain visibly and actively in his firm, so that if embarrassment had to be faced it could be faced at once. In the office he never avoided an interview, but he avoided his club. This brought him home more and was a further trial to Pearl. Sometimes she considered despairingly why she had tried so urgently to save him, had not left him to face the consequences of his act. From discreet inquiry and by keeping her ears open, she learned that the charge might then have been murder. Quite possibly it would have meant several years in prison, as he had said at the time. Would she have been able to live with herself, known to the world as a guilty wife and knowing that her husband was languishing, perhaps dying, in gaol for an act which she had precipitated? That way at least she would have been free of him, free to live her own life, as she had often fervently wished. But would it have been a life at all?

In Cannes, after a splendidly extravagant summer in the best hotels on the Riviera, Viscount Vosper bought a £30,000 yacht from Prince Nicholas of Lithuania – a bargain at the price – and announced that he would spend the next three months in it cruising in the Aegean. At home Sir Francis Hone ordered a large extension to his house in Eleuthera in the Bahamas and opened negotiations for the purchase of a private plane. Simon Portugal bought his wife a Mercedes 250 SL, hoping this would salve some of her discontents. In Handley Merrick, from dawn to dusk, one could hear the whine of chain saws cutting down the beech woods behind Merrick House.

In Jude Davis's stable there was one absentee. The boxing world had closed over Little God, and soon he might never have been. His name disappeared from the ranking lists and Goodfellow's, after two meritorious wins, took its place. Jude Davis never talked about him, Prince sometimes missed his arrogant good humour the way one misses a thorn in one's shoe. Only Bushey referred to him often. 'Godfrey. Remember Little God. Man, he was a type. He might not have been everybody's favourite, but he was go, go. You won't see another like him.'

Perhaps it was a suitable epitaph. The only other person who had ever been close to Little God, if she had heard Bushey's comment, would have bitterly, fervently, sadly agreed.

The trial of Wilfred Angell for the manslaughter of Godfrey Brown came on on the 9th October, which was a Thursday, at 10 o'clock in the morning, before Mr Justice Smedley. It had been arranged that the case should be heard before Smedley, as he and Angell were completely unknown to each other professionally.

The police were scrupulous in the evidence they offered and the way it was presented. No bias, no prejudice appeared in Prosecuting Counsel's voice as he told the tale and examined the witnesses. Eric Bergson, Q.C., and Mr Evan Roberts for the defence were equally courteous and impartial. Bergson called only four witnesses for the defence: Fred Heath, the chauffeur, Dr Amersham, Pearl Angell and the accused. Mr J. C. Harvill, Q.C., for the Crown established the fact that Heath had not actually seen the attack on the accused, and from Dr Amersham he elicited that Angell's injuries on that occasion had been superficial.

After Pearl had gone up to the box and taken her oath a heavy-jawed man at the back of the court whispered: 'Holy Moses, I know where I seen her before!' 'Where?' asked Jude Davis, sitting beside him. 'I seen her at the gym one day. She came in and asked for Godfrey. Round about last

March it was, not long after his fight with Kio.' 'Well, didn't you see her photo in July?' 'It didn't look like her then. Honest to God, you wouldn't've known.' Jude sighed and rested his chin on his hands. 'So what? So what, Pat? Maybe they were up to monkey tricks, her and Godfrey. It would be like Godfrey to be up to monkey tricks. But it wouldn't change anything now if you stood up and said so.' 'Holy Moses,' said Prince. 'From the photos I'd never've known.'

In the box Pearl was taken through her story and presently was faced by a deferential and kind Mr Harvill. He, it seemed at first, was only anxious to spare her the distress that her present ordeal was giving her. It was only after a while that some of his questions were barbed so subtly that she wondered if the jury understood them. She would not have understood them herself had she been as innocent as she claimed, and for a few minutes, until the judge stopped him, she walked upon a dizzy tightrope not knowing if she would fall.

When Wilfred went up he gave his evidence in chief with a quiet candour and composure that surprised her and clearly confirmed the jury in all they had so far been led to believe. She had not quite realized that Wilfred was so much on his home ground. Nor would he be rattled by Mr Harvill in cross-examination. Yes, he recognized the revolver that was in court. No, he had never seen it before the evening of the 22nd July. No, he had never owned a revolver, not even during the war. They were not issued to non-commissioned ranks. No, he had never handled one before. No, he did not know where the safety catch was. Yes, he saw it now, but it must have been already lifted when he seized the revolver. No, he had only pulled the trigger once. Oh, yes, he was certainly in fear of his life; the young man appeared to him to be insane with rage.

Angell was asked to describe again how he had wrested the revolver from Brown and how Brown had jeered at him that the revolver would not fire. No, he had no personal reason for disliking Brown. Brown had never wronged him in any way. No, neither physically nor morally. He *feared* him because he feared personal injury and even death; he also feared for the safety of his wife. No, his act of pulling the trigger was simply an act of self-preservation.

During all this Mr Justice Smedley had been growing impatient, and in the end he cut Mr Harvill short as he had done during his cross-examination of Mrs Angell. The closing speeches were brief and the judge instantly began his summing up, as if he had been waiting for this moment.

'Members of the jury, you have heard the evidence in this case, and I will not detain you long. We have before us a man accused of manslaughter and rightly standing his trial. He has admitted that he fired the bullet which killed Godfrey Brown so these facts are not at issue. No man may take the life of another without suffering the full examination of the law.

'The accused man, as you know, is a solicitor, well known, respected, and the head of his law firm. His character all his life has been of the highest.' The judge lifted his body off its plush seat and lowered it again, frowning his approval of Angell's character. 'He served during the War with distinction in Europe and in Africa. But by choice he is a man of peace and of refined tastes. Into his life came a young man, brought up in an orphanage – though no worse for that – but with a record – not a police record, but a history nevertheless – of violence and intimidation. A boxer by choice, he had served one sentence of suspension by the British Boxing Board of Control for attacking his manager in a fit of temper.

'Mr Angell, the accused man, in the nature of his profession, must tender advice from time to time, and last year he advised a sick woman – since dead – that she was being deceived and imposed upon by this young boxer, Godfrey Brown. As a result of this advice – or so at least Brown thought – he did not come in for the legacy he expected when the sick woman died. So he built up in his own mind a resentment and a bitterness against the accused for giving this advice, and resolved to revenge himself as best he could.

'You have heard of how he attempted to do this – by threats and later by actual assault – so that Mr Angell, a man in middle life following the sedentary occupation of the law, was knocked about by a trained and vicious assailant twenty-five years his junior.

'Now let us come to the evening of Tuesday the 22nd July of this year. Brown, arriving at Angell's house directly from a fight in which he broke the nose of an opponent – though this I understand was only in a training bout – forced his way into the house in which Mrs Angell at that time was alone. He terrorized Mrs Angell, and might well have done her injury had not Mr Angell then returned. Mr Angell, hearing the commotion upstairs and not knowing its cause, went up and discovered Brown in his wife's bathroom breaking up the mirror glass . . .'

It's all right, thought Pearl, he's on our side, he's accepted our story, hook, line and sinker, he is as good as retelling it from our point of view. It's all right. She glanced at Wilfred. It's all right, Wilfred, after all these months. She glanced at him sitting in the dock, sitting with hand to chin, fingers touching the heavy lips, his face more haggard than she had ever seen it before – not as puffy or as flabby as at the time of Godfrey's death; stress had refined it, made it more human; over the cheeks it had narrowed, become overcast with shadows. He was better looking for it; his hair had not greyed; she could see his distinction, could see how it impressed judge and jury. She knew that distinction was very real, but she felt certain that nothing in this harrowing experience would fundamentally change him. It's all right, Wilfred, my lies, our lies have come off. Do you already know it? Are you already breathing free air?

'Counsel for the Crown has cast some doubts upon the accused's story of his struggles with Brown. How did Mr Angell wrest the revolver from Brown – a small man but one of great strength – and retreat sufficiently far from his attacker to fire the revolver at a distance of about six feet?' The judge half stood up and lowered himself again, as if ready for the break that soon must come. 'I think you will find, however, that Mrs Angell in her evidence has said that she diverted Brown by trying to reach the telephone, and that it was at this moment that the accused, driven to extremities of force by fear for his own life and the safety of his wife, snatched the revolver and backed away. The prosecution has been unable to bring

405

any evidence to disprove this explanation. It is for you members of the jury, to decide whether you accept it.

'Now, members of the jury, you have to decide the facts and I have to direct you as to the law. The prosecution has to prove the guilt of the accused, and the standard of proof required is that you should all feel sure that his guilt has been established. The defence here is self-defence. A man is entitled to defend himself and his wife if attacked or under real apprehension of imminent attack. The real test of self-defence is that a man who is genuinely defending himself does not want to fight. The force he uses must be in reasonable proportion to the violence being offered against him. He has a duty to retreat if possible, in order to escape his assailant; but if in a confined space he can retreat no further, he is entitled to act in his own defence. The plea of self-defence having been put forward here, it is for the Crown to disprove it. If you think that it either is or may be the case that when Mr Angell snatched the gun from Brown and fired the fatal shot he feared for his life and safety or that of his wife's, he is entitled to be acquitted. It is only if the Crown satisfies you so that you feel sure that that was not the case, that you should convict.'

Mr Justice Smedley looked at the clock. 'It is now one-fifteen. I will keep the court in session for fifteen minutes more. If at the end of that time you have not arrived at a decision you will please inform my clerk and I will adjourn until two-thirty.'

The jury were out ten minutes. During that time Angell was taken below but Pearl would not move from her seat. 'Come outside for a few minutes, Mrs Angell,' Mumford urged. 'It passes the time; moving about is always a help on such occasions.' She shook her head. 'When this is over,' said Esslin, 'take him away for a long holiday. We are over-worked anyway in the firm so a little more will do no harm. He will need the change.' She nodded without speaking.

'Holy Moses,' said Prince. 'I only seen her that once, but when the coppers showed me their picture it didn't look like her at all. An' any road Godfrey'd always got some girl or another hanging around.' 'He'd always got

ome girl or another,' said Jude Davis. 'So what the hell.
That was his undoing. He's dead.'

'I'm by no means an expert,' said Mr Friedel, 'but I
thought it a very fair summing-up. I thought the judge was
very impartial. It makes one glad to be in England. Ah,
I see they're coming back.'

They were coming back. Unanimously they found the
accused not guilty. The case had taken just three and a
half hours. At one-thirty Angell was discharged. He immediately collapsed and it was two o'clock before he could
be helped to a waiting taxi. Pearl and Mr Friedel took
him home. Later in the afternoon he was able to eat a
satisfactory lunch.

Chapter Fifteen

They did not take Esslin's advice until January.

They had stuck together somehow, more from the centripetal forces of routine than from any stronger motive. And lacking, after this long enforced period together since Godfrey's death, the new disruptive moment. The hatred and loathing of those first days had passed. They were used to each other again. Angell worked hard and prospered greatly. The Handley Merrick scheme was going to make him richer than he had ever been before. The strains and stresses he had been through had left no appreciable mark except that thinning of the face. He returned to his club and soon overcame its embarrassments when members wanted to talk to him about it. In a little while he found it not altogether displeasing to have had his moment of notoriety. In his own eyes he was quite willing to see himself as the brave householder of Pearl's tale, not the wronged and cuckolded husband but the simple Englishman defending his life and his wife and his property against a little thug. Only once he bore a whiff of this attitude home, but Pearl's reaction was instant. 'Never, never talk about it to me. And never, never, never in that way.'

So at home he held his tongue – as he had learned to hold his tongue about so much. There were so many areas in their lives now in which silence was the only preservative.

Yet their life together was by now not entirely an unpleasant one. Their interests, which had often seemed similar in the early days of their marriage, continued to develop. Pearl was learning all the time about art and architecture and furniture and silver and glass. She often prospected in antique shops and told Wilfred what she had found, and they would go along together and see it and possibly buy it. They were frequently at the sale-rooms together, and sometimes Wilfred considered withdrawing a day a week from his firm to have more time for his enthralling hobby. Pearl still enjoyed being rich and cultured, and found this way of living better than any she had previously known. She was a good cook and enjoyed her own food. He enjoyed it too.

In December he began to sleep with her again, now at regular intervals of ten days, which he found suited him best. Sometimes she was passive, calm, acquiescent, as she had been in the early days, sometimes over-passionate and demanding. These times put a strain on his health, but in retrospect they flattered him.

A new warmth – like the sun they found – came into their relationship on their holiday. They went in late January for three weeks to Tenerife. For Christmas he had bought her two more pieces of jewellery, and because of this and the early Georgian silver they had acquired he said they could not afford to be too extravagant, so they took a package deal, flying on a slow turbo-prop and getting a slightly inferior bedroom at the modern steel and concrete hotel. Otherwise it was all the same at half the price.

They sat by the swimming pool each day garnering a sun denied them in England. Wilfred, because of his size, did not like to sun-bathe – he described it as the new mindless religion – but he sat under a parasol reading his art books and was content.

Pearl, having scarcely believed it possible to find such warmth in February, gradually unfolded herself like a crumpled flower, to lie stretched all day in a very small bikini, browning and receiving the admiring glances of the male population of the hotel. Lunch could be eaten either in the hotel or at a buffet by the pool, and Wilfred discovered that, while second helpings were not quite the thing in the restaurant, at the buffet table one could pile one's plate as high as the fourteen storeys of the hotel for all anyone cared, and even then go back for more at no extra cost. So every day they ate by the pool, Pearl discreetly, knowing that she had put on seven pounds since Godfrey died, Wilfred ravenously, pushing food into his mouth like a nervous householder stock-piling before a siege.

In the evenings Wilfred found friends to play bridge with, and Pearl, soaked with sun and air, was happy to retire with a book to bed. Life was easier now, quieter, undisturbed by violent sexual demands. Godfrey's death had left a terrible vacuum but also a sense of peace. One drifted

along pleasantly enough, easily, respectably, Mrs Wilfred
Angell. A rich solicitor's wife, with a place in the world,
a position to maintain. One could become concerned about
the quality of the Spanish wines, the temperature of the
pool, the availability of chairs, the demand for tables at
dinner. One did not argue about, or even consider, being
treated like a chattel, being dragged by the arms naked
across a bed, being summarily ravaged by a wild little man
and summarily dismissed. Nowadays one had one's position
to think of, not the savage excitements of last year.

The clientele of the hotel was cosmopolitan: a high percentage of English, Germans and Swedes, together with
modest numbers of Danes, Norwegians, Italians and
French. There were even a few representatives of the proud
and stiff-necked country which owned the island. One day
when it was very cloudy and rather cool, Wilfred and
Pearl took deck chairs strategically near the luncheon
table, and there arrived in the next two deck chairs two
Frenchmen of inimitable appearance. They were in their
thirties, muscular, assured, hair en brosse, well bred,
monied, sophisticated. They gave off the impression which
Frenchmen often give, of knowing more about food and
women, and how to enjoy both, than anyone else in the
world. The taller of the two, who was addressed as Gaston,
celebrated his arrival by doing some extraordinary gym-
nastics on the arms of his chair: raising himself bodily
upside down apparently by the strength of his wrists;
and this he did, as no person of another nationality could,
as if he were alone in the world, as if other deck chairs,
other people, other watchers did not exist. It was unself-
conscious, yet arrogant. After it was over he lowered himself and smiled encouragingly at Pearl. She glanced quickly
away. Now and again during the morning the smell of
Gauloises and Ambre Solaire drifted across.

Wilfred had hired a car in the afternoon and they drove
up to Tiede, breaking through the cloud barrier at 2,000
feet and coming into brilliant sunshine. They explored the
great craters of the extinct volcano and returned to the
hotel at seven.

At dinner Wilfred ate more lightly than usual. Pearl
looked surprised and he said: 'I have been thinking, my
dear, I owe it to myself, I perhaps even more owe it to you,

410

to bring down my weight again. I'm still in my prime, and some discretion in middle life is probably a good thing. D'you know. An active life such as I lead, and such as I hope to lead for many years to come, makes demands on one's fitness, and I would be no worse for being half a stone lighter.'

'Oh,' said Pearl. 'Yes, well, I need to watch my weight too. Perhaps we can help each other.'

'You?' said Wilfred gallantly. 'Oh, no, not at all. You're so young, and a fraction of added fulness lends an extra attraction.'

Pearl sipped her wine. 'Well, that's nice of you, but *I* think I need to watch myself.'

They ate in silence and with new-found dedication. Wilfred said: 'The Wests and the Rowlands have asked me to play bridge at nine-thirty. They're good players but not as good as I am. And the stakes are modest. Will you come and watch?'

'No, thanks. I'll go to bed. Wine always makes me sleepy.'

'Just as you wish, my dear.'

The dining room was crowded, and the scene a gay and animated one.

Angell eased his stomach against the table and said: 'What an extraordinary lot of people there are in this hotel. Abroad, I think the English are seldom seen to advantage – and this stratum of English society shows up almost the worst: that is the well-to-do lower middle-class. Of course one has to admit that most of the people here are enjoying the benefits of a package deal, so that they are experiencing a higher quality of hotel than they are normally used to –'

'Like us,' said Pearl, to tease.

He frowned but was not put out. 'Ours is a special case. What I was endeavouring to say was that these English people show up so badly against the other people here. The women's dress is quite appalling, the men tip the head-waiter and then expect to be treated like lords. They fuss about the food as they would never dare to do at a comparable hotel in England; they complain as if they were used to something better instead of something worse. They talk in loud voices, they try too hard to impress. They have no *taste*. Above all they have no taste.'

Pearl looked at him in affectionate amusement. She hadn't seen it like that, but now it was pointed out she did see it like that. Yet it was not so long since *he* used to talk loudly in restaurants. This was one of the ways in which she had been able to influence him. They learned from each other. *Her* own taste, she thought now, had been pretty awful two years ago. It was fantastic how far and how quickly one progressed. Wilfred, she thought, must have been more badly smitten than one realized, to have overlooked her gaucheries at that time and have married her in spite of them.

Wilfred was still muttering. 'I suppose it's more difficult to judge other nationalities, but there are not more than ten English in this hotel I would care to talk to. One wonders at the acreage of prosperous desolate suburbs in which these people breed.'

They were near the end of the meal when the two Frenchmen were shown in to a recently vacated table. The big one, Gaston, half bowed to Pearl as he was sitting down, but she averted her eyes.

Wilfred said: 'I think of these very pleasant things we have to go back to. How lucky we were to get that Queen Anne snuffbox. It's in such rare condition – and the price was reasonable. Someday we must try to get one of the Archbishop Sancroft type. Although they *are* so dear, one is almost certain of a continuing rise.'

'There was a George III box in a shop in Beaumont Street. But it had bits of gold on it and it seemed overpriced.'

'Oh, that's a Linnit. You should get one of those for £250.'

'That's what it was! How clever of you to know. But I thought for George III it was a bit much.'

They finished their meal.

She said: 'Are you playing bridge tonight?'

'Yes, I told you.'

'Who is it with?'

'The Wests and the Rowlands. They're civilized people. But I told you that too.'

'Did you? Sorry. I think I'll go to bed. All that scrambling over rocks.'

He took out a cigar. 'One of the signal virtues of collecting silver is that it has an intrinsic value apart from its value to the collector. The intrinsic value of a painting, to put it crudely, is the value of the frame and the canvas. Values of the paintings themselves can therefore fluctuate with the taste of the time. Values in antique silver can hardly depreciate, (a) because only so much of it has ever been made, and (b) because the price of the metal is constant or more frequently rising.'

'Wilfred,' she said, 'when we get home let's go over *all* your things once again, piece by piece, just to see if there *is* anything you can part with – to sell at a good profit. Unless we buy a new house there just isn't going to be room for anything more.'

He looked at her speculatively over the top of his glasses, which he had put on to cut his cigar. He noticed that she was wearing the diamond clip he had recently bought.

'We've been over this before, my dear. You know how I hate to lose something I've grown fond of.'

They were still looking at each other, and the words came to be double charged.

She smiled. 'Well, yes, but there *are* things. Apart from me. That lacquer secretaire, for instance. If we selected a few things carefully it might give us a couple of thousand to spend on something new.'

'Very well,' he said. 'We could do it together.'

'Yes, we could do it together.'

He lit his cigar and said expansively between puffs: 'I think we should try a French wine tomorrow. This is a pleasant table wine but it lacks finesse.'

Pearl finished her glass, gulping it rather quickly. 'All right. What I would like now, though, is a liqueur. Would they have a Green Chartreuse?'

'Of course.' He ordered the liqueurs and she sipped it appreciatively. Her eyes were lighting up.

He said: 'We have ten more days here, with really nothing to do except sit in the sun. Do you think you will be bored?'

'No, oh no, I'll not be bored! If you aren't. I adore getting brown!'

'I think I like you looking sun-tanned,' he said.

They sat in silence while he finished his cigar. When it

was nearly gone his table napkin slipped off his knee. The waiters were all busy so he bent to pick it up for himself. As he did so Pearl happened to meet the eye of the big Frenchman sitting at the nearby table. He was eating lobster, and his white teeth seemed very much in evidence.

He again inclined his head slightly at Pearl, and this time she smiled back at him over her husband's shoulder quite, quite brilliantly.

Winston Graham

'One of the best half-dozen novelists in this country.' *Books and Bookmen*. 'Winston Graham excels in making his characters come vividly alive.' *Daily Mirror*. 'A born novelist.'
Sunday Times

His immensely popular suspense novels include:

After the Act

Greek Fire

The Little Walls

Night Journey

The Walking Stick

The Sleeping Partner

The Tumbled House

Fortune is a Woman

The Poldark Saga, his famous story of an 18th Century Cornish tin-mining community:

Ross Poldark

Demelza

Jeremy Poldark

Warleggan

And:

The Grove of Eagles

—a swaggering novel of Elizabethan Cornwall. 'Masterly story-telling.' *New York Times*

 *Fontana Books*

Helen MacInnes

Born in Scotland, Helen MacInnes has lived in the United States since 1937. Her first book *Above Suspicion*, was an immediate success and launched her on a spectacular writing career that has made her an international favourite.

'She is the queen of spy-writers.' *Sunday Express*

'She can hang up her cloak and dagger right there with Eric Ambler and Graham Greene.' *Newsweek*

The Salzburg Connection

The Venetian Affair

I and My True Love

North from Rome

Above Suspicion

Decision at Delphi

The Double Image

Assignment in Brittany

Pray for a Brave Heart

Horizon

Neither Five Nor Three

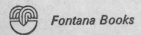 *Fontana Books*